THE WICCHE GLASS TAVERN

SEANA KELLY

The Wicche Glass Tavern

Copyright © 2021 by Seana Kelly

Ebook ISBN: 9781641972123

KDP POD ISBN: 9798517940513

IS POD ISBN: 9781641971768

NYLA Publishing

121 W. 27th St., Suite 1201, NY 10001, New York.

http://www.nyliterary.com

ONE

Um, What the Hell?

The new engagement ring sparkled as I wiped down the already gleaming bar. Today was the day. My Slaughtered Lamb Bookstore and Bar was reopening. The construction crew had done much of the work while Clive and I had been in New Orleans. It wasn't the same. It'd never be the same, but The Slaughtered Lamb 2.0 gleamed in the light of the setting sun.

Thankfully, the wolves who had destroyed the original hadn't compromised the window wall overlooking the San Francisco Bay and Pacific Ocean. Seawater splashed against the thick glass four feet above the barroom floor. Kelp bobbed and swirled as large fish swam by.

"Hey, boss. I put away those last two carts of books, but I got a call that another shipment is being delivered tonight." Owen, my friend, assistant, and wicche extraordinaire, was helping me get ready before we opened up for the first time in two months. "The shelves are pretty light. We should be getting back to normal soon, though."

The wolves had been thorough in decimating my home. Very few of the books were able to be salvaged. They'd destroyed rare, ancient grimoires and first editions, irreplaceable items. I pushed away the sorrow and outrage. They didn't have a place here tonight.

Dave, my half-demon cook, came out of the kitchen carrying a plate of treats. He knew me so well. When he dropped the chocolate coconut caramel bars in front of me, Owen dove for the plate as Dave turned back to the kitchen.

"Wait. Don't you want a drink?" I held up his preferred brand of cinnamon schnapps.

He paused at the swinging doors and looked over his shoulder. Dave's shark-like black eyes zeroed in on the bottle in my hand. "Later. I don't want that scent in my head while I'm cooking." The door swung closed a moment later.

"Have you been in the kitchen yet? Do you know what he's making?" Owen snatched the bottle from my hand and returned it to its spot in the colorful, sparkling wall of cascading bottles behind the bar, aligning it so the label faced perfectly forward, as he had with every other bottle on the wall.

"No idea. I've been banished from the kitchen today." I took a bite of the treat and groaned.

"Makes it difficult to get to your apartment if you're not allowed in the kitchen." Owen glanced around the bar, looking for anything that needed doing. I knew because I'd been doing the same thing all day.

I'd been in business for seven years before my home had to be gutted and rebuilt. This wasn't my first day on the job, but I was nervous as hell. Instead of opening at noon, as we normally did, we postponed the grand reopening to five in the evening to make more of a party out of it.

Checking my watch, I admitted—if only to myself—the fear that had been losing me sleep. What if no one came? It had been months. Habits changed. Maybe they'd found new places to hang out that they liked better.

"It's time," Owen said.

Nodding, I pasted on a smile, braced for silence, and opened the wards protecting my bookstore and bar. They were magically linked to me and responded to my thoughts. A moment later, many footsteps pounded down the stairs and something tight and scared in me disappeared. Owen grinned, kissed me on the cheek, and went to greet our customers.

First in was Grim, an aptly named dwarf who had been sitting on the last stool at the bar every evening since I'd first opened. He wasn't a drunk. He was a man who enjoyed a tankard of mead at the end of the day. As he hopped onto his regular seat, I slid the tankard in front of him. And just like that, things were back to normal.

The bar filled quickly, with patrons overflowing into the connected bookstore. They collected scattered chairs and positioned them around a sofa in front of the glass wall. I wasn't the only one excited to see and talk with friends.

The first hour was a rush. People who never would have thought to hug Sam 1.0 were squeezing my hands, embracing me, even kissing me on the cheek. To say the last few months had been life altering was not an exaggeration. Whether by necessity or design, I'd kept myself separate and isolated. But now…well, right now, Owen's gorgeous boyfriend George was swinging me in a circle as his sister Coco shook her head, grinning.

Coco had never been here before. She was the extraordinary dragon shifter who had fashioned the choker I never removed, the one created to keep my mind safe from outside influence. My aunt, who was hell-bent on erasing me from existence, had used her considerable power to pull me into horrifying visions, ones intended to stop my heart. Coco had spelled an exquisite protective choker that kept my mind under my own control.

Not as tall as George, she had his broad shoulders, warm brown skin, and piercing green eyes. She was also a recovering alcoholic, which was why she had never visited before. Once George had set me back on my feet, Coco shook my hand.

"It's even more beautiful than I'd imagined." She kept her back to the bar, her gaze on the view. "I can't stay. Just wanted to wish you well on your first night."

"To thank you properly for coming, let me get you something."
When I reached behind her toward the bar, her eyes jittered.
"No, thank you. I'm fine. I should probably—"

I held out the plate of chocolate coconut bars that Dave had made, offering my last two to George and Coco.

Releasing a gust of air, she nodded, taking a bar and a bite. The groan made me smile. George took the last bar and finished it quickly, all the while keeping a strong arm around his sister.

"I'm going to take Coco home. I'll probably be back near closing to pick up Owen."

Coco elbowed her brother. "You don't have to babysit me. I'm fine. Stay and have fun."

"Are you crazy? It's Springboks versus All Blacks. It's rugby night, woman." George gave me another kiss on the cheek, his arm never leaving his sister's shoulders. He waved at Owen before escorting Coco up the stairs and out.

An impact tremor rippled through the floor. When I turned, I found Meg drawing in her wings and glaring at the person sitting on the barstool she normally occupied. This was the drawback to having incredibly powerful patrons. They weren't used to waiting their turn. Meg was one of the Furies. She was an ancient Greek goddess of vengeance. I needed to get her a whiskey and a stool before a scourge appeared in her taloned hand.

Motioning to Owen, who was making drinks behind the bar, I pointed at the stool I kept in the corner. It was the one I used on quiet nights. He picked it up and passed it over heads to me. I set it down at the end of the bar, near Grim. As neither Meg nor Grim were talkers, I figured they could tolerate each other well enough. I waved Meg over to the empty stool as Owen slid a double of her favorite whiskey in front of her. Annoyed but placated, Meg sat.

The kitchen door swung open and Dave started scribbling on the menu board we'd recently installed. It was best for all involved when Dave didn't interact directly with customers.

In honor of Sam's recent trip to New Orleans, tonight's menu is

Po'boys—crab, shrimp, hot sausage, or roast beef, served with fries or onion rings. No substitutes. Don't piss me off.

When Dave went back in the kitchen, Owen began circulating, taking orders. A low, fierce "Fuck" was breathed to my right. When I turned, I found Meg glaring at the bottom of the stairs.

"Nice place, kid."

I spun to find Stheno scanning the bar with her one good eye. With a yelp of excitement, I raced around the bar and hugged my favorite gorgon. She was stunning in a long white tank dress with high slits on either side that showed off glowing, olive skin. Her black corkscrew curls fell to the small of her back. She was still sporting an eye patch, but this one matched her dress.

"You came!" I'd really missed her.

"Said I would." She gave Horus—who may or may not have been the Egyptian sky god—I didn't like to pry—a long look. I'd never seen him anything but stoic. At Stheno's lascivious gaze, his dark skin colored. "You remember," she murmured, causing Horus to choke on his black and tan.

"I'm so happy to see you! Do you need a place to stay? My apartment is in the back."

Patting my arm, she said, "Thanks, but we're good."

"We're? Is Gabriel with you?" I was surprised he'd leave New Orleans when his Alpha was taking over as Master of the City.

"No, but that is one hot wolf. The things he could do with— well, this probably isn't the place to get into it." She winked. "Ask me later. No, 'we' is my sisters. Every century or so, we get together for as long as we can stand each other."

"Wait. Both sisters? I thought Perseus cut off Medusa's head."

Cackling, she said, "He wishes. Men. Do they ever stop exaggerating their exploits? Or the size of their cocks?" She rolled her eyes. "Not including that wolf, because oof."

I stepped back behind the bar. "What can I get you?"

Nial, a tall, dapper elf with grass-green eyes and long, silvery blond hair, stood and offered Stheno his stool.

She looked him up and down, a hand trailing over his arm as

she thanked him. "I think I'd like something tall and cool." She winked at Nial and then sat.

Nial put his lips to Stheno's ear and whispered something that had her eyes dilating.

"Yes. I'd like that very much. I need to talk to my girl first. After that, you're on." She fanned her face as he bowed formally and then moved to the steps to wait for her.

I slid a tall, pink drink in front of her. "So, that whole beheading Medusa story was a lie?"

"Mostly. He saw her reflection in his shield and then wet himself and ran." Shrugging, she took a long sip. "Mmm. So anyway," she said, looking over her shoulder at the hot elf waiting for her. "I need to go, but I wanted you to know we rented a house in Sea Cliff, a mile or so away. I'll bring Euryale and Medusa with me next time. Make sure you have lots of wine on hand. It's all they drink."

She hopped off her seat. "I'll be back. Just stopping in to say hi." Flipping off Meg—who I hadn't realized she'd seen—she dropped a twenty on the bar, collected her elf, and headed out. I'd missed her.

Later in the evening, the place was still crowded, but they'd settled in. I was cutting lemon wedges when I noticed Liam, a selkie and one of my regulars, push up through the water entrance. I'd been wondering where he was. He removed his seal skin, shifting to human. Ignoring the privacy robes I kept hanging by the ocean entrance, he walked toward the bar.

People called out greetings, a few whistling, but Liam didn't respond. Confused, I pushed aside the cutting board and grabbed a pint glass, drawing his favorite lager from the tap. This wasn't like him. True, many in the supernatural world had no issue with nakedness, but I knew for a fact that Liam did. He was the main reason I kept robes available for the water fae.

"Is everything okay?" I slid the beer in front of him.

Head cocked to the side, he stared, uncomprehending. A split second later, he snatched up the knife I'd dropped and dove over the bar, knocking me down. My head slammed against the hard wood floor. Momentarily stunned, I didn't react until I felt the knife slice into my neck. Claws drawn, I knocked his arm away, breaking the bone. Eyes still blank and uncomprehending, he wrapped his good hand around my neck and squeezed.

His eyes were wrong. I knocked his other arm and again heard a break. Not a second later, he was yanked off me and was hanging from Dave's meaty grip. Flames ran down Dave's arm, burning Liam, but still he hung limp and unresponsive.

"Stop! Drop him."

Dave complied but pinned Liam under his foot. "What the fuck was that?" he snarled.

I hadn't realized the bar had gone quiet until I stood and heard the collective gasp.

"Sam, you're bleeding!" Owen raced around the bar, clutching a bar towel. He pressed it to my neck, trying to stem the flow of blood.

Holding my hand over his, adding pressure, I studied Liam. "Look at him. He's not in there."

"Mom." Owen waved over his mother Lydia with his free hand. "Is it a curse?"

Dave dropped to a crouch and laid his hand on Liam's unblinking face.

When Lydia looked like she was readying a spell, I stopped her. "He's tracing it. Don't do anything."

A moment later, Liam jolted, curled into the fetal position, and shook.

Dave stood, his expression grim. "She's back."

TWO

Liang, Liang, Liang

I t was close to eleven when Clive and Liang arrived to find me sitting at a table in an empty, darkened bar, staring at the waves and wondering what the hell.

"I'd assumed there'd be more people." Liang, a visiting vampire and one of Clive's gorgeous exes glanced in the bookstore entrance, no doubt looking for a hidden crowd.

Of course he'd bring Liang. Yes, she was an old and very powerful ally, one who was committed to helping Clive find out who was targeting him and his nocturne of vampires. Did she have to be so freaking beautiful and perfect all the time, though? Stupid luminous, unscarred skin, golden brown eyes, glossy black hair, she was the worst.

"Where is everyone?" Clive pulled a chair over and sat beside me, his hand resting on my thigh. "I called earlier. It was so noisy, Owen couldn't hear me."

"Yeah." I picked up his hand and held it between both of mine. "It started off great." I watched Liang inspect my bookstore bar. Squeezing his hand, I added, "Everybody came, and most brought friends. We were packed."

Leaning over, he kissed my temple. "I told you."

8

The kitchen door swung open and Dave stalked out, causing Liang to freeze. "Yeah, it's all fun and games until someone tries to slit your throat." He slid a plate with a shrimp po'boy and fries in front of me. "Eat. What the fuck am I supposed to do with all the food I cooked?"

Ignoring a stiff, blinking Liang, he went behind the bar and poured himself a tumbler of cinnamon schnapps and me a soda.

"I guess the shelters are going to be enjoying Cajun food tonight." I hadn't thought to eat earlier, but he was right. Now that the food was in front of me, I was starving.

Dave dropped into the chair on my other side.

"What are you talking about? Who had their throat slit?" Clive's voice chilled the air.

Dave pointed to the side of my neck opposite Clive. Owen's sister Lilah, a healer, had already worked on me. I was fine, although I now had yet another scar.

Biting into the po'boy, I shrugged. "Little cut." Turning to Dave, I added, "So good," around a mouthful of spicy shrimp.

He tipped his glass to me, acknowledging the compliment, before finishing half the booze in one gulp.

I didn't see him move. Clive was suddenly crouched next to Dave, his finger lightly tracing the new scar on my neck. "Who attacked you?"

"Liam." Dave downed the rest of his drink and shook his head. "A fucking selkie gets the drop on her. The bar's filled with just about every powerful being in San Francisco and the asshole swims through the ocean entrance, walks across a crowded bar—naked—and jumps over the bar, trying to kill her."

"Liam? Why in the world would Liam attack you?" Clive was fuming, I could sense it, but he kept his voice and body language in check.

Swallowing first, I said, "Not his fault. Abigail's back—Dave traced the spell—and she's apparently going for friends since she can't get me." Taking a sip of soda to wash down Dave's incredible food, I added, "Everyone was shocked. No one moved. Dave was in the kitchen and he was still the first to help, to pull him off me."

I stared at my food, wanting to eat but knowing Clive needed answers. "You know Liam. He's quiet, thoughtful. Slight. He was the first one here a few months ago when I was shot. The mermaid who'd rescued me told him and he raced here to help. He's a sweet person who's well-liked."

Dave nodded in agreement. "The place was festive as fuck. They didn't see a threat when they looked at him."

"I doubt anyone even saw him snatch the knife when he dove over the bar. I didn't yell for help because I didn't need it." Clive opened his mouth to respond but I shook my head. "I didn't. He's a selkie. I could have taken him easily, but it's Liam. I didn't want to hurt him. I could see there was something wrong with him. I ended up breaking both his arms to get him off me. The sound was horrible. Thankfully, Lilah was here and able to heal them. If he wasn't able to swim, he'd probably die. A selkie can't be separated from the water for long."

A heavy silence was broken when Liang asked, in her stupid, perfect British accent, "Who is Abigail?"

I let Clive handle that one while I finished my dinner.

"Abigail is Sam's aunt. She takes exception to Sam's existence." He ran a hand down my back in comfort, rising and returning to his seat while spearing Dave with his gaze. "If you were able to track the spell, why are you here and why isn't Abigail dead?"

Dave blew out a breath, angled himself toward the ocean, and snaked his foot around the legs of an empty chair, dragging it to him. "I don't answer to you, son, so watch your tone." He put his feet up on the chair, ignoring Clive's anger. "And don't try and pull your Jedi mind tricks on me. That shit only works when I'm not paying attention."

"He tried," I said.

"Fucking-A. Bitch felt me tracing and broke the spell. She's nearby, but that's all I got. She probably had to be close to control him."

Liang finally moved to our table and sat on Clive's other side, her hand briefly on his arm as though encouraging him to calm. The presumption of laying hands on my mate made me want to tear off her arm and smack her across the face with it.

"Why does your aunt desire your death?" Liang asked, all quiet concern and interest.

If I hadn't recently discovered my own necromantic abilities, I might have bought it. Yearning for Clive lurked behind her every word and gesture.

Since Clive and Dave were pissed off, I finished the last of the fries and responded. "My father was a born wolf—as you know—and my mother was a Corey wicche, an ancient and powerful line of wicches. My aunt believes my mother bespoiled a long, pure line of wicches with me."

Dave snorted, "Bespoiled."

"Couldn't your mother—"

"Dead."

Liang leaned forward. "Your father, then. He—"

"Dead." This conversation was just getting more and more depressing.

"Surely you have some family member who could aid you." Again with the quiet concern. I wanted to flick her right between the eyes.

Dave chuffed a laugh and stood, taking my empties up to the bar. He returned a moment later with a cocktail for me.

I took a sip. A perfect lemon drop. "Thanks."

Nodding, he put his feet back up, crossed his arms, and watched the waves swirl around the glass.

Both Clive and Dave were letting me decide how much to share. I was self-aware enough to understand that my issues with Liang stemmed from my own insecurities. The other vampires in the nocturne loved her, wanted her to be Clive's special someone. Mostly, I didn't care. It just got to me sometimes.

Vampires were all about the long game. Clive might love me now, but she doubted he'd feel the same in a few years, a few decades, a century? Biding their time, for good or ill, was a hallmark of their creed.

After another sip, I reluctantly responded. "As far as I know, I'm the last Quinn, and she and I are the last Coreys. I think. Honestly, I have no idea." I toyed with the martini glass, turning it this way and that, catching the moonlight. "She's more skilled and more powerful than me."

"Not more powerful," Clive began.

"She's a fucking sorcerer," Dave cut in. "That power isn't all hers."

Shrugging, I continued, "Regardless of how she has it, she's stronger than I am and has been training for this her whole life. I've only had access to my wicche heritage for a few months. I have no idea if I possess any buried skills that can best her."

I also had no intention of telling Liang, or any vampire, that I was a necromancer, that I could sense the presence of vampires, read their thoughts and emotions, even control their actions. I didn't have a death wish. The only vampires who knew were Clive, his second Russell, and his third Godfrey, none of whom would betray me—I was pretty sure—and none of whom actually knew the extent of my abilities.

I hadn't even told Clive that I'd once searched deep in my own mind and found cold, green vampire blips in small groupings across the planet, or that I'd read the thoughts of a vamp half a world away. I'd tell him—I would—once the implications of what that might mean didn't leave me in a cold sweat.

Clive rested his hand on mine. "I assume Liam's murder attempt put a damper on the evening?"

"Yeah. They all started leaving after that." They'd been so happy—well, except for Grim, naturally—when they'd arrived. I couldn't stomach the looks of dread and pity they'd given me when they left.

"How is he now?" Clive asked.

"He's been better. When he came out of the trance, he curled in on himself, shaking horribly. If Lilah hadn't been here to help, I don't know what we would have done. In the end, we helped him slip into his seal skin and return to the ocean."

"Probably the best thing for him," Dave said. "Might heal better."

"Yeah." Poor Liam. I hated my aunt, truly hated her. She didn't care who she hurt in order to get to me.

"All right." Clive stood, tugging on my arm. "Up you get." When I rose, Clive slid an arm around me and snugged me close. "We'll go home. You'll sleep. And we'll meet here tomorrow after closing to discuss what's to be done about your aunt."

"Kill her," Dave grumbled, kicking the chair.

"Maybe we could get Coco to make a spelled chain that encircles The Slaughtered Lamb, so everyone who visits is in control of their own mind." Like the choker she'd made me kept *my* mind safe.

"Sure," Dave said, hitting the lights. "And then what happens when you walk out the door? You don't live in the back of your hobbit hole anymore." He started up the stairs. "It's not even midnight. Maybe I'll take Maggie dancing." He was through the ward and gone.

Clive tugged my braid, tilting my face up to his, and gave me a kiss. "I'm sorry the evening didn't end well. Now"—he gave me a quick squeeze—"where's your jacket?"

"Um." I glanced around the bar, retracing my steps, trying to remember when I'd taken it off. "On the couch in my apartment."

Clive went to retrieve it, leaving Liang and me alone.

"Your establishment is magnificent. Clive mentioned this was your brainchild." Her perfect features glowed in the moonlight. She was, quite simply, stunning.

I struggled to build a wall against her emotions, struggled and failed. "Yes. If the rules of the mundane world didn't need to be adhered to, I imagined what was possible. I didn't really know Clive then, but he put me in touch with the people who could make my dream a reality."

Liang nodded. "This seems to be a comfortable and rewarding

life you've carved out for yourself. Congratulations." Smiling, she turned to watch the waves.

As I couldn't completely block her, I also knew she thought that, unlike the bookstore and bar, there was nothing particularly beautiful or extraordinary about me. Clive's attachment baffled her.

THREE

Just So We're Clear, I Was a Straight-A Student

I wasn't sure how she did it, but Liang always positioned herself at Clive's side, whereas I seemed to forever be lagging behind, the sulky teenager, angry with the world. Of course, it didn't help that every vamp we passed thought Liang powerful, deadly, brilliant, beautiful, and perfect for Clive. I wouldn't get into what they thought about me. I was already feeling down.

Russell was waiting for Clive in the foyer. "Sire, Godfrey and I had a thought."

"My study." Clive and Liang sailed ahead while Russell walked with me.

"I didn't expect you back so soon, Miss Quinn." He kept pace with me, quiet solicitude in every word and expression.

"We had a spot of trouble." I didn't want the whole nocturne to know my woes. The schadenfreude was strong in this crowd.

"I'm sorry to hear that." He held the door open for me before closing it firmly behind us.

Clive sat behind his desk with Godfrey in one chair and Liang in the other. Russell and I would either need to stand or sit farther from the action. Godfrey stood immediately, gesturing for Russell to take his chair. Liang, who had no official place in the nocturne and therefore should have moved, remained seated.

15

Godfrey pulled two chairs from the table at the opposite end of Clive's study and brought them to the desk, as a kind of second row. I patted his arm in thanks but ignored the chair, instead prowling around the room, restless.

Voices in a nocturne were always kept low to avoid eavesdropping. We all had excellent hearing, including any who might have an ear to a door. None of the rooms in the house were soundproofed. Clive had explained to me when I'd moved in—when the Slaughtered Lamb had been destroyed and I'd had nowhere to live —that soundproofing was the quickest way to be ambushed. If someone was coming for him, he wanted to hear it.

So I wandered the far side of his study, picking up rare treasures, examining them, and putting them back. Their discussion, like the hundreds that had come before, seemed to spiral away in too many directions. When you're a thousand-year-old vampire, like Clive, you make a lot of enemies. They'd long since exhausted primary possibilities, those he may have battled or bested. They were now exploring secondary and tertiary connections.

Most vampires were long-lived. Was it the lover of a rival he'd killed? The underling of that lover who had been brooding about his master's defeat for a century or two? The possibilities were, as I was discovering, endless.

"Yes, but I contend Leticia is older than she admits." Godfrey was leaning forward, intent.

I'd been letting their voices wash over me until now, as I hadn't known anyone they were discussing. This name I knew. Leticia was the vamp in Clive's nocturne who'd had it out for me. She'd blamed me for her lover Étienne's death. Bélisaire Lafitte, Étienne's brother, agreed, attacking the nocturne and luring us to New Orleans. Clive had killed Étienne when he'd failed to follow Clive's order to guard me. When I was seventeen and just building the Slaughtered Lamb, I'd been attacked by a kelpie, almost killed, and it was Clive who'd had to rescue me. That fucking kelpie was nothing but trouble.

"You've mentioned this before, but I don't see how she could be," Russell responded. "She was thoroughly investigated before she was accepted into the nocturne."

"Yes, but who was doing the investigating? Remember, she arrived when we were going through a changing of the guard. Greta was returning to Europe and Nicolette was taking over the job."

A weighted silence filled the room.

"What?" I asked, moving back toward the discussion. "Why is that important?" I ignored the empty second-string chair and instead settled onto the tufted bench along the wall to the right of Clive's desk.

While Clive considered the question, Russell turned to me. "Nicolette only held the job for a few months, while we looked for a researcher who possessed the age and experience needed to do the job properly." Expression strained, he continued, "Nicolette was one of the members of the nocturne who fought on Lafitte's side when they attacked."

"You say you believed her to be older than she said. Why?" Liang rested a hand on Clive's desk, turning to Godfrey.

"Her speech," Clive said.

"Yes." Godfrey nodded, waiting for Clive to continue.

Clive blew out a breath and turned to me. "Her phrasing, but only rarely, was archaic."

"Yes." Godfrey stood, excitement forcing him to move. "And never when speaking directly to either of us. I only noticed it a handful of times over the years, and only when I overheard her deep in discussion with others."

"Exactly," Clive said. "I'd heard her once or twice use a word or a phrase that made me think of home. I thought it odd for one as young as she to use it. It happened so rarely, though, I'd assumed she'd merely picked up the expression from someone older."

"We can be magpies with language," Liang agreed.

"Sure, but doesn't that prove Godfrey's point?" I pulled up my knees, wrapped my arms around them, and wished I had a blanket in here. The cold window at my back was chilling me to the bone. "I do the same thing. I listen to ancient supernaturals chatting in the bar and sometimes pick up the expressions that interest or tickle me. If it's a fun word, like Grim referring to musicians as troubadours, I consciously make the switch in my head, wondering which troubadours I might listen to as I stock the shelves in the bookstore. I haven't altered my lexicon. I've merely overlayed a word I find more joy in."

All four vamps stared at me, Clive smiling, so I continued. "I knew the word from books, but it wasn't until I heard Grim using it that I wanted to adopt it. For him, it wasn't a fun, archaic word. It was the proper word for musicians of his time. He wasn't doing any code switching or making a joke. When I use it, I'm consciously playing with language because it's not my word. It belongs to another age."

Clive rose while I spoke and opened a cabinet door, pulling out a folded gray and white throw. He wrapped it around me before resuming his seat. A line formed between Liang's eyebrows and she blinked twice in rapid succession, a sure sign of distress.

"If, as you say, Leticia only used the archaic language when lost in a discussion with others, not with you, when she'd be more inclined to be circumspect, it might be indicative of those words being part of her own learned language. She may have known to hide her native diction when being overheard could prove danger- ous. And I think it's safe to say she found you three dangerous."

"I understood you'd barely graduated high school." Liang's comment hung in the room.

Clive turned his attention to her, a troubled expression on his face. "Were that the criteria for discussion, none of us—save your- self—would be able to speak."

Liang held herself stiffly and inclined her head toward Clive. "I apologize. I intended no disrespect to anyone in the room. I was taken by how she expressed herself, given her limited, and more modern, education."

"Not happy about the 'barely graduated' comment, but to

answer the question I believe you were asking, I'm neither stupid nor illiterate. Bookstore owner equals book nerd."

"Of course," she said.

The temperature in the room dropped a few degrees, which warmed my heart. None of my guys were happy with the swipe Liang had taken at me.

"Russell, see if you can locate Greta. I need to know if she left of her own volition or if she was coerced into leaving her post. Godfrey, as this was your idea, you run with it. See what you can find out about Leticia, how old, who she's connected to, and why the hell she's aimed at me." Clive stood. "That'll be all for now." He held out his hand for me and we left without a word or backward glance at Liang.

I thought we'd be heading upstairs, but instead Clive walked us down the hall and into my favorite room in the whole mansion. The library put the Beast's to shame. Bookshelves soared to the ceiling. A spiral staircase in the corner rose to the walkway that encircled the second-floor landing. Ladders slid on rails, making it easier to find any book in a room that had to be four times the size of my own bookstore.

Every time I walked in here, I sighed. It was involuntary.

Clive closed the door, tapped and swiped at the discreet control panel. The door lock clicked, the lights dimmed, flames shot up in the fireplace, and soft music played. He guided me to the center of the room, pulled me into his arms, and we began to dance.

Resting my head on his shoulder, I breathed in my mate's scent as tension drained from my limbs. His right arm held me close, his left hand cradling my right against his chest. Slowly, we let the threats preying on both of us slide away.

A year ago—Hell, a few months ago—I'd have been in my apartment, blanket up to my nose, completely, painfully alone.

Abigail may be back, but I had allies this time around. Russell and Godfrey would do whatever they could to back me up. I had friends. Dave, Owen, Stheno, and Meg would stand beside me when the battle began. And I'd found my forever love, the one who, no matter what, no matter how prepared I was, how unlikely I'd be hurt, would step in front of me to take the hit. He wouldn't be able to help himself.

I was going to make sure that didn't happen. I was going to figure out how to be a proper necromancer. I was going to hone my considerable talents and take out my aunt, preferably before any more of my friends were hurt.

For now, though, I was going to dance with my betrothed, his quiet humming rumbling in my ear.

"In the past," he began slowly, "when I knew trouble was on the horizon, when I knew forces were gathering against me, I was steady. I knew I'd triumph. Others may be lost, some dear to me, but I never doubted I'd survive. As Stheno once told you, she and I have lived as long as we have because we put our own survival first. Always. We're ruthless and self-centered and will do whatever it takes, no matter how heinous, in order to be the last one standing."

Swaying in the firelight, surrounded by low, bluesy music, I asked, "Are you trying to scare me off?"

Pulling back, he stopped moving but kept my hand in his. "No. I'm explaining that a thousand years of muscle memory, of survival at all costs, has been altered. I'll still do whatever it takes to survive, but your safety is now tied to my survival.

"I've had millions of discussions like the one tonight, trying to ferret out the enemy and planning an attack. Since you, though, my perspective has changed. It's no longer about vanquishing the enemy in so bloody a manner that any comer pauses. Not only that. Now, there's an underlying fear that never existed before. If the battle ends and you aren't standing beside me, I'm not sure I could muster the desire to go on." He gave a quick shake of his head. "It's new and unsettling, but it's there. In my bones, in my blood, I can't live without you."

Eyes glassy with tears, I said, "It's a pretty good thing we're getting married then, huh?"

"It is, indeed."

I slid my arms around his neck and pulled him down for a kiss. Gentle, tentative—like this new love for both of us—the kiss turned heated. We grappled with the clothes in our way.

"Wait," I panted. "The doors are locked and no one can get in, right?" I looked into dark corners of the room. "No one's lurking?"

He chuckled, his lips brushing the column of my neck before his fangs skated over my skin, causing me to tremble and go up in flames all at once. "You tell me."

I reached out, found all the cold, green blips in other parts of the house, and let it go. "Must you wear so many clothes?" I tore open his shirt, revealing a sculpted chest, but his tie was still tight around his neck. I resisted using my claws to slice through it, instead using more restraint than I thought possible at the moment to slowly slide the knot down and then drop the tie at his feet.

Eyes glowing in the low light, he dove for me. We ended up naked and rolling around on the carpet in front of the fireplace, laughing and desperate for one another. Skin rising and falling against skin, lips and tongues exploring, we took our time, the need becoming almost painful. Finally, when I thought I'd lose my mind, he rose over me and slid inside. Caught in his gaze, I wrapped myself around him, meeting him stroke for stroke until neither of us could hold back any longer.

Later, stretched out on top of Clive while he lazily drew designs on my back with his fingertips, I closed my eyes and sought the little green blips again. This time, I found Liang in the hall outside the library door. Deciding I was far too content to care, I snuggled in.

FOUR

A Rare Moment of Reflection

A few restless hours later, my eyes opened in the dark. Clive was at my back, his arm around me. Did vamps die during daylight hours? Clive certainly believed they did. Me, not so much. Given enough of an emergency, Clive could be roused. He wasn't on top of his game, but he was up. He believed that was due to his strength and age. I contended if he could move or speak at all, he wasn't dead.

When we were in New Orleans, I'd experimented on one of Laffite's vamps who had broken into our townhouse. Stheno had caught him and placed him in Clive's holding cell in the basement. When I did a deep dive into his mind, I found synapses firing. Slowly, sure, but there had been mental activity. I believed vamps were in a kind of regenerative stasis during the day, not dead.

All that was to explain how I knew it was daylight now. The vamps were out. The low level of resentment that hounded me every moment in the nocturne turned off when the sun rose. You'd think that would mean sounder sleep for me during the day, but you'd be wrong. The sudden absence of hostility actually made me acutely aware of how ever-present and exhausting it had been. Constantly bracing for attack was my life in the nocturne. I wanted to be with Clive, but it was a lot.

When I tried to slide out of bed, Clive's arm tensed, holding me close. See? He hated it when I left during the day. I grabbed my phone and headed to the bathroom. It was only a click past sunrise, but I was wide awake. A huge shipment of books had been delivered yesterday and I was looking forward to unpacking and processing them. I decided to use my restless energy for a good purpose.

Cleaned and braided, I headed for the closet. Whichever minion Clive had given the job to had been steadily filling the huge walk-in closet since I'd arrived. There were plenty of fancy duds mixed in, but I loved that whoever was doing the shopping had been given the memo that Sam wears jeans and long-sleeved tops every day. The jeans actually fit properly—a revelation for me —the tees were of a much finer quality, and the sweaters were soft as a dream, but they were all suitable for work.

The same went for shoes. There were pretty boots and high heels in here, but my personal shopper had given me a rainbow of running shoes, a pair to match every top or hoodie. I needed to remember to ask Clive who did the shopping. Whoever it was didn't seem to hate me.

Dressed and ready, I slipped silently through the dark house. Norma, Clive's human liaison who took care of business during the day, wasn't due to start work for a few hours. I considered standing outside Liang's door, as she did to us last night, so I could read her mind, but what would be the point? I knew she considered me riffraff, as most vamps did, and I knew she wanted to take my place in Clive's affections. None of that was worth losing my sight over.

My necromancer abilities meant I had an affinity for the dead— in this case, vampires—but it didn't come without a price. The way I understood it, invading another's thoughts or emotions threw the natural balance out of whack. In order to restore balance, a payment had to be extracted. For me, that payment took the form of temporary blindness. What I'd learned, though, I'd read in books. I needed to find a necromancer who would be willing to train me, preferably before my aunt succeeded in killing me. The problem was that necromancers were really freaking rare.

The nocturne was in Pacific Heights, only a few miles from The Slaughtered Lamb. Clive had been bugging me to drive one of his cars to work, trying to keep me safe on my commute. I'd been refusing, reminding him that I loved running. Werewolf. The thing was, though, I didn't know how to drive.

I knew I should've told him at the first suggestion, but I was embarrassed. He was this old, powerful, been everywhere, done everything, killed everyone kind of guy and I was a book nerd who'd been in hiding most of my life, one who'd been dumped in San Francisco to live or die on her own when she was seventeen. When would I have learned to drive?

Anyway, Dave had promised he'd teach me. I'd tell Clive once I knew how.

The early morning run was chilly and wet. Lots of houses along the way had holiday lights glowing steadily or just winking out. The cheery whimsy of colored bulbs lightened my mood. Too bad we didn't celebrate every season with colored lights.

When I got to the Slaughtered Lamb, I went straight to the kitchen in search of leftovers I could have for breakfast. Dave didn't disappoint. There was a covered plate of cinnamon rolls with a note reminding me to save one for Owen. Heh. We'd see.

I ate at a table in the bar, watching the ocean swirl against the wall of windows, the sky above still holding onto hints of pink. Sometimes it hit me out of the blue. After spending my childhood always on the run, always hiding, I had a home of my own, a stable one. For seven years, I'd had my very own place in the world. My aunt wasn't going to wrestle it away from me.

After I put my dirties in the dishwasher, I loaded the first few of many book boxes onto a handcart and wheeled them into the bookstore. It was like Christmas morning as I opened box after box, pulling out beautiful new books. I checked off titles against my order, entered them into the inventory software, and then organized them on carts for different sections of the bookstore.

I hadn't realized I'd been at it for hours until I felt a gentle pressure on my wards. I checked my phone. It wasn't time to open. There was a text from Owen, though, asking to be let in. He was early. I opened the ward and heard two sets of footsteps heading down.

"Sam?" Owen called.

"In the bookstore."

Owen and his mom Lydia appeared in the doorway. "Dang, you've been at it a while. What time did you get here?" Owen went to the carts and started picking up books, studying covers and reading the back copy, a true bibliophile.

"A while. Good morning, Lydia. Thank you again for your help last night." I emptied another box. "I don't know what we would have done without you and Lilah."

Lydia waved my thanks away, crossing the room to kiss me on the cheek. "I'm just sorry no one realized what was happening until after he'd attacked you."

Owen put down the books he'd been studying and came to stand next to his mom. "Listen, we're here early because Mom found you a necromancer."

"What?" My heart leapt at the idea of defending not just myself, but my friends against Abigail.

"I don't want to get your hopes up," she said, patting my arm. "She hasn't agreed to train you. She's willing to meet you, though, and that's a good sign. Owen will take over here so I can drive you."

"Oh." If she didn't think I was worthy or whatever, I was back to battling Abigail with only what I could learn from books. "When do we leave?"

"Now, dear." Lydia stood patiently, a stylish little handbag on her arm, a black trench over a sweater set and trousers, with pearls at her ears.

She made me miss my mom. Lydia was a very different woman than my mom, but the protective, mama-bear love was the same. Sometimes the pain and grief over losing mine hit like a physical blow.

"Owen, these three carts can be shelved. I haven't added the books piled on the counter into the inventory yet. Once you've freed up the carts, transfer these piles to the carts and tuck them back into the storeroom. I don't want people browsing through books I haven't processed yet."

"You got it, boss." Owen spun one of the carts and pushed it toward the memoir display.

"Thanks." I slipped an arm through my peacoat. "I'm not sure how long this will take. I either leave the wards open now or close them again until I return."

"Leave them open. No one will know to come early. I should be able to get the shelving done before Grim stomps down the steps."

Patting my pockets for my wallet and phone, I nodded to Lydia, ready as I'd ever be.

Lydia drove a safe and sensible sedan. Knowing I'd need to learn how to do this soon, I studied her every move. It wasn't until she got on the freeway that I thought to ask where we were going.

"So, who are we meeting?"

Lydia flicked her turn signal, craned to see in her rearview mirror, and then switched lanes. "Her name is Martha. She runs a bar—The Wicche Glass Tavern—in Colma, which makes sense. That's really all I know, and I had to do quite a bit of hunting to get that. She's a crone who keeps very much to herself."

"If she runs a bar, she can't be too cut off from the wicche community," I said. I'd hardly ever left my bar until recently, but all the supernaturals in town knew my name. When you run a bookstore and bar, people either know you because they're patrons, or they hear about you from friends.

"It's a fae bar. That's how I finally found her. Owen's cousin is dating a water nymph."

We weren't on the freeway for long before Lydia was exiting. "You said of course her bar was in Colma. Why? What's the significance?" Fog blanketed the town as Lydia took the offramp.

"Hmm? Which lane…" Lydia drove slowly, looking for arrows

on the pavement. When she turned left, away from a mall, she responded, "It's been around since the early 1900s, an unincorporated area of nothing but cemeteries. I remember hearing, even now, there are more dead than living in Colma. There are houses and stores now, but this town is still known for its dead."

The road she drove down was filled with single-story mortuaries, religious supply shops, florists, a sandwich shop or two, a couple of bars. The street ended at a cemetery, one that went on as far as I could see, curving over a distant hill and fading from view. There was a guidepost on the sidewalk with the names of a few nearby cemeteries and arrows pointing in different directions. A Japanese cemetery was to the left, a memorial park directly ahead.

Lydia pulled to the curb in front of an out-of-business monument maker's storefront. The windows had a light washing of white paint on the inside, but you could still see the silhouettes of sample tombstones in the dark building.

She checked the address on her in-dash GPS system and then continued around the corner, pulling into a parking place at the Colma Historical Society. When she turned off the engine and got out, I followed, confused. Where the heck was this bar?

"Keep your head down, dear," Lydia whispered. "We're going for solemn and bereaved."

Right before we turned the corner back onto the street we'd driven down, she made a sharp turn, walking through—quite literally *through*—the rickety Employees Only gate, leading to the back of the out-of-business monument shop. It was a ward, like the ones at my own place. At the Slaughtered Lamb, mundane humans walked down the public steps to the Land's End overlook. Supernaturals winked out of sight at a turn in the path, continuing down the stairs and into my bookstore and bar.

Here, any passerby who was interested enough to look over the six-foot wooden fence would see an enclosed construction area with a chipped block of granite and a small, rusting forklift that had already been stripped for parts.

I followed Lydia through the closed wooden gate and found

myself in a fairytale courtyard. A forest surrounded the clearing on three sides. White twinkle lights were strung from tree to tree overhead, lighting the sturdy wooden tables and chairs that filled the space. At the far end of the courtyard stood the biggest tree I'd ever seen in real life. It had to be at least thirty feet wide, with massive, gnarled roots that rose up through the ground, snaking around the dining area, separating it from the encroaching forest. Its branches, covered in thick green leaves with wisteria-like purple blossoms hanging down, formed a kind of canopy over the tables.

At the base of the tree was a split door, the bottom half closed with the top thrown open. Although it was midday out on the street, it was twilight here, with fireflies dancing in the surrounding forest. What I could see of the room beyond the door was dark, but light flickered in the curtained window to the right of the door, as though there was a fire banked inside.

"Hello?" Lydia ventured.

"Have a seat," a whispery voice responded. A moment later, the curved form of a woman who couldn't lay claim to fewer than a hundred years appeared at the door. Her thick white hair was in a long braid that hung over her shoulder. She was barely tall enough to look over the half door, but when she met my gaze, I stilled, caught in a fight or flight response to the power she held.

"You stay here," she said to Lydia. "We'll bring you some tea while you wait." Turning her gaze back to me, she said, "And you, girl, come with me."

FIVE

Where's Strider When You Need Him?

She was an old crone. I could totally take her, and yet I felt my feet dragging, not wanting to get any closer to her. When I reached the door, she stared a moment longer and then finally stepped back, allowing me to enter. Once I stepped inside, she slammed the door closed. Flames roared, flaring past the edges of a stone fireplace, before settling again.

Lanterns hung from the low wooden ceiling. I had to duck to avoid smacking into the one closest. The room was filled with long tables and benches, all dark wood. It felt like I'd walked into the tavern scene in *The Lord of the Rings*.

A tall, willowy woman with long silvery-blonde hair stood behind the bar. She wore a plaid flannel shirt with baggy jeans and was putting together a tea tray. She looked up once, nodded to me, and then continued her work, adding a scone to the tray.

"Who are your relations?"

I jumped. I'm ashamed to admit it, but it's true. The reedy voice was gone. Her question was a loud clap in the room. When I turned, I was eye to eye, not with the doddering old crone who'd shown herself earlier, but with a powerful wicche, still clearly in her prime, white hair and wrinkles notwithstanding.

"Ma'am?"

29

"Your relations, girl. There are no Quinn wicches."

"Wolves," the woman behind the bar said.

"Aye, wolves. But this one's a wicche. I can feel her power. Odd scent, though." The crone looked me over again and sniffed.

The barmaid shook her head, picking up the tray. "Wolficche." The crone took a quick step back, disgust evident, as the barmaid threw open the door and went to deliver Lydia's tea.

"Who are your relations," she asked again, her expression hard.

This was a bad idea. I already had Abigail wanting to erase me because of my mixed blood. I didn't need to add this wicche to the list of people who wanted me dead. When I turned to leave, the door slammed shut again, barring my way.

"Don't make me ask again, girl."

"Corey," I said, keeping my distance. "My mother was a Corey wicche and my father a Quinn wolf." I released my claws, six inches, razor-sharp. She wasn't taking me without a fight.

Her eyes flicked down to my hands and then back to my face. "Was," she breathed. "What was her name?"

"Bridget."

Closing her eyes, she let out a gust of air. "Damn." She strode behind the bar, pulled a shot glass out from beneath it, snatched a bottle of whiskey off the counter behind her, and poured a shot. She looked up, mumbled something in a foreign tongue, and downed the whiskey.

When the barmaid came back, the crone poured another shot and slid it down the bar to her. "Bridget's dead."

"Ach." The bartender said the same phrase the crone had— Elvish, perhaps—and then downed the drink.

"As you're Bridget's girl, I guess introductions are in order. I'm your great-aunt Martha. My sister Mary was your grandmother. This," she said, flicking a hand to the barmaid, "is Galadriel. She's an elf and my bar manager."

My brain stuttered to a stop at her words. I had a great-aunt? "Galadriel?" I'd walked into *The Lord of the Rings* and found family.

Rolling her eyes, the bartender said, "It was my name first. The idiot names a character after me, and suddenly I'm the one who has to deal with everyone wanting a magical gift." She moved the shot glass back under the bar and pulled out a mug. "Tea?"

"Yes, please." As no one appeared to want me dead, I snicked my claws back in.

Martha waved me to a table in the corner of the room. "I'm not in contact with my family." At Galadriel's snort, Martha side-eyed her and then continued. "I hadn't heard about your mother. Was it recent?"

"No." Mind reeling over the thought of a real family member who maybe didn't want me dead, I sat at the table she indicated and studied a mirror on the wall beside me. I sat directly in front of it, and yet there was no reflection. A fragrant breeze blew across my face. When I stared into the elaborate frame, its silvery surface became clearer, a window into a deep, verdant forest.

I held out a finger to touch it. Martha and Galadriel both shouted, "No!" Flinching, I drew back my hand and decided to move to another table, to put distance between myself and the portal that beckoned.

"Sam, is it?" When I nodded, she sat and took a sip from her own mug, settling in. "Spin us a tale, girl."

Light from the fire flickered in the dim room as I told her of my mother and father, of my aunt's psychotic mission to end me, of Mom and me trying to keep a few steps ahead of my aunt, moving from place to place. I told her about the protective amulet my mother had put around my neck as a child and how all hell had broken loose when I'd lost it. And I told her how I'd begun to develop necromantic abilities. When I got to Clive, a look passed between Martha and Galadriel. Deciding I'd probably told her more than enough, I picked up my mug and took a sip of the now tepid tea.

"Who made that necklace you're wearing now?"

I said, "Coco Drake," at the same time Galadriel said, "Dragon."

"Well, that was quite a tale. Wicche, werewolf, vampire lover, demon cook, and dragon jeweler." She lifted her brows and tapped her fingers on the table in a steady tattoo. "And you've come here, expecting me to train you. Is that it?"

"Asking, not expecting." Family. I had living family. She was probably going to toss me in a minute, so I wanted to memorize everything about her.

"Gad?" Martha watched the bartender, who was cutting lemons. The woman stared through me a moment and then shook her head.

Damn. "Look, even if you don't want to train me, can I visit sometime? I just—I haven't had any family in a really long time." Sudden tears blurred my vision. Embarrassed, I blinked them back quickly.

"No one's throwing you out." She paused, studying me. "All right. You can come in the mornings, before we open. If you come too early, before the door is unlocked, you can sit outside. I'll be along soon enough."

"Thank you." A tear leaked out and I quickly swiped it away. "I really appreciate it."

"First lesson," she said, leaning forward and pinning me with a stare. "You don't have to go blind every time you use your powers."

"I don't?" My heart leapt at the idea of not being left vulnerable to attack, as I had been in New Orleans.

Galadriel delivered a fresh pot of tea, with a new mug for me. Mine had gone cold. As she poured, she said, "When I heard you were coming, I asked around about you."

"Oh?" I swallowed and thought about that head shake she'd given Martha.

"I'm told you broke Liam's arms." She replaced the pot on the tray with more force than necessary.

My stomach dropped. "I did."

"That all you have to say for yourself?" She crossed her arms and waited, violet eyes sparking in anger.

In that moment, I knew it was over. No visits with my great-aunt, no lessons, no family. "Yes, ma'am. I broke both his arms."

Galadriel shook her head, picked up her tray, and headed back to the bar. "Are you sure she's one of yours?"

Martha let out a breath. "I was wondering the same thing."

"I'm also told," Galadriel continued, "that you could have killed him right off when he attacked, that that scar you're sporting on your neck is because you were trying to figure out how not to hurt him while he was pinning you down, knife to your throat."

"It wasn't his fault. Abigail had taken over his mind. She was pushing him to kill me. He's a kind man. He'd never have done that without her influence."

"Aye. Which is why you stopped your demon from burning him and asked that woman out in the yard to help heal him before you returned him to the sea." She put her forearms down on the bar, leaning forward. "When I shook my head at Martha about you, I wasn't saying to toss yer ass out. I was telling her there was no black in your aura."

"Unlike some others in our family," Martha added, pulling her shawl tight around her shoulders. "Back to your problem. My guess is your mind came up with the loss of sight as payment and you've never redirected it. Do you have a deep-seated fear of going blind?"

I flashed on being tied and blindfolded in that shack seven years ago, on being tortured and having no idea who he was. "Yes, I guess I do."

"Frame it in another way. Accept the payment freely but direct it differently. When you use your power, focus on the payment you deem acceptable. Headache, stomachache, sore joints, gray hair, withered features. You offer it up and see if it's accepted."

"Is that why your hair is white?"

Galadriel snickered.

"No. I'm just old." She pursed her lips before continuing. "You can also go the tried-and-true method of getting a familiar."

33

"A cat?" I was pretty sure a cat wouldn't want to hang out with a wolf.

"It can be any animal you create a bond with. You channel the payment through your familiar in order to avoid the pain."

I'm not sure what kind of horrified expression I wore but it was enough for Galadriel to drop off a plate of cookies. "Do people really do that? Torture animals?"

"Yes. I would venture to guess my niece has gone through a shelter's worth of familiars."

Low cursing sounded from the direction of Galadriel's retreating back.

"What I recommend for you is a piece of jewelry that can be used to store the pain. In battle—for instance, with a homicidal aunt—you can access the reserve of pain and aim it like a weapon."

On the one hand, that sounded amazing. I'd have a way to fight back. On the other, it felt like a slippery slope to becoming my aunt.

"You can't use the necklace you have. Dragon-made won't do. The item must be wicche-made with a spell for this exact purpose. I'm guessing, because of your other form, rings and bracelets won't work."

I shook my head no. As it was, I worried all the time that I'd need to shift suddenly and lose my engagement ring.

"I know just the thing." She glanced at Galadriel, who'd made a strange noise. "I'll give it to you. Next time you come." She tapped the table. "We need to open, so you should run along. The fae don't take easily to new people."

I stood and carried my mug up to the bar. "Thank you. I'll be back as soon as I can."

Nodding, Martha rose as well. "Don't take too long. Your aunt won't. All right." She waved me toward the door. "Enough visitors for today. We have work to do."

My throat was tight as I nodded goodbye. A great-aunt. I had a great-aunt who wanted to help me. I was feeling lighter as I walked across soft, mossy ground under the twinkle-lit twilight of the courtyard to collect Lydia.

"Oh, thank goodness," she said. "I was worrying that I'd delivered you to your death while I sat out here drinking tea." Standing, she brushed a few stray crumbs from her coat and grabbed her bag. "Owen's been texting me every half hour, begging me to go look for you."

"Wait." I checked the time on my phone. "How long was I in there?"

"Two and a half hours," she responded as we walked back through the gate.

"Two and a half hours!" I checked my phone again. "But it only felt like twenty or thirty minutes, at most."

Lydia hit a button on her key fob, causing the car to chirp and the doors to unlock. "Time runs differently in faerie. That bar must have a foot in Underhill for it to exist out of our time."

I thought of the large mirror on the wall and decided Lydia was probably right.

SIX

Gorgon vs Demon

W hen I returned to the bar, it was busier than a usual afternoon. Some of the cheer from the previous evening had returned. Owen, looking harried behind the bar, was mixing two cocktails, brewing a tea, and making a cappuccino. A wicche walked out of the bookstore and plopped a book on the bar. Owen had been covering it all without me. It was my business and I'd left him to handle it all on his own.

Patting his back, I stepped up next to him. "I'm so sorry. Time runs differently in a fae bar."

He grunted, which was very unOwenlike. Poor guy was probably ready to pull out his hair.

"Listen, tell me what orders you're working on and then move to the bookstore and relax. Sorry I left all of this for you to handle alone."

Rubbing his forehead, he recited who ordered what and left without ever looking at me. Damn, that wasn't good. As soon as Dave stomped down the stairs a couple of hours later, I told Owen to take off. His bad mood had cleared out the bookstore. Consequently, the bar was standing room only again.

Nigel, a normally quiet and staid regular, was sitting in a large group of wicches, most of whom had forgone their usual tea for cocktails. His pure, true tenor led the group in an amazing rendition of Heart's "Magic Man." Dave actually came out of the kitchen to lean against the wall and listen, which was high praise, indeed.

The afternoon crowd left, including our singers, and the evening crowd began pouring in. Like last night, the bar patrons annexed the bookstore. It was nonstop all night, but I didn't care. It was a second shot at our grand re-opening.

Stheno and her sisters arrived a little after ten. The volume of voices dropped appreciatively, which is what tipped me to their arrival. I doubted most knew who they were, but they knew dangerous predators when they saw them.

"Stheno!" I came around the bar and hugged her. She seemed baffled by the show of affection but accepted it. Mostly, I was trying to let my patrons know she was okay and this wouldn't be a repeat of last night.

Dressed in a short, tight, black dress, Stheno was a stunner. "Sam, these are my sisters Euryale and Medusa."

I heard a couple of gasps in the room, but we ignored it. "It's so lovely to meet you both. Stheno said you don't all get together too often."

"Thank the gods," Euryale mumbled as she scanned the room.

All three sisters had a fierce beauty, with long, black corkscrew curls that fell almost to their butts. They were olive-skinned, with the same light, golden brown eyes, although Medusa's tipped more toward hazel. All three had long, sharp noses and full lips. Although no one would ever confuse them as anything but sisters, they weren't identical.

Euryale, tall, thin, and stern, was wearing a filmy white dress that skimmed the floor and seemed to be the leader. At a guess, I'd say she was the oldest. Stheno was curvier, with a smirk on her lips and a come-on in her eyes. Medusa, I guessed, was the youngest. They were all thousands of years old, but she had an air of adolescent resentment, complete with ripped jeans and a band tee.

"Is the bitch here?" Medusa asked.

Stheno used her one good eye to stare daggers at her sister. The one behind the eye patch had been damaged in New Orleans. She told me it'd be back to normal in a century or two. I was horrified, but she'd shrugged it off. I supposed a century to a being that lived millennia wasn't a big deal.

"She's not," I responded, though the question hadn't been directed at me. I was pretty sure Medusa was referring to Meg.

Euryale walked to a corner table in front of the window and stared at the two men sitting there until they both got unsteadily to their feet and scrambled away. Medusa, apparently tiring of harassing Stheno, went over to sit with her sister.

"Wine," Stheno said. "We're going to need a lot of wine. If it looks like it's going to be a mean drunk night, I'll try to get them out before they destroy your place." She patted my shoulder and went to sit with her sisters.

Once the gorgons were seated, the other patrons seemed to feel it was okay to speak again, until, that is, Liam arrived a few minutes later. He rose from the water, shed his seal skin, donned a robe, and walked meekly across the bar to me. You could have heard a pin drop.

Stepping out of the kitchen, Dave watched, his black, shark-like eyes zeroed in on the selkie.

Liam stood contritely at the server's station, where no one sat, his eyes enormous and filled with remorse. "Please forgive me. I have no idea what came over me. I've never wished you harm."

"None of that was your fault, Liam. None of it. In fact, I apologize to you." I came out from behind the bar. "It was my aunt who cast a spell on you. That wasn't you trying to kill me. That was her."

"Is that who was in my head?" His soft voice trembled. "It felt like poison running through me. Trapping me. I couldn't move, couldn't speak. She used me like a puppet."

"I'm sorry." I took his hand and squeezed. "So very sorry."

He nodded slowly, glancing around, seemingly just realizing that we were the focus of the room. "I can't stay."

I squeezed once more and then dropped his hand. "You're always welcome. I hope you'll feel comfortable returning."

After Liam departed, the mood of the room was far more somber. Damn Abigail. I'd never understand how people could carelessly destroy lives in the pursuit of their own wants. I held up a finger to Stheno's table and then followed Dave back into the kitchen.

"Fucking bitch needs to burn," Dave grumbled, pulling a baking sheet out of the oven.

"Same page," I responded, stalking into the storeroom for bottles of wine. Not wanting to piss off a gorgon, I went for the best bottles I had. I carried an armload back to the bar and noticed fewer people in the room. Grabbing three glasses, a corkscrew, and a bottle of red, I made my way to Stheno's table.

I set down the gasses and then held out the bottle, label up, waiting for approval before I uncorked it. Euryale nodded and I set to work.

"So, what was that about?" Medusa asked.

"Sam's got a homicidal aunt who wants her dead," Stheno offered. "She possessed the selkie?"

Nodding, I poured. "Last night—after you left—she used him to attack me."

Pointing to my neck, Stheno asked, "Is that how you got the new scar?"

Shrugging one shoulder, I topped off her glass and put down the bottle. "What's one more? Ladies, due to unforeseen circumstances, Dave is making po'boys and fries again tonight. Menu's right over there." I pointed. "If you'd like anything, let me know."

"Shrimp," Euryale said, taking a long sip of wine.

"Yeah, same," Medusa said.

"Crab for me and we'll need a few more bottles lined up over here."

I put in the order, dropped off six bottles, and then took care of the dwindling crowd. A few minutes later, Dave dropped off food at the sisters' table. He nodded at Stheno, who winked back. Euryale looked him over in a way that made me uncomfortable to watch, like she was trying to decide if he was worth fucking.

"Demon," she breathed.

"Gorgon," he responded, clearly unimpressed.

Medusa was the one who pushed it too far, though. When he pulled a roll of napkins out of his back pocket and dropped them on the table, she slid her hand up the back of his thigh. Not a second later, she screamed in pain, cradling her burned palm to her chest.

"Watch the hands," he said with more annoyance than anger.

When he turned to leave, Euryale leaped to her feet, blocking him. Stheno and I both jumped to intervene, but Euryale was already high-beaming him.

I stopped, the blood draining from my head. I barely registered the light shooting out of Euryale's eyes or the shock on Stheno's face before slamming my eyes shut and crumpling to the barroom floor. *Nononononononono.* Not Dave. Choking on a sob, all I could think was, *Not Dave, too.*

I pressed my face to my knees and searched out the gorgon signatures in my head. They weren't dead. It shouldn't have worked, but three barely perceptible purple afterimages surrounded a blip of pure, unrelieved black. I picked out Euryale and squeezed, imagining my magic like a boa constrictor. When I heard choking, I squeezed harder. The bitch deserved to die for turning Dave to stone.

"Gods damnit! I can't take you bitches anywhere." Stheno's snarl was followed by a grunt and a crash.

The one constant grumpy guardian in my life for the last seven years was gone.

"Come on, you. Cut it out," Dave murmured. He gathered me up and rose, carrying me from the room.

My eyes flew open, staring at his deep red skin, his shiny black shark-like eyes, and then I was hugging him hard enough to choke. "You're okay?"

"Fuck, I'm fine. I know how to close my eyes too." He kicked open the swinging kitchen door and then put me down on the island before grabbing my chin and staring into my eyes. "How did you do that?" he mouthed.

I shrugged, shaking my head. "Did I hurt her?" I mouthed back.

He nodded. Seeing my horror, he whispered, "She'll live." He closed his eyes a moment, as though listening, and then curled a lip. "Sorry, kid. The place cleared out again."

Sighing, I hopped off the island. "I can't even blame that one on Abigail. I'm the one who tried to pop the head off a gorgon."

Dave pushed through the door and went behind the bar to pour himself a tumbler full of cinnamon schnapps. "Yeah, well, maybe I shouldn't have burned the bitch's hand, but I've dealt with enough of that shit in my life. I'm not their fucking demon whore." He downed the liquor in one and then turned back to me. "Maybe we both overreacted."

I stared at him a moment, realizing I had no idea what Dave had had to endure in his life. He was my grumbly, foul-mouthed, half-demon cook. From what I'd picked up over the years, he was old, maybe even as old as Clive. Being neither fully human nor fully demon must have made those many years difficult. Given his violence to Medusa's grope and his *demon whore* reaction, those years may have been more than just difficult.

"No overreaction on my part. Anyone who hurts you deserves to lose her head."

I couldn't read his expression, but he blew out a breath before putting his preferred liquor bottle back under the counter. "Come on, kid. Let's close it up and go home."

"Oh, um."

Leaning back against the bar, he crossed his arms and eyed me warily. "What?"

"Remember how you said you'd teach me to drive?" Smiling hopefully, I waited.

"Fuuuuck," he drew out. "You're going to strip my gears. When I said I'd teach you, I meant on someone else's piece of shit car, not my baby."

"Oh. Right. Fair enough." I went to get my coat. It was about ten miles to Colma. If I tried to keep my pace to at least close to human speed, it'd take me over an hour each way. With time being wonky in Faerie, I had no idea what time I'd be able to open my own place. Damn.

When I returned to the bar, Dave was waiting, keys in hand.

"Really?"

"Don't make me regret this." He tossed me his keys and hit the lights while I ran up the stairs, excited to finally be learning how to drive.

SEVEN

In Which Sam Learns the Difference
Between Second Gear and Reverse

"This is a 1965 Shelby Mustang. It's worth more than your life. If you fuck it up, I *will* have to kill you."

I stared at the shiny black muscle car as my confidence drained out of me. "Isn't it dangerous to leave an expensive car just sitting out here all night?"

"It's not without protections." He grabbed the keys back from me and unlocked the driver's door, leaving it open before walking around the back and dropping into the passenger seat.

Warily, I approached the open door, stared at the pristine red leather seats, the chrome shined within an inch of its life, the gleaming wood of the steering wheel, and felt sick to my stomach.

"Never mind. I'm good." I was pretty sure my internal organs were liquifying. "I can run to Colma. Given the way we keep clearing out customers, no one may even notice if I open late."

"Sit down, quit being a baby, and tell me why the fuck you have to go to Colma." He cricked a finger and I finally sat.

There was no console between the seats, only a carpeted hillock running the length of the car with a long metal stick shift rising from the hillock. The gauges on the dash only concerned themselves with the running of the engine. The small AM radio seemed like an afterthought. Unlike Lydia's sedan with a touchscreen integrated system that allowed drivers to access apps from their phone, this one monitored speed, temperature, fuel, oil, RPMs, and that was it.

"Okay." He pointed to the pedals coming through the floorboard. "The one on the far left is the clutch. Use your left foot on that one. And don't even *think* about changing gears without that pedal on the floor."

I nodded quickly, trying to hold off his anticipatory rage. "Do I press it down and then shift gears, or does it need to be at the same time?"

"Get out," he growled.

I popped out the still open door like I was made of springs. "Good first lesson," I said, backing away.

"Get in the passenger side. I'll drive and narrate what I do. You watch the patterns and timing. Got it?" He dropped into the driver's seat and then fired up the engine. Cursing, he turned it back off again. "Force of habit. We'll start from the beginning."

I closed the door, pulled the single seatbelt across my lap, secured it, and then focused all my attention on Dave.

"Put your hand on the gear shift."

I did and he put his over mine. "Feel that?" He wiggled the shift. "See how there's a little give? That means you're in neutral. It has to be in neutral before you start the engine, so always remember to check. Once you know it's in neutral, press the clutch down with your left foot and turn the key in the ignition."

The engine roared to life. I started to pull my hand away, but he kept it in place under his own. "I can only do this because the car isn't moving and I still have the clutch down, okay? This is a standard H stick. The top of the H is first gear. Feel that? Slide straight down for second gear. Now go up halfway, feel the give there? That's the crossbar over to third and fourth. Up for third and down for fourth. Now, slide back left along the cross bar and then push down for reverse. Feel that?"

When I nodded, he let go of my hand.

"Back up to first. Now I ease up on the clutch as my right foot presses down on the gas. Feel that? It's in gear now."

I did feel it. The sound of the engine changed and I felt a purpose in the rumble through the seats. The car moved forward and we were off. We drove through the parking lot and then along the dark, empty streets while he explained everything he did. I was feeling pretty confident when he drove back into the parking lot above The Slaughtered Lamb.

He shut off the engine. "Okay, you try now." He got out and went around to my side of the car. When I didn't move, he opened my door. When I still didn't move, he leaned in, unbuckled my seat belt, dragged me out by my arm, and shoved me toward the driver's side.

"I'm going. I'm going." My life flashed before my eyes as I slowly trudged to my death. Watching was exhilarating. Imagining doing it myself was terrifying and I wanted no part of it.

"Quit being a fucking baby and get in."

I'd like to say I nailed it, but that would be a lie. I didn't get the timing right and stalled it on my first try. If I hadn't been desensitized by years of exploding rage, I might have jumped out of the car and kept running. Instead, I blocked him out and tried again, trying to feel that tension, that readiness I'd felt when he shifted gears. I ended up stalling three times, but no gears were stripped.

It was almost two in the morning when Dave had me drive to the nocturne. I had a few truly terrifying moments when I had to stop on a hill and then start again, but I did it, even with a demon forcefully advising me in the next seat.

I put the car in neutral, engaged the parking brake, and then shut off the engine, handing him back his keys. "Thank you. I know—"

"Shut it, kid. You did good. Now," he said, tapping his fingers on his thigh, "why the hell do you need to go to Colma, of all places?"

"Oh, right. It's been so busy and, well, weird at work, I forgot to tell you. Lydia found a necromancer in Colma."

"Makes sense." He nodded.

Ignoring the vamp at the gate who was watching us, I continued. "She owns a fae bar called The Wicche Glass Tavern."

"Heard of it," he said, scratching his cheek. "Never been there."

"It has a foothold in Faerie, so time is off when you visit." I'd read enough fantasy to be appropriately frightened of being trapped for all eternity in Faerie.

"Hadn't heard that part." He stared out the windshield, lost in thought. "Having a door to Underhill nearby…that could be very bad." After a long pause, he shook himself out of his reverie. "Listen, make sure you tell Clive that the fae have access to Underhill. Locally."

Turning his focus back to me, he added, "All the fae aren't like the elves or water sprites who visit the bar. Hell, even that grumpy old bastard Grim is nothing compared to the monsters lurking in Faerie. Doors work both ways. We don't need any of their horrors walking into our world."

"Right. I should sleep well tonight. Thanks."

"What does this have to do with your necromancer? Is she fae?"

"No." I shook my head, still not quite believing it. "She's my great-aunt." I couldn't stop the smile. "I have family. I mean, that doesn't want to kill me."

"Are you sure?" Dave's black eyes glowed in the low light. "How do you know?"

"She told me. Her name's Martha Corey. She has my mom's eyes."

"I get it, kid. I understand the lure of finding family, but what we know is you have an aunt who wants you dead. Now some long-lost relative, one involved with the fae, wants to meet with you? Nah, I'm not buying it."

"I believed her." It wasn't until Dave tried to block her that I realized how badly I wanted to see Martha again. "She didn't trust *me*. An elf named Galadriel was with us the whole time. I think she was guarding Martha in case I was the psycho trying to kill a relative."

"Galadriel," he echoed thoughtfully. "I've heard of her. Silver hair, purple eyes?" At my nod, he continued. "Bloodthirsty warrior. A general, of sorts, in Faerie."

"In this world, she's Martha's bar manager."

He took a deep breath and blew it out. "I don't trust any of this. I'll go with you," he decided.

"No. I need you to open the bar on time, in case time slips sideways and my thirty-minute lesson ends up taking five hours. I'll be fine." I patted the dashboard. "Like this car, I'm not without protections."

"I don't like it." He climbed out and circled around to the driver's side. Pulling the door open, he said, "See if Owen can drive you tomorrow. At least you'd have some backup if things turn ugly. He's good in a fight. I'll go in early and cover until you get back."

I hugged him quickly before he could protest. "Thank you." Holding up my hand in farewell, I made my way to the disapproving vamp manning the front gate. We stared at each other a moment before he finally relented and opened the gate. Asshole. They were all assholes.

They could hear my heartbeat the minute I walked in. As I walked across the foyer, tension in the house amped up in response. We'd weeded out all the ones who wanted me dead. What we were left with was a mansion filled with vamps who were offended by my presence, disgusted that their Master, for whom they had a healthy mix of respect and fear, seemed to actually love me, and flabbergasted that perfect, powerful, beautiful Liang hadn't been their Master's pick.

Hungry but unwilling to hang out in a communal area, I bypassed the kitchen and took the stairs up to the third floor, to the bedroom I shared with Clive. He wasn't home. I didn't feel his, Liang's, or Russell's signatures in the house. Sighing, I closed the door, flopped onto the bed, and pulled out my phone, hitting Owen's contact.

When it went to voicemail, I remembered what time it was. "Sorry! Hopefully I didn't wake you up. Are you able to take me back to Colma tomorrow morning? Maybe nine or so? Dave said he'd open and cover until we got there. I hope you're feeling better. Goodnight."

Two minutes later, I received a text.

Owen: Seriously? You call at 2 in the morning? It's just all about you, right, Sam? No, I can't be your chauffeur tomorrow. I feel like crap and I'm staying home.

Me: Sorry to disturb you. I hope you feel better soon.

Feeling queasy, I sat up. Owen must have been really sick. He'd probably finally fallen asleep when my stupid phone call had woken him up. I was becoming too used to the vamps' inverted clocks.

I changed into leggings and a hoodie, grabbed my phone and some cash, and went for a run. Being out from under the vamps' suffocating disdain felt wonderful, as did my muscles warming up and stretching out. I ran aimlessly, up and down hills for no other reason than the exertion.

My phone buzzed in my pocket as I was nearing Coit Tower. I sprinted around the empty parking lot and leaned against a low wall, not wanting to get too close to the edge. Lights shimmered along the Embarcadero as the first hints of dawn had stars winking out. I pulled out my phone and saw a missed call from Clive. I called him back and he picked up on the first ring.

"Are you all right?"

"Yeah. On a run."

"Still? It's almost dawn. I'd hoped to see you tonight."

Feeling guilty for letting the house get to me, I sat on the wall and felt my stomach swoop. I hated heights. I kept my eyes trained on the windows beginning to light—people waking for the workday ahead—as I shuffled back from the edge. "Me, too, but you weren't there. It'd already been a rough night and then being surrounded by vamps who hate me…" I shrugged, not that Clive could see me. "I guess it got to me."

He was a long time in responding. "It's selfish of me, I know. I keep waiting for them to come to their senses, to finally appreciate this rare gift they've been given. While we wait, though, you're forced to live in a dangerous and unfriendly home." He sighed. "I'm sorry."

"Me, too." I bounced my heels off the low wall and wished Clive and I could live alone, separate from all the vamp politics and rivalries.

"If you need to move back to The Slaughtered Lamb, I understand. I'll visit as often as I can, but it'll mean I don't get to wrap myself around you every night. You've become a kind of tether. When I—well, you believe I sleep, so I'll use that word. When I sleep during the day, I sometimes hear you, feel you nearby. Sometimes it's just your heartbeat I hear. It's like a tether keeping us connected across time and space. I've come to rely on that tether. It leads me home."

Wiping away a tear, I swallowed down the emotion. Hopping off the wall, I began sprinting back to the nocturne. "I'm on my way. Try to stay awake."

Dawn was just breaking as I took a lightning-fast shower, put on my favorite silk pajamas, and slid into bed. Clive pulled me close, his arms wrapping around me on a sigh, and then he was out.

EIGHT

I Forgot About the Freeway

The alarm on my phone went off at nine. By rights, I should have been exhausted, only having slept a couple of hours, but I woke clear-eyed and alert. Dave may have been wary about an out-of-the-blue relative backed by the fae, but not me.

I considered my options. Owen was out. Maybe Lydia would be willing to drive me again? Remembering her sitting for hours in the courtyard yesterday had me dumping that idea. George? No, he was usually at work by now. The San Francisco Zoo opened at ten. As a large exotics veterinarian, he went in long before visitors began showing up. As I considered everyone I knew and their ability to take a few hours out of their day to chauffeur me, the more sick and helpless I felt. It wasn't anyone else's responsibility but mine. Dave said I did good last night. I could do this on my own. It wasn't far.

Avoiding a plea for help made me feel better, stronger, as I went to find Norma, Clive's human assistant. She worked days, while the vamps were out of it, and had an office down the hall from the kitchen. I stopped there first, starving. I'd taken money with me last night, planning to stop at an all-night diner for food. Instead, I raced home to be with Clive.

I checked the fridge. The vamps hated buying food for me, so the pantry was empty. Since Clive insisted there be food for me in the kitchen, whoever did the shopping usually picked up ready-made dinners they left in the refrigerator. Finding meatloaf, mashed potatoes, and green beans, I piled a plate high and put it in the microwave. There was also a chocolate cake in there, one that would be a crime to let go stale.

After I scarfed my dinner-for-breakfast plate, I cut two slabs of cake. I ate mine with a tall glass of milk and then brought the other down the hall to Norma's office.

When I appeared at her door, she jumped.

"Sorry!" I held out the plate. "I didn't mean to startle you. I assumed you'd heard me in the kitchen."

"Oh, Miss Quinn. Whew, that took ten years off." She shook her head, dark curls bobbing, as though shaking off the fright. "I just got off the phone. I didn't realize you were up yet."

"I come bearing cake." I put the plate and fork down. "And to ask if I can borrow one of Clive's cars." I really hoped she hadn't been tipped to my non-driver status.

"Of course. Mr. Fitzwilliam has been very clear. You have access to everything." Norma started typing on her laptop. "Which car would you like?"

"Can I just go to the garage and look around? I don't know car names. I want whichever one is the safest and easiest to drive, as I don't do it often." Understatement.

"Absolutely." Norma popped out of her chair and a blanket hit the floor. She was wearing leggings and warm, puffy boots paired with a red silk blouse and pearls. She looked down at herself and her warm brown skin pinked. "Um, ninety-nine-point-nine percent of the time, I'm alone in my office. When I have to take part in a video call, they only see from the chest up."

"Understandable. If Clive knew you were cold, he'd add a heater or adjust the thermostat, or something."

She grabbed her keys from the corner of her desk and led me down the hall toward the garage. "I don't mind." At my look, she continued. "If it's too warm, I get sleepy, especially since I'm all by myself. If the room is chilly, it keeps me awake. When I'm not on phone calls, I usually have podcasts playing to keep me company."

"Smart." Did she know she was working for vampires? I needed to remember to ask one of the guys.

"Here we are," she said, opening the garage door. She hit the light and I was stunned by the number and variety of luxury sportscars, but not by the lack of color. Almost every car was black, with a few silver ones mixed in. They were so on-brand, it was ridiculous.

"Seriously?" It was like a freaking showroom, some on lifts, some on the ground. "This is embarrassing."

Norma laughed and raised her eyebrows in agreement without actually saying anything negative about her employer.

"I'm not driving any of these things. Doesn't he have a nice, quiet sedan in the bunch?"

She walked me to the far corner. Here was the Mercedes Russell had driven me in a few times. There was also a BMW and a Volvo. I pointed to the last one, the least assuming of the bunch. "Those are supposed to be safe, right?"

"Absolutely. The key is in the cup holder. Don't forget to take it with you, as the car won't lock if you leave it inside. When you start the engine, the garage door automatically opens. Once you're out, it will close after you."

"Perfect. Thank you so much for the help." I needed her to leave while I tried to remember how to drive.

"You're welcome. If you need anything else, there's an intercom on the wall behind you." With a nod, she left.

I approached the car as I would a dangerous predator. The door opened soundlessly, the black exterior giving way to supple tan leather and a black dash. I sat, closed the door, and panicked. This was nothing like Dave's car. Breathing slowly, I realized it was a great deal like Lydia's. No perfect clutch timing required.

This was stupid. And dangerous. I should call a cab or download one of those ride sharing apps. Pulling the phone from my pocket, I remembered Liam's empty gaze as he leaped over the bar, knife in hand, hell-bent on killing me. Liam, a selkie with his own inherent magic, was unable to fight off Abigail and her pet demon. What chance did a mundane human have? And if she attacked while the driver was in traffic, even more people would die.

Sighing, I pushed the button to start the engine and it quietly purred. The garage door opened as I studied the gauges, buttons, and switches, trying to remember everything I saw Dave and Lydia do.

I could do this. I was twenty-four, almost twenty-five. I should be able to drive a damn car. Tamping down the fear, I looked up the address of the Historical Society where we'd parked yesterday, as The Wicche Glass wouldn't be on the internet. The display on the dashboard asked if I wanted to pair my phone. I hit yes and a map popped up on the screen.

"Beginning route to 1500 Hillside Boulevard. Turn right and proceed to the route."

Deciding it was a sign, I put the car in gear and eased out of the parking place toward the garage door. Once out, on the slate drive, the door closed. I had a moment of worry as I approached the gate, but then it slid open. The cars must carry a chip the gate recognized.

Following directions, I made it across town without incident. Well, there was that car pulling out from a side street that I thought was trying to get in front of me. In hindsight, judging by the loud, sustained honking, stopping to let him in was not the right choice, but I still contend it was the polite one.

It wasn't until I was directed to merge onto the freeway going south that I started to panic in earnest. Thank goodness none of the other drivers wanted to start their day in a collision. A few honks and middle fingers later, I was in the flow of cars.

I was just starting to relax when the computer voice told me to take the Serramonte Boulevard exit. Following her directions, I put high-speed terror behind me. I ended up on a road that ran parallel to the freeway before it crossed the 280, becoming the road that bisected Colma. I passed the out-of-business monument shop, turned the corner, and ended up back in the Historical Society's parking lot.

Putting the car in park, I shut off the engine and breathed. The last thirty minutes of my life were equal parts petrifying and exhilarating. Sometime in the future, I'd know how to do this properly, and I'd then have the freedom to go anywhere I wanted, whenever the whim hit me. I wouldn't need to check with anyone, ask for a ride, or keep it within running distance.

I'd always wanted to see the snow. I could drive to Lake Tahoe, take a run in the snow, and then drive back. Bubbles of giddiness filled me. No more relying on others to get me somewhere or me just deciding it wasn't worth going.

Sighing, I remembered to grab the key before I got out. I looked for a way to lock it, scanning the door for a keyhole, like Dave's car had. Finding nothing, I studied the key and saw a locking icon. I hit the button and the car chirped. That hurdle cleared, I went in search of my great-aunt.

The gateway was passed as easily as last time. The light in the courtyard was different, though. It was as if the perpetual twilight had edged a bit further into night. Voices whispered in the distance as I weaved through the tables toward the door in the magical tree. Knocking, I waited, the whispers pausing.

"Come in, dear," a reedy voice called.

The voice raised my hackles, but I didn't know why. I recognized Martha's voice. Unable to pinpoint what was spooking me, I opened the door and entered.

Martha sat by the fire. The large mirror—the one I suspected of being a window into Faerie— hung behind her, the reflective surface darker than it had been last time. Was there a link between the courtyard and the mirror? Was it Faerie's pull that had me uneasy?

Firelight flickered in the dark room. Martha hunched under a shawl, her head tipped forward. Galadriel was nowhere to be seen. Scalp prickling, I knew Dave was right. I'd been set up.

A withered finger rose from the folds of her clothing, beckoning me foreword. "I've been waiting for you."

Retreating a few steps, I turned to leave and found the door gone. *Fuck me.*

"Oh, don't leave." The voice had changed: deeper, more guttural. "I haven't had my breakfast yet." Not-Martha rose, shedding the shawls, and kept rising. The top of his head brushed the wooden beams of the ceiling. He had been wearing some kind of glamour that concealed his size and bulk. Rippling muscles glistened in the firelight as he moved toward me.

Ogre? Troll? My mind raced through all the fae monsters I could think of, trying to place this one, trying to remember weaknesses. He most closely resembled an Orc. This was the problem with learning everything from books. I had to rely on others' knowledge and accuracy. The fae weren't big on anyone knowing their secrets, though.

The question for right now was: Did he resemble an Orc by happenstance? Was this his true form or did he know I'd had nightmares about Orcs ever since I first read *The Lord of the Rings*? Was he playing on my fears, as my aunt had?

Fingering the necklace spelled to keep my mind safe, I backed away and cast out to see if I could find him in that part of my mind where my necromancy lived. Nothing. Either my brain was on the fritz or he was neither undead nor an immortal.

Unleashing razor-sharp claws, my face distending to accommodate a wolf's big, sharp teeth, I motioned the monster forward. I might die, but I wasn't going down easy.

He chuffed a laugh, flexing his arms and rotating his head. He picked up a ten-foot wooden bench and swung.

Ducking at the last minute, I rolled toward him and shot out a hand, raking my claws across the back of his ankle, hoping Orcs had Achilles tendons. He was bellowing when I popped up behind him. Unfortunately, he was also swinging a massive slab of wood.

The bench slammed into my side. I felt my left arm break, heard the sickening crack as I went flying over the bar. I don't recommend crashing into alcohol bottles. The broken glass cuts you to shreds as the alcohol stings like a mofo.

Blocking it out, blocking all the pain and fear out, I slowly righted myself and stood. Blood seeped into my eyes, but I could see my own death staring at me clearly enough.

NINE

Orcs are Assholes

G rinning, he plucked me off my feet by my neck. I let my face
go slack as he bared broken, blackened teeth.

Hanging limply, trying not to telegraph the move, my good
arm shot out, my claws raking across his face, tearing through his
eyes. Screaming, he dropped me and clutched his face.

While he was distracted, I scrambled up the table behind him,
trying to match his height, and then jumped onto his back. I
snapped my jaws around the back of his neck and tore with as
much force as I could muster. It was like trying to bite through an
armadillo.

Fearing even my slashing abilities wouldn't be enough to cut
deeply through his hide, I instead used the claws on my right hand
like spears, jabbing them into his neck and then drawing my
fingers slowly into a fist.

He spun, pounding my sides with his huge, meaty fists. I was
hanging down his back, so although he couldn't get a clean shot at
me, those fists still hurt like hell, especially when they landed a
blow on my already broken arm. If there was one thing I knew
how to do, though, it was float above the pain and horror. This
wasn't even close to the worst that had ever happened to me, and
I'd survived that. I'd fucking survive this, too.

SEANA KELLY

Blood oozed over my fingers and down my throat. Angered to have any part of him in me, even his foul-smelling skin and blood, I shook my head viciously, gnashing my wolf's teeth. The problem was his neck was so freaking thick, I wasn't finding his spine.

While my claws slowly cut through the gristle of his neck, he spun again and slammed me against the wall. I lost my breath, feeling like I'd been dropped ten stories. Ribs broken, body battered, head ringing, I dug in deeper. It wouldn't be long. Once he knocked me unconscious or broke too many bones for me to move, I'd be at his mercy. I had to fight like hell while I still could.

Desperate, knowing he wasn't dead so it shouldn't work, I imagined my magic as a coil in my chest, the way Lydia had taught me. Claws ripping, teeth constricting, I imagined that coil wrapping around his neck, cutting off his air.

His strangled gasping caused hope to bubble in my chest. Pulling tighter, imagining the coil cutting through his hide, I felt more blood ooze over my fingers. When he dropped to his knees, I knew in my heart I'd survive this, too.

A few struggling moments later, his neck caught in my jaws, I ripped out his spine and watched his dead body slump to the floor.

A world of hurts made themselves known as I sat, rather abruptly, on the barroom floor, my back to the wall. No one can sneak up on you if you have your back to the wall. Cradling my broken arm to my chest, struggling to breathe, I stared at the mountain of dead Orc. I knew my head had been slammed against hard surfaces quite a lot recently, but none of this made sense. Why the hell were fae monsters after me?

I understood my aunt, sort of. I even understood the vamps wanting to take me out. What the hell had I ever done to the fae? My mind flashed on Liam. Was I being blamed for Abigail possessing Liam? Shit. That was *so* unfair.

Movement out of the corner of my eye had me flinching. A leg emerged from the mirror on the wall. A moment later, a tall, armored warrior stood over me, studying me. When he dropped into a crouch to get a better look, the claws on my right hand slid out again. His eyes flicked to the claws and then returned to my face.

"Just barely survived that one." He paused a moment, listening. "Punctured lung." Standing, he moved to the dead Orc. "Interesting." Grabbing the Orc's legs, the elven warrior looked me over one last time, said, "You're not at all what I was expecting," and dragged the carcass back through the mirror.

I sat in a daze, wondering if more monsters would be emerging from the mirror soon or if Faerie was done with me for the moment. The elf had carried a sword. If he'd wanted, he could have killed me. I took his disinterest to mean I could sit here a bit longer.

Barely five minutes later, the door opened. I hadn't noticed it reappearing. Galadriel flicked on the lights and held the door for Martha. "What's the horrible smell?" Both women stared at the destruction a moment.

"Totally not my fault," I wheezed, causing Martha to start.

"Samantha?" She cautiously approached until she got a good look at me. "Oh, good Lord. Gaddie, help me." She rushed over and dropped to her knees beside me.

Galadriel hung back. "Arm's broken, ribs, lung, concussion. She's a mess."

I started to nod and then winced.

"Gad, please." Martha ran her hand over my head, grimacing when her fingers touched the big knot on the back.

Galadriel, like the elven warrior, crouched beside me, her gaze taking it all in. "Whose blood is that?" She gestured to the pool of foul-smelling blood, her eyes following the smeared trail to the floor before the mirror.

Shrugging my good shoulder, I said, "No idea. He looked like an Orc."

Making a sound of disgust in the back of her throat, she scoffed, "Tolkien again."

"Looked like one." I used the sleeve of my working arm to

wipe more of his blood from my face. Stomach roiling, I tried not to think about how much of it I'd probably ingested. "His head brushed the ceiling. Musclebound. Skin so thick. Hard to bite through." I couldn't get the air I needed to speak. I whispered in short bursts. "He pretended to be Martha. As soon as I walked in. The door disappeared. He dropped the glamour."

"A soldier?" Martha turned to Galadriel. "Why would Faerie send one of her soldiers here?"

Galadriel continued to stare at the smeared blood on the floor, expression strained.

"After I killed the Orc. Warrior stepped through the mirror." I had to stop talking for a minute as I struggled to take in breath. They needed to know, though, in case more were coming. "Warrior said I was interesting. Dragged the Orc back through the mirror." There. Hopefully I was done talking for a while. Not being able to breathe easily made me *very* focused on my next breath.

"Faerie finds you interesting." Galadriel shook her head, staring warily at the mirror.

"Gad." It wasn't said as a question, but Martha was clearly asking for something.

Galadriel stared at Martha, her expression softening. "You know what that means."

Martha's eyes filled with tears and nodded. "I wouldn't ask if she weren't so bad."

Galadriel blew out a breath and then laid one hand directly over the break in my arm and the other over my ribs and lungs. Heat and pain mixed for a moment before I went numb. I could feel something happening, but pain wasn't associated with it, which was a nice change. A few minutes later, her inner light dimming, Galadriel's hands slipped from me.

Martha rushed over to help the elf to her feet. "You sit down now and rest. I'll bring you some tea."

Galadriel patted Martha's hand. "That won't do it this time."

"No. It'll be okay. I'll fix you right up. You'll see." Martha was pleading now.

"I'll always give you what you need, my love." Galadriel bent, softly kissed Martha, and then stepped through the mirror into Faerie.

Martha sagged against the wall, a quiet sob choked off. Feeling better than I had in quite some time, I popped up and helped Martha to a nearby bench. Tears silently ran down her face as she stared into the mirror.

"I'm so sorry."

Martha turned to me, wiping her face dry. "Whatever for?"

"I don't understand everything that just happened, but I get that Galadriel was hurt by healing me and that she's had to return to Faerie because of it." I would have rather dealt with the broken arm, concussion, and internal injuries than see the unadulterated misery on Martha's face.

She patted my hand and then stood. "I'll make us some tea. It seems we have much to discuss."

When she had filled a tea tray, I went to the bar, intending to carry it back to one of the long trestle tables. Instead, she motioned down the back hall. She brought us to a snug room with over-stuffed floral chairs and a comfortable-looking couch.

I placed the tray on the tea table between the chairs and poured. Handing her a sturdy mug, I tried to give her time to settle. Photos filled the walls and most of the flat surfaces. I crossed to study them. Some were taken in the bar, some in the courtyard. Most were people I'd never seen before. One looked very much like my mother as a child, sitting behind a birthday cake, a huge smile on her face. Her sullen-looking sister stood in the background.

The vast majority of photos, though, were of Martha and Galadriel. In the earliest, they looked to both be in their twenties, arms around each other, laughing. In one, the women were on a motorcycle, Galadriel driving, Martha hanging on, both so happy. They'd traveled the world together. Smiling, hand in hand, in front of the Eiffel Tower, the Globe Theater, Sacre Coeur, Notre Dame, Incan pyramids, Egyptian pyramids, the Serengeti...so many images chronicling their long life together.

As Martha aged, Galadriel remained young, beautiful, and vibrant. Fifty years and what had never changed, not in any of the photos, was the love and devotion the women showed for one another. Martha had to be in her seventies, but Galadriel still looked at her as she had in the earliest photos, a woman deliriously in love. I hadn't realized I'd been crying until Martha said my name.

"What have I done?" Sitting next to her, I reached for her hand. "Please, tell me how to get her back."

"That was me, not you. I made the decision." Grief-stricken, she stared into her mug. "Time is so unpredictable in Faerie. She might return in a few minutes or it may be fifty years after I've passed."

Swallowing down the tears, she continued. "It happened once before. My cousin, a black wicche like your Abigail, hunted me down. The spell she cast should have killed me. Galadriel stepped in front of it, giving me time to send the dead after my cousin. She ran, but Gad was mortally wounded. She had to return to Faerie to heal. I thought I'd lost her forever and then three years later, she walked back into my life."

Wiping away more tears, she took a sip. "I'll just need to make sure I live long enough to be here when she returns, that's all."

"Clive could make you a vampire. Or I could make you a were-wolf! I have no idea how, but I could try. Then you could stay together." I couldn't stop the tears running down my face.

"Nonsense. I'm too old for all that. No." She shook her head, staring at the wall of photos. "It's been a better life than I could have ever hoped for." Glancing at me, she said, "Here now. Stop that. I got fifty-two years with the love of my life. How many can say that? And who knows? She might be back soon.

"So." She put down her mug and straightened her shoulders. "You're here for a lesson, so we should get started."

"Oh, no," I said, putting down my own mug. "Never mind about that."

"I absolutely mind when people try to kill my grandniece." She reached for a small wooden box on a bookshelf to her left. "I have something for you." Handing it to me, she picked up her tea again.

Opening the lid, I found a small glass ball on a long chain. Filaments of glass crisscrossed through the interior of the iridescent ball. I brushed a finger lightly over the cold surface. It was too beautiful not to touch it, and yet I feared even that might crack the glass.

"Put it on."

Startled, I met her eyes. "I don't want to break it."

"Nonsense. It's tougher than it looks. Go on." She waved a hand to move me along.

Lifting it by the chain, I watched the light infuse the glass, bouncing it this way and that around the room. Taking her at her word, I put it over my head, pulled out my braid, and let the glass ball rest against my chest. It was definitely spelled. Its harnessed potential thrummed through me. It was neither good nor evil, merely powerful.

"Good. Now wrap your magic around the glass. In your mind, picture your magic—"

"Lydia told me to picture it like a thread coiled in my chest. I've been doing that."

"Okay, good. We'll go with that. Picture your magic wrapping around the glass, completely cocooning it."

Closing my eyes, I did as she said. I pictured a golden thread looping around it, like the God's Eye ornaments I'd made as a child.

"Now, pull it into yourself. Your magic has claimed it. Make it your own. Pull the coil back into your chest, with the wicche glass nestled inside."

Again, I did as she said. There was the briefest moment of cold before the heat of my magic subsumed it, making it mine.

"Yes, good. Now, when you need to use your necromancy, you trap the payment in that wicche glass."

"But—"

"No. Survival does not deserve punishment." Her hand fisted on the arm of her chair. "Gad and I have had this discussion more times than I'd care to count over the years. It's not right. No other magical being is punished for being who they are. Elves feel no pain when they do magic. Gad wasn't weakened today for using her magic. She claimed your injuries as her own. And now, back in Faerie, she's good as new.

"The rest of the fae feel no pain. White wicches theorize about balance and payments, but they don't suffer as we do. Black wicches *should* feel the pain, but they channel it into familiars or victims. Why are we punished simply for being different?" She let out a gust of breath. "No. Pain should not be the payment for existing. You use that wicche glass."

Nodding, I said I would, not really knowing if it was the truth.

TEN

No Easy Answers

The drive back was better. I was feeling too raw to maintain a constant state of panic. Consequently, I made fewer mistakes. I went straight to the Slaughtered Lamb, as it was already an hour after opening. Maybe I could get Dave to give me a lesson with this car so I could make the trips to Martha's more safely. I also needed more than my natural weapons, in case Faerie sent me more monsters.

I parked, remembered to take the key, and jogged down the stairs to The Slaughtered Lamb. Halfway down, I passed a man rubbing his forehead. I paused, not wanting him to see me fade from the mundane world as I passed through the ward. I was completely unprepared for his fist shooting out, trying to coldcock me. Thankfully, my reflexes being what they are, I ducked his fist and pushed him off the stairs into the brush.

I braced myself, ready for him to attack again, but he lay still, eyes glazed a moment before blinking rapidly. "I'm—did I just try to hit you?"

"Yes."

"Oh, my Lord." He scrambled to his feet and stepped over the rope boundary marker, keeping walkers from wandering into protected nature areas. "I'm so—I have no idea what just happened."

"It's okay."

"No. It's really not. I'm so sorry. I just..." The poor man wandered away, no doubt questioning his own deep-seated violent tendencies when it had to have been Abigail, using random humans to attack me.

I continued down the stairs, wanting nothing so much as to smack my aunt really freaking hard. Untold damage; she lived a life of untold damage.

Owen was in, tending bar. Three people. There were only three wicches sitting together and drinking tea. Damn. I glanced in the bookstore. No one. This wasn't good.

I was about to tell him what had just happened but he was looking haggard, which was so unlike Owen. "Hey, how are you feeling?" His dark brown eyes were glassy.

"Fine. Can't shake this headache. I have a doctor's appointment this afternoon." He checked his watch. "Actually, is it okay if I leave now? As you can see, the place is dead." There was an edge to his voice I didn't like. He must have been hurting quite badly.

"Sure. Take off. When you're done at the doc's, go home and rest. Dave and I can cover."

"Yeah. Thanks." Rubbing his forehead, he added, "I will."

Once Owen was gone, I checked on my tea drinkers and then went in search of Dave. He was sitting at his desk, a new addition to the remodeled kitchen. He now had an office area, tucked behind the door.

"Hey, something really weird just happened." I opened the refrigerator door, looking for the lemonade he sometimes made for me. No luck today. When I closed the door, I found him standing a foot away, his face lined in anger.

"What?"

"What do you mean what?" He grabbed me by the neck of my sweater and yanked me forward. "Owen was here at opening. When I mentioned I thought he was driving you today, he didn't know what I was talking about. I called your cell. No answer. Then." Little flames seemed to light his black eyes. "I called the house and Norma said you'd taken one of Clive's cars out."

"Oh."

"You could have died!" he roared in my face. "And you could have taken a bunch of innocent people with you. You *told me* you'd call Owen for a ride. You lied to me."

"No, I didn't." Slapping his hand away, I backed up a step and pulled out my phone. "See?" I showed him the text messages.

Carrying my phone back to his desk, he dropped into his chair. "What the fuck? I asked him why he wasn't with you and he acted like he had no idea what I was talking about."

I hopped up on the island. We'd hear if anyone came down the stairs into the bar.

"He looks like shit," he mused. "I thought he was fighting with George."

"You think maybe Abigail's working on him?" The idea of it had been keeping my stomach in knots. I pulled up my legs and wrapped my arms around them. I didn't want anyone else hurt because of me.

"Fuck if I know." His fingers drummed on the counter. "I'll stop by his apartment after work. See if I can pick up anything." He tossed me my phone. "Now, get your feet off the counter. What's the matter with you?" He pulled me off the island and pushed me out the door. "And no more driving!"

More people arrived in the evening, but it was still quiet. Possessed selkies and angry gorgons were probably more than the average patron wanted to deal with as they unwound with a drink. Sighing, I unnecessarily wiped down the bar for the hundredth time.

We closed early again.

"Am I gonna have to start thinking of this as a part-time job?" Dave snarked as he flicked off the lights.

"Ha ha." I trudged up the steps, worrying he was right. We'd been closed down for almost two months for the remodel. People had probably formed new habits. And who wanted to worry about being stabbed or turned to stone while they drank their tea and read a book?

"At least you didn't steal one of his sportscars," Dave said when we hit the parking lot.

"I'm not a moron." I just felt like one. "Can you open again? I'll run to Colma tomorrow."

"Call an Uber," he said a moment before his car shimmered into view.

"I thought about it, but if she can get to Liam and maybe Owen, a regular person—like that guy who tried to punch me earlier—would have no chance. If she pushed him to attack in the middle of traffic or on the freeway, even more people could die."

Leaning against his car, arms crossed over his chest, he studied me a moment. "Shit. That's true. And what guy tried to punch you?"

I explained the weird confrontation earlier and then turned to walk home.

"Fuck it. Get back here." When he moved away from his car, it winked back out of sight. "It's not good for my relationship to be home too much. Maggie can only take so much of me. Go on." He pointed to the Volvo. "Lesson number two. This time with an automatic."

I pulled the key from my pocket and hit the unlock button.

When it chirped, he shook his head. "You don't need to do that. With these kinds of cars, just having it in your pocket will trigger the lock. When you put your hand on the handle, it unlocks."

"Nice," I said, sitting in the driver's seat.

Dave crouched down at the open driver's door. "See these buttons here on your armrest? This will unlock the passenger side door." He tapped a knob higher up. "This moves the side mirrors." He spent the next ten minutes showing me how everything worked before having me push the ignition.

Checking the rearview mirror and then looking over my shoulder, I put it in reverse.

"Wait. Look at your screen."

Turning back, my gaze dropped to the screen and I saw the car from a bird's eye view. It must have cameras front, back, and sides. "Cool!"

"Yeah. It'll blink and beep if you get too close to anything. Now, back us out nice and smooth and take us for a drive."

After an hour or so, during which I had to get on and off the freeway multiple times, deal with every one-way street downtown, and relay what had happened at the Wicche Glass, I was finally headed back to the Slaughtered Lamb.

"Go to the nocturne. You're not driving by yourself until you have a license. I mean it, Sam." Since he was using his growly, serious voice, I nodded. "And as for your necromancy lessons, ask your boyfriend to loan you a sword and show you how to use it." Shaking his head, he looked out the window at the dark houses we passed. "What the fuck, Sam? Now Faerie is after you?"

"Right? Lowly little book nerd over here." Putting on my turn signal, I looked both ways and then turned down the dark street leading to the nocturne. "I'm a friend to the fae. Why is Faerie sending her monsters?"

Pausing at the gate, I eyed the vamp guarding it a moment before the gate slid open. Asshole. "I'd say he was a rogue looking for breakfast if he hadn't been waiting for me, pretending to be Martha."

I took the slate drive around to the back of the mansion. The garage door opened as we approached. Using my new skills, and the cameras, I backed into the garage, right back into the proper space.

"Good. Put it in park and turn it off." Once I had, and the garage door closed, he continued. "Stay where you are. Let's test that wicche glass she gave you. They probably can't hear us right now," he whispered. "They'll hear the heartbeats, but not the words."

"You want me to read someone's mind?" I unbuckled but didn't move to leave the car.

"That's right. And while you do, focus part of your mind on channeling payment to the glass ball around your neck."

"Okay." Closing my eyes, I found all the cold, green blips in the house around us. I looked for the most familiar ones. Clive, Liang, and Godfrey were in his study, discussing Leticia. Russell was moving toward the back of the house, toward the garage. "The jig's up. Russell's on his way."

"What's he thinking?"

"He's worried. They had an argument earlier. Russell knew I couldn't drive. Clive didn't. Apparently, his Master got an earful about that."

"Clive called the bar to check on you. I assured him you were an idiot, but a safe one."

"Thanks."

The door to the hall opened and Russell stood, silhouetted in the light.

"How's your vision?"

Grinning, I elbowed Dave in his beefy shoulder. "I see a disapproving vamp clearly enough."

"Good."

We got out and crossed the huge garage. My focus was on the lecture I could feel coming. Dave, on the other hand, was taking his time, admiring the cars we passed.

"Miss Quinn." Russell nodded respectfully, but I could hear the disappointment in his voice. Damn. That was worse than anger.

"Russell," Dave said as he patted my shoulder on his way out.

Russell stared at me for a long moment. "If I might have a word with you?"

Sighing, I followed him down the hall and into the library. He gestured to one of the chairs by the fire and I sat while he remained standing.

"Miss Quinn," he began.

Letting out a gust of breath, I said, "I know. Dave already yelled at me. He's been giving me lessons, you know." The plural was a lie. "Okay, lesson. I'd had one before I borrowed the car." I studied his dark, disapproving face. "Please, sit down."

When he did, I continued. "I need to learn how to use my magic if I have any hope of surviving Abigail. The only necromancer around is a wicche who turned out to be my great-aunt. She lives in Colma. Her bar The Wicche Glass Tavern has a foot in Faerie, so time is inconsistent. Anyone willing to drive me needs to give up hours of their day. You guys are all sleeping during the day. Lydia had already given up much of yesterday to help me. I asked Owen. He said no in a way that made me feel like an asshole for asking."

My heart clutched even thinking it. "Abigail may be trying to spell him, like she did Liam." I swallowed. "Dave's going to try to find out for sure. If I tried a ride sharing app, I'd be endangering innocent humans. If I'd ran, I'd be hours late for the Slaughtered Lamb opening, leaving Dave to cover for both Owen and me."

It wasn't like I was joyriding around town. I understood where it was coming from, but I was starting to resent being treated like an errant teen. "I calculated the possibilities and felt I could make it to Martha with the least risk and fuss if I drove myself. And FYI, I did. No one was hurt and no scratch on the car."

Standing, I went to the minifridge hidden behind a panel in the wall. It was filled with blood bags, but now also had water bottles. Taking a long drink, I went to the window and stared out into the night.

"What would you have me do, Russell? Live my life being babysat by an array of supernatural guardians, hoping my aunt goes away? She wants me dead and doesn't care who she hurts or kills along the way."

I turned back to him and sat in my window seat. "I don't know how to protect myself against her magic, let alone anyone else. Unlike her, I *do* care about the well-being of everyone else."

"You could close The Slaughtered Lamb, take away her targets." His deep, measured words felt like a hit to the chest.

"It's selfish of me not to, isn't it?" I felt sick even contemplating it.

"Not selfish. It might be prudent, though." He watched me struggle, his dark gaze compassionate.

"Prudent," I echoed, nodding slowly, lost in thought. "It would be that. It would also break my heart."

"Sometimes the only path forward is one of heartbreak."

ELEVEN

Russell's Story

"Are the lessons with Martha helping?" Russell sat by the fire, watching me.

I was a long time in answering, not because I distrusted Russell, but because I was still deciding. Eventually, I told him everything, including my fight with the Orc and Galadriel's departure, not knowing what, if anything, needed to be censored and worrying the detail I held back was the one needed to find the answer.

Russell had become agitated as I spoke. Consequently, he'd taken to wandering the room. "Dave is correct. If you're going to be battling fae monsters, we need to give you more weapons. Clive is the best with a sword, but I can teach you to shoot. We can do that tonight. Get you a gun."

"Thank you." I pulled up my knees again. Hugged them.

Waving off my thanks, he asked, "Does it work, the wicche glass?"

Resting my chin on my knees, I grinned. "Well, I knew you were coming to the garage to lecture me."

"No vision loss?"

I shook my head.

"Excellent. That makes you far less vulnerable."

"I'm not sure I should use it, though."

He swung around and pinned me with a stare. "Why?"

Shrugging, I wrapped my arms more tightly around my knees. "Those books I read said there had to be balance. What I'm doing is wrong. I'm invading someone's personal thoughts." Lowering my voice even further, I added, "I'm pushing people to do something against their—"

Russell hissed over the top of my words, glaring at me to shut up.

That answered one question I had. Russell knew what I could do, and he was making sure no other vamp with an ear to a door found out. Closing my eyes, I searched for blips. "No one's listening at keyholes," I whispered.

Crossing the room, he sat next to me in the window seat. "Your concern is that you will not be punished severely enough if you use the wicche glass?"

"Appropriately. If I violate a person's privacy, his will, with impunity, what's to keep me from becoming my aunt? The blindness—or Martha said I could channel the payment differently—is a reminder, an immediate one, that what I did was wrong."

"And who determines right and wrong?" he asked softly.

"Human decency?" I thought this was pretty basic stuff.

"We're not human," he countered.

"Sure we are. You may have fangs and I may get furry, but we still have our humanity. Or we should, anyway."

He leaned back against the bolster, studying me. "I should be punished for drinking blood? Clive? What about our long lives, our strength and speed? Should we be punished each time we use our gifts?"

"No, of course not. I just meant that I—"

"That *you* deserve to be punished. Is that it?"

Forehead to my knees, we sat in silence until I finally whispered, "Maybe."

The library door opened and closed. "No." A low, weepy,

instrumental began playing a moment later. "You always forget the music."

Russell stood. "Sire, I'll leave you now."

"Sit," Clive said. He moved to the window seat, shifted pillows, sat on my other side, and pried my arms from my bent legs, pulling me against him. "No," he said again, kissing my temple. "You do not deserve to be punished."

"None of this, Miss Quinn, has been your fault," Russell said. "Not Owen, not Liam, not Galadriel, not the women those wolves attacked, not your father." He paused, tapping a hand on the cushion next to me. "Not your mother."

Clive squeezed the arm around my waist.

"Existence is not grounds for punishment," Russell said.

"Hear, hear," Clive murmured.

Russell studied his hands for a moment. "If you will allow me, I'd like to tell you a story."

Nodding, I curled up, leaning against Clive's chest as he wrapped both arms around me.

"I was born on a plantation in the Orleans Territory. Enslaved from birth. When I was a young man"—he gave a barely discernable shrug—"seventeen, eighteen, I heard the owner talking with the overseer. He was planning to sell a few of us for an influx of cash. We all knew he was short on funds. New wife, oldest daughter ready to enter into society. The buyer was in South Carolina.

"I'd tried to escape when I was a few years younger and was caught by the patrols, dragged back, made an example of." His dark eyes gleamed in the low light. "I'm not discussing that." At my nod, he continued. "I wasn't clear on the geography of the states, to be honest, but I knew South Carolina was the opposite direction of where I needed to go.

"It was a miracle, really. It was the wee hours of the morning on a moonless night. I'd made my way across the fields when I heard a huge commotion up at the big house. I learned later that the owner, drunk and unsteady, fell down the stairs. The dogs went running toward shouts for the doctor, and I travelled west as far and as fast as I could.

"I crossed streams to throw off the dogs I knew were then on my trail. I ran at night and found small, hidden, dark places to sleep during the day."

"Even then," Clive said, humor in his voice.

Russell inclined his head, a shadow of a smile, there and gone.

"I was somewhere in Texas when a group of patrols found me."

At my gasp, he reached out and patted bent knees. "I'm right here, Miss Quinn."

"But I've read. I know what they did to runaways." I knew he didn't want to discuss it. I understood, as I never wanted to discuss what had been done to me, either. Reaching out, I grabbed his hand before he had a chance to move it. "I'm sorry."

He squeezed my hand, nodded, and then pulled away from me. "I'd been with them for going on two days when the vampires attacked, glutting themselves on the patrols."

"Yay."

He glanced over and shook his head. "You'd think, wouldn't you? Turned out the undead were just as mired in white supremacy as the living. They wouldn't drink from a Black man."

"Whatever keeps you breathing," Clive remarked.

Russell grunted in response. "I'd been trying to keep as still and quiet as possible, hoping they'd forget about me. It almost worked. As they were leaving, one paused and cocked his head."

"Your heartbeat," Clive said.

Russell nodded. "Yes. He pulled a knife from the waist of a dead patrol and moved toward me. He'd just lifted his arm when another ragtag group of vampires arrived. They'd been following the patrols and had had their dinner stolen. They fought, tearing each other, limb from limb. I'd never seen anything like it. It was horrifying. I understood that they were the damned. And yet, I wanted to possess that kind of power.

"They'd all but killed each other off. There was one left, but he was a mess. I made a bargain with him. If he'd make me one of them, I'd drag him to safety and care for him until he healed." He glanced over again. "I had no idea what first thirst would be like, what would happen to me.

"In hindsight, I realize he was merely a fledgling himself. It shouldn't have worked, but the following night when I awoke, he was dead and I was ravenous. I could hear and smell everything. The night was alive around me and I was out of my mind with thirst."

"Yes," Clive murmured.

"I ran so fast, it felt like I had wings. I found another group of patrols, three white men with two female runaways. I pulled the bastards off the sobbing women, broke two necks with more ease than should have been possible, and drank the third dry. When my brain was working again, I saw the two women, naked and huddled together, their eyes like saucers in the firelight. I told them to get dressed and run, pointed west.

"For weeks, I was on my own patrol, killing the paddyrollers and setting the runaways free. I'd become the ghost story they told by the fire at night. When they jumped at noises in the dark, it was me they imagined." When he smiled, I understood why so many feared Russell.

"Eventually, I ran across other vampires. Strangely enough, when they were starving, the color of my skin became less important." He made a sound of disgust in the back of his throat and then continued. "Smartest, strongest, the one who reliably found food, it wasn't long before I'd been made Master. I hated them as much as they hated me, but I can't deny the bone-deep pleasure of having white men do my bidding.

"A week or so into my tenure, I found a huge group, twelve patrollers with twenty-three runaways. I planned the attack down to the smallest detail. They knew the rules. The runaways were always released. There were only five of us. The twelve patrollers were more than enough to sate us for days.

"It all went as planned. The following evening, though, when I went in search of the next patrol group, I found three runaways drained dry, their dead bodies barely hidden beneath tree branches. Leaving the vampires I led, the ones pushing me farther and farther east in order to find larger parties, I retraced our journey west. It wasn't long before I found more dead runaways.

"On the second night, I found an abandoned barn in a field gone fallow. I'd been hearing whispered voices, cries, that led me to them. When I saw—I've never felt such rage. All the runaways I'd thought I'd been freeing were being scooped up by another party of vampires, the rest of the group I was working with. The dead bodies of runaways were stacked like cordwood along the walls, while five, still breathing, clung to one another in the center of a pen, eyeing the vampires surrounding them with abject terror."

Russell leaned forward, resting his forearms on his thighs. "Well, the details aren't important. I went in like the hand of God and slew them all. The runaways were near catatonic when I opened the pen and tried to set them free. That's when I realized that fangs trump melanin.

"I went back and found the ones I'd been traveling with. They were outside a plantation, pitifully trying to plan an attack, as only the criminally stupid can. I killed them all easily but felt no triumph. I'd thought I'd been using my newfound strength and speed to right wrongs, to find justice. Instead, I was just another Black man unwittingly being used to betray his own people."

"You betrayed no one," Clive said softly.

He shook his head. "Tell that to the ones who'd thought they'd finally broken free, only to be used—admittedly, in a bloodier and more immediate way—by different white oppressors."

We sat in silence for a moment.

"I traveled west after that, following my original plan. When I ran across vampires, I killed them. It didn't matter what nocturne they belonged to or who they fed on. They were a reminder that no matter what I did, what strengths or talents I had, I'd never be seen as anything but less than.

"Moving at night, I eventually made it to San Francisco. I heard about this limey bastard." He aimed a thumb at Clive. "And planned to take him out." He chuckled, and this time it was absent rancor. "I'd barely made my first move when I was flying through the air and bouncing off a tree. I'd never seen anyone move so fast. He overpowered me in a laughably short time. I waited for him to take my head, a little relieved if I'm being honest, but he asked who I was and why I had my heart set on his demise."

Clive's chest rumbled against my back as he laughed. "Seemed an important piece of information."

"As I assumed I was moments from being put out of my undead misery, I spewed every filthy thing I could, accusing him of all the heinous things other vampires had done. Instead of taking my head, though, he gave me a hand up and invited me to have a pint on him, as it sounded as though I'd been having a rough time of it."

He turned to me then, pinning me in his gaze. "Did I deserve to be punished, Miss Quinn? According to all laws, to the prevailing beliefs, the color of my skin meant I was little more than a work horse, a thing to be used up for the betterment of white society. I rejected their version of human decency. I upended their take on the natural order by stealing myself and others, depriving them of the ones they needed to step on in order to feel superior. Should I be punished for that?"

"Of course not," I breathed.

"So, it's just you? You should be punished for doing everything you can to survive?"

TWELVE

Is It Me, or Does the Word Swordplay Just Sound Dirty?

R ussell was right. It broke my heart, but the Slaughtered Lamb needed to close while I dealt with my aunt. Otherwise, I was offering up my friends as targets. I called Dave, who grumblingly agreed, texted Owen, who ignored me, and left a message for the wicche who had created my wards, to add some kind of "closed until further notice" message on the bar entrances.

Deciding it was the best I could do in the middle of the night, I went in search of Russell and Clive, who were setting up a training session for me down in the basement. I would have much preferred to stay in the library and read, but we didn't always get what we wanted.

I was pleased to realize how easy it was now to track their signatures. They were in the basement, the large room at the end of the east wing. Normally, I avoided the basement at all costs. The style and elegance of the floors above continued below. It wasn't that it was a dark, scary place. It was that this was where most vamps lived, their resting places beneath the ground.

When I exited the circular stairway, I had to walk through a posh undead living room. The vamps no doubt heard my heartbeat coming, so I was greeted with bored stares of disdain. I closed off my mind to their thoughts, but a few of the more persistent ones still slipped through. Most could be filed under the heading "Why Liang is a better mate for our Master than you."

Sighing, I passed through the group and turned right at the hall leading toward Clive. Great. I felt Liang's signature behind the door at the end of the hall as well. Peachy.

The room was huge, much larger than I'd expected. Stairs led down to a floor covered in tan matting. Because of the dropped floor, the room was almost two stories high. Russell arranged assorted swords and handguns on a black-draped table. Liang stood nearby but wasn't speaking to him. Her eyes were glued to the middle of the room. When I began to descend the stairs and the whole room came into view, I saw why.

Clive, shirtless, shoeless, stood in his black trousers, swinging a broadsword with the skill and ease of an ancient warrior, which he was. As much as I couldn't stand Liang, her fixation was understandable. The way he moved, muscles bunching and lengthening, was making it hard to think.

He looked up and found me staring a moment later. Grinning, looking younger and lighter than he had in a while, he motioned me forward. "Lose the shoes and hoodie and we'll begin."

His shirt and jacket were draped over a long leather bench along the wall. I toed off my shoes, peeled off my ankle socks, and pulled my hoodie over my head, leaving it all beside his clothes.

The mat felt odd beneath my bare feet. It wasn't like the ones in high school gyms. This one was thinner and made of some kind of woven material that meant no slipping.

Clive, looking more gorgeous than anyone had a right to, waited for me, the flat of the blade resting against his shoulder. When I got close, he pulled me into a fierce kiss that had my brains leaking out of my ears.

"I caught the tail end of what you were thinking as you came down the stairs," he breathed against my lips. "Shall I dismiss them?"

I pushed away. "No." I knew my cheeks were flaming with our audience. "Later," I mouthed, causing him to laugh loudly.

"Try the swords I pulled for you. See if you like the feel of any of them." He resumed his practice swings while I moved to the table.

The swords were amazing, some long and thin like the kind used in fencing, some short and broad. I couldn't walk down the street with a huge sword strapped to my back, so while I had fun swinging the big ones around, I ruled them out quickly.

There was one, about the length of my forearm, that I liked the feel of. It had a good heft but wouldn't weigh me down in a fight. It was double-edged, with a word etched down the blade.

"*Fìor*? Does that mean fire or flower?"

Pausing midswing, Clive said, "True. It means true in Gaelic." He returned his broadsword to the table with a grin. "And I knew that was the one for you." He picked up something made of leather straps. "I even brought the sheath." Kneeling before me, he adjusted the straps so it fit securely around my waist and thigh.

"I feel like a gunslinger with this thing."

"Gunslinging is Russell's forte. Swordplay is mine." He stood, guiding my hand and therefore the sword to the sheath. "Practice sheathing and unsheathing, over and over, until you can do it smoothly and without thought."

"FYI, that swordplay comment sounded super dirty," I whispered.

"Leave us," he commanded. Both Russell and Liang moved toward the exit immediately.

I held up my hands. "Stop. He was kidding."

"No I wasn't."

"You, hush," I said, waving my hand in his face. To the others, I motioned them back. "As you were." Russell, I could tell, found us funny. Liang, on the other hand, was shocked I'd countermanded the Master.

"Okay," I said to Clive. "Teach me how to use it."

He was a relentless instructor, demonstrating the proper form for countless moves, explaining when to use them. He corrected any deviation on my part as he watched me practice over and over.

What felt like hours later, exhausted, I dropped to the mat. Handing me a water bottle, he let me pant on the floor while he discussed my progress with Russell and Liang.

When he felt I was ready, we moved on to sparring, me with a sword, him weaponless. I worried I might accidentally cut him while we grappled, but I needn't have. I never got close. He was that fast.

It was close to dawn when we stopped. Russell's lessons were pushed off to the following evening. As much as I wanted to learn as quickly as possible, my muscles were too tired to hold a gun steady.

Liang stepped forward. "Clive, we have time to make a few more phone calls. Perhaps we could contact—"

"Not now." Clive grabbed my hand and led me to a discretely designed elevator I hadn't noticed.

I had a moment to register Liang staring after us, her expression blank, before the doors were closing and my back was to the wall, a Master vampire's lips on mine. Hours of desperately wanting him and we were finally alone. Far too soon, I heard the doors open.

His hands slid down, palmed my butt, and hiked me up. Wrapping my legs around his waist, I let him carry me to our room, our mouths fused. He kicked the door shut and then my back was pressed to the door. I couldn't get enough of him, my hands dragging down his arms and chest, in his hair. Hours of foreplay were finally at an end.

He yanked my top over my head and all I could think was *Thank God*. My bra had disappeared. Damn, he was good. He tore my jeans down the center and then impaled me to the door. Even his mouth on mine couldn't muffle the groan. We had a moment, the briefest of moments, to stare into one another's eyes, stilled, savoring the instant of finally being exactly where we'd wanted, before his hands were on my breasts, fingers rolling my nipples.

Fangs skimming down the column of my neck, he plunged into me over and over. Muscles straining, I kept pace. He was perfect.

When I couldn't hold back a moment longer, I drew his head back to my neck. His fangs pierced my skin, I clenched down hard on him, and then we were both flying.

A few minutes later, still shaking, I unlocked my legs from around his waist. He adjusted our positions, making me groan again, and then carried me into the bathroom.

"Not done with you yet." He finally put me down and then turned on the shower. While he adjusted the heat, I disposed of the shredded jeans, which had fallen around my ankles. How did he always look so good? I was sure I was a mess. Glancing in the mirror beginning to steam, I caught my reflection. Huh. When had my hair been unbraided? I was looking more tousled and sexy than sweaty mess. Yay me!

He pulled me into the hot, steamy spray and then ran slick, soapy hands all over me. Getting a handful of rich, creamy foam, I followed suit, my hands eventually wrapping around a part of his anatomy I was quite fond of. The look in his eye made my stomach quiver.

Once we were both thoroughly cleaned and sated, again, we toweled off and finally made it to the bed. Window shields descended. Dawn was only a few minutes away, but my fella wasn't a master vampire for nothing. This time, the urgency was gone and what was left was a gentle reverence. Slowly, softly, we kissed and stroked one another, both finding love and home.

When we joined in the dark, it was on a sigh. I loved him so much, I felt near to bursting. And when gentle contentment burst into flame, we clung to one another. All the vamps in the house had already winked out when I rolled us and came up, straddling Clive. His clever fingers kept me tight and needy. And when I started to fly, it was his hands, interlocking with my own, that kept me tethered to the world.

Later, wrapped around one another, we finally slept.

Too many nights of too little sleep did me in. I'd forgotten to set an alarm. As a result, I didn't wake until almost two in the afternoon, long past when Martha said we could conduct lessons. Annoyed with myself, I dressed and began the long run to Colma.

It felt good. It had been a while since I'd gone on a good, long run in this form. What with The Slaughtered Lamb's opening and the drama since, alone time to run had been shunted aside. Ignoring the route my phone suggested, I created one of my own that took me through the most green spaces.

I ran through Golden Gate Park, down past Lake Merced, West-moor Park, crossed over the freeway, and eventually ended up back in the fog, jogging past one cemetery after the next. The Wicche Glass Tavern had been open for hours when I walked through the false gate. As it was a fae bar, I had no idea what sort of welcome I'd receive.

When I'd made my way past the old monument shop's work area and into the bar's courtyard, I wondered if fae time was finally working for me. The area was empty, the overhead twinkle lights dark. The door to The Wicche Glass was closed; no firelight flickered in the window.

I went to the door and knocked. Martha had just lost Galadriel. Perhaps she'd decided to close her bar, too. When I heard movement inside, I knocked again.

"Martha? I know it's late, but can I talk with you?"

Shuffling feet and then the door squeaked open. A sad blue eye stared at me through the crack. "Not today," she croaked, the door closing with a soft finality as she shuffled away.

Damn. What was I thinking, coming for a lesson the day after she'd lost her love?

Not wanting to run home yet, I went to one of the sturdy trestle tables, the one closest to the unimaginably huge and gnarled tree roots that encircled the courtyard. Crossing over the roots into the adjacent forest felt dangerous, so instead I sat cross-legged on the tabletop and studied what I believed to be the boundary to Faerie.

I let the quiet seep in. I had no proof, but the air, the light, even the scent, felt very familiar, like the breeze from the mirror in the bar. If I had to guess, the mirror was a doorway into the heart of Faerie, whereas this border was one of the outermost edges.

Once healed, would Galadriel be able to step back through the mirror or would she need to trek weeks or perhaps months across the fae lands in order to cross over this border?

Closing my eyes, I tried to shut out the heartbreak hanging heavy in the air. Martha said she lived here because she was close to the dead. Could I feel them as she did? Could I call them to me?

THIRTEEN

The Quick and the Dead

M artha was right. The air felt charged. I searched my mind for the dead—not the cold, green blips of vamps, but the haze of the spirit world. My stomach dropped. A lightheaded swoop of dizziness meant that a moment later I was flat on my back, staring up at the undersides of branches.

The black void of the dead swirled in my mind in a kind of vortex. Afraid I'd soon be sick, I rested my hands on my stomach and breathed deeply. It was too much. I'd done this in New Orleans as well. When I'd tried to find the dead in St. Louis Cemetery #2, I'd opened myself to a darkness too vast to navigate.

I did now what I'd done then. I pulled back, focusing on the dead in close proximity. Mind awash in gray mist, I tried to differentiate the spirits crowding around me. They were legion, but I methodically discerned and acknowledged each one, and in doing so, helped them to regain individual forms.

Remembering I wore the wicche glass pendant around my neck, I pushed the nausea into the glass ball and felt better instantly. Sitting up, I found myself surrounded by hundreds of ghosts jostling for position, trying to get close. Positive I'd gone about this all wrong, with pale, ghostly eyes staring at me, I said the first thing I could think of.

"If anyone would like to pass on, I can help. I've done it before. You need only reach out and touch my hands."

As one, the crowd stepped back. Well, that was clear enough.

"What on earth do you think you're doing?" The crowd parted as Martha glared at me. "You couldn't leave me in peace for one day?"

"No. I'm sorry. I wasn't—I didn't intend to disturb you. You'd said there was power for us here, so close to the dead, so I was trying to teach myself how to find them, to call them."

"Too strong for your own good," she grumbled as she made her way across the courtyard. "All of you, scat!"

A ripple went through the ghosts, but most remained where they were standing.

She sat at a small table with chairs in the center of the courtyard. "You called them. You get rid of them."

Staring out at hundreds of hazy faces, my stomach dropped again. "How?"

She drummed her fingers on the table, waiting for me to figure it out. Okay, I could do this. Channeling my inner Clive, I adopted an imperious tone and said, "You may all leave us now." I added a mental push and they scattered. Nice.

"Good. Did you use the wicche glass I gave you to hold the payment?" She studied me from across the courtyard and I suddenly felt stupid sitting on a tabletop.

"Of course." I slid off and took the seat across from her. "I mean, eventually. Once I thought of it, yes."

Giving an exasperated shake of her head, she pulled her shawl close around her shoulders. "Judging by the recent crowd, you've learned how to locate and call the dead. Good."

Shrugging one shoulder, I explained, "I have no idea if what I'm doing is correct. I found them the way I find vampires. Self-taught over here. I could be doing it all wrong."

"It worked, didn't it? That's all that matters." She ran a fingertip along a shallow groove in the wood. "Are there specific spells for what we do? Yes. Do you need to learn them? No. Given your little experiment, you've already proven you have enough power to call all the dead on the West Coast to you."

Her gaze slipped off my face as she stared over my shoulder, into the vast, dark forest. "There aren't many true necromancers left. A few who've inherited a bit of power, the ones who need the spells. Once every few generations, a Corey is born with our gift." She paused, shifting her gaze back to me. "We usually aren't alive at the same time. This overlap, as far as I've been able to determine, is quite unusual."

"How do you research something like that?"

"I have the Corey grimoire. The first few pages contain a family tree that goes back centuries. I'll pass it to you, but not yet. I'm still searching for a way to deal with my niece. I'm sure there's something in the book that will work against her. I just haven't found it yet."

A low, almost inaudible murmuring emanated from the forest. I turned sharply, staring into the trees, the deep shadows. I saw nothing, but I could feel a presence.

"What is it?" Martha asked.

"There's something out there, watching, listening." I angled my chair to the side, not wanting the forest, or anyone hiding in it, to be at my back.

Martha closed her eyes, tipping her head to the side. Almost instantly her shoulders lost their tension and she called, "Pippin, come out."

There was a full minute of silence while we waited. A mad rush of twittering sounded before a loud, "Shh," and then a tiny person climbed up the gnarled tree root and stared at us.

"I'm closed today, Pippin."

"Why?" His voice was high, the word little more than a bird's chirp. He appeared to be dressed in leaves and blossoms. He looked like a tiny, six-inch-tall human with light hair, pointed ears, and soft green skin.

"Is he a pixie?"

"I'mstandingrighthere." His voice was a bright bell in the stillness and so fast, it took my brain a moment to catch up.

"Sorry."

He sneered at my apology and turned his attention back to Martha. "Whyareyouclosed?Where'sGaladriel?"

Martha's hand clenched on the table, but her voice betrayed no distress. "Gad had to go back home. She'd been hurt badly."

After a flurry of tiny chirping sounds coming from every direction, Pippin asked, "WhohurtGaladriel?"

"I guess I did," I explained. "Something that looked like a troll or an Orc came out of the mirror yesterday and attacked me. Galadriel healed me."

"Whoareyou?WhyisFaerieattackingyou?"

"This is my grandniece Sam. As to why, we have no idea."

"NevergoodwhenFaerietakesadisliking." Frightened chirps accompanied that statement.

"If you hear anything in the wind, in the rustling of the leaves, you will tell me, won't you?"

Pippin looked over his shoulder at the multitude of pixies I could hear but couldn't see, and then turned back to us. "Betcha." He hopped off the log and returned to invisibility.

"I'll get out of your hair now." Poor woman; she just wanted to be left alone and I had to cause a commotion outside her door.

When I started to rise, she waved me back down. "The next part is extremely important. You know how to find and call them, but you must always remember to give them a choice." She paused, letting that sink in.

"Choose your words carefully. It must always be a request. If you start commanding the dead, given your power, you will create a mindless army. They will be compelled to do your bidding. In overtaking their will, you will become a black wicche."

"Got it." I went cold at the thought. "Always put it in the form of a question."

"Yes. It's also quite helpful to create a relationship with one particular spirit, one with whom you share an understanding, one who can be trusted. The dead, like the living, have their own histories, their own wants and needs. You could be giving valuable information to one who passes it on to any number of mildly talented spell casters."

That could be a real problem, considering the number of powerful people I kept company with, people who wouldn't thank me for my inadvertent breech of secrecy. "So, how would I go about finding someone trustworthy?"

"Has anyone already made themselves known to you?" At my head shake, she continued, "I have Rose. We were children together, neighbors and best friends. When we were teenagers, there was an accident. We left at three in the morning to drive to Tahoe for a ski day. After a week of temps in the fifties and sixties during the day, there'd been a cold snap overnight. Rose hit a patch of black ice and we slid, spinning, across the freeway.

"We hit an eighteen-wheeler going south. Driver's side. Rose was killed instantly. The big rig sustained minimal damage. There was so much blood, bright red against the white snow. I had whiplash and a concussion, but that was it. They told me Rose had died on impact. She appeared to me for the first time while I was in the hospital."

She tied the ends of her shawl in a knot. "I thought they'd lied to me, that it had been some cruel joke. She looked fine. Beautiful, really. No blood, no damage of any kind. It took a long, very confusing conversation—one I assumed was caused by my concussion—for me to understand that she was dead. She was dead but I could see and speak with her."

"I'm so sorry about your friend." Poor teenaged Martha, her best friend dying beside her.

"Hmm? Oh." She patted my hand. "Thank you. It took me by surprise, you see. Up till then, I'd shown no gift for magic. I was a failure at every lesson. My sister Mary was the star pupil. I was the family disappointment, the one they didn't discuss, the one who never seemed to make it into family pictures."

She let out a gust of breath. "And who would have guessed I

was still harboring resentment over that?" Shaking her head, she continued, "Once it was discovered that I was one of the rare Corey necromancers, I was welcomed back into the family with open arms. I knew their true faces by then, though. Aside from my sister, your grandmother, they could all go to hell for all I cared.

"But that's neither here nor there. The point was Rose. She was my dear friend, in life and in death. I can call her and ask for help when I need it. Your homework," she said with a smile, "is to think of someone, now dead, who would be loyal to you. Someone restless, who never left this plane. Don't ever try to call someone back who's crossed."

She stood, a bit shakily, and raised a hand in farewell to the pixies in the woods. "Enough for now. I want to rest." She shuffled off, back toward the Wicche Glass tree. "Gad waits for me in my dreams," she murmured.

When I stepped through the spelled gate, I checked the time on my phone. That couldn't be right. I checked the date, to make sure I hadn't lost a full day. Nope. I walked out of the Wicche Glass Tavern one minute after I'd walked in.

Wondering why time was on my side today, I set out on the long run home. The Slaughtered Lamb was closed until further notice. The vamps wouldn't be awake for training for hours yet. I had the afternoon free. Altering my route, I ran along Skyline Boulevard and the Great Highway, straight to the San Francisco Zoo.

FOURTEEN

In Other News, Giraffes Hate Sam (and the Lemurs Aren't Happy with Her Either)

A huge group of children was gathered near the entrance, a few chasing each other around a large oval planter while chaperones tried to count heads. Skirting the kid who was terrorizing his friend with a very realistic-looking snake, no doubt purchased in the gift shop thirty feet away, I headed to the ticket windows.

"That'll be twenty-five dollars." The older woman behind the glass had short brown hair and an SF Zoo jacket.

I pulled out my cash and paid. "Is it possible to find out where George Drake is working right now?" At her blank stare, I added, "He's one of your vets. I'm a friend."

"Oh. I haven't met all the vets yet. Just a sec." She left the window and picked up a walkie talkie.

I could hear both sides of the conversation but glanced around the entry area, pretending I couldn't. A couple with a toddler went up to the other window while I waited.

"Dr. Drake is working with a grizzly right now. He asked if you could wait for him right inside at the African Savanna exhibit. You'll see giraffes near the fence."

I took my ticket and thanked her. The area she directed me to was busy, people going in and out of bathrooms, strollers rented for the day, camera phones out as a giraffe stood right inside the enclosure fence, eating leaves off the tall trees.

After a few minutes, the chaotic crowd had dispersed, some going into the zoo, some heading to the parking lot. The couple with the toddler, who'd entered when I had, were the only ones left with me. Dad stood on the bench by the enclosure fence, his son on his shoulders. The little boy gleefully shouted, "Graff! Graff!"

The mom was trying to get a pic with the giraffe and her son in the same shot.

"I can do that for you."

The mom hesitated, but the dad said, "That'd be great. Thank you. Come on, honey. Climb up here."

I held out a hand to help her up, then moved back, framed the shot, and took a few. The poor dad was going to have a sorely bruised chest, considering how often the toddler drummed his feet in excitement every time he saw a new animal.

After the family moved on, I hopped onto the bench myself, to look out over the huge enclosure of African animals. The giraffe nearby blew a puff of air out his nose and stamped his feet before moving quickly toward the opposite end of the savannah.

Feeling guilty for scaring the giraffe, I hopped down and crossed the entry area, finding an open bench by the gift shop.

"Hey, this is a nice surprise." George, dressed in black pants, black boots, and a teal SF Zoo jacket, reached out a hand and pulled me up. "What are you doing in my neck of the woods?"

"You mean besides scaring giraffes? I wanted to talk with you."

George glanced over at the people standing on the bench and taking pictures of the animals. No giraffes were in sight, though. "Oh. I hadn't considered that."

Lowering my voice to barely a whisper, I said, "My other form is nothing compared to yours. Why aren't you scaring the daylights out of every animal in here?"

"Come with me." Leading the way, we headed up the main path, past the gatehouse, where I showed my ticket. The lemur exhibition area was just inside on the right. When they started screeching, George changed places with me, putting himself closest to the enclosure.

He cut down a narrow path to the left, away from the lemurs. "We'll stick to the areas without animals." The path curved to the right and ended at the carousel. While parents with small children rode the carved wooden animals, George and I sat under a tree on a bench away from the hubbub.

"To answer your question, they know wolves. Me? How would any of them know what I am? What they know is that I'm a preda-tor. The type? No. It makes it easier for me to handle the more dangerous animals. They show me a proper respectful fear." He chuckled. "It drives the other vets nuts. We had a new one a few months ago who almost had his throat ripped out because he thought the tiger I'd been examining was tame."

"If you could do it, he could do it?" I ventured.

"Exactly. Idiot." He relaxed back onto the bench. "I love it here." He nodded to the carousel. "I take my lunch here a few times a week."

We listened to the pipe music, the shouts of children's names as parents tried to get their attention and take pictures. All the while, the beautifully carved and painted animals went round and round. "Do you get side-eyed by the parents?"

He tipped his head, chagrined. "Unfortunately. Pedophiles ruin everything."

I elbowed him. "You should put that on a t-shirt."

"Yeah." Instead of laughing, he watched the carousel with sad eyes. "I've always wanted children."

"Oh." Reaching over, I took his hand, light and dark fingers intertwining.

"Yeah," he said again. "It's hard enough as a gay man to adopt or find a surrogate, but if I want my child to be a dragon?" He shook his head. "Forget it. Plus," he added. "Owen isn't sold on the idea."

"Which brings me to why I'm here."

George shifted his gaze from the carousel to me. "You want to talk about why Owen is content in an uncle-only role?"

"No. I'm worried about him."

Sighing, he squeezed my hand. "Me, too. I saw that text he wrote when you called in the middle of the night. He was angry on my behalf. I'm here by seven on workdays. Middle of the night calls always wake me. I'm a light sleeper and it's hard for me to fall back. He was being protective, but it was too much."

"I'm sorry. It was thoughtless of me."

His shoulder bumped into mine. "I was more concerned with the anger. He was spitting mad, which isn't Owen."

"No, it isn't." I brew out a breath. "I think Abigail may have targeted him, like she did Liam."

"What?" George crushed my hand in his grip. "What do you mean targeted?"

When I wriggled my fingers, he instantly let go. "Abigail is trying to get someone to kill me. She wants to avoid the Corey curse against familicide. I have no idea what the curse is, but it must be bad for her to go to these lengths to avoid it."

"What's she doing to him?"

"I don't know. My guess is that it's something similar to what she did to me a few months ago, invading my thoughts, making me see and experience things that aren't there. Liam didn't say much, but I didn't get the impression he'd been caught in a vision. For him, it seemed more like constant psychic battering. He said he'd had terrible headaches."

Fear jumped in George's eyes. "Owen's been downing aspirin like there's no tomorrow. His mother's taking him to the doctor today to see if they can get him migraine meds."

"My guess is she hammers at her target until they're too tired or in too much pain to fight back. Then she takes over and uses that person as a kind of puppet to do her bidding."

George stood. "I'm going to talk with the director, get some time off." He thought a moment. "And call Coco. Maybe she can make something for Owen like she made for you, something to keep his mind safe."

He turned to leave and then stopped himself. "Do you need a ride somewhere?"

"No. I got it. Take care of Owen and let me know what I can do, okay?"

"Yeah." He nodded but wasn't really paying attention. "I'll take him somewhere. She can't turn him into a puppet if I take him to the other side of the world, right?" The desperation in his eyes broke my heart.

"No. I think she needs proximity."

"Okay. That's what I'll do." Leaning over, he gave me a quick kiss on the cheek and then took off at a run in the opposite direction.

Being winter, the sun was already starting to go down. I considered going straight back to the nocturne so I could begin training with Russell, but then I thought better of it. They'd need to conduct their vampy business first, so I headed to the Slaughtered Lamb.

It was dark and empty, but home. I stood in the bar, looking out the window at the swirling rush of waves capsizing against the glass. The distant hills of the North Bay were pink in the disappearing light. The stillness and silence helped to settle my nerves. George would protect Owen. Abigail wouldn't be able to hurt him.

Stomach growling, I flicked on the lights and went in search of food. Dave had left a well-stocked kitchen. Cleaning out the leftovers, I heated up four huge po'boys and inhaled them. The gnawing hole in my stomach finally filled, I raided the cookie jar and filled a plate with chocolate toffee cookies and made myself some tea.

Taking my spoils into the bookstore, I set to work on the order I hadn't completed inventorying. I'd been at it about an hour when my phone pinged.

Clive: Where are you? With the SL closed, I hoped you'd be here when I rose.

Me: @SL. Busy day, lots to tell you, but I'll let you guys do your vampy thing first.

Clive: That word.

Me: Busy? Anyway, I haven't finished processing a book order from a couple of days ago. I'll work for another hour or two. I need to fill these sad, empty shelves. Then I'll be ready for gun practice.

Clive: Which reminds me, why is your dagger sitting on the nightstand in our room? The point was that you be armed at all times.

Me: Running 10 miles—each way—with a dagger strapped to my leg did not seem like a great idea.

Clive: But returning to the Wicche Glass, where Faerie has a foothold, without your weapon seemed like a better one?

Me: You might have a point. Maybe a sheath on my back?

Clive: Come home and we'll figure it out.

Me: Soon.

Clive: I'd prefer sooner to soon.

Laughing, I slid the phone aside and rolled the cart of books from behind the counter, happy to finally be putting them in their proper places. Normally, I'd do the computer work while Owen shelved the new books, all while chatting about whatnot. I missed him terribly.

A few hours later, I was optimistically a third of the way through processing the shipment. Thankfully, the shelves were looking far less empty. Someday soon, when my aunt was gone, we'd be open for business again and the bookstore would be ready. Flicking off the lights, I stood silently in the center of the bar, hypnotized by the undulating ocean.

Prickles of fear ran down my spine. The water seemed to be staring back at me. My fingers went to the choker I wore, the one fashioned by Coco, George's sister, the one that kept my mind under my own control, not Abigail's.

The Kraken had not returned. This was something else. Had she targeted one of the merpeople this time? I didn't see anything out of the ordinary. Perhaps I was feeling her focus on me as she worked her spells. Maybe it was her demon.

Abigail was a sorceress, not merely a black wicche—although that would be bad enough. She'd aligned herself with a demon who amplified her magic and took his payment from the agony and death she caused. I prayed tonight's agony wasn't courtesy of Owen.

The full moon was still almost a week away, but fur prickled beneath my skin. Something was watching, lying in wait. If I ran up those stairs right now, something or someone would be poised to attack.

Closing my eyes, I searched my mind for what it might be. A hazy form hovered just outside the ward. Odd. Odder still was the cold, green blip that waited farther off. The vamp wasn't familiar. It wasn't one of Clive's. Who the hell was up there waiting for me?

FIFTEEN

Beware Strange Vamps Bearing Gifts

D eciding a strange vamp lying in wait was always a bad thing, I went to my apartment, grabbed my wolfpack, stripped out of my clothes, including my ring, stuffed them in the pack, strapped the pack on, and then fell to my hands and knees and allowed my wolf to take the fore. Being a wicche allowed the shift to happen quickly and without too much pain.

A minute later, I shook myself, fully inhabiting my other form. I trotted over to an empty bookcase in my living room, tapped the hidden release with a paw, and then was running through the tunnel that led deep into the Presidio, a former military post near the Golden Gate Bridge.

When I reached the magical barrier, a black marble monument in the San Francisco National Cemetery, I paused to scan again. I didn't want to jump through the ward only to find myself surrounded by strange vamps. Hazy forms? Yes. It was a cemetery, after all. No vamps, though.

Hopping through, I took off at a low run, keeping headstones between me and the nearby deserted road. Keeping to the shadows, I traversed the Presidio, stopping at a large grove of trees near its border. I could hear a homeless man sleeping under low branches and snoring. Skirting him, I secreted myself away, shifted forms, cleaned up, and got dressed. I'd started carrying baby wipes in my wolfpack, and it was a game changer. No more dirty hands and feet when I shifted back.

As I left the Presidio to jog through the streets, I checked again. The vamp and ghost were both gone. Interesting. The nocturne was only a few miles from The Slaughtered Lamb, so it was a nice, easy run home.

The vamp at the gate seemed more tense than usual. I would have asked why, but they were all such dicks, I couldn't bring myself to do it. The energy in the house was buzzing. Heading to the stairs, in need of a shower, I searched the nocturne in my mind and located Clive in his study. He was with Godfrey, Liang, and the strange vamp who'd been outside The Slaughtered Lamb. Huh. Maybe the newcomer was trying to check out the Master's new mate.

Pausing on the stairs, I closed my eyes and tried to eavesdrop. Channeling the payment into the wicche glass, I listened intently, skimming through Godfrey's thoughts. The new vamp was an old friend from England who was visiting the States and had dropped by to see Godfrey. She was merely paying her respects to Clive at the moment.

Feeling better, I pulled out of Godfrey's thoughts and headed for our bedroom and a hot shower. Cleaned, dried, and dressed in my softest jeans and sweater, I went down to wait in the library for Russell and tonight's lesson. If I had to meet this new vamp, I was presentable. If not, I was comfortable for a night of training. I'd even traded my usual running shoes for boots and left my hair down, instead of in its constant braid. See? Totally presentable as the Master's mate. Mostly.

Grabbing the mystery I'd been reading, I settled into my window seat, adjusted a few pillows, and dove back into nineteenth century Boston. The killer was the housekeeper. It had to be. She was a woman who held grudges for decades and was deeply, personally, offended by breaches in etiquette. She probably—

Bomb!

The word was shouted from three different minds, Clive's the first. Bolting off the cushion, I raced to the door, only to see it engulfed in a ball of fire that rocked the foundations. Lifted off my feet by a concussive wave of heat and flame, I flew across the library, and then nothing.

———

"SAMANTHA?" SOFT LIPS TOUCHED MY BATTERED HEAD. I COULDN'T open my eyes. I seemed to have forgotten how.

"Sire, Dr. Underfoot has been contacted. He's on his way." Russell's deep voice helped to settle my nerves. If both Clive and Russell were fine, hopefully no one had been hurt in the explosion.

"If I could just—" Liang began.

"OUT!"

I flinched at the rage in Clive's voice, setting off a million hurts and causing a whine to escape.

"Sorry," he whispered, as a feather-light kiss brushed my lips. "Help is coming."

"I also called Lilah Wong, Sire. She's an excellent healer." Russell sounded angry, as well.

"Good."

"Shouldn't we move her to the couch or your bed? She can't possibly be comfortable lying in rubble." Godfrey had a good point. I hurt everywhere, but part of that seemed to be the pointy-edged rocks I was on. And yay, Godfrey was fine, too.

"I don't know what's broken," Clive said, his voice strained.

"He could cause more damage if she's hurt her spine," Russell said. "Look at the blast radius and where she is now. She had to have been thrown ten feet before slamming into the stone of this fireplace." He paused a moment. "It's a miracle she's not dead."

"I should have taken her head instead of banishing her," Clive ground out.

My eyes fluttered open. Hey, they did work. "What...

happened?" My voice had become part whisper, part creak, and all ouch, like I had inhaled the flames.

"Sam," he breathed. Clive was looking singed himself. Ash marred his jaw. His clothes were torn…and smoking.

"Ow."

"What hurts?" he asked, concern etched in his features.

My eyelids drifted closed of their own volition. They were being real assholes today. "Kinda one big hurt over here." Talking was overrated and far too ouchy to do on the regular.

Russell crouched down on my other side. "Does anything feel broken, Miss Quinn?" Before I could answer, he rose like a shot and barked, "Downstairs! Everyone downstairs. You'll be called if you're needed."

"What's wrong?" My eyes slitted open for a moment and I saw the rest of the vamps who were standing in what used to be a doorway walk down the hall. Russell was usually the voice of calm reason. Why was he shouting?

Russell and Clive exchanged a look before my eyelids dropped yet again.

"Godfrey," Clive began, "check the perimeter. Make sure we're protected. We have no idea if our visitor was working alone or in league with others. When you're done, if we're secure, please go downstairs and make sure everyone feeds."

"Sire." Godfrey's footsteps retreated from the room.

Oh, got it. "I'm bleeding, huh?"

"Head wounds do, unfortunately, bleed quite a bit, Miss Quinn." Russell crouched down again. "Anything feel broken? Numb?"

I considered how I felt after the Orc whaled on me. "I can't speak for internal bleeding, but I don't think anything's broken." Broken. *Shit*. I tried to move my arm and hissed in pain. "The wicche glass. Is it broken?" It was such a delicate ball of spun glass, how could it have survived the blast?

Clive pulled the chain around my neck. A moment later, the wicche glass spun before my eyes, sparkling in the low light.

"How?"

Gently tucking it back into my sweater, he lifted his eyebrows. "Magical object?" Turning to Russell, he said, "Spread a blanket on the couch."

"Please," I reminded him.

"Please," he echoed.

As carefully as he could, Clive picked me up and deposited me on the couch.

"Did you already…" I pointed a finger that didn't hurt toward my head.

The tension on Clive's face eased a fraction as he tried to smile. "Yes, I sealed the head wounds. Blood did, however"—he glanced over at the rubble that had been a fireplace—"drip onto the stones."

"Hence the vampy interest in my well-being." Figures the only time they'd actually care if I was okay is when my blood was up for grabs.

"That word." Crouched beside me, humor had finally taken the place of fear in his eyes.

"Hence?" Every word hurt, but playing with Clive felt good. From the couch, I could finally see the full extent of the damage. I tried to choke off a sob but wasn't quite successful. Clive and Russell were instantly alert.

"What?" Clive demanded.

"Look." At his confused expression, I pointed. The door to the library had been blown apart, taking the whole wall with it. Bookshelves had been destroyed. Torn, scorched books were scattered over half the library. The blast had taken out at least a third of the former ballroom.

"Things can be replaced, Miss Quinn. We're more concerned with you right now."

My head was feeling woozy and floaty, like I was hovering over myself. I could still feel the pain, but it was almost separate from me. Dr. Underfoot and Lilah would be here soon enough. I didn't need to tell these two about the floaty pain. They were worried enough as it was.

"So, who was the strange vamp and why does she want me dead?" Maybe I could move their focus from me to the blast.

"Not you, me," Clive said. He slid a chair over and sat beside me, while Russell murmured into a phone. "She was an old friend of Godfrey's, said she was swinging through the city on a visit."

"I heard you all shout bomb—"

Russell hissed over the top of my words again.

"They're all downstairs or outside, aren't they?"

"You tell us." Clive studied me intently.

I didn't think my battered brain was up to it, but I closed my eyes and tried to find the cold green blips of vampires. They were all where they were supposed to be, out of earshot. What wasn't supposed to be here was the ghostly haze by the former fireplace.

"Hello," I ventured.

Both vamps went on instant alert, suddenly standing between me and the fireplace.

"It's okay, guys." I patted the backs of their legs. "You're in the way."

Clive inched right as Russell inched left, giving me a window. Focusing my power on the hazy cloud, it began to take form. It was the ghost I'd felt outside the Slaughtered Lamb tonight. Was she working with the vamp?

A moment later, the haze coalesced into a human form. A woman. It was the ghost that had warned me a party of vamps from New Orleans was coming to kill Clive last month.

Reaching out a hand, I said, "Thank you for your help before."

She nodded, her eyes glued to the vamps in fear.

"You don't need to worry about them. They can't even see you."

Reluctantly, she tore her eyes away from my guardians and looked at me.

"You're the one I pulled from the ocean, right? Well, tried to anyway. I failed horribly, as I was being shot at. It was a mermaid who rescued you, which is far cooler."

"Do you know who she's talking to?" Russell whispered.

"I believe so." Clive glanced down at me and back across the room. "This is the ghost of the tortured werewolf, the one who warned you about the New Orleans attack, is it not?" He patted Russell's shoulder, letting him off guard duty, and then resumed his seat. Vampires could do nothing about ghosts.

"What's your name?"

Moving closer, her eyes continued to dart to the vamps in the room. She mouthed something.

"I'm sorry. I didn't get that. Last time when you touched me, it helped me hear."

Hesitantly, she moved to the end of the couch and placed one finger on my bare foot. What happened to my boots?

"Charlotte."

"I'm Sam."

A smile came quickly and was gone. "I know."

"Do you have another message for me...or are you just visiting?" I didn't want to make her feel unwelcome. She had helped us before. "If you're ready to move on, I can help."

She was already shaking her head before I'd finished my offer. "Not yet." She glanced over her shoulder toward the hall. "That dead bloodsucker. She was prowling around your place. I was keeping an eye on her." She wrung her ghostly hands. "I missed the bomb, though."

"That's okay. No one was hurt."

Clive could only hear my half of the conversation, but that last comment still earned an incredulous look, one Charlotte mirrored.

"I mean no one besides me."

"Why would I care about a bunch of bloodsuckers dying?" Charlotte was clearly questioning my sanity and I couldn't blame her. Other than myself, I doubted any werewolves would shed a tear over a dead—a well and truly dead—vamp.

I relayed to Clive what she'd told me.

Russell stopped speaking midsentence and came around the back of the couch, pocketing his phone. "Our bomb-wielding visitor went first to your establishment?" He turned to Clive. "Were we wrong about her purpose?"

"I don't think so. I felt her intent as she pulled that package from her pocket. She wanted my death. My guess is that if she could inform me of my mate's demise before she ensured my own, it would be that much sweeter."

"Wait." I glanced around the room, remembering Clive's shout of "Out!" earlier. "If she was the one with the bomb, why was Liang tossed?"

SIXTEEN

We Meet Again, Dr. Underfoot

"She's fortunate that's all I did," Clive ground out.

Clive and Russell wore matching expressions of fury.

"But if it was the other one..." I wished they could read my mind so I wouldn't have to talk. It wasn't that I minded Liang's banishment, but I wondered why.

"Miss Quinn, we always know where you are. You don't even need to be in the house. If you're on the grounds, we hear your heartbeat. We may have been in the study exchanging pleasantries, but we all knew when you returned for the evening."

"When you paused on the stair a moment, I assumed you listened for me," Clive held my hand gently in his own. "We knew when you showered, dressed, came downstairs, and went to the library."

"We can hear the change in your heartbeat that means you're reading," Russell offered.

"Do they get how creepy they are?" Charlotte whispered.

"We're telling you this to explain that every vampire in this house knew you were reading in the library. We were just leaving the study when the woman took the bomb out of her pocket. It was wrapped like a gift, but I heard the tail end of her thought and knew what it was. I gave her pain, driving her to her knees to incapacitate her."

"If we'd been able to interrogate her, we might even now know who's been behind all these attacks," Russell interrupted.

"Yes." Clive's voice had hardened. "Liang, who has always been a brilliant strategist, ensured that wouldn't happen by simultaneously taking the woman's head and swatting the bomb down the hall, directly into the library door."

I thought about that look Liang had given us the previous evening, as Clive and I were getting on the elevator, the way she found reasons to touch him, her standing outside the library, listening when Clive and I were alone. "She loves you. Her only thought was probably neutralizing the threat. The strategy came as an afterthought. Get rid of the competition."

"There is no competition."

I tried to shrug and then whined in pain. "In her mind, there definitely was. I don't know how to explain it so you'll understand."

"I saw it," Russell volunteered.

Clive turned sharply, studying Russell. "You saw what?"

"She wanted you back, Sire. And she couldn't fathom you honestly intended to bind yourself to Miss Quinn. I believe she saw Miss Quinn as an odd experiment and of the moment."

"She's not a villain. You didn't misjudge her. She just wouldn't have been heartbroken if you'd kicked me to the curb."

"Tossing a bomb in your direction is not a passive act," Clive contended.

"Yeah, but that *was* of the moment. She needed to keep you safe from the explosion. My guess is that it was done with no more thought than, 'I need to get rid of the bomb and maybe I can make her go away, too.'"

We all heard a car pulling through the gate at the same time.

"I'll check." Russell rushed off to hopefully find Dr. Underfoot. Instead, he returned a few minutes later with Owen's sister Lilah.

Making her way carefully through the rubble, she darted

glances this way and that. Right. I doubted too many non-vamps were invited into the nocturne.

Clive rose. "Thank you for coming so quickly. Please, take my seat."

Lilah was clearly nervous but, holding herself stiff, she walked farther into the vampires' lair in order to help me. I wouldn't forget that.

Sitting next to me, she held one hand over my head and the other over my heart. "Concussion. Dislocated shoulder. A broken collarbone. First-degree burns. Cuts and bruises." She opened her eyes. "The collarbone has already begun to knit together. I can help with that and the concussion. The shoulder should wait for Dr. Underfoot. I don't want to make it worse."

"Any help you're able to give," Clive said, "we will gratefully accept."

"How are you feeling, Sam?" Her voice was calm and even, but I could tell she was worried I was in a dangerous situation and needed an extraction.

I patted her hand. "I was in the wrong place at the wrong time," I assured her. "I was in a lot of pain initially and feeling really floaty, like I was watching myself bleed, but I'm doing better now."

"I've been blocking your pain," Clive said.

Right. Forgot. "In that case, I have no idea how bad it is."

"Okay." She looked directly at Clive, the first time since she'd arrived. "Would you like Dr. Underfoot to check her first? Once I get started, it's difficult to pause without losing ground."

"In that case—"

Russell walked back in, this time with Dr. Underfoot, a dwarf who stood four feet tall with dark hair, ruddy skin, and an impressively bushy beard. Dr. Underfoot wore a three-piece tweed suit and carried a large leather bag.

"Miss Quinn, Miss Wong. It's good to see you both, although I'm sorry for the circumstance." He studied the library before focusing on me. "Your skin is red, although I don't see any blistering."

"There was," Clive said. "The explosion threw her back into the fireplace. It took us a couple of minutes to put out the flames so we could get in the room. She was over there, in the rubble. Her head was at a bad angle, blood running down the side. Her skin was bright red and blistered."

I could see his hands fisted in his pockets and I felt for him. Clive needed control. I held out my hand to him and he took it.

"I was able to stop the bleeding and deal with her pain, but I didn't feel confident in doing anything else. Miss Wong says she has a concussion, a broken collarbone, and a dislocated shoulder."

When the doctor touched my shoulder, I felt a stab of pain and a whine slipped through. "And Miss Wong is correct. Be ready to help with the pain, Mr. Fitzwilliam." He kept one strong, hairy hand on my shoulder while the other lifted my arm at the elbow.

Before I had the time to brace for pain, he'd popped it back into the joint. I had one brief moment of intense pain and then I was floating again.

"Before Miss Wong begins her work, let me do a quick exam." He prodded and poked and flexed my limbs, not finding any injuries in addition to what Lilah had already identified. Talking was getting easier, but I pointed to my throat. He had me open my mouth and declared the soft tissue a bright, blistered red.

Once he moved aside, Lilah resumed the chair and began to work on me.

"Is Owen okay?"

She paused. "I believe he will be. His headaches are lessening. Relax, Sam. Let me work."

I must have fallen asleep because when I eventually opened my eyes, I was lying in bed, Clive sitting up next to me reading. "The last time I had a concussion, I woke to find you sitting with me. Different room. Different bed." The light in the room was low for me. I didn't know how he was able to make out the words on the page.

"Sadly," he began, closing the book and tossing it on his night-stand, "the common denominator is me." He brushed a stray hair from my face. "I braided your hair. I know you don't like sleeping with it loose, but I didn't do a very good job."

"You braided my hair?" If we'd been in a cartoon, little hearts would have been circling my head.

"Perhaps we should say the attempt was made." He reclined beside me, his head propped on his hand. "It's only fair to tell you, as my future wife, that I will never be a hairdresser."

"That definitely narrows our options."

"Indeed." His fingers gently feathered across my forehead and temple.

"I suppose we'll need to muddle through as we are. In your case, though, I think job options at the unemployment office for a former Master vampire are going to be pretty limited."

"Pity."

I wasn't ready to leave the silliness behind, but I needed to know. "Does knowing who the bomber is help pinpoint our nemesis?"

He sighed, a long, strong finger sliding down my nose and over my lips. "No. Godfrey's been acquainted with her for centuries. When living in England, he occasionally ran into her, but she's thoroughly forgettable, neither too powerful nor too weak and therefore not noticed."

"But we think she's connected? She's not just some random mad bomber?"

He grinned and dropped a kiss on my nose. "We don't think so, no. Now, tell me how you're feeling."

"A little muzzy and sore, but nowhere near as bad as I thought I'd be feeling." When I moved my shoulder, there was a quick zing of pain and then nothing.

He reached back, turned off the light, and then settled in. "I'm still controlling your pain. When I go out, though, that's going to disappear. You have meds and a water bottle on your nightstand."

Normally, he'd pull me into his arms, but I was too battered for that. He, instead, wrapped his hand around mine in the dark. "I'll stay awake as long as I can. Try to sleep. If we're lucky, you can go back under before I'm out."

We were not, unfortunately, lucky. When Clive went out, a million pains made themselves known. As gingerly as I could, I slid out of bed and turned on the bedside lamp. The bright light felt like a hammer to the head. I took the meds and used the bathroom, realizing Clive must have showered me, cleaning off the dirt, soot, and blood before putting me in my favorite pjs and braiding my hair. For a ruthless bastard, he was pretty sweet.

That brief jaunt exhausted me. Shuffling back to bed, I clicked off the lamp and slid under the covers. Thankfully, the meds did their job and I was pulled back under.

Hours later when I awoke, I was feeling better. Natural were-wolf healing, augmented by Lilah's magic and Dr. Underfoot's medicine meant that, while not back to normal, I was on the mend. All that healing also meant I was ravenous.

I donned slippers and a baggy hoodie I wore over my pajamas and then shuffled down the hall to the elevator. There were two flights of stairs between me and food.

Norma was probably in her office, but I avoided it, going straight for the kitchen. I didn't want to have to explain why I was stiff and covered in bruises. I found a steak, asparagus, and rice plate in the refrigerator.

Feeling even better after eating, I chose the stairs this time. One long, hot shower later, I dressed in my softest, loosest yoga pants and hoodie, slid back into slippers, and left my hair long. My shoulder wasn't up to braiding at the moment.

Not wanting to avoid it any longer, I walked slowly down the stairs and straight to the library. Grief was like a vise in my chest as I took it all in. The library had been cleaned out. The furniture on the far side of the enormous room remained, along with my window seat. The rest—the stone, wood, and plaster rubble that had shot across the room—had been cleared. All the broken, singed books that had been scattered across the floor, removed.

The beautiful wooden floor was scorched. Rebuilding the library was going to be a gargantuan task. Wanting to do something to help, I went to the edge of the blast zone, where books still sat precariously on shelves, and began to cull. When I found one that had been damaged too badly to keep, I reached into my pocket to take a picture of the cover. I wanted to compile a list of the titles we needed to replace. My pocket was empty and I remembered my phone was gone. Slamming into shards of marble was not, it seemed, compatible with tech.

After hours at it, the meds were wearing off and I was exhausted. I should have gone upstairs but didn't have the energy. I'd hit the wall.

"Excuse me, Miss Quinn."

I turned to find Norma standing at the missing wall. "Yes?"

"Should you be up? Are you feeling okay?"

Her genuine concern helped battle back the overwhelming sadness of these ruins. "I'm okay. I'm just fading fast." I gestured to my destination, the window seat.

She crossed the blackened floor to me. "I was told you needed a new phone. It was just delivered." She handed me a small handled bag containing a box.

"Thank you. I'll set it up later."

"Already taken care of. You're good to go."

"Even bigger thank you." I was having a hard time keeping my eyelids open.

Norma took my arm and guided me. "I programmed my number into the phone. If you need anything, you call. Okay?"

"You bet." Zombie walking to the window seat, I wrapped myself in a throw, fluffed a pillow under my head, and promptly fell asleep.

SEVENTEEN

Cherchez la Femme

I awoke hours later to the sound of soft voices speaking far away. Turning my head, I found Clive, Russell, and Godfrey deep in a conversation so quiet, even I couldn't make out their words. My heartbeat must have changed because they turned as one. If I didn't like them all so much, it would have been terrifying.

"She lives," Godfrey joked.

A moment later, Clive was sitting on the edge of the window seat, his hand on my forehead. "No fever. How are you feeling?"

Testing, I moved and flexed, finding sore spots. "Mostly fine. Collarbone still hurts. Shoulder feels fine. Head's not quite back to normal, but no more than a headache. I'm okay."

Leaning over, he kissed me. Soft, gentle, its own kind of healing, the kiss quickly changed from sickbed to boudoir. It was some time later, when we were plastered against each other, that I remembered we had an audience.

Pushing him away, my face no doubt flaming, I searched the library for the men. "Where did they go?"

"I sent them away."

Smiling, I brushed my fingertips down his perfect jaw. "Oh." His lips were on mine again, and I lost all thought until coming up for breath again. This time I was on top of him, staring down into his stormy gray eyes.

"There's no wall. Anyone could walk by and see us."

"Not when they've been ordered away." His gaze was heated as he dragged his hands down my back before landing on my butt. "Which they have been."

Straddling him in my yoga pants, I gave one quick grind that had him groaning. His hands went up my hoodie and found my breasts, no bra in his way, as I hadn't wanted to deal with one earlier. When his thumbs flicked my nipples, I came close to throwing off my clothes and yanking down his pants, but there was no way I was going to get naked in such an exposed place.

I put my hands over his, stilling them. "Upstairs. Not out in the open like this."

He opened his mouth to counter that and then really looked at me. "Of course." He gathered me up and then all but flew up the stairs to our bedroom. I'd made a lot of progress since the attack. I loved and trusted Clive. I could bare myself and be intimate with him. I had not, however, come so far as to be exposed and vulnerable with others around. The fear would have kept me fighting off nausea and distracted from everything he was doing.

Once we were alone, behind closed doors, the tenor of our lovemaking changed. The silly, grappling speed downstairs had morphed into long, healing strokes upstairs. Our clothes dropped to the floor as he walked me backward to the bed.

By the time we hit the sheets, some of the silliness and urgency had returned. He could always do this, heal and inflame with a kiss, a caress. When his fangs slid down my throat, I'd shaken off the unease. Rolling us over, I straddled him again, grinding down the length of him, desperate.

Fingers entwined with his, I braced, changed positions, and took him in, made him a part of me, of us. We found our rhythm quickly and when his hands were on me again, I was flying. Still in the throes, he rolled us back over, hammering hard and fast, taking us both over.

He rolled off and I snuggled in. "Wait. If everyone can hear my heartbeat, does that mean they all know when we—ah, fuck it."

"There's the right attitude." He grinned, his hand possessively on my hip.

"So, what was the deep conversation I interrupted?"

"Hmm?" His hand lazily stroked my back. "Oh, we were discussing the bomber. She's no one important on her own. She's not behind Amélie's scheme in New Orleans or this. No. She's working for someone."

"Lots of women," I mused.

Clive stilled. "What do you mean?"

I glanced up at his very intent expression. "Just thinking. I mean, we started with Leticia, then Amélie, then possibly Liang, now—what's this one's name?"

"Anne."

"Right. Now Anne. I mean, look around your own nocturne. There aren't many female vampires. Is your nocturne different from other ones? Do you just have an unusually large number of men here?"

"No. There are more male vampires than female. It's similar to the gender disparity in werewolves."

"Okay, pushing aside the fact that women are clearly smarter to avoid all the supernatural bullshit, you have a lot of women working together in a plot against you when there are few of them in total. That seems like an important clue to me."

He rolled me over and kissed me soundly. "Brilliant."

Feeling energized and only a little achey, we cleaned up and went back downstairs, where Russell and Godfrey waited in the study. They discussed many women and their possible rationales for plotting, but as I knew none of them, my mind wandered.

"Wouldn't it make more sense to ask a woman?" I interrupted.

All three men stared at me.

"What? You're in here trying to figure out who has it out for you and why. You're men, though, men who have existed for hundreds of years. Chances are, you were oblivious to the initial insult or you brushed it aside, as it was just a woman."

All three had the decency to look uncomfortable.

"Since you're trying to remember or piece together something you probably forgot as soon as it happened, wouldn't it make more sense to ask a woman? You have a whole nocturne of vampires you could tap for info. Why do these discussions only involve the three of you?"

"We had a coup last month, Miss Quinn," Godfrey said simply. "Trust isn't high right now."

"I understand and I know I'm part of the problem." I turned to Clive. "I should just move back to The Slaughtered Lamb. The remodel is complete. My apartment—"

"No."

"You're being stubborn. Do you really want to deal with your own people revolting while you're trying to figure out who's behind the attacks? Your people will settle down if I'm gone."

Clive was about to launch into an argument when Russell spoke first. "I disagree, Miss Quinn. You and the Master will be taking a blood oath soon. It is a sacred ceremony for our people. They need to know that this is permanent. You are joined forever-more. You leaving the nocturne opens up questions about the committed nature of your relationship."

I sat with that for a minute. "Okay." I turned back to Clive. "But just so you know, it was Russell's sound argument that changed my mind, not your 'No.' I can't tell you how to behave with your nocturne, but you're not allowed to shout commands at me." I gave him my angry squinty eye so he'd know I meant it.

"Apologies." His face relaxed into amusement.

"Uh-huh. Back to the original point. You have some female vamps here; why not just ask them? Or, better yet, have a big house meeting, lay it out—these attacks affect them, too—let them bounce ideas and connections off each other. You won't be any worse off than you are now."

I settled onto the bench by the wall that I always claimed when in these meetings. I liked the positioning. I was to Clive's right. Sitting in front of him meant positioning myself with his under-lings, and when you're the Master everyone is an underling. To the side meant I had some share in the power while maintaining my ability to stay aloof if I chose.

All three men sat quietly with varying expressions of disgust.

"What now?"

"That's not our way," Godfrey finally said.

"What's not?" They were killing me.

"Open-air discussions." Russell took over the explanation. "I'm not sure how to explain to one so young. Barring violence, we are extremely long-lived. During those hundreds of years of life, allies and enemies are made and remade. We need to be aware of every possible relationship before we share sensitive information, as that information may end up in an enemy's lap moments later."

"So, you don't trust your people?"

"It isn't trust so much as caution," Russell said. "Any informa-tion we share could be deemed important and therefore worth torturing one of our people to get, or even one of those allies I just mentioned. What would Clive do if someone contacted him to say they had you in their possession and, in exchange for your life, they wanted information on Godfrey or myself, information that would directly lead to our true deaths?"

"That's easy. I'd kill the people who took me and we'd all live happily ever after."

Clive swung his chair around, a grin tugging at his lips. "I'd help in any way I could."

"Perfect. I'd have Clive as backup." I folded my legs up on the bench. "I get what you're saying. I do. My point is the reason you have no idea who's attacking you is because you trade in whis-pers. You keep to the shadows and hoard secrets."

Godfrey scoffed, "Tell us what you really think."

"Not you guys in particular," I assured him. "I meant all vampires."

"Ah." Russell's face broke into a smile. "I feel so much better."

"It's like the kidnapping scenario. How do you win? You don't play by the rules. How about we use a wildcard instead?"

"Not you," Clive said quickly.

I narrowed my eyes at him. "That was dangerously close to the barked 'No' I just outlawed."

"I don't bark," he ground out.

"In your own vampy way, you do."

"That word."

"Way? That's an odd one to object to. Anyway," I said, rolling my eyes. "No, not me. I don't have anything to do with ancient vampire grudges. How the heck am I supposed to do anything when I only know a handful of you guys?"

"Then what are you suggesting?" Clive asked, more relaxed now that he knew I wasn't planning to swan dive into the middle of a vampire war.

"Don't do what you've always done. All those covert phone calls and veiled conversations, have you gotten any real information from them? No. So why continue to do what doesn't work?"

Godfrey stood abruptly and began to pace.

"I'm not trying to tick you guys off. I'm just offering a different opinion. If I'm gumming up the works, I can head to the Slaughtered Lamb. I still have carts of books to process."

"You misunderstand, Miss Quinn. You're voicing a strategy that Godfrey has been arguing for a while," Russell explained.

"I imagine," Clive began, "it would be extraordinarily frustrating to have us listen to your ideas when we've been ignoring his." He stood and crossed to Godfrey. "I apologize, my friend. I get too set in my ways."

Godfrey took Clive's offered hand and clasped it. "She helps with that."

"That and many other things." Clive shook his head and returned to his seat.

Godfrey remained standing. "We have a secret weapon," he said, gesturing to me. "We hold a group briefing with the whole nocturne. We ask for any input. All the while, she's doing her thing. If we have people who know something but are resistant to say it, she pulls it out of them."

I sat up straight and hugged a pillow to my chest. "Yes! I love this idea."

"Reading all those minds takes a toll on you," Clive said, clearly concerned.

I could feel my face scrunching up in disbelief. "I'll take a nap. Besides," I added, holding up the wicche glass hanging around my neck, "I have a way to avoid the pain now."

"What is that?" Godfrey asked.

"I have secrets, too," I said, dropping the ball back under the neck of my sweater.

EIGHTEEN

*Still Sounds Dirty

Deciding where to have the meeting took longer than getting everyone there. It turns out that vampires don't lollygag when their Master calls them. So, since the library was a wreck, they all met in the practice room where Clive had taught me swordplay.*

As I didn't need to be with them in order to read vamp minds, I went to the window seat in the library, directly above the practice room. Pulling one of the tattered curtains closed, I sat with my legs folded up, leaning against the side wall, in the dark.

Staring out the window into the moonlit grounds and the distant Golden Gate Bridge, I began to mentally cast out for all the cold green vampire blips in the house. Finding no one lurking where they shouldn't be, I concentrated on the glut of vamps below. I channeled the pain from invading others' minds into the wicche glass, which meant I didn't need Clive's help to mask it.

This was far more complicated than anything I'd ever done before. I was trying to monitor thirty-four vampires at the same time. Since I knew what Clive, Russell, and Godfrey knew, I ignored them and focused on the other thirty-one vamps' reactions.

I knew when Clive began to talk because they all lit up at once. It was a little like being in The Slaughtered Lamb, surrounded by countless conversations, but needing to hear one drink order. Most vamps were experiencing varying forms of disbelief that their Master was briefing them. I was heartened by how many wished they knew something they could share. More than a few were running through every blonde vampire they'd ever met. There! One of them just thought the same image I'd seen in the memory of the NOLA vamp.

Ignoring the others, I dove deep into the vamp who'd thought of our mystery woman. She was still cycling through possibilities. She didn't know she had the right one. Casting out to the larger group again, I monitored for a few minutes. No, she was the only one thinking of our mystery vamp.

Diving back in, I tried to direct her thoughts, by sharing a quick image of my own. She remained calm and thoughtful, not picking up on my interference. I'd been practicing with Clive. I didn't want to remain as ham-handed as I'd been when trying to read St. Germain's mind. If I couldn't slide in and out undetected, I wasn't much of a secret weapon.

A synapse fired beside me. I jumped into the memory before it disappeared.

Leticia and…Audrey. The vamp whose mind I was reading was Audrey. They were standing in a large, ornate room. The clothes, the furniture, it all belonged in a period film. The mystery woman stood imperiously before them.

"No, Mother. I told you. I don't want any part of this," Leticia said.

"Audrey, wait for my daughter by the carriage. She and I have personal matters to discuss."

Audrey curtsied. "Of course, my lady." As she left the room, she heard one final comment.

"I won't do it."

I pulled out my phone to text Clive.

Me: Talk to Audrey. She doesn't know that she knows anything.

I plucked it out. The woman we're searching for is Leticia's mother. Audrey met her.

A few minutes later, the large group broke up. As the vamps left, their minds were still fixated on finding the woman Clive sought.

I dove into Clive's mind, something I was only able to do because he allowed it.

Hi.

Hello, love. I've asked Audrey to stay back so we could speak.

Perfect. Going completely by historical romances, I think she met Leticia's mother in the 1700s and they were all speaking English. With English accents, that is.

Leticia isn't English.

She was in the 1700s.

Interesting. Godfrey and I both thought her speech patterns belied the age she claimed. Neither of us picked up on her being English, though. Rather embarrassing, given we both are. Go ahead and move to the study. We'll be up in a minute. I assume you'd like to be present when I talk with her?

Yes, please.

Good.

Picking up a book at random, I went down the hall and took up residence on my usual bench near the wall in Clive's office. I sat cross-legged, put a pillow in my lap, and propped the book on it, opening to the middle. Slouching, I tried to look as though I'd been in here reading for a while. Not long after, Clive, Audrey, Russell, and Godfrey filed into the room.

"Hello, darling. I'm meeting with the contractor later this evening so we can get started on repairing the library. Would you care to join us?"

"Absolutely." I really hoped that was true and not a mock conversation to help Audrey relax. She appeared quite nervous, being called into the Master's study.

"Good." He turned his attention to Audrey. "Have a seat. I just have a few questions for you."

Bowing her head, she breathed, "Liege," and sat on the edge of one of the two chairs in front of his desk.

Russell took the other chair, leaning back comfortably. They were doing what they could to set her at ease.

Godfrey came to my bench. "Budge up," he said, waving me over.

I slid to the end, making room for him. This was new. No one ever sat over here with me. It did make this whole meeting seem chummy, though, which may have been the point.

"Audrey, I'd like to ask you about Leticia. I believe you two have been friends for centuries. Is that correct?" Clive leaned forward, his hands clasped on his desk, the picture of calm reserve.

"Oh." She glanced at Russell before turning back to Clive.

I dipped into her mind. The poor thing was terrified she was going to be given her final death because of her connection with Leticia, who had betrayed Clive.

"Yes, Sire." Her fingers trembled.

"We believe the woman I'm looking for is related in some way to Leticia, so I would appreciate any insight you could give me."

She thinks you're going to kill her because of Leticia.

"Let me also say, in our very long lives, we meet and befriend many people. Unless you, too, were working against me, I don't hold you responsible for what Leticia did."

"No, Sire! I would never. I—" She glanced around the room uneasily. "I'd never betray you, Sire. I love it here. Even with…" Her eyes darted to me. "Even with some of the problems we've had lately—many of them because of what Miss Leticia was doing —this is the best, the safest, nocturne I've ever lived in."

She means every word.

"I'm glad you feel that way. I'd like to keep it a safe home for us, which is why I'm asking you to tell me everything you know, or suspect, about Leticia. For instance, where and when did you meet?"

"In London, Sire. I was her lady's maid." Clive's words had

dispelled some of the anxiety, but she still sat ramrod straight on the edge of her chair.

"You were human when you met?"

"Aye, Sire, I was. As for when, I'm a little muddled on dates." Her eyes shot to Russell and then Godfrey, as though seeking help.

"I understand. Time can be strange for us, can't it? A general period is fine. Who was on the throne?"

"Oh, George III, Sire. He'd just been crowned King of Britain, and so young, too. I remember all the coronation parties. It seemed like Miss Leticia was getting new ball gowns every day. I needed to care for them—and quite a fair bit of work that was—and create new hair designs to complement each. I was much sought after, Sire, for my skill with hair." Being able to discuss what she was proud of had stopped the tremble.

"1760—"

"Aye, Sire. That was it." She was beginning to warm up to the conversation. "I'd thought she was a lazy layabout, like her mother. I didn't know, you see? They went out to dinners and parties and balls every night, sleeping all day. And they never ate. When I asked Miss Leticia about it, she shouted to wake the dead. I'd overstepped my place. It wasn't for me to ask, you see?"

"Yes, I see."

"I mean, ladies weren't supposed to eat a lot, but still, something, you know. I thought perhaps she stuffed herself at the parties—which they were never supposed to do, it being unlady-like. They'd often send us to the kitchens, though, to get some food to nibble on in the retiring rooms."

"Oh, is that why they stayed in there so long?" Godfrey asked, a grin on his face. "I'd assumed they were taking naps."

A shy and grateful smile brightened Audrey's face. "Only the elderly ladies fell asleep. Most gossiped and tried to relax. I sometimes felt a little sorry for my employers, always on display, every word, every gesture, every ribbon being judged. They couldn't move without someone finding fault. Of course, then one would slap me for brushing her hair too hard and all that sympathy dried up." She started to roll her eyes and then caught herself. "Sorry, Sire. I'm sure you don't care about any of that."

"Actually, it's quite interesting. How was Leticia as an employer?" Clive asked.

"Oh. Well." She stared down at her hands a moment. "Miss Leticia was very much like other ladies. I have some thoughts on that, if you don't mind my saying."

Clive nodded for her to continue.

"What I was saying before about being under the magnifying glass, having no say in any part of their own lives, being pushed into marriages that are advantageous for the family, but rarely for the girl, all of that. I think it made them strike out at the servants, the only ones with less power than themselves. So, slapping, spilling scalding tea, stepping on feet, waking us in the middle of the night to straighten the bed linens, all the mean petty things that made our lives miserable were done because they were miserable."

"I believe you're quite right, Audrey," Clive said, earning a tentative smile. "Was Leticia like that, filled with secret hostilities?"

"Aye, Sire. That's exactly it. Her mother was a fierce, angry, disapproving woman who kept Miss Leticia under her thumb."

"Any personal information about her mother, her background, relationships, habits, anything you can remember would be helpful to us," Russell said.

Eyes large and a guileless blue, she stared a moment too long. Oh, Audrey seemed to have it bad for Russell. Wholly unnecessary and yet far too tempting, I dipped into her mind again. Yep. She'd come with Leticia almost eight years ago and had fallen in love with Russell almost from the start. She kept it well-hidden, but she thought he was just about perfect in every way.

She nodded awkwardly, still staring at him, and then turned back to Clive, breaking the spell. "Lady Atwood is a very severe woman—"

"Is?" I interrupted. "Is she a vampire, too?" The vamps normally got super pissy if I spoke to them, but Audrey didn't seem to feel the same animosity toward me that others did.

"Yes, miss. Like I said before, I didn't know why they slept all day. It wasn't until they decided to move from London back to their home in Canterbury that I saw my opportunity to leave their employ. I had a friend who worked for another family. They had a daughter who was debuting soon. They wanted my skills with hair to set her apart.

"When I broached the subject with Miss Leticia, she flew into a rage, saying she'd just finally trained me properly, which seemed a bit much, if you don't mind my saying so. I had quite a good reputation before they'd hired me. I'd only left my former employer when her husband gambled away the family fortune and they needed to let staff go." She looked embarrassed to have shared information about her former employer's financial troubles.

"Audrey, you need to remember, none of us are from the aristocracy," Clive said gently. "None of us will fault you for speaking ill of your employer."

"She sounds a right bitch," Godfrey added, his accent sounding more street urchin than usual.

"Oh, aye. When I tried to leave, she backhanded me hard. She'd just had an argument with her mother and was riled up. I should have waited to tell her." She shook her head, still annoyed with herself after two hundred and fifty-plus years. "I guess she broke my neck. When I woke up, I was on fire." Her gaze darted to Russell and then away. "First thirst, you see. Miss Leticia shoved Mary—one of the maids—at me and..." The poor thing faltered, remembering.

"We know what happened," Russell said. "It wasn't your fault."

"I wish I could say I agree with that." She sighed. "Well, that's when I found out what was really going on. Her mother was fit to be tied, but Miss Leticia wanted me to stay with them, so she made sure I did."

"Why *did* you stay?" Godfrey asked.

"At first, I didn't know what else to do. She'd made me a demon. I'd been a good, God-fearing woman and now I was a monster, preying on the living. I felt too hopeless to do anything but what they demanded. It was like sleepwalking. It wasn't until Miss Leticia left a couple of months ago that the hopelessness disappeared. She left and I woke up the following evening feeling as I had when I was living." She shook her head in wonder.

"So," I said, "are we all thinking the same thing?"

"That that bitch Leticia had been messing with Audrey's mind for two hundred and fifty years? Yeah, I think we are," Godfrey said.

Audrey flinched. "What?"

"Some vampires are gifted with special abilities," Russell began. "Our Master, for instance, can talk to us in our minds. He can deliver pain with only a thought. We believe Leticia was augmenting the natural bond between a dame and her fledgling to keep you subservient to her."

The outrage on Audrey face heartened me. She was no longer nervous. She was pissed off. "She…"

"If I didn't want to kill her so badly myself," Clive said, "I'd give you the honor."

Audrey shot out of her seat and stalked around the room. "She…"

"A good way to get even is to tell us everything you know so we can hunt them down," Russell explained.

"Oh, aye." Audrey marched back to the chair and sat down. "Let's do."

NINETEEN

Wherein Ancient Connections Are
Discovered

"You said 'Lady Atwood.' Has she always gone by that name or has it changed over the years?" Clive asked.

Audrey struggled to get her rage under control before answering. "For as long as I've known her, Sire."

"And you said they had a home in Canterbury. Did you visit it?"

"Yes, Sire. It's near Blean. Quite grand."

Staring at his desk, lost in thought, Clive tapped his index finger. "Did you ever meet a Lord Atwood? Did Leticia have brothers?"

Audrey was shaking her head before Clive finished the question. "No, Sire. There was never mention of a husband. Miss Leticia, though, once told me they were gone now. Her father and brothers, that is."

"Were there two brothers?" Still staring at his desk, he seemed to be piecing something together.

"Aye. Begging your pardon, Sire, I can't be certain. She didn't give me details, being a servant and all. She said brothers with an s, and I feel like she may have used two names once, but it was so long ago and meant next to nothing to me at the time."

Nodding slowly, Clive turned to me, eyes full of sorrow,

before focusing once more on Audrey. "I understand you may not know or remember, but when she spoke of her father or brothers, was it with fondness or perhaps sorrow at their absence?"

She didn't answer right away. Brow furrowed, she, too, stared at the top of the desk. "I don't think so. It's just an impression, you understand, and she could have been annoyed about something unrelated. I got the feeling, though, that she didn't like them, was happy they were gone. It felt like that was part of the tension between her and Lady Atwood." Audrey looked up. "But I could be wrong, Sire."

"What is it?" I asked Clive. "You've figured something out."

"Possibly. Audrey, do you have any idea where Leticia or her mother are right now?"

"No, Sire. Last I heard, Lady Atwood was still in England, and thank heavens. I haven't heard from Miss Leticia since she left the nocturne."

"All right. You needn't stay any longer. If you think of anything else, no matter how inconsequential it seems, please let me know." Clive stood, walking around the desk, and extended a hand to Audrey. Helping her to her feet, he added, "I appreciate your insight a great deal."

She gave a quick bob of a curtsy before she remembered where and when she was. "I'll go now, Sire, but if there's anything I can do…I just want to help."

Placing her hand on his arm, he walked her to the door of the study. When he smiled down at her, her expression went blank a moment. "Once we have a plan, I'll find a place for you in it."

"Thank you, Sire!" She was so flustered, she almost walked right into the closed door.

Clive pulled her back while opening the door, and did it so deftly, I doubt she noticed what she'd almost done. Once he'd closed the door and was crossing the study back to his desk, Godfrey got up and took the seat she'd recently vacated.

"Well?" Godfrey asked.

Clive turned to me. "Do you remember what happened to my sister?"

"Of course." How could I not? It was the parallels between his sister's story and my own that caused Clive to take an interest in helping me.

"Your sister?" Godfrey sat back in his chair. "She was attacked and killed when you were human."

"She was the reason," Russell put in, "that he sought the dark kiss."

"Yes," Clive said. "Well, the reason I accepted it. I had no idea vampires existed, so I hadn't been seeking it. My father had passed the winter before. When Elswyth was raped and killed—you have to understand, Elswyth was the kindest and gentlest of souls. She was forever trying to adopt injured animals, nurse them back to health—when I brought her brutalized body home, my mother collapsed. I held the farm together as best I could, but my mother wasted away, heartbroken. When she finally succumbed a few months later, I buried her next to my father and sister. And I then began a new, bloodier chapter of my life."

"You hunted the men down." And wrong or not, it made me feel good to know those men had had their lives cut short, too.

"Yes. I could have stayed on the farm, married. None of that mattered anymore, though. Rage and grief ruled the day. I packed a few things and went in search of the men who'd destroyed my family."

"Leticia's father and brothers are these men?" Russell asked.

"It follows. I tracked down the ones I believed killed Elswyth. Atwood was their name. When I confronted them, they overpowered me, three to one. More anger than sense," he said, shaking his head. "As they were kicking my prone body, one of the sons make a comment about Elswyth taking a pounding, too. A tradesman on horseback happened upon us and the men laughed, mounted, and rode away.

"The tradesman helped me to my feet, even offered me some work while I healed. Edwards. He was a kind man. When I was strong enough, I left in search of them again." Glancing at me, he said, "If you're interested, I'll tell you the story of my turning. To Russell's point, yes, I accepted the dark kiss, the forfeiture of my soul, and an eternity of night so that I could kill the men who had brutalized and murdered my sister, consequently causing the death of my mother as well."

"Was your farm near Canterbury?" Sometimes it was difficult to think of Clive as a farmer. Other times, like now, the vision came easily. Him, in trim breeches, a coarse tunic, working in the fields.

He nodded. "I hadn't considered them. It happened so long ago."

"So you became a vampire to kill her husband and sons and then she became one to kill you? What the heck? Did you have a drive-thru vamping station in town?"

Godfrey laughed. "Fair point."

"I have no idea where and when they were turned," he said.

"Why wait so long?" Russell asked.

Nodding, Clive said, "Exactly so. That was why I'd never even considered what was left of the Atwoods as being behind the attacks. What purpose is there in waiting so long?"

"She said no," I volunteered.

The men stared blankly at me, so I relayed Audrey's brief memory of Leticia and her mother.

Grinning at me, Clive stood. "Always sitting over here quietly, listening attentively, and putting it all together." He sat next to me and held my hand in his lap. "She said no. That's what Audrey remembered."

"It could have been, 'No, I won't go riding today,'" Godfrey argued.

"Could have, but the timing fits. I have no idea why the mother didn't come after me herself, but she tries to send her daughter. Daughter says no and keeps saying no until I hand Étienne his true death. Then Leticia changes her mind and says yes."

We sat silently, considering.

"And we'd still be sitting here," he continued, "spinning our wheels, no idea who was behind it all if you hadn't told us to ask a woman." He kissed my hand. "And then plucked out the exact one we needed to make the connections."

I knocked him with my shoulder. "I'm kind of awesome."

"You kind of are." He held my hand, the one sporting his engagement ring, between both of his.

"You should probably marry her, Sire," Godfrey said.

"I probably should."

Russell stood abruptly and left, Godfrey in his wake.

"What was that about?" I thought we were having a planning meeting.

"Oh, that," he said, pulling me down so we were reclined on the bench. "I told them to leave us." His hand traveled up my side before resting on my breast. Running his nose along my jaw, he said, "I hope you don't mind."

Pulling his shirt out of his trousers, I ran my hands up his back, reveling in the feel of him. "I'll survive." When I tried to unbuckle his belt, I almost fell off the side. "I do kind of mind how narrow this thing is, though."

"Easily fixed," he said as he rolled us onto the exquisite rug below, making sure he took the brunt of the fall. When he kissed me, I forgot about everything but him.

I had just sat up to pull off my sweater when my spidey senses started tingling. Straddling Clive, I stilled his hands, closed my eyes, and cast out for who was nearby.

"What is it?"

"Shh." There were no vamps on this floor. They were all below or outside on guard duty. A hazy form hovered outside Clive's window. Opening my eyes, I hopped up and stalked to the window. This better not be Charlotte or we were going to have words about boundaries.

Clive stood at my back, waiting.

"Give me a minute. We have a ghost voyeur." Without being able to touch her—and she definitely felt like a her—I stared into the dark glass where she was standing and concentrated. She was familiar. I was sure I knew—"No!"

Racing out of the study, I flew down the hall to the patio door and tore through it. She was fading. *Nonononono.* I reached out and she grabbed my hand. "Why?"

"I'm afraid I underestimated my niece."

I tried to stifle my sob. Abigail had killed Martha.

"What's happened?" Clive asked.

Tears flooded my eyes. I'd *just* found her, a great-aunt and a mentor. Family. I'd had family for a blink and then Abigail had ripped her from this world. Martha had lost her love and her life because of me.

"Martha's dead."

Clive's arms wrapped around my waist as I continued to cling to Martha's hand, even as it lost its form.

"In the Wicche Glass, in my snug, is the family grimoire. You must find it…behind Gad…"

I was barely able to make out her words. She was fading. Moving on, as she should. "She didn't know who you were, did she?"

"No…knew I was teaching you. She's weakened now…" I felt a soft, barely there brush across my cheek and then she was gone.

Turning toward Clive, I crumpled and wept. She'd been in hiding from Coreys most of her life, and for good reason. I'd barely known her a week and had ruined everything. Clive comforted and soothed but couldn't touch the grief that felt like an open wound. After seven long years without my mother, I'd had family. For a few days, I'd had ties. I hadn't been adrift and alone.

"Neither of us will ever be alone again," Clive promised, picking up on some of my thoughts. "We're our own family."

"Yes." I tucked my head in the crook of his neck, his scent settling something jumbled up inside me. Mate. No Coreys, no Quinns, but I had my partner in this world. "We need to go. I need to take care of her and find something she left me."

"Then we'll go." He gave me a soft kiss and then took my hand, walking me back into the house where Russell was waiting.

"Sam and I are going out. She's lost her great-aunt. There are some things that need taking care of." We continued down the hall to the garage, Russell accompanying us.

"I'm terribly sorry, Miss Quinn." He rested his hand on my shoulder briefly in comfort.

Nodding my thanks, we left Russell at the door.

Clive chose the charcoal gray sportscar he favored, opening the passenger door for me. Settling into the black leather, I waited, hollowed out, afraid of what we'd find. What had Abigail done to Martha?

Clive slid in, started it up, and had the roadster slipping under the rising garage door a moment later. "Colma, wasn't it?"

I nodded.

"I thought the Corey Curse meant she couldn't kill a family member herself. It was why she got the wolves involved, trapped you in visions, and pushed Liam to kill you. Don't the same rules apply to Martha?" Clive quickly made his way across town to the freeway, as traffic was light at this late hour.

"Martha believes Abigail didn't know who she was. Martha left home young. Like me, her necromantic abilities hadn't made themselves known early. The family thought she was without magic and therefore ostracized her."

Downshifting, he glanced at me. "So, whatever this curse is, Abigail tripped it? She's been weakened?"

"Martha says yes."

"We need to find out what the curse is and strike before she realizes her vulnerability."

I'd been thinking the same thing. "I need to figure out how to win before I confront her."

"*We* need to figure out how before *we* confront her." He reached over and squeezed

my hand before taking the Colma exit.

I directed him to the Historical Society parking lot, grateful he was my we.

TWENTY

Requiem

I hadn't been in Colma at night before. It made quite a difference. The dead were thick on the ground, adding to the fog crawling over the hills and blanketing the cemeteries. Getting out of the car, I felt stronger, the magic coiled and ready in my chest.

Clive took my hand and we walked down the deserted street to the side gate of the out-of-business monument shop. I had a moment to wonder if the gate would admit a vampire and then he was pushing through the ward. Passing the remnants of the old business, we made it to the courtyard.

It was dark and empty. No fairy lights glowed above, no flicker from a fire in the windows of The Wicche Glass Tavern. She was gone.

"You described it, but I hadn't imagined properly. It's magical, isn't it?" Clive silently prowled the courtyard, taking in the massive, gnarled tree that housed the bar, the gargantuan roots snaking their way around the yard, protecting it.

"Very." I didn't want to go in, didn't want to see what had been done to her. Please, let it have been fast and painless. *Please.*

Clive took my hand again as I made my way to the door, hanging askew off its hinges. Holding my breath, I pushed it open and stepped inside. Hazy moonlight streamed through the windows, illuminating the wreckage. It was like The Slaughtered Lamb all over again. Tables and chairs busted, the bar splintered, bottles broken, glass littering the buckled wood of the floor.

The scent of alcohol was heavy in the air, but so, too, was death. Following my nose, I stepped over and around shards of wood, making my way to her snug, the little sitting room she kept behind the bar.

The door was open, so we were hit with the full impact at once. A lifetime of mementos and memories smashed to pieces. Most of the photos of Martha and Galadriel that had decorated a full wall were now broken on the floor. The few that still clung to the wall bore a similar center hit, the glass spiderwebbing out, obscuring the life the women had shared.

In the center of the room, stripped and covered in burns and cuts, lay Martha. Abigail and her demon had tortured a woman in her seventies. Holding in the sob that wanted to break free, I went to her. Kneeling in blood, I covered her, gathered her in my arms, and rocked. Tears streamed down my face as I silently prayed for her.

I'd done this before. Pain split my head as I recovered a stolen memory. I'd been kneeling in my mother's blood, her torn and broken body in my arms. I'd come home from school and found her in the living room of our tiny apartment. A homeless man had lain crumpled in the corner, dead. He'd probably been used to torture my mother, as Abigail would have wanted to keep her hands clean.

When I stood with Martha in my arms, Clive tried to take her, but I couldn't let him. She was mine to carry. Shuffling through the bar, I went back out to the courtyard. I'd bury her here, where she'd been happiest with Galadriel. Laying her on one of the long tables, I studied the area. I wanted her to have a view of The Wicche Glass Tavern tree and the side of the courtyard that led to Faerie, to Galadriel.

"What can I do?" Clive asked.

I'd forgotten I wasn't alone anymore. "See if you can find a shovel?"

Clearing leaves and rocks from the moss where I wanted to dig, I unspooled the magic within me and sent it deep into the earth, asking if I could use this place to inter Martha. I was on the border of Faerie. I didn't want to do anything to piss her off.

A feeling of peace and calm settled on me and I had my answer.

Clive returned a few minutes later, shovel in hand.

"Thanks." When I took a closer look, I saw it was brand new.

"There were no shovels around here, so I took one from a nursery a few blocks away."

"Handy."

"I am." He brushed a stray hair off my face before dropping a soft kiss on my lips. "Let me do this for you."

I hugged him tightly and then stepped back and took the shovel from his hand. "This is mine to do."

Nodding, he sat on the bench next to Martha and waited. It didn't take me long. When I turned to retrieve Martha, Clive was there, holding her. We laid her in the hole together. He took up the shovel and moved the earth back in, covering her. I went to the closed monument shop storefront. They had to have something I could use as a headstone.

Dust swirled in the air as I yanked open the back door. No one had probably stepped foot in here since Martha and Galadriel bought it to use as a front for their bar. Cobwebs swayed as I walked through the dark building. I finally found what I was looking for on a shelf behind the register.

It was a soft, almost periwinkle blue stone that had already been partially carved. It was maybe a little over one foot square, perhaps two inches thick. A large tree of life dominated the stone plaque, leaving a smaller area open for personalization.

Taking the stone, I walked back to Clive, who had filled the hole and replaced the layer of moss I'd put aside. I sat at the nearby table, concentrated on the claw of only my index finger, and soon had something to carve with. It wasn't professional looking, but it felt right.

Martha Corey
Beloved of Galadriel

Not knowing when she was born, I left the dates of her life blank. Besides, this seemed the most important pieces of information. She'd lived, been loved, and will be missed. I placed the plaque on the ground and pushed it firmly into the moss.

"Did Martha tell you where to look for the grimoire?" Clive asked. "If she believes it's important in defeating Abigail, we need to find it."

I opened my mouth to respond and then heard a soft, strange noise. Glancing around, I found Pippin on the gnarled tree root, looking down at the plaque.

"She'dlikethat."

Again, it took a moment for my brain to catch up with the pixie's fast, high pitched speech. "Good. Were you here when it happened?"

He shook his head, anger lining his face.

"When Galadriel returns, can you tell her what happened? Tell her I'm so very sorry."

"Sorry about what?" The beautiful elven warrior hopped over the tree roots on the far side of the courtyard. She focused first on Clive, her hand lifting to the sword strapped to her back, and then her head lifted, scenting the wind.

On a strangled scream, she tore across the courtyard and ran into The Wicche Glass. Knowing what she would find, I started to follow.

"Sam," Clive was by side, a hand on my arm stopping me. "She needs time to grieve."

"She'll have questions. I want to help."

"The dawn is coming. We must leave." He gripped my hand and tried to pull me away.

"I can't just leave. You go ahead, beat the dawn. I'll run home later."

"I'm not leaving you with an angry, heartbroken warrior. She'll kill you just to feel something other than pain."

"Excellent idea, vampire." Galadriel stood in the doorway, her face a mask of rage, a huge sword in her powerful hand. Her purple eyes flashed as she stalked down the stairs, long silver hair streaming behind her.

"You." She pointed her sword at my head. "She was safe until you. I'd kept her safe. All these years, I've kept her from your kind. Then you show up and—" She faltered, her eyes becoming glassy. A blink later, they were clear and fierce. "You show up. I'm forced to leave. Then she's tortured and killed."

Clive stepped in front of me, into the path of the sword. "It's not Sam's fault. Sam's aunt—Martha's niece—is a sorceress. She's evil."

"And *you* led her here!" she roared, her sword still pointed over Clive's shoulder at me.

She was right. It didn't matter whether it was intended or not. I'd led evil to their door. Martha was dead and Galadriel heartbroken. "I'm so sorry. I wish I'd never bothered either of you. Truly. If I could go back and do it again, I wouldn't have come."

"Keep your guilt. I want my love, but I'll settle for your blood."

When she started forward again, Clive held up a hand. "I won't let you hurt her. Unlike Martha, Sam has been hunted since she was born. The only reason she survived torture as a teenager is because of her father's wolf blood. Sam is not the villain in this story. Abigail is. Sam and Martha found family after a very long time alone. Your anger is misplaced. *But* if it would help…" He pushed me away from him. "You'll find me a more experienced adversary."

"Done." She slashed the huge sword through the air, nearly taking Clive's head off, but he was gone before the weapon completed its arc. Standing behind her, his fist swung toward the back of her head. She must have sensed it coming because she was flipping over his head, landing on a table behind him, the sword coming down at an angle to hack him in half.

Before the sword could touch him, he'd spun and punched, causing Galadriel to fly across the courtyard and bust a table and some chairs. Wiping the blood from her brow, she charged at him again. They were too fast. Much of what they did barely registered after the fact. It was like talking to Pippin. It took my mind a moment to catch up with what I was seeing.

Which is how, a short time and many broken tables and chairs later, Galadriel stood behind me, her sword to my throat. Clive rose from where he'd been thrown and crossed the courtyard to us. Rage poured off him. It wasn't until his calm was gone that I realized it had been like a practice session to him. She needed to work off the grief and he was the only one equal to her skill. The disinterested expression was gone.

"You overstep," he said, his voice like ice.

"Mercy and forgiveness are despised by the fae. We prize revenge. A love for a love. It's time for you to lose yours." The grief in her voice was her only show of emotion. Her breathing remained steady. The huge sword at my throat never wavered.

"That I cannot allow." He spared me the briefest of glances before focusing once again on the woman who held me.

Please don't hurt her.

I may not have a choice. If that sword moves, she's dead.

Have you tried giving her pain?

She'd convulse, cutting off your head.

I can stop her.

See that you do. Now.

Faster than a blink, I wrestled her arm from my neck as Clive gave her pain that dropped her to her knees. Clive had me ten feet away, wrapped in one arm, while the other held Galadriel's sword. He stared down at the sword a moment and then dropped it, his hand red and blistered.

The distraction was enough. Galadriel popped up, intent on continuing the battle, when something caught her attention. Pausing, she looked to the left at Martha's grave. Shoulders slumping, she dropped back to her knees and rested a hand on the stone.

"Just leave." The defeat in her voice broke my heart.

The dawn was fast approaching and Galadriel needed space, so we left. Clive raced home, the streets thankfully quiet in the early morning. The sun was just rising as the garage door slid down. We'd made it.

I waited until the engine was off and then grabbed his hand. The blistering was gone, but it still looked red. "What caused it?"

He got out and waited for me, taking my hand as we entered the dark, quiet house and made our way to our room. "I've heard of elven metal that can be spelled for one owner. It's possible only Galadriel can touch her own weapon. I've never held elven steel before. It's just as possible that vampires can't touch it without burning."

"Handy."

"For them, yes."

When we reached our bedroom, we both headed for the bathroom. We cleaned up quickly and were sliding into bed shortly afterward. Clive had time to pull me in tightly, kiss the top of my head, and then he was out.

Wrapping myself around him, I settled in to sleep, trying not to think about death and grief, responsibility and regret, and the grimoire I needed to combat Abigail, the one Galadriel would never let me have.

TWENTY-ONE

It's Getting Hot in Here

I woke midday, feeling at odds. I needed the grimoire to prepare for Abigail, but it was now out of reach. *Wait.* There were grimoires in the shipment I hadn't finished processing at The Slaughtered Lamb. They weren't the ancient Corey book of spells, but they were something.

I got cleaned up, dressed, grabbed the two necromancy books I had picked up in New Orleans, and ran to the ocean and down the steps into my bookstore and bar.

Dark and empty, it was like coming home and being cut adrift at the same time. Abigail had to be defeated, her influence gone, so that these beautiful rooms could be opened and filled with friends again.

Grabbing a soda, I dropped my necromancy books on my favorite table by the window and then went in search of the grimoires. I remembered unboxing them, so they had to be on one of the book carts in the storeroom.

It didn't take long before I was walking back to my table with five grimoires of varying ages. I'd left the newer ones, the ones that had been published by a company, on the cart, taking only the rare handwritten ones. These were the kind I kept locked in a glass-fronted cabinet in the bookstore.

The first one had peeling leather and an ornate lock. Unfortunately, it also had cramped writing in a foreign language that may or may not have been Welsh. It was something with a shit-ton of Ys. Pushing that one aside, I carefully took the next. This one appeared to be even older. Thankfully, this one was in English, although the script was nearly impossible to read.

Carefully turning delicate pages, I found one spell that was a bit easier to make out. It used the word *spirits* multiple times. Perhaps this was my kind of wicchey spell. Reading the page over and over, I finally got the gist. It was about calling spirits to drag an enemy away. The words that had given me the most trouble to decipher were Latin. Thank you, Internet translator.

I hopped up and went to Dave's desk in the kitchen for a piece of paper. I wanted to add bookmarks to the spells I needed to memorize and practice. Lydia, Owen's mom, might be able to help me make sense of them.

When I opened the third grimoire, I felt a push on the main ward. I knew a notice had been added to the ward, letting people know I was closed, but the push came again. It was probably Grimm. The old dwarf did not take no for an answer.

Climbing the stairs, I passed through the ward to find a pissed-off gorgon instead of a pissed-off dwarf.

"What the fuck, Sam? Why is this place always closed?" Stheno tried to march past me but ran into the invisible wall again. "You're working my last nerve, Wolfgirl."

"Sorry." Mentally opening the ward to her, I followed in her wake as she stomped down the stairs.

"Make me a drink and tell me why you've gone into hiding." She plopped down on a barstool and drummed her fingers, waiting.

Grinning, I went behind the bar and started pulling bottles. As I made us a pitcher of blackberry lemon drops, I told her the whole story, the part that related to me, not Clive. I wasn't going to tell someone else's secrets.

Carrying the pitcher and two glasses back to my table, I sat and poured. "So, as I don't want to encourage Abigail to possess my friends, I decided to lay low."

"How hard can it be to take this bitch out? I don't get it." Stheno downed the first glass in one gulp and poured herself a refill.

"She keeps to the shadows. I've only ever seen her once in person, when she was handing me off to the wolves to be killed. I think that demon of hers keeps her hidden. She works through others so she can technically keep her hands clean."

Stheno pulled over a chair and put her sandaled feet up. "But since she killed her aunt, she's fucked, Corey-wise?"

Nodding, I finished my first and poured another as well. What the hell. Might as well get drunk.

"So, the plan is to wait for her to come out of hiding again and then take her out?"

Nodding, I took another sip. Motioning to the grimoires spread out on the table, I said, "I'm looking for spells that might help."

"Let's just go grab the one your great-aunt wanted you to have. If the elf gives us trouble, I'll turn her to stone."

I was shaking my head before she stopped talking. "No. She's right. I led Abigail to them. She's lost her wife. I'm not going back there to bug her."

"You're too soft, kid," she said, grabbing the nearest book. "Have I taught you nothing?" She studied the faint design on the cover. "What are we looking for in these things?"

"Anything I can use to either protect myself or hurt her. I don't care about spells that do anything else. At the moment, I just want spells for battle." I pulled the book I was looking through earlier into my lap. This was nice. I had to keep reminding myself I wasn't alone anymore.

"We need snacks," she said as she poured a refill.

"Good call. Let me see what Dave left in the kitchen." I popped up again and headed for the kitchen.

"Ha! This one's for making a guy's cock drop off." Her cackling followed me into the kitchen.

"Bookmark it!" I shouted back, opening cupboard doors, looking for snacks. I returned to the bar with a large canister of nuts—the ones I put out for customers—the last of the cookies Dave had baked on the last night we were open, and a bag of chips. Dropping them on the table, I said, "There's also ice cream and microwave popcorn in there. I'm not sure if the food in the fridge is still okay, so I didn't chance it."

"This works." Stheno tore open the bag of chips, grabbed a handful, and turned the page.

"Wait! No greasy fingers on rare grimoires!" I ran for napkins and came back with a roll of paper towels.

She grumbled about prissy wolves, but she wiped her fingers before touching the books. "Hey, this one is cool. It can cloak you, for short periods of time."

"Mark it. Honestly, this may be a waste of time. I'm not this kind of wicche, so I may not be able to do these spells, but I want to ask Lydia, see if any of them are within my reach. I did a cleaning spell to get rid of the evil sap from the convent in New Orleans. That worked. And I did an opening-doors one to break the window to let the ghost escape. So I seem to be able to do some spells."

Shrugging, I added, "Before we knew I was a necromancer, Lydia was trying to teach me to be a normal wicche, and I was a dismal failure."

"I could have told you you weren't normal, kid," she cracked, filling up our glasses again. "And we're out."

Pushing the grimoire aside, I took the empty pitcher back to the bar and started mixing again. "I think I'm going to need to call Clive for an extraction when the sun goes down. Walking may be right out by then."

Snickering, Stheno turned the page. "Ooh, I like this one. It forces the truth from a liar's mouth."

"Handy, but probably not a lot of help in a fight."

"Oh, I don't know. The truth can be quite powerful, especially when it's being hidden."

SEANA KELLY

"Good point. Mark it."

It turned out the first grimoire I couldn't read *was* written in Welsh, which Stheno could read. So, while she searched for spells in that one, I went back to look at some of the pages I'd marked.

"You're Greek. How is it you know Welsh, anyway?" My feet were up on a chair as I flipped through spells. I kept coming back to the one that called spirits to drag away an enemy, trying to figure out how I could make that work for me.

"Thousands of years, sister. You pick up a lot of shit. Didn't I French braid your hair in Lafitte's? I know all kinds of crap. You want me to explain 401(k)s? I can do that, too."

"Not right now, but thanks. So why didn't you ever learn to drive?"

Cringing, she turned the page. "I had a bad experience."

"Would you care to elaborate?"

Ignoring me, she continued scanning the cramped handwriting and flipping pages. Finally, she said, "No."

Thirty minutes later, the snacks were gone and I was behind the bar, mixing another pitcher of blackberry lemon drops. I was also more than a little drunk, but it was just Stheno and me. No one else was here to take advantage of my being impaired. I could sleep in the back or call Clive. Feeling safe and relaxed, I asked Stheno if we should transition to ice cream.

"Fuck yeah we should." She turned the page and continued reading. The drinks weren't affecting her as they were me. Thousands of years building up a tolerance, I supposed.

"Are your sisters going to be pissed you're with me this afternoon?" I was doing a piss-poor job of muddling the blackberries, but whatever. Neither of us were picky about presentation.

"They probably haven't noticed I'm gone." She tipped the chip bag and shook the crumbs into her mouth. "Euryale has a stick so far up her ass, I'm surprised she hasn't ruptured vital organs. Feeling superior takes a lot out of her, so she sleeps most of the day."

I snickered. That was exactly how I'd pegged her older sister.

"And Medusa, shit." Stheno dropped her head back in exhaustion. "Oh my gods, she hoards slights like a dragon does treasure. She remembers every insult, every gesture, every fucking eye roll, and she trots them out daily to prove how put upon she's been her entire life. If I have to hear one more time how my sleeping with her boyfriend ruined her life, I'm gonna lose it!"

I cringed. "Well, jeez, that does sound bad."

"Only when I phrase it the way she does. The truth is she tried to steal my favorite boy toy while I was away. I come home, make a date, and then she's busting into my room, crying about how he's cheating and I'm ruining her life." Stheno shook her head. "The drama. For almost two thousand years, I've had to hear about how I stole her one true love. Typical middle child desperate for attention."

"Wait. She's the middle child? I thought that was you." I poured the fresh lemon juice into the shaker.

"Nope. I'm the baby and the only normal one in the group. Giving them alone time means they get to bitch about me to their heart's content and I don't have to listen."

Heavy footsteps pounded down the stairs and I jumped, my heart in my throat. I wasn't prepared. My brain was too fuzzy to think straight, to defend myself.

Black boots and then jeans. Dave. Blowing out a breath, I slumped against the bar.

"What the fuck are you two doing here?" His tone was off. He was always grumpy, but he sounded genuinely angry.

"Fuck off, Demonboy. It's her bar. She can do whatever she wants." Stheno turned the page, never once sparing him a glance.

When he came around the back of the bar, though, she put the grimoire aside and stood.

Clutching a hand to his bald head, he slammed a fist on the bar. "You're not supposed to be here!"

Panicking, I backed slowly away. This was Dave. He'd been my grumpy security blanket for seven years. Now, though, his shark-like black eyes held nothing but hate. Stheno moved in behind him and I held up a hand.

"Don't," I said to her. She couldn't kill him. No matter what Abigail was doing to him, he was Dave.

"Don't what?" he snarled. "Always where you're not supposed to be."

Adrenaline and fear were clearing my head. "You're stronger than she is. Don't let her turn you into a puppet."

"What the hell do you know? Hiding behind your vampire, leaving the rest of us to deal with constant fucking pain and never-ending whispers." He smacked his head again.

"I'm sorry."

"Fuck your sorry. I need it to stop!" he roared, hand whipping out, grabbing me around the neck, and squeezing.

Stheno reached for her eyepatch and I held up my hand again. Dave wasn't dying because of me, not like Martha.

Flames jumped from his arm and I knew what he intended. Unleashing my claws, I raked them down the side of his face, trying to snap him out of Abigail's spell. He didn't flinch at the pain, though sweat had popped out at his temples and his whole body shook. The hand around my neck convulsed, cutting off my air before releasing a hair's breadth, letting it back in again. The fact that I was breathing at all meant he was fighting her.

The flames crawled slowly down his arm, the heat already burning my face. If she'd had complete control of him, I'd be engulfed in flames.

"I'm not just going to stand here and watch him kill you!" Stheno shouted.

I tried to wave her off a last time, but when the flames hit my skin, I screeched, clawing at his arm. I wouldn't kill him. Abigail couldn't force me to kill him. I wrapped myself in my own magic and recited what I could remember of the spell I'd been practicing.

Shadows shot up from the floorboards and swarmed around Dave. He let go. When I dropped to the floor, I scuttled away. Opening and closing his mouth, eyes wide open, he flailed, trying to fight them off, but they swirled ceaselessly around him, slashing his skin and taking little bites.

There was one moment when he seemed to be looking at me—Dave not Abigail—and then the shadows dragged him down and off this plane.

Stheno was crouched beside me. "Can you breathe?"

Air trickled through my crushed, scorched throat, but I could breathe. Sort of. I tried to nod without moving my neck, which was an excruciating mistake.

What was that spell, and what had I done to Dave?

TWENTY-TWO

Wherein Clive Discovers the Joys of Duct Tape

S theno was on the phone. As the sun was down, I assumed she was speaking with Clive. My wards knew to always let Clive in, so I didn't even flinch when he raced in a few minutes later. And just like that, the pain was gone.

"The scarring around her neck is going to be severe. Can't you do something? I thought bloodsucker spit healed." Stheno was kneeling by my head as Clive crouched beside me.

"Hold her shoulders down for me."

Closing my eyes, I concentrated on breathing slowly and not on his fingers scraping at the charred skin of my throat. Stheno pulled something over my head and shoved it in my pocket before they sat me up. Clive moved around me, peeling away what was burned and blistered. Unfortunately, his ability to mask pain only went so far. I held in my whimpers as best I could. Only later did I realize I had Stheno's hand in mine. She didn't even bitch when I repeatedly tried to crush it.

When I felt Clive's tongue, I knew we were through the worst of it. I also knew it must have been bad, as Stheno wasn't making any dirty jokes.

I felt a push on my ward.

"Russell's here. Can you let him in?" Clive asked.

I opened my eyes to a very concerned Clive. Russell hurried down the stairs a moment later. I wished I'd kept my eyes closed, as I'd have avoided the split-second look of horror on his face.

"Sire, I've brought the car. Dr. Underfoot and Miss Wong have both agreed to meet us at the nocturne. Is Miss Quinn able to be moved?"

"She's fine," Stheno said, unceremoniously lifting me to my feet.

My knees buckled but she held on until I steadied myself, standing under my own power.

"Thank you for calling me," Clive said to Stheno.

She shrugged her acceptance.

"Would you like to come with us? I can guarantee your safety in the nocturne." He reached for my hand and I took it.

"I don't need your help to protect myself, bloodsucker. And no, I don't want to sit around and watch her heal. I've got shit to do." She looked around the bar. "I'll clean this up before I go. Your wards will let me out, right? I don't feel like getting stuck in here all night."

Yes.

"She says yes."

"Good enough. Somebody grab the old books. She needs to study those."

Russell went to the table and collected the grimoires.

When I started to move toward the stairs, she grabbed my arm, spinning me toward her. "And the next time somebody is trying to kill you, don't you fucking wave me off!"

I couldn't let her kill Dave.

"You may not have noticed, but Dave is a kind of father figure for Sam." He gave me a sad smile when he saw my eyes filling with tears. "Perhaps a foul-mouthed stepfather would be a better description. She just lost her great-aunt. She couldn't let you take him, too." He lifted our joined hands to his mouth and kissed my fingers.

I think I killed him myself.

Dave is very hard to kill.

We slowly made our way up the stairs. Holding my neck completely still was proving to be quite difficult. When we hit the cold night air, I thought my head was going to snap off. The cold pierced my exposed muscles and veins, settling into my spine.

I must have made a sound because both Clive and Russell were trying to block the wind and move me as quickly as possible without jostling me. Getting into the car without bending my neck was near impossible. Soon, though, we were on our way. Clive sat in the back with me, his hands wrapped tightly around one of mine.

What happened?

Stheno and I were going through the grimoires that were in my last book order. And drinking heavily, which might be helping to dull the pain. Dave arrived, started shouting about how I wasn't supposed to be there.

Perhaps that's why he was there.

What do you mean?

He may have known that Abigail was infecting him, so he tried to keep to places he knew you weren't. In that way, he couldn't be forced to hurt you. Then there you were, exactly where you weren't supposed to be.

I know she didn't have complete control of him, He could have killed me in an instant. Instead, he was shaking with the effort to not hurt me.

He did well enough.

No. I clawed him, down his face and arms. Then I used a spell I'd just read, not knowing what it really was, and called dark spirits up to rip him apart and drag him from this plane. I gave him over to be tortured.

I couldn't stop the tears from falling, couldn't care about the fiery sting as they rolled over my exposed throat.

I will say again, Dave is very hard to kill.

But he can feel pain.

Dr. Underfoot and Lilah were waiting in Clive's study when we returned. Lilah gasped when she saw me, but Dr. Underfoot, who had no doubt seen far worse in his very long life, opened his bag and set to work. Lilah held her hands a few inches from my neck, her lips moving rapidly. The itching began almost immediately. I clamped down hard on Clive's hand and a new wave of pain relief washed over me.

When Lilah, looking exhausted, finally dropped her hands, my eyes cut to Clive.

Better.

"As always, Miss Wong, it is a pleasure working with you," Dr. Underfoot said. "You are able to do what I am not, and because of that, there is now something I *can* do to help. Until the subcutaneous tissue was regrown, there wasn't much I could do. Now, however, as dermis growth has begun, I have a balm that will help." He pulled a chewing tobacco tin from his bag.

At my raised eyebrows, he chuckled. "They're just a handy size, so I collect them." He popped off the top and showed us a cloudy ointment. "Wait another few hours. We want the restructuring of the epidermis to begin before using this. Even a soft breeze is going to hurt, so wait until you can handle it and then lightly brush over the new growth. It contains an anesthetic you will need once the sun rises and Clive is no longer controlling your pain. It also contains herbs for healing."

Thank you.

"Sam and I thank you both for coming so quickly." Clive inclined his head toward each. "We also hope not to see you again anytime soon," he added on a smile.

Except at our wedding.

"Except, of course, at our wedding. You would both be honored guests."

Lilah perked up at the news. Dr. Underfoot merely nodded in acceptance.

Once they'd left, Clive took my hand and led me to the elevator. "We need to figure out how to keep your neck from touching anything while still allowing you to rest."

Duct tape.

Excuse me?

We're going to have to jury rig something, which means duct tape.

When the elevator doors opened, we stepped out.

I have no idea if we even have duct tape in the house.

By the time we got to the bedroom door, Russell was waiting for us with a roll of duct tape in his hand.

Speedy.

He is.

"Thank you. Let's see what we can do about finding a way for Sam to rest." He took the tape from Russell as we passed. I stiffly made my way to the couch, as I knew the bed was right out.

Slide the couch all the way to the left, against that wall. Then duct tape the pillow to the wall at head height.

Clive must have asked Russell for a pillow because one was flying through the air a moment later. "Hold that side," he said to Russell. "If I tape the sides up and let the middle hang, it'll act as a kind of hammock for your head, helping to keep you from slumping one way or the other in your sleep."

As carefully as possible, they had me recline against the arm of the couch with my legs stretched out along the sofa so they could position the pillow properly. Once they were done and I was as comfortable as it was possible for me to be, Russell held out his hand for the tape, intending to leave.

"This is extraordinarily useful. Can you ask Norma to buy more? I want a roll in each of my cars and another in my office."

Russell barely hid his grin as he gave a short bow and said, "Yes, Sire."

Once he'd gone, Clive helped me up. "Let's get you changed into more comfortable clothes."

"I'm guessing showering is out." Which was too bad, as I felt grimy. Near immolation could take a toll on a body.

"Perhaps not." He turned on the shower and then quickly undressed us both. Grabbing a face towel, he led me into the spray, careful not to jostle me and to keep the water pointed low on my body. When he wet a towel, wrung it out, and gently cleaned my face, I could have wept.

He twisted a bath towel into a roll and then wrapped it around my shoulders, to help block stray drops of water from hitting my neck. He then soaped and rinsed us both, quickly and efficiently.

Better?

Yes, I thought on a sigh.

Good. He turned off the water and then dried us off before leading me to the closet. He dressed me in my softest pajamas and then led me back to the couch, pulling the comforter off the bed and wrapping it around me.

It's too early for the medicine. Are you hungry?

I've been thinking about something. I was going to try earlier, but Stheno, and grimoires, and a lot of cocktails happened. If Leticia has decided to work with her mother against us, maybe she's nearby.

You've tried before and never found her. Why would now be different?

I started to shrug and then caught myself. *She's figured out a way to hide, to cloak her signature. I used to think I could only sense the dead, but sometimes I feel other immortals. Now that we know Leticia is definitely involved, I want to do a deep dive, searching for the wall she's hiding behind or the person who's cloaking her.*

What can I do?

Just keep the pain relief coming.

Done.

He sat on the couch, and then a hand snaked under the comforter and wrapped around my foot. Being tethered to him helped me make the leap.

Don't let go.

Never.

Closing my eyes, I tapped into the deep reservoir of magic that lived in me. Mentally unspooling a magical thread from my chest, I imagined wrapping it around my neck and then thought the simple healing spell Lydia had taught me. I wasn't a healer, like Lilah, but I figured it was worth a try.

Casting out in my mind, I didn't try to filter for vampires or ghosts or anything in particular. I mentally took a walk through San Francisco, searching for anything unusual. I found what I thought was probably Stheno and her sisters. There were three unrelieved black dots with a hazy film of purple over the top. They were in their beach house.

When I got to the North Beath neighborhood, I found Meg. At least I think I did. The signature felt familiar, and, again, purple over black. I couldn't see the wicches at all. They were living and mortal. My abilities didn't extend that far, so I had no idea where Abigail was. Besides, she had a demon keeping her hidden.

Later, I found black blips with a faint overlay of green; I guessed they were the fae. Perhaps immortality was the link to what I could sense. The faintly green beings were in the parks and the ocean, as well as some residences in town. They felt like sunshine and growing things.

I was traversing Golden Gate Park, surrounded by black and green blips, when I felt my body being moved. Clive was still with me, so I ignored it. When I felt his cool fingers brushing ointment over my throat, I knew it must be close to dawn. Still, though, I searched.

Concerned I was overstepping boundaries, I told myself to forget the immortals' dens I'd found on my search. They deserved their privacy.

Exhausted, close to giving up, I felt a pull in the North Bay. Crossing over the water, I bypassed what I believed to be the fae and followed a subtle draw up the coast. I passed over the same spot multiple times. There was nothing there, and yet I kept coming back to it. Why?

And then I knew. At the exact moment I felt the whole nocturne blink out, I felt a similar winking out in that spot in the North Bay. I couldn't feel her, couldn't sense her, but I knew when her consciousness shut down at the rising of the sun, when that almost imperceptible white noise stopped.

I couldn't pinpoint anything, sitting here in Clive's nocturne. We needed to go for a drive up the coast. Something was hidden up there, something, I was willing to bet, that was undead, with big sharp teethies.

TWENTY-THREE

The Clive Effecttm

I awoke late in the afternoon, Clive still seated on the couch at my feet. He was out, but he'd stayed with me, a hand wrapped around my calf. Tentatively, I reached up and touched the skin of my throat. It was incredibly sensitive but felt like skin.

The head hammock worked. I didn't appear to have moved while sleeping. When I tried to sit up, I was stiff and sore, but alive and with skin, so win-win. Extricating my leg from Clive's grip proved more difficult than usual, but then I was the one who told him not to let go. I'd meant that I'd wanted a mental tether to my body, but he seemed to have taken me literally.

Giving him a kiss, I stood, moving more gingerly than usual. I picked up the tin Dr. Underfoot had left and made my way to the bathroom.

Terrified at what I'd find, I turned on the light and looked in the mirror. And then pulled open my collar and looked again. The skin of my neck was smooth and scarless. Even the new scar Liam had given me was gone. Getting close to the mirror, I lifted my jaw. Stretching the new skin stung, but I wanted to see what I was dealing with.

My body was covered in scars left from the attack seven years ago. Because of that, I perpetually wore long-sleeved, crew neck tops to cover them. Only a few scars snaked outside the lines of my clothing, a few light traceries peeking out. I'd thought for sure I was going to need to adjust my self-image to include red, rippled skin to my jaw, an illustration of pain continuing its journey to overtake me. Instead, the scarring had been beaten back.

Taking off my pajama top, I studied myself in the mirror. It was odd, almost like I'd been wearing a collar seven years ago. All the scarring stopped at an invisible line. There was a new, thin ridge along the underside of my jaw, old skin meeting new. I could feel the ridge, but when I wasn't tipping my head up, I couldn't see it.

It wasn't that I missed my scars. It was that they were *my* scars and now they were gone. I'd spent so long obsessing over them, memorizing them, trying to hide them, and now a few inches had been erased, leaving me off-kilter.

Staring in the mirror, I told myself, *This is what I look like now.* I could have died, but I didn't. I saved myself, and then a dwarf, a wicche, a vampire, and I worked together to heal me. So, *this* was what I looked like now.

Okay, enough. Pushing out a deep breath, I turned my back on the mirror and finished undressing. A hot shower would help loosen stiff muscles. By the time I'd finished washing and was letting the steaming water pound against the muscles in my back, Clive walked in.

"What are you doing up so early?" Sometimes—okay, often—the man took my breath away. This was one of those times.

Dropping his pajama bottoms, he stepped into the shower with me. "Winter." Taking me in his arms, he kissed me thoroughly before leaning back and checking out my neck. Running a finger lightly down the side, he asked, "Does this hurt?"

I had to fight off a shiver. "Not hurt. It's just really sensitive."

A mischievous light leaped into his eyes. "Is that so?" His hands roamed, enticing and exciting, while his lips dropped soft kisses along the column of my throat. When his fangs barely glanced over my skin, the shiver became a jolt—and he was only getting started.

By the time I staggered out of the shower some time later, my muscles were definitely warm and loose. "Oh! What with naked shower games, I forgot to tell you. I may have found Leticia."

Clive was suddenly standing directly in front of me. "Explain, please."

Stepping back, I secured the towel around me and headed for the closet. "You know that freaks me out when you move so fast."

"You didn't say that a minute ago." He came up behind me and pushed my wet hair aside, dropping kisses along my shoulder.

Clenching low at the mere thought of what he could do, I tried to shake off The Clive Effect™ by gathering random clothes.

"If I'm not mistaken, we promised to meet back here if we survived the attack by the NOLA vampires." When he tugged at my towel and palmed my breasts, the clothes fell from my hands, forgotten.

"I'm pretty sure that was the closet in my room, not yours." Head dropping back to his shoulder, I trembled at his touch. When his fingers found me hot and wet and desperate for him again, I reached back and took him in hand, squeezing.

He walked me over to a small bench, his fingers still exploring, and then pushed my shoulders forward. "Put your arms out and brace yourself."

Bent at the waist, I clutched the cushioned bench, quivering in anticipation. One hand between my legs while the other lay flat against my stomach, he lifted me to my toes and slid in with excruciating slowness. When he slid out even more slowly, my knuckles whitened against the black leather.

"Clive!" If I could, I would have kicked him.

"Yes?" His voice vaguely disinterested as he slid in slower than a glacier. "Problem?"

"Hurry the fuck up!" I was going to kill him. Screw him blind and then kill him.

"Quite literally, yes?"

When I started to laugh, he slammed home hard and fast, turning it into a groan.

Slowly pulling out, he said, "So, you don't always hate it when I move fast."

"I know I've got a stake around here somewhere," I said, starting to stand up.

He pushed my shoulders back down and then showed me exactly how mind blowing fast and hard could be. When he leaned over me and pierced my shoulder with his fangs, we clung to each other, quaking.

Afterward, I reached for my underwear drawer, absently admiring the beautiful jewelry box on the shelf above when it hit me. Hand flying to my throat, I began to panic. *Shitshitshit.* Stheno. She'd pulled something from my neck the night before. I dove for the hamper and pulled out my dirty clothes.

"What is it?" Clive watched me, tucking his dress shirt into his trousers.

Fuckfuckfuck. "My necklaces." I stuffed my hand into the pocket of my jeans and came up with the wicche glass, but the choker Coco had made me to protect my mind from Abigail was gone.

Clive turned over the hamper, looking for the choker, but it was gone. He stared at me in horror. "Given the boundaries of the new skin, his hand would have been right over the necklace."

I pulled the wicche glass over my head. "That was probably why she pushed him to burn my neck, to get rid of the protection."

Clive patted his pockets and then looked around the closet. "I have to call Coco, get you a replacement."

"We will. I feel fine. No visions are trapping me. She could have screwed with me last night, when I was weak, but she didn't. Either she doesn't know or she's not as strong."

"More likely, you've become stronger." He gave me a quick kiss. Grabbing his phone off his nightstand, he dialed.

"I like that better."

"No answer," he said. "I'll try again in a bit. I don't want to leave a message about this."

I nodded. "The necklace will take a while to make and spell

anyway. Let's deal with the Leticia crap first and then we'll circle back."

Dressed and ready, we finally left the bedroom. We needed to tell Russell and Godfrey what I'd learned snooping around last night.

I didn't know I'd been doing it, but when Clive turned to me, eyebrows raised, I realized I'd been swinging our joined hands, like we were a couple of teenagers on a date. He grinned and it felt like sunlight was warming me from the inside.

Russell and Godfrey waited at the base of the stairs, Russell staring straight ahead at the wall opposite, Godfrey watching us and smirking.

"We expected you down earlier, Sire, but I suppose you needed to check on Miss Quinn's health and well-being," Godfrey said.

Russell's hand shot out, doubling Godfrey at the waist.

"Thank you. You've saved me the trouble," Clive said, walking us past them.

And it hit me again that everyone in the nocturne knew every time Clive and I had sex. I knew my face was flaming as we walked into the study. Clive noticed and squeezed my hand. When Godfrey walked in a moment later, Clive shot out a hand that had Godfrey doubling up again.

Straightening, he choked out, "Apologies."

We need a cold room.

Do we?

Yes! It's mortifying that every vamp in the joint knows when we're having sex.

Think of it as evening the playing field, darling. You can read their minds. All they can do is hear your heartbeat.

I thought about that a moment. He was right. Hearing my heartbeat wasn't anywhere near as invasive.

I still want a cold room.

As you wish.

"It's very good to see that your neck has healed, Miss Quinn."

Russell inclined his head to me and then sat in his usual spot in front of Clive's desk.

I'd taken up roost on my favorite bench. Well, maybe not my favorite, I thought, remembering the one upstairs.

"Gentlemen, leave us."

Both popped up and headed for the door.

"Cut it out and get back here." I gave Clive my squinty-eyed disapproving face. Once the men had settled back in their chairs, all eyes were on me. "I've been kicking around an idea. I wasn't sure if it'd work, though."

Unfolding the throw at the end of the bench, I wrapped it around myself. It was chilly down here. "Since I had to remain immobile for a few hours, I decided to give the thought a try."

"What was your thought?" Russell asked.

"Right. Sorry. Leticia has to be nearby. If she's intent on causing Clive trouble, she's not going to be doing it from Albuquerque. So, I blocked out everything except the signatures of supernaturals. In my mind, I walked the streets of San Francisco, searching for supernatural signatures."

Russell leaned forward. "You can find others of us, not just vampires and ghosts?"

"I wasn't sure. But when Stheno's sister high-beamed Dave, I thought she'd killed him. I found her in my mind and choked her."

Clive jumped up from his seat, followed a split-second later by Russell and Godfrey. "You never told me this. We have a gorgon after you?"

Taken aback by three angry vampires, I pulled the blanket closer around my shoulders. "I don't think so. Stheno never mentioned Euryale was after me or anything. Those women regularly beat the crap out of each other. I don't think a little choking is going to cause a fuss. Besides, Medusa started it! She groped Dave, who then burned her hand. Euryale jumped in to defend her burned sister by high-beaming Dave, which was complete overkill. When I saw her eyes go bright, I closed mine, thinking she'd made Dave a statue.

"I kind of went a little crazy. I found three black voids with a purplish overlay. Assuming they were the sisters, I wrapped my magic like a boa constrictor around Euryale and squeezed. I heard choking and gasping, but my eyes were closed. Turned out Dave was fine and he carried me out."

Clive had begun pacing between his desk and the window. Godfrey, on the other hand, flew out of the room, almost faster than I could track.

"What? I'm sure it's fine. Those women spend all day bitching at each other and drinking. She's probably forgotten all about it." I started shivering. Why the hell was it so cold in here?

Clive was suddenly crouched in front of me. Voice barely a whisper, he said, "If you can hurt an immortal, you can kill one. If you can kill one, members of our community who never gave you a second thought will now view you as an adversary. We don't need more targets on you."

Russell stood with his back to us, but close, acting as a body-guard. "Miss Quinn, imagine how the New Orleans battle would have gone if Stheno and Meg were fighting against us, rather than with us?"

"But Stheno knows. She was right there."

Clive rose and crossed to his desk, tapping up the volume of the music he always had playing in the background.

"Our only hope is they believe it was Dave who did it," Clive said. "No one really knows what he's capable of. Even I'm not sure how old or powerful he is. He says he's a half-demon cook, but I don't believe it."

Clive crouched again, putting his hand on my knee. "He came to me when you opened, asking to be your cook. Owen was there to keep an eye on things, and I sent my people in regularly to check on you. It all seemed to be as he'd said. He wanted to cook. Eventually, I was happy you had an extra layer of protection."

"If they believe it was Dave, it'll help keep her abilities hidden," Russell whispered.

"Why did Godfrey race out?" Russell and I were staring at the open door to the study.

"We needed him to make sure no one heard what you said," Clive responded.

"Godfrey is very good at insinuating himself into situations without causing people to question him or become defensive. If either Clive or I were to search the nocturne, looking for eavesdroppers, the whole house would know and feign innocence."

"Why didn't you say so?" I closed my eyes and scanned the nocturne. No one was on this floor but us. Guards patrolled outside, none by this window, though. The rest were either out or downstairs. I tapped each of the guards, to see if any of them had been by Clive's window and overheard anything. Nothing. Each was thinking of his own issues: thirst, perceived insults, sex, disgust with me...

"I think we're okay." I did a quick spot check on the vamps down below and didn't hear anything alarming. "At ease, gentlemen." I pulled the throw up to cover the lower half of my face, trying to warm up.

"Why are you so cold?" Clive grabbed my chin, staring into my eyes. "Is someone in there with you?"

TWENTY-FOUR

Future Clive's Going to Have His Hands Full

My heart lodged itself firmly in my throat. My aunt was trying to worm her way in.

Clive was up and pacing again, his phone at his ear, finally getting through. "I'm sorry to disturb your evening, Coco, but we're in rather desperate need of your help again." He paused. "Yes, thank you. I doubt you've heard yet, but there was an altercation at The Slaughtered Lamb last night. Sam's neck was severely burned—yes, she's fine now. We've just realized, though, that the choker you made her was melted in the struggle. We need a replacement, as quickly as you can make it. I can double your fee."

He listened intently and then said, "I see. Are there alternatives?" He stared out the window and my heart sunk. When he stood straighter, I began to hope. "I would consider it a personal favor, one you may count on me to repay as you see fit."

Russell's head turned at that. There was something about the phrasing that worried me.

"I'll await your call." When he turned, pocketing the phone, Russell and I were staring at him. He gestured to the doorway a moment before Godfrey walked in, closing the door behind him.

"We're clear," Godfrey said, dropping back into his chair. He looked between the three of us a moment and sighed. "Now what's happened?"

"Miss Quinn's necklace was destroyed. She has no protection against her aunt at present," Russell said.

Godfrey stared at me for a long beat. I smiled uncomfortably in return. "I don't understand. If her aunt has access to her mind, why isn't she trapping her in a vision again or telling her to jump in front of a car?"

Now all three men stared at me. "Stop with the staring! I'm not going to explode."

Clive crossed the room and sat next to me, one arm burrowing under my blanket so he could hold my hand. "A lot has happened in the last few months. Sam is no longer defenseless. When Abigail first attacked, Sam didn't even know her aunt existed or that she herself was a wicche."

He squeezed my hand. "She's worked hard to not only embrace her wolf side, but her necromantic one, as well. Sam was blindsided. Now she won't be."

"I'm sitting right here." Stupid men talking about me, rather than to me.

"You were in a different place, just trying to survive, occasionally peeking out of your hobbit hole before ducking back in."

"You say that like it's a bad thing," I grumbled.

"No, indeed. It was a necessary, healing thing. You're different now. You run into danger instead of away from it, much to my eternal pride and horror."

"You took on a nocturne of vampires in New Orleans," Russell volunteered.

"You fought off killer ghosts and crawled through a collapsed tunnel in order to rescue me," Godfrey added.

"I killed my rapist," I said, feeling more confident than I had when I'd realized the necklace was gone. "And I called a legion of ghosts to me with only a thought."

Clive turned to study me while Russell and Godfrey glanced uncomfortably around the room. "When was this?"

"In Colma. Being close to the dead makes me stronger. It's why Martha's bar is there. I was trying to train on my own, sitting in her courtyard. I asked them to come to me and when I opened my eyes, there were more dead than I could count. Martha came out, annoyed I was causing trouble when she was trying to grieve Galadriel's return to Faerie. She tried to shoo them away, but it only caused a ripple in the ghosts."

I met the gaze of all three men. "Not gonna lie, I was pretty sure I'd royally screwed up and would have a phalanx of ghosts surrounding me for the rest of my days." Grimacing, I added, "That would have put a real damper on closet dates."

"On clos—" Godfrey began before Russell's hand shot out, smacking him in the head. Godfrey shook it off with a grin and asked, "Is that what you two crazy kids call it?"

"How did you get rid of them?" Clive asked, ignoring the other two.

Shrugging, I said, "I asked them to go."

"That's all? You just asked and they left?" Russell resumed his seat, as we no longer required a guard.

I nodded, pulling Clive's hand further under my blanket and then wrapping both of mine around his. "Clive's right. I'm more aware now than I was then. I don't think she could sneak in again without my knowing."

"Knowing and actually fighting her off are two different things, though," Godfrey said. "What are we doing about getting a replacement for the necklace that was destroyed?"

"I spoke with Coco while you checked the house. She would start now, but she doesn't have the stones she needs. She can get them—already has them ordered, in fact—but they won't arrive for a few days."

"Oh." Okay, I could keep her out for a few days, assuming she wasn't already in and listening to this whole conversation. Clive was right. I was stronger now. I had new abilities, abilities I didn't want anyone to know about, least of all her. If she could control me, she'd have a unique weapon.

"But," Clive continued, "she knows of a protective stone she could get immediately. It's one of her grandmother's treasures."

Russell and Godfrey both made sounds I couldn't interpret.

"What?"

"Dragons don't part with their treasures. Ever. Even for family," Clive explained.

"And that was why he pledged to help her in any way she saw fit," Russell said.

Godfrey stilled. "He did what?"

"Sam must be protected." Clive's tone put an end to the discussion—with his own vamps, but not with me.

"Explain why those two are concerned."

"Aside from being overly cautious, you mean?" When he tried to stand, I pulled him back down to the bench with me.

"I'll accept that Russell can be cautious, appropriately so, not overly." Russell inclined his head at my words. "Godfrey, though? No. I don't accept that the one who's already been smacked three times this evening for mouthing off is overly cautious."

Settling back on the bench with me, he pushed out a breath. "It indebts me to the dragons. I offered a favor to Coco, but she could ask on behalf of another dragon—or all of them. If they need help —any sort of help, including battle—I've promised to aid them in their cause."

"Even if that cause is wiping out all vampires," Russell added.

Oh. "I was all ready to say, 'Hell yeah, we fight on the dragons' side,' but I can see how that could get sticky." We sat in silence a moment. "Call her back. Tell her never mind. I'll be fine."

Godfrey snorted. "Never going to happen, luv."

"I'll deal with what comes," Clive said, resolved.

"It's future Clive's problem."

He glanced over, brows furrowed.

"Nothing. So, since there's not much to be done on the Abigail front, should we get back to the Leticia problem?"

Crossing the ankles of his outstretched legs, Clive said, "By all means."

"Okay," I began. "If Leticia has finally agreed to bring Clive down, it makes sense that she's nearby. Coordinating attacks on multiple fronts is more difficult from farther away."

Russell nodded that they were following my logic.

"That being the case, I decided to try to find her."

"I thought you'd already tried," Godfrey said, his fingers drumming on Clive's desk.

"Right. I did." I kicked off my running shoes and sat cross-legged, tucking all of me under the blanket.

"If you're cold, does that mean Abigail's in there listening?" Godfrey asked.

"No. I think this is just her pushing at boundaries. I'm not sensing anyone up here with me," I said, tapping my forehead. "Anyway, back to Leticia. If she's here, she's found a way to hide her signature, or someone who can do it for her." I held up a finger and searched for any eavesdroppers. Nope. We were clear. "That being the case," I continued, "I used my enforced downtime last night to mentally walk the streets of San Francisco, looking for any and all supernaturals."

"If I might interrupt, Miss Quinn. I thought your necromantic abilities allowed you to sense and manipulate the dead. How are you sensing all supernaturals?" Russell's soft, deep voice rumbled in the quiet room.

"Not all. I can't see wicches. My guess is that it has to do with immortality. I didn't expect to be able to sense Stheno and her sisters. It was faint, barely there, and maybe my heightened emotion in the moment helped, but whatever the reason, I saw them and could use my magic on them."

"I see," he said, though he looked troubled by the information.

"So, I took a walk to see who I could find. Vamps and ghosts are easy to find. Also, just to set your minds at ease, we have no zombies."

Clive made a sound in the back of his throat that I recognized as almost a laugh. "At least we've staved off the zombie apoca-lypse a bit longer."

"Right? Focus on the positive, people. Anyway, again, it was really faint but I also found immortals like Meg, Horus—by the way, does anyone know why he's here?" When they all shook their heads, I continued. "I found the fae, on land and at sea. Immortality seems to be the common denominator.

"Eventually, I decided to cross the bay and begin looking north."

"She was at it for hours," Clive said.

"There's a pack in the North Bay, but I couldn't see them."

"Werewolves are immortal," Clive stated, a little more forcefully than was necessary.

Shrugging, I said, "Owen once told me that they couldn't see werewolf auras. They—oh, I guess we, although I've never seen an aura—wicches believe it's the duality of man and wolf that obscures the aura."

"Perhaps what you're seeing in your mind is a kind of aura," Russell volunteered.

Huh. I hadn't thought of it that way. Interesting. "Anyway, I didn't sense anything other than the fae." I let the blanket fall to my waist, no longer freezing. Maybe Abigail had given up.

"I always know when the sun rises because you all wink out at the same time."

Clive turned to study me. "We do what?"

"I'm not sure how to explain this. Since I've been living here, there's a constant background hum in my head. You guys are like fanged white noise machines. *Except* when the sun is up. Your consciousness winks out and it's completely silent."

All three men seemed lost in thought. I supposed when you were hundreds of years old, learning something new about yourself was a good enough cause for a pause.

"So," I eventually continued, "I was searching the coast up near Bodega Bay when I felt the house wink out. What was interesting, though, is that I felt the same thing up there. I couldn't sense a vamp, couldn't sense anything, but when the sun rose, I felt an almost imperceptible drop in background noise. I could totally be wrong, but I don't think so."

Godfrey stood, rubbing his hands together. "Road trip."

"No," Clive said, standing and pulling me up with him. "I won't leave the nocturne unprotected if Leticia is nearby. Sam and I will drive north. You two will protect our people."

Russell inclined his head a moment before Godfrey repeated the movement.

"If we find anything, we'll call." Clive moved to his desk while I sat back down to put on my shoes.

I ran upstairs, got coats, and met Clive by the door to the garage, his topcoat in my hand.

"Thank you," he said, slipping it on when the phone in his pocket buzzed. He pulled it out, glanced at the display, and answered. "Coco, do you have good news?"

He listened for a tense minute while I wondered if protection from my aunt was coming.

"Yes, of course. May we visit now?" He paused a moment and then said, "We're on our way." Pocketing the phone, he took my hand and led me into the garage. "We're visiting the matriarch of the Dragon clan. She'll decide then if she's loaning us the relic."

TWENTY-FIVE

In Which Sam Has Been Measured and Found Wanting

"No pressure, though, right?" Great. Now I had to hope that the Queen of the Dragons didn't go nuclear on my ass.

"Quite a bit of pressure, actually. Do try to be extraordinary, won't you?" Clive led us to a metallic pale blue roadster with a soft top.

"Wow," was all I could think to say. It looked like a Bond car. "What is it?"

Clive opened my door. "BMW 507. Since you're no longer chilled and we'll be taking the coast route, I thought we could drive with the top down."

I sat, glad I'd put on the long leather trench I'd bought for New Orleans but had never worn. I'd even grabbed a scarf and gloves in case my aunt tried to break in again. Why had she gone for cold like she had a couple of months ago? Hot and itchy would have been worse. Perhaps she had issues with the cold. I'd need to think about that and how I could use it against her.

Clive slid into the two-seater and started the engine. It roared to life and I was thrown back in my seat as he raced out of the garage and around the house, a grin pulling at his lips. The full garage clearly pointed to a man who appreciated cars, but watching him drive made me realize it was more of a profound love. Leaning over, I kissed his cheek as he sailed through the main gates, waiting open for us. The guards at the gate bowed as Clive shot out onto the street.

"You're cute."

His eyes cut to me before he downshifted and executed a perfect turn. "Cute? I don't believe I care for that."

"Too bad. I calls 'em like I sees 'em."

He hit a button and the soft top roof slid back, opening us up to the night. I pulled my gloves out of my pocket and pulled the scarf up so it covered my head before wrapping the soft weave around my neck.

"Too cold?" Clive asked, his hand hovering by the button to close the roof.

"Perfect." It was a clear night, stars bright above us, and I was feeling too good to be worried about a dragon's fire-breathing judgment at the moment.

Far too soon, though, Clive turned down Sea Cliff Drive, an enclave of the ridiculously wealthy. The mansions we passed had to be worth ten, more like twenty million, each. It being San Francisco, though, meant that they were crowded close together.

Clive parked in front of the grandest on the street. It soared four stories high, but no doubt had a few more below ground, as these houses were built on a cliff overlooking the ocean.

A dusty Jeep was already parked on the street in front of the mansion. "Good," Clive said. "Coco's here." He closed the top as we both got out. "Ready?"

Nodding, I took his hand. "As I'll ever be. If she says no, we'll figure it out."

"We will," he agreed. When we passed through the gate, more of the house, hidden by a wall and large trees, opened up. The façade was austere and dour, but I had a feeling, like good dragons, they hid their treasures on the inside.

The doors opened before we reached the steps leading to the grand entrance. A man dressed in black stood in the open doorway.

"Thank you, Fyffe. I can handle this." Coco came out from a side room, wearing her usual flannel shirt, jeans, and work boots.

The butler glided out of sight.

"Grandmother knows you're here. She'll be down shortly. Please come in."

The entry was elegant, with lacquered black flooring and smoke gray walls. Enormous blown glass flowers hung from the ceiling, casting sparkling light in the dark foyer.

"We can wait in the living room." Coco beckoned us into an adjacent room with floor-to-ceiling windows overlooking the ocean, the Golden Gate Bridge lit up in the distance.

I'd started to follow her in when I saw movement to the side. Pausing, I looked up the swirl of stairs leading to the second floor as a woman began to descend them. Clive and Coco had already moved into the living room, but I waited at the base of the steps for the lady of the manor.

Like Coco and George, she had flawless, deep brown skin and knowing green eyes. Her hair was swept back in a chignon. She wore flowing silvery-gray slacks and a white silk blouse. Large, faceted rubies with pearl drops decorated her ears. She was stunning and I was horribly underdressed for this meeting.

Her gaze traveled over me, assessing, from my braided hair down to my running shoes, and I was consumed by the desire to point at Coco and shout, "But she's wearing flannel and scuffed boots." Thankfully, I held it in.

"So you're the one causing all the trouble." If I hadn't already known this woman was formidable, her voice would have settled it. This was a woman who suffered no fools, and I was currently feeling quite foolish.

"Yes, ma'am." I stopped myself from curtsying, but just.

"Grandmother, you're here." Coco rushed in, with Clive right behind her. "Let me introduce you to our guests."

"I'm well aware of who our Master of the City is, Coco. This one," she said, looking down her nose at me, "you may introduce."

"Of course. Grandmother, this is Sam Quinn. Sam, this is my

grandmother Benvair Drake." Coco's nervousness was not helping to calm my fears.

"It's an honor to meet you, ma'am."

"Hmm." From the look of disdain on her face, we wouldn't be progressing past introductions.

Clive circled around behind Coco to stand beside me and wrap an arm around my waist.

"I see," she said, looking away from the two of us. "Let's sit down and you can explain why I'm being asked to loan you a family heirloom. Coco, have Fyffe bring in the tea."

"Yes, Grandmother." Coco disappeared down the hall.

Benvair led us into the cavernous living room with high ceilings, and the same black lacquered floors and smoky walls as the entry. Flames blazed in a black marble fireplace. More crystal-bright blown glass flowers hung from the ceiling, like treasure hoarded in a dark cave.

Benvair sat in a high-backed chair, upholstered in a charcoal gray and silver damask. A small sofa in dark gray sat opposite her, with an exquisite black coffee table between us. Clive and I sat on the sofa. Coco returned a moment later and took a bench in front of the window.

"It'll just be a moment," Coco said.

Her grandmother inclined her head. "It's been quite some time since you've visited, Clive. And now, after so many years, you've come to ask a favor."

"I have," he said. "I hope my absence wasn't interpreted as a lack of interest in your well-being. I try to give the members of our community the freedom to live their lives as they see fit, assuming nothing is done to call our existence into question."

Ignoring Clive's response, she turned to the entry as Fyffe rolled in a tea service.

Handing Benvair a delicate cup and saucer patterned in gold filigree, he turned to Coco. "Miss, may I serve you?"

"No, thank you, Fyffe."

This seemed like a breach of etiquette to me. Shouldn't Clive have been asked next? Maybe it was because they knew he didn't drink tea, but I thought it had more to do with dragons being held above all others.

Fyffe nodded and then turned his attention to me. "Miss?"

"Miss Quinn and I will both have a cup. It smells wonderful," Clive said.

Ha! I saw it. The slightest of hesitations as she brought the cup to her lips. Clive just threw her off her stride. As a rule, vampires did not eat, nor did they drink anything but blood. It was a mark of one's age and power to consume food and drink without becoming sick.

Fyffe passed each of us the same sublime cups and saucers containing a light gold tea with a tantalizing fragrance.

Clive breathed in the scent and murmured, "Silver tips," before taking a sip.

"Yes," Caught off guard again, Benvair set the cup and saucer on the table. Shrewdly, she studied Clive and then me.

"If you are a connoisseur of fine teas," he said, "I could have a packet of Da-Hong Pao sent over. As a thank you for meeting with us this evening."

Slow blink. "You have Da-Hong Pao? I've found it quite difficult to acquire."

Clive took another sip, savoring it a moment before placing his cup on the table as well. "The right connections can be useful, can't they?"

I felt like a spectator at a tennis match, watching the advantage passing back and forth between the two. Content to drink the most amazing tea I've ever tasted in my life, I left them to it.

After a pause, heavy with calculation, she replied, "They can." Turning her attention to me, she asked, "I was under the impression my granddaughter had already given you a treasure to keep you safe."

"Coco made the most exquisite necklace I've ever seen, let alone owned." At her smile, I knew praising Coco first was the right way to start. "Unfortunately, I have an aunt who's a sorceress."

I heard a hiss, though neither dragon appeared to move her lips. "A particular skill of hers is mind manipulation. When Coco made me the necklace, it was to take the place of one my mother had spelled to protect me."

"I was under the impression that you were a werewolf. Was I misinformed?" The way she said *werewolf* told me all I needed to know about her views on the subject.

Feeling less inclined to be polite, I said, "No, ma'am. That's correct." I put down my cup and sat straighter. "I'm the last of the original line, a born wolf on my father's side and a wicche on my mother's."

Tipping her head to the side, she pinned me with a stare, sparks of red dancing in her dark gaze. "Is that so?"

"Yes. I'm sure George would vouch for me, were that needed."

Blowing out a breath, she looked out the window. "George is off with his…friend."

It was the pause between 'his' and 'friend' that did it. I stood, ignoring the dragons. "We should go now." Because fuck her and her disapproving pause.

Clive stood and took my hand. "I believe you're correct. Good evening, ladies."

Coco rose, as well, reaching for my arm. "You misunderstand. Grandmother has no patience for any of us if we're not producing baby dragons."

When I returned my gaze to the matriarch, her features were pinched but her chin was high. "We are dying out and I won't have it!"

I understood the fear, but… "Will you die more slowly by being an asshole?"

I heard a deep intake of breath from Coco and felt amusement from Clive.

Red flickered in her glare and I could swear wisps of smoke puffed out of her nostrils, but she didn't attack. Turning to the window, she seemed to watch the white caps race toward the shore in the moonlit ocean. "Sit." Still not looking at us, she added, "I love my grandson and I won't have that called into question. I'd just like great-grandchildren as well."

"Perhaps you'll get them." George's desire for children was his to share or not.

"I don't like uncertainties." She turned back to us. "Enough. Sit down."

Your decision.

Let's give her another chance. She continues to be an asshole, though, and we're out of here.

We resumed our seats and she picked up her tea again.

"Having an aunt who's demon controlled doesn't explain why Coco's creation has disappeared." She took a sip, pinning me with a predator's stare.

"She possessed a friend who has a talent for fire. He did his best to fight her, but he had my neck in his grip when flames ran down his arm. Later, we realized the choker was gone. We assume it was melted."

Benvair showed no reaction. "Why then aren't you covered in burns?"

"I was, but as Clive mentioned earlier, the right connections can be quite useful." I had no idea if I was doing this whole we're-powerful-but-we-need-your-help thing right. If I misstepped badly, I was counting on Clive to whisper something in my mind.

"Your connection being your...friend Clive?"

She was a master of the pause. This time, it was all about me being a trifling gold digger.

"Her fiancé Clive," he corrected, causing another slow blink. "And I am just one of the many powerful friends Sam enjoys."

Benvair stared into her tea a few moments. When she took a sip, her gaze shot back to me. "I don't approve of a man paying the debts a woman incurs. Whether or not I loan you this heirloom will depend on what *you* can do in repayment, not him." Her fingers flicked in Clive's direction. "I have no use for a werewolf. What talents can you claim as a wicche?"

Do I tell her the truth?

I believe you're safe to do so. Don't mention immortals, though.

"I'm a necromancer."

She put down her cup and walked out of the room. "Do keep up, child."

TWENTY-SIX

In Which Dragon Humor Is Lost on Sam

I glanced at Coco, who nodded and waved her hand for me to follow her grandmother. We all went out to the entry and found Benvair down the hall, standing by a framed mirror. Once she saw us, she put her hand on the mirror and a wall panel slid to the side, revealing an elevator. The doors opened and she walked inside, with us following.

"I'm taking you to the crypt. My mate died years ago. Unfortunately, he took the whereabouts of an important document to the grave with him. Find it and you may borrow my treasure."

"I'll try. Spirits often don't linger." At her glare, I added, "But if he's around, I can talk to him."

The door opened and we were deep underground in a dark tunnel carved into rock, lit by torches. Who knew the dragons had their own catacombs? She walked us to the end of the tunnel, to an enormous stone room. Displayed in the center were the curled-up bones of a dragon. Two torches by the entrance flickered over the bones, giving them the impression of movement.

"Ddraig, I've brought someone to speak with you." Benvair extended her hand, allowing me to enter.

The skull alone was bigger than me. I went to it, though, sitting on the floor and resting my forehead against his jawbone. Closing my eyes, I searched my mind for the dead. Dragons, like other immortals, manifested as a black void, but they had a faint red afterimage.

There were only two dead dragons down here. There was probably an ancestral catacomb in the Old World that held the rest.

Ddraig?

Fire blazed behind my eyelids and his massive jaws, filled with razor-sharp teeth, snapped at me, almost taking my head off.

I flipped up off the ground, somersaulting in the air, dropping down eight feet away from the head. Claws unsheathed and jaw distended with wolf teeth, I registered Clive standing in front of me, crouched for battle. The dragon bones lay inert. Laughter chuffed in my ears.

"What the hell was *that*?" When I noticed Benvair studying me a little too interestedly, I snicked in the claws and reshaped my face.

Clive stood straight, keeping me behind him. "What happened?"

"Stupid dragon tried to set me on fire and eat me!" I'd expected horror, maybe apology. Nope. Both women started to laugh uncontrollably. Coco was bent at the waist, wheezing, while Benvair wiped tears from her eyes.

"I've missed you, Ddraig." Benvair finally said.

How is my Queen Ast? His voice was a deep, gravelly rumble in my mind.

"He asked how his queenest is, but I probably misheard that last word. He has a rather strong burr."

Benvair's eyes glowed as Coco explained. "You heard correctly. Ast is Welsh for bitch."

Why do I have a wolf and a bloodsucker in my crypt?

"I'm a necromancer and your mate has a question for you." Tapping Clive's shoulder, I had him move aside. The old dragon wanted to mess with me. He no longer had the ability to hurt me.

Aye, what say you, Benvair?

"He wants to know what the question is." I didn't need to be close to hear him, so Clive and I moved to the side of the cave while Benvair moved forward. She rested her cheek on the skull and whispered something I couldn't hear, even in a room with stone walls.

Tell her it's in my desk, in a hidden compartment. The claws on the right leg. Tap first third first third. Tell her true or I'll burn you in your dreams.

"What is it with you two? Why do you always lead with the threats?"

"Saves time," Benvair and Ddraig said in unison.

"Whatever. He said it's in his desk, in a secret compartment." They were right bastards, both of them, but knowing how much they missed one another made my heart hurt.

"Coco, take them up to the office. If she finds it, loan her the treasure. If not, kick them out." Benvair hadn't moved.

We left them and returned to the elevator.

Once the door closed, Coco said, "I'm sorry. I know Grand-mother can be a lot."

"She mourns for her mate," Clive said, taking my hand. "Survival often depends on biting first and asking questions later."

The elevators doors opened almost as soon as they'd closed. We weren't up at ground level yet.

"Grandfather's office is down here." Coco led us down a carpeted hall, walls plastered the same smoky gray as the main floor. Light fixtures that appeared ancient but used electricity hung from the tall ceiling above.

At the end of the hall was a thick wooden door. Coco tried the knob and it opened soundlessly. She flicked on the light and we all stared at the massive desk.

"Did he sit at this in his dragon form?"

Coco laughed. "Grandfather was a very large man, even taller and broader than George." She held out her hand, inviting me to have at it.

"Okay, he said the claws on the right desk leg." I walked around to the chair, pushing it aside. The desk legs were carved to resemble a dragon's. "Was your grandfather right-handed or left?"

"Right," Coco said.

"Just making sure. He said right leg." Crouching down, I studied the claws at the base of the leg. Clive and Coco watched as I pushed on the claws in the order he'd said. When I finished, I heard a quiet click.

Clive crouched down next to me, running his hand along the leg, feeling for a catch. "Got it," he said. A section of the leg, carved with muscle and sinew, pulled forward, revealing a hollow in the center. Clive reached in and pulled out a rolled-up document. Without giving it a glance, he handed it to Coco.

Coco spread it out on the desk. It was a deed of some sort. She heaved a great breath. "Yes. This is what we need." Rolling it back up, she held it tight and led us from the room. "Grandmother's given me permission to loan you the pendant. Well," she added, hitting the call button on the elevator, "it wasn't a pendant before, but it is now."

We returned to the living room and Coco left the deed on the fireplace mantel and picked up a leather box. She opened it and showed us the contents. It was a carved black stone dragon's head with cabochon ruby eyes. The craftsmanship was astounding. The dragon was so realistic, I half expected it to start breathing fire.

"It's obsidian, which is best for keeping you safe from sorcery. It's also a stone that's been in our possession for centuries, so it is infused with the magic of generations of dragons. I added a bit to protect your mind specifically from your aunt and put it on a spelled chain, in case you need to shift."

When she tried to place it around my neck, I stepped back. "I can't. What if I lose it or break it? I'd never forgive myself and your grandmother would be well within her rights to burn me alive. And that would cause a war between the dragons and the vampires, or at least one very pissed-off vampire. No. I can't take that. I'll figure something else out."

"Put it on." Benvair appeared at the doorway and went

straight for the deed rolled up on the mantel. Like Coco, she read it and let out a breath. When I continued to hesitate, she pinned me in her dragon stare. "You've recently become useful to me. Don't die," she ordered as she strode back out of the room, deed in hand.

Clive's hand was at my back, urging me forward. "I've seen my future. Put the damn necklace on."

Knowing he was right, I leaned forward. Coco secured it around my neck, the flat, obsidian disk lying below the notch at the base of my throat. "It's warm."

"Dragons." Coco shrugged. "We like the heat."

Clive and I thanked her and left. The night air had lost its chill. Either Abigail had been continuing to mess with my temperature or I now had a personal heater. I was pretty sure it was the latter.

Once we were back in the closed car, Clive leaned over and kissed me. "Well done, you." Starting the engine, he put the top down again, put it in gear, and drove us out of the neighborhood before he spoke again. "You now have dragon allies, and not the grandchildren who hold little sway. The grand dame finds you useful." He squeezed my knee before turning onto Lincoln Boulevard.

Clive turned on low, bluesy music and we settled in to the drive. I had a bad moment when he crossed the Golden Gate, the lights flashing as we passed beneath. The last time I'd been on this bridge, I'd been paralyzed in the flatbed of a truck with three wolves hell bent on torturing and killing me.

Clive took my hand and kissed it, no doubt picking up on my thoughts. Placing my hand on his thigh, he shifted gears as we came off the bridge and shot off into the dark. We passed through a tunnel and then were driving through Sausalito, a gorgeous little town on the bay, filled with shops and restaurants on the water. On a Sunday afternoon, the outdoor tables and nearby walking paths were overflowing with tourists.

Clive's phone lit up, Liang's name on the screen. He tapped the phone, declining the call.

"We're not going to have another enemy gunning for us, right?"

He glanced over at me and shook his head. "I'm still too angry to speak with her. Perhaps in a few years I'll accept her call. Russell has spoken with her. She's back in New York. She understands that while I have chosen not to deliver her true death, I have chosen to cut her from my life. If she ever raises a hand against you again, nothing will stop me from taking her head."

"I'm sorry."

"None of this is your fault. Come now; let's forget about her."

Cutting to the west, Clive left the 101 and took Highway 1, the coast route. It was after midnight and the road was empty. White-caps broke on the ocean, rushing toward the shore to crash on rocks and wash up on beaches. Tall grasses on either side of the lonely road whipped back and forth in the wind. And above it all, a waxing moon silvered the landscape. A few more days until it was full, but even now the desire to set my wolf free was powerful.

He pulled to the side of the road and turned to me. "Would you like to drive?"

Giddy at the thought, I studied what was no doubt a ridiculously expensive sportscar. "Are you sure?"

"The only way you learn is through practice."

"Yes!" I jumped out of my side and met him in front of the car

He smiled down at my obvious delight. "Your eyes have lightened, more wolf gold than Sam green."

"Soon," I said as we climbed back in. "Although now I have two necklaces to keep track of. Good thing I'm a lone wolf. Can you imagine the snickers from the other pack members if I showed up for a moon run wearing jewelry?"

Clive laughed and my heart bubbled. Nothing made me feel better or more right in the world than the sound of Clive laughing. It was a little unicorn of joy. A millennium of battle and death and scheming and betrayal had worn Clive down. He was powerful, feared, and Master of the City. What he hadn't been, according to Russell, was happy. Russell feared Clive was losing what was left of his humanity. He believed that had changed when I arrived in San Francisco and Clive began taking an interest in my well-being.

The scarred, beaten, terrified little wolf I'd been had pulled at his heartstrings, as I'd reminded him of his brutalized little sister. Things had changed between Clive and me months ago, when the attacks began. No longer stern vampire and bookish bartender, we opened up and fell in love. Perhaps my aunt deserved a thank-you for that.

"No," he said, catching the tail end of my thoughts.

The engine was still running. Remembering everything Dave had taught me about driving a stick shift, I put it in gear, pressed down on the gas, let up on the clutch, and stalled it. Clive said nothing, looking out at the moonlit night, while I restarted the car and tried again. This time, I got it going. Alone on a deserted highway, I was flying down the road in no time. Freedom.

"Heartbeat about a quarter mile ahead."

I eased up on the gas and dropped the speed back to the posted limit. "Handy skill for avoiding speeding tickets."

"Isn't it?" He grinned.

Once we passed the black and white cruiser tucked into a side road, I opened it up again and we flew down the road. As we approached Point Reyes, I saw a sign for Drakes Bay.

Pointing, I asked, "Our Drakes or a different one?"

"Hmm? Oh, ours. They've owned this outcropping of land west of the highway for hundreds of years. Officially, it's a marine conservation area, a large, pristine estuary. Unofficially, it's where the family comes on moonless nights to shift and fly out over the ocean."

"I'd love to see that." Imagining it made me happy.

"Shall we discuss the wedding?"

When my hand flinched on the stick shift, he laid his over the top and squeezed as we raced up the dark road toward Bodega Bay.

TWENTY-SEVEN

A Few of Sam's Fears Are Made Known

N erves, fear, excitement, dread all fizzed through my veins at the word *wedding.* "Uh, sure."

Grinning, he glanced over. Whatever he saw had him laughing out loud. "As bad as all that?"

"No, of course not. It's just a lot. Lots of attention and focus and staring and pictures and… I could call up the ghost of a priest or something and have him marry us. No one even needs to know about it." A lifetime of invisibility had ill-prepared me for a life in the spotlight.

"You could. It's an option. I've waited a very, very long time to get married, though. I want the world to know that I love and cleave unto you."

"I like that part. Then all those ridiculously gorgeous exes of yours will know to go cleave themselves."

Chuckling, he brushed the back of his hand down my cheek. "I don't believe you're using that word correctly."

"Oh, it's correct. Especially when they rub up on you and end up with a cleaver in the face."

"A blood ceremony will be required," he said, watching me. "Weddings are lovely but mean nothing to my kind. The ceremony, an ancient ritual in which our blood is combined, is a kind of metaphor for becoming one. It's performed rarely, as trust is always an issue. One never knows when today's lover will become tomorrow's foe."

I glanced over, trying to read the beautiful man I loved with all my heart. My mate. "Does that mean you can't conceive of a future where I'm your enemy?"

"Never. If you and I are on opposite sides of a battle, I'll know I've misstepped badly and need to reassess the situation. Not that you're perfect—"

"Hey."

"But what you are is completely loyal, unfailingly kind, and generous to your own detriment. If you and I are on opposite sides, one of us is missing key pieces of information."

I liked that. If we were at odds, it was because we weren't seeing the full picture. "Back up. You said combined blood. I have no desire to become a vampire. I've already got mixed-up blood as it is. I'm not interested in adding a third strain. Plus, the vampire blood will probably be a dick and try to kill off the wicche and wolf blood."

"I'll have you know my blood is quite noble. It's not a dick," he said in his snobbiest, most upper-crusty English accent. The farther we got from the nocturne and his responsibilities, the lighter and funnier he became.

"Fine. You plan the wedding. I'll buy a dress."

"Done. As to your concerns about my dickish blood trying to conquer yours, I won't be giving you enough to change your body chemistry. Given how quickly both of us heal, it's unlikely more than a few drops will mingle. As I said, it's ceremonial and symbolic of our union."

"Okay." I thought about what I knew of weddings. "Do I buy you a ring?"

Clive lifted his left hand and studied it a moment. "I'd like that."

"Do I surprise you with it or have you pick it out?"

"I have no idea." Under the words was happiness at wearing my ring.

"Maybe we should go to a jewelry store?" I was so out of my depth.

"Yes. We'll need to find a quiet evening when we're not being attacked or visiting dragons to pop into a shop."

The highway had cut inland while we talked. We passed long stretches of green, interspersed with houses, low outbuildings, a restaurant, later a wine tasting room. I was beginning to worry I'd missed a turn on the dark, lonely road when it cut back toward the water. Once we hit the coast, businesses started popping up: a motel, a café, a winery, a couple of gift shops, a kite store. I pulled over onto the narrow shoulder of the road. "We should switch so I can look for her."

A moment later, I was back in the passenger seat. I missed the control but was happy at the moment to relinquish it. I had a vamp to find.

Accelerating onto the empty road, Clive asked, "Any idea where we should go now?"

I didn't feel anything. "Maybe slow down even more and drive from one end to the other, then snake up and down the streets. I'll see what I see." Closing my eyes, I put away thoughts of love and marriage, instead focusing on hate and death.

While Clive called Hollis, Alpha of the Bodega Bay pack, to let him know we were visiting his territory, I continued to search. Opening my eyes, I tilted my seat back and watched the dark, quiet town slowly slip by. After circling around the tiny town, Clive retraced our path on Highway 1, turning inland again.

"Are we giving up?"

He rubbed my thigh. "Not at all. Just giving you a new perspective. The pack territory is in this direction. It's isolated, which might make it a good place to hide."

I'd just settled into our drive when I shot up straight in my seat. "Holy crap! Go back!" I pointed at a white clapboard building. "That's the schoolhouse from *The Birds*. I forgot it was filmed here. Damn, that movie scared the heck out of me as a kid. To this day, birds freak me out."

Clive had stopped across the street from the schoolhouse. "I have no idea what you're referring to."

"Hitchcock? *The Birds*? Really? We'll need to watch a movie, too, on that quiet night we shop for rings."

"That sounds perfect. Are you picking up on anything besides birds?"

Was I? "Nope. Can you go back to town? This feels like the wrong direction." Closing my eyes, I breathed slowly in and out, trying to focus as Clive sped back to the bay. And then it occurred to me. "Pull over," I said, pointing to the narrow parking strip for the beach.

Clive did as I asked. Hopping up on the seat, I sat on the head-rest, wanting more of my body out the top of the car. No idea why. Closing my eyes again, I searched for the dead, calling the ghosts to me. We weren't in Colma, so an army didn't arrive. Instead, eight ghosts of varying strength arrived. A few looked too insub-stantial to have retained sentience. With them was my insubstan-tial new friend Charlotte.

"Are you saying I didn't need to call everyone? Wait. Are you always around?" That kind of creeped me out. I didn't need an invisible audience when I was doing private stuff.

No. Mostly I'm just in a dreamy hazy place and then you call and I'm here and aware. She shrugged transparent shoulders, at a loss to explain her type of life after death.

"Okay, everyone," I said to the assembled ghosties. I spoke aloud for Clive's benefit but kept my volume at a whisper. "We're looking for a vampire who's been hanging out around here. Has anyone seen anything out of the ordinary?"

A frisson of awareness sang in my blood. "Who knows what?"

It's the little one in the back. She's seen something that scared her, so she's stayed away. Let me see if I can get her to show me where it was. Charlotte and the faint spirit of an old woman in a faded house dress merged into a fog. Whatever the old woman showed them scared them enough to have seven ghosts streaking away into the night. I could have called them back, but why?

It's down at the water. At the base of a cliff, there's a narrow cave entrance only accessible at low tide. She's heard screaming in there. When she went to investigate, she saw something that horrified her.

I relayed the information to Clive. "Perhaps I should come back during the day at low tide, so I can investigate while she's sleeping." I'd need to check the tide tables.

"No. We do this together." Clive looked along the coast. "Does Charlotte know where the cave is?"

Yeah, I think so.

She pointed to a rocky outcropping that appeared disconnected from the cliff, a kind of craggy, stone island. Waves pounded against the rocks. In the best of conditions, this would be dangerous. Now, with the surety of a churning ocean slamming us into jagged rocks, it seemed more like a suicide mission.

Clive drove up the coast, away from the old-fashioned storefronts in downtown Bodega Bay, tucking onto a service road. We walked to the edge of the cliff and stared at the crashing surf below.

"Ideas?" I had none that didn't lead directly to death.

"One or two. Could you ask Charlotte to investigate? The ideas are pointless if what we're looking for isn't down there." Tilting his head, Clive crouched, his face a mask in concentration. "I hear something."

"Charlotte?" A filmy fog at my side took form. "Could you do some reconnaissance for us? Is there a cave down there? Does it hold something that can terrify the dead? You know, stuff like that?"

On it. And she was gone.

Dropping down next to Clive, I rested my hand on his knee for balance. The wind was so strong, it almost knocked me on my butt. "What do you hear?"

"Irregular heartbeat. Growling."

"How in the world can you hear that over the roar of the ocean and this wind?" The man was ridiculous.

Grinning, he kissed me soundly. "I thought you knew. I'm extraordinary."

Laughing, I stood, pulling him up with me and using him as a wind break. "I hadn't heard."

A moment later, I felt Charlotte's return, although I couldn't see her. "Charlotte?"

You have to go help him. Voice high and panicked, she whispered close to my ear.

"Who?"

A wolf. He's chained with silver. He can't heal. He's covered in bites. And there's...there's something wrong *with him.* The way she said *wrong* had my scalp prickling.

"Wrong how?"

Help him. Or kill him. Just make it stop. Please.

I relayed her report to Clive.

"Where's the cave?" he asked.

Charlotte pointed.

"On the far side of the rock, facing the open ocean." How the hell were we going to cross this crevasse between the cliff and the outcropping? It had to be a hundred-and-fifty-foot drop onto sharp, jagged, pointy things and a churning ocean. We couldn't jump across, as it was seventy or eighty feet away from the edge of the cliff.

I was still contemplating going back to the beach and swimming out when Clive picked me up and swung me around so I was on his back. He moved back to the car and then sprinted to the edge of the cliff. Holding tight, I closed my eyes as I felt us go airborne. After what seemed far too long, we jolted as Clive's feet hit rock.

Terrified, I didn't move.

"Are you shaking?"

Reluctantly, I slid down so my own feet were on the top of the uneven rock. Gusts of wind tried valiantly to blow me off the rock.

Leaning into the gale force winds, I attempted to talk myself out of my fear of heights. We hadn't even gotten to the hard part yet and I was paralyzed. This wouldn't do.

"Sorry, love. I didn't realize. Sit here. I'll go check it out and be back."

"No. I'm good. I'm fine." I wrapped my hand around his. "Lead the way."

We crossed the top of the uneven rock. When we got to the far edge, I had a bad moment of vertigo, going lightheaded as my stomach dropped. All I could see was my own shattered body on the rocks below. I was tipping forward, balance gone, when a change in the wind pushed me back, almost knocking me off the side of the rock.

Clive looked over the edge and I fought my need to snatch him back. "I don't see the cave. It could be underwater." He turned to look at me and then wrapped me in his arms. "I can take you back to the car and do this on my own."

"I can do it."

"I've never seen someone with a heartbeat quite this pale. You're allowed to be scared, Sam."

"I'm staying. What's the plan?" My brain wasn't currently working. Clive was on his own, plan-wise.

"You're sure?"

"I'm sure."

"Back up you go, then. Hold on tight and close your eyes. I've got you." He cupped my face and kissed me. "I will not let you fall."

He swung me unto his back. It was a good thing he didn't need to breathe, as I had a death grip on his neck. Eyes squeezed shut, I tucked my head down, my nose against the skin of his neck. His scent never failed to soothe. My head and stomach swooped in opposite directions as I felt him drop off the edge of the rock.

Clive's arms moved up and down as he descended the rock wall. If I hadn't been petrified, I'd have been impressed. Winds tore at me, trying to separate us, but my arms were locked around him. He'd be lucky if I let go an hour from now. When sea spray hit the back of my neck, I knew we were getting closer to the ocean.

"I still don't see a cave. When we get near the bottom, I'm going to find an edge for you to hang onto while I plunge into the water. Once I've located the entrance, I'll come back and get you."

Umm.

Sooner than I was ready, Clive was prying my arms from around his neck and guiding my hands to a sizable ridge on the rock. "Hang on. I won't be long." Pushing away from the cliff face, he dropped into the raging ocean below.

TWENTY-EIGHT

Was it a Mercy?

The scent of wet stone and ocean brine filled my nostrils. Frustrated with myself, I opened my eyes and stared at the water running down the dark gray rock inches from my face. Steeling myself, I dared a glance down and watched a massive wave crash onto the rocks twenty feet below.

Clive hadn't resurfaced. Shouldn't he have resurfaced? How long had it been? Fear was screwing with my head. A few seconds? Minutes? Had he found the cave? Been impaled on a rock below the foaming surface? Was he fighting Leticia now?

I tried to find him in my mind but couldn't. Fear was quite literally blinding me. I had to suck it up. How long had he been gone? Partners are supposed to stick together. One wasn't supposed to be cowering while the other did all the work. Seriously, it had to have been a half hour by now or maybe five minutes. Hard to tell.

Channeling my inner drill sergeant, I berated myself quite loudly and viciously in my head and then started to move my damn hands. Ledge to shallow ledge, I slowly made my way down the cliff face. When seawater started splashing against my legs, I knew I was close.

Taking a deep breath, I dropped down into the ocean and was immediately slammed against the rock. Keeping my arms against the side of the outcropping, I was able to brace against another head injury while pushing myself farther under water.

Opening my eyes, I felt the sting of salt water but also saw a dark open area to my right. Hoping there was air in the cave because my lungs were about to burst, I waited for a wave to move out and then dove down, fighting the pull of the ocean, and swam into the mouth of the cave.

Popping out of the water a moment later, I gasped for air and waited for my eyes to adjust. The cave appeared empty. *Shit.* Were there two caves? And then a growl rent the still air. I swam toward the edge of rock, smelling blood and werewolf.

Climbing out of the water, I went to a body chained to the rock. He was almost unrecognizable as a man, body ripped and torn, covered in vampire bite marks. When I knelt beside him, his eyes flew open.

"Kill me. Please."

His eyes held flashes of red, as Clive's sometimes did when he was angry.

The chains were too thick for me to break. George may have been able to do it with his outsized dragon strength, but not me. When I moved to check the bolts in the rock, he writhed and growled, the sound reverberating off the walls. I scrambled back to check on him and saw long, pointed fangs sliding over his lips.

Hissing, he pulled at his chains, desperate to attack me. Heart sinking, I knew what she had been doing. I moved to his head, placed my hands on his temples, and dove in. Pain. Fiery, agonizing pain. She'd been feeding on him, keeping him chained in silver so he couldn't heal, and then forcing the change on him. He didn't know how long he'd been held captive, but it was long enough to have lost track of the days.

She was turning him into her undead pet, giving him just enough of her blood to begin the change, but withholding what he needed to quench his tormenting thirst. His mind was a raging torrent of pain.

"Shh." I rested my forehead against his, trying to calm the vamp and the wolf. He snapped again and again, desperate to feed on me. I considered offering up my blood, but it would never be enough. She'd painstakingly created a killing machine, a weapon to use in her war on Clive. She was going to set this poor creature loose and let him carve out a killing path to the nocturne. Clive would be so distracted, dealing with an undead werewolf, he wouldn't see her move in.

I could see it all in his tangled mind, what she'd said and done to him. He couldn't be set free as he was. I'd been able to manipulate vampires in the past. Perhaps…

Uncoiling the thread of my magic, I imagined roping it around the part of his consciousness that spoke to mine, the undead vampire part. Gathering it close, looping my magic around and around, I tried to tear it out of him. His heart stuttered to a stop. I released my grip, and it began again unsteadily.

"Kill me." His hoarse words echoed in the dark cave.

I didn't let myself think about it, didn't second-guess it. Unleashing my claws, I raked them across his throat, taking his head and ushering his spirit to the other side.

Clive emerged from the water a few minutes later. "Thank the gods! I thought you'd dropped into the ocean and were washed away." Crouching in front of me, he tilted my head. "You're bleeding." His kissed it to staunch the flow.

"Oh, that. I hit it on the rocks out there."

He followed my gaze to my bloody hands. "What—" Then he looked to the left and saw that the werewolf we'd come to rescue was minus a head, thanks to me. "You put him out of his misery, Sam. It was a kindness, a mercy."

"Kind? No, I don't think that was kind of me. I gave him what he asked for because I couldn't fix what she'd done to him. I tried to extract the vampire, but it would have killed him, making him exactly what he didn't want to be. Look how decomposed he is now. She'd been slowly torturing him, turning him by inches." I found his gray eyes in the dark. "Why? I mean, I know that she wanted a pet monster, but why draw it out?" I felt hollow inside.

"Two reasons, I think. One was to drive him insane. There'd be no logic to his attacks and no way to trace him back to her. The second is only a guess. You said you couldn't find her in your head. It's possible she was too far away. It's also possible that feeding exclusively on wolf was muddying her signature."

"That happens?"

He took my hand and pulled me away from the dead wolf. "There have been experiments, rumors. Russell explained to you that Lafitte had a theory about drinking from wicches and psychics in order to absorb their talents. I don't know that it's possible, but still the rumors continue to circulate.

"Come on." He pulled me toward the water's edge. "Let's talk elsewhere. No more cliffs for you. We'll swim to shore instead. Swim fast and hard straight out and then turn toward the beach to avoid the rocks." Laying a hand on the side of my face, he wiped away my tears. "Ready?"

Nodding, I took in a deep breath and dove back into the ocean. Clive stayed right beside me as we ducked under the stone lip of the cave and swam away from the rocks. When I had to break the surface for a breath, he wrapped my arms around his neck and shot off through the water.

Once we hit the sand, I remembered the time. "How long until the sunrise?"

"We'll make it." He took my hand. "Let's go get the car and I'll tell you what you missed."

It wasn't until we hit the road that I noticed Clive was barefoot. "How about if I give you a piggyback ride this time?"

"I think not."

Stopping, I pulled on his arm. "So, this is all one-sided, huh? Only you can help me?"

The Wicche Glass Tavern

"Sam, I love you, but I don't need your help."

He tried to tug me forward, but I wasn't having it. "Roadsides are always littered with glass."

"I'll survive." When I remained unmoving, he sighed. "If we ran, we'd already be at the car."

"If you stopped being a vampy manbaby and take the ride, we'd already be at the car."

"That word." Glaring, he leaned in and nibbled on my lower lip. "How would this even work? I'm taller than you."

"Just climb on and quit being weird."

Once I had him on my back, his arms around my neck, I pulled his legs up on either side of me and sprinted up the hill. My running shoes squeaked wetly, but we were back at the car in under a minute and Clive's feet were uncut.

I drove us home, as it was dangerous to drive without shoes. At least that was my argument. Clive gave up his token protest rather easily. He was sweet on me and knew I wanted to drive again. The conversation this time, though, was less about making plans for the future and more about dealing with the present. Discussions of weddings and rings had been replaced by all things Leticia.

"When I swam into the cave, her scent was too strong not to have just been there. I knew she wasn't in the water, so I examined the back of the cave and found a narrow cut in the wall. I tried to follow and got stuck."

I grabbed his forearm. "I was hanging on a cliff while you were stuck in rock?"

"In my defense, she's a petite woman. Anyway, I eventually made it through."

"Wait. You were stuck and instead of pulling out, you pushed forward?" I was pretty sure I was hyperventilating as I took a curve in the road at too high a speed. Forcing myself to both calm and slow down, I said, "We're getting married. You need to start asking yourself, 'Would Sam be okay with this?' And the answer is hell no, she would not!"

He patted my knee and I punched him in the thigh. "I'm perfectly fine. Anyway, the passage led to a far smaller cave. I followed her out into the water, but I'd been stuck in the passage for too long. I lost her."

"Do either of us have a phone that wasn't just destroyed in the water?"

He pulled his from between the seats. "I took it out of my pocket before we went to explore underwater caves. I'd assumed you'd done the same."

"Well, aren't you so smart?" It was a brand-new phone. Damn. I was trying to stay on Norma's good side. "Can you dial Hollis for me?" Even with the top down, we'd be able to hear each other on speakerphone.

"What?" I flinched at his angry growl, remembering too late that the rest of the world slept at night.

"It's Sam Quinn. I don't know if you remem—"

"Yeah, I know who you are and why you're on that bloodsucker's phone." The disgust was palpable. He'd been growly but kind when we'd met a few months ago. Of course, that was before anything had happened between Clive and me.

Clive rubbed my thigh in comfort.

"Right. I'm calling to ask if you're missing any wolves." I'd heard a name in all the snarling chaos in his head. I was pretty sure it was his name, but it could have been someone he was thinking of.

"Why?"

Is it okay to tell him about Leticia?

As she's targeted one of his, I think we have to.

"There's a vampire who's causing horrible problems—"

"They're bloodsuckers. Evil comes with the territory."

"Listen, asshole, I'm reaching out to give you information. How about you stop bashing my betrothed." When I saw the corner of Clive's mouth kick up, the nerves in my stomach settled.

"Betrothed?" I felt his growl through the phone. "Just tell me what you need to tell me so I can go back to sleep."

"A vampire named Leticia, petite and blonde, took a wolf and kept him captive in a cave in Bodega B—"

"What!" I heard crashing in the background. "What the fuck are you talking about? Who does she have? And where?"

"Just let me tell it, okay? We came to Bodega Bay because we had reason to think she might be hiding up here."

"What reason?" he spat out.

"Stop interrupting, and none of your business. If you're going to be an asshole about vampires, I don't need to pass on any vamp secrets." Or my secrets. "We came up and started searching. We received information that she was hiding in a cave."

"A cave? What the fuck cave?"

"You're really not good at shutting up. A little north of town, there's an outcropping of rock maybe a hundred feet?" I turned to Clive and he nodded. "A hundred feet from the edge of the cliff. On the far side of the rock, there's a cave that's underwater except at low tide."

"I know where you mean."

"Good. We went to investigate and found a wolf chained in silver." I heard a hiss through the phone. "He was covered in bite marks, unable to heal because of the silver."

"Fucking bitch!"

"That's not even the worst of it. She was trying to turn him into a vampire, feeding him just enough to keep him mindlessly in pain."

I almost swerved off the road at the sound of his anguished howl. Distant howls answered his. "Who does she have?" His voice was unrecognizable. He was probably very close to shifting.

"Had. Clive chased her off. I stayed with—I think his name was Rob. She'd turned him into a mindless, undead killing machine with the strength of a wolf. I took his head so she couldn't bring him back."

A mournful howl wailed through the phone and then it went dead.

"I may have just added a pack of wolves hell bent on taking me out, but I had to tell him."

"He needed to know. If his misplaced anger is directed at you, we'll deal with it."

Nodding, I released the breath I'd been holding. He was right. We'd deal with it. That quiet evening of ring shopping and movie watching seemed farther away than ever.

TWENTY-NINE

M + G
___

We made it home about an hour before sunrise. The vamps were shocked, in a low-key vampy way, to see us both wet and Clive barefoot. My running shoes squeaked loudly on the marble floor of the entry. Clive and I went straight upstairs to shower and change.

I held onto Clive in the hot spray, seeing that poor man writhing and snapping, desperate to kill right up until I sliced through his neck. Stomach roiling, I burrowed into my betrothed. He held me, almost too tightly, just as I did him.

Eventually, he began unbraiding my hair, stiff with saltwater, and then shampooed it. We tended to one another in every way before we settled into bed. The briefing would need to wait until tomorrow.

"I love you," he said, wrapping his arms around me.

"I know." Grinning, I dropped off almost immediately.

___

I awoke midafternoon, wrapped around Clive, his scent helping me to sleep. Staring into the dark, I finally forced myself to consider what I'd been avoiding. Dave. Did I kill him? Did I banish him to some other realm? What had I done and how could we get him back? His girlfriend Maggie was definitely going to kill me this time.

Hunger finally dragged me out of bed. I dressed and went in search of food. While I was raiding the refrigerator, Norma walked in.

She made a quiet squeak. "Oh, I didn't hear you." She paused at the door. "I came to make more tea, but I can come back later." Like last time, her top and bottom didn't match. She wore a crisp white shirt with a wine-colored blazer and pearl jewelry. Her face was perfectly made up and her dark curls gleamed. On the bottom, she wore yoga pants and slipper boots. If there was a need for a video conference, she was ready. Otherwise, she was comfortable.

"Don't be silly. Are you hungry? We seem to have some kind of calzones today." Hopefully, they were meat-filled.

"No, thank you. I already had my lunch. You know, if you want to leave me a list of food you like, I can make sure we have it stocked." Norma filled the kettle and put it on the stove.

"Really? Not just ready-to-heat stuff, but anything?" The vamps were so put out by my existence, I considered myself lucky not to be poisoned. There was already enough tension in the house. I wasn't going to make a fuss about food. "That would be fantastic. Oh, my goodness, I'm unreasonably giddy about this. Anything?"

Norma took tea packets down from the cupboard. "Would you like a cup?"

"Yes, please."

"It's an orange pekoe." She held the second tea bag over the second mug.

"Sounds lovely."

Nodding, she dropped it in the mug. "Miss, what you need to understand is that you're the Master's fiancé. I've been given very specific instructions. Anything, and I do mean *any*thing you want, you get."

Damn. "So, if I wanted to add a carousel to the back patio?"

"I'd call the contractors."

I unpackaged the calzones and found a baking tray to cook them on. "Now that you've become my new best friend in the house, I hope there will be no judgment—at least out loud—about my eating both calzones." I slid the tray into the oven and took the steaming mug she offered me.

Laughing, she picked up her mug and wrapped her hands around it. Poor thing said she was always cold in the house. "No judgment, only anger and jealousy over skinny girls who

can eat anything they want."

"That being the case, the first on my list of demands is that you raise the temperature in this joint. Is there a way to at least make the first floor warmer?"

Nodding, Norma stirred her tea. "You're good people, Miss Quinn. I'll go see what I can do about that."

"Perfect." While my lunch cooked, I found a paper and pen and began my very long wish list. It was glorious. I added a phone to the bottom of the list, embarrassed to tell her I needed another one.

I'm going for a run. Clive didn't respond, but I was positive he heard me.

I'd been thinking while I was eating. Leticia and Abigail were attacking at the same time. It wouldn't make sense for them to be connected, but they were certainly taking advantage of the other one's distractions. Abigail needed to be dealt with once and for all. She'd already done too much damage. Had I destroyed Dave while trying to fend her off? My very full stomach sank. He had to be okay. I couldn't live with any other possibility.

I needed Martha's grimoire. She'd said there was something in there that would help me defeat Abigail. It was the Corey family grimoire. I wanted it, even if it meant going toe to toe with Galadriel and her sword. With any luck, she wouldn't be there and I could slip in and out without her knowing.

The run felt good. When I'd been living and working at the Slaughtered Lamb, my nightly runs after closing were consistent.

Since the world went topsy-turvy, I couldn't fit them in as regularly. I missed my bookstore and bar. I had to get rid of Abigail so I could have my life back without my friends being menaced.

The sun was setting as I ran past the out-of-business monument store's front window. Sliding through the ward on the side gate, I strode past the abandoned tools behind the store and into the courtyard of The Wicche Glass Tavern. Empty.

I went to Martha's grave first, snapping a sprig of wisteria off a branch hanging over the gigantic tree roots separating the mundane world from Faerie. Placing the flowers by the grave marker, I knelt, laying my hand on the moss, wishing I'd had more time with her. A cool breeze slid along the back of my neck.

It was quiet in the permanent twilight. Would Galadriel open the bar again? Maybe she'd returned to Faerie. The door to the bar was unlocked. It was dark: no overhead lights, no fire in the fireplace. I slid my hand up and down the wall, looking for a switch. Nothing.

The mirror on the wall gave off a faint silver glow. Not wanting to attract Faerie's notice, I averted my eyes. The place was still a mess, so no one had bothered to clean yet. I would have stayed to do it myself if I weren't afraid of running into Galadriel.

I headed straight for Martha's back room. The smell of blood hit me before I entered. Martha's blood still stained the floor. Stepping around it, I went to the wall of photos. Martha had said she'd left the grimoire behind Gad. She'd been fading, but I'd heard that much. It could have meant anything, but this was my first thought.

She used to sit in this snug little room, drink tea, and look at these photos, remembering a lifetime with her love. Most of the photos had been knocked off the wall and left smashed on the floor. A few remained, including a large one in the middle. It was a picture of a much younger Martha with her arm around Galadriel, standing in front of The Wicche Glass.

Feeling around the edges of the frame, I tried to find a catch. It was firmly affixed to the wall, not hanging on a small nail, like all the rest of the images. I tried using the spell Lydia had taught me for opening things. Nope. I dragged a sharp claw around the edges of the frame, trying to slice through the seal. Nothing.

Martha wanted me to have the grimoire she had hidden from everyone else. If it was secreted somewhere only I could access…

"Charlotte!"

Charlotte appeared beside me, glancing around. *Where are we?*

"Fae bar. I need to get a book that I believe is hidden behind this picture. Can you look, see if there's a compartment back there?"

She glided through the wall and was back a moment later. *Yeah. There's a wall safe behind the frame and it has an old book in it.*

Perfect. How did I get it, though? "Do you see anything in there that would help us open the safe?"

Charlotte disappeared for a minute and then came back. *There's a note on the book. Her handwriting is hard to read, but I think it says pull the right corner, then push the release at the bottom.*

Upper right? Lower right? I kept my left hand flush along the bottom of the frame while I fiddled with the right corners. A small button popped out. I pressed it and the frame swung open, revealing a keypad.

"Any other directions on that note?"

Charlotte disappeared again. I couldn't see her, but I heard her. *Yeah. It says push the hashtag button and then 13+7 and then the hashtag again.*

I followed her directions and held my breath. The keys went green and the safe unlocked.

"How did you do that?"

I spun to find Galadriel in the doorway. Her sword wasn't drawn, giving me hope.

"Martha came to me when she died—"

"Was murdered," she said flatly.

"Yes. She told me to get the family grimoire, saying it was hidden behind Gad." Shrugging, I motioned to the wall that had once held a lifetime of adventures. "This was the first place I thought of. Charlotte, the, uh, ghost who's with us now, she looked inside the safe and read the note Martha left me."

Galadriel pushed me out of the way and opened the door. Snatching the note, she scrutinized the message and then flipped it over, looking for more. Her shoulders dropped as she handed me the paper. Reaching in, she grabbed the cracked-leather grimoire and handed that over as well.

Once the oversized book was out of the small safe, an envelope remained. Galadriel dove for it, read the name on the front, clutched it to her chest, and walked out.

"Thanks, Charlotte. I'm good now. Since Galadriel doesn't seem bent on killing me, I'm going to clean up around here."

Okay.

I felt her fade away. I didn't normally feel that. It must be because I was so close to the dead. Martha had made her home here because this was where she was most powerful, which gave me an idea.

After cleaning up the blood and glass, extracting the photos from the wrecked frames and leaving them for Galadriel, righting what hadn't been broken, and hauling what had to the area behind the monument shop, I decided to put my theory to the test. I'd been trying to find Leticia in my head for some time but couldn't. Maybe here, where my powers would be at their strongest, I could.

I sat on a table in the courtyard, closed my eyes in the gentle twilight, and searched for the cold green blips that meant vampire. My head was filled with the hazy forms of ghosts, but I pushed them aside and searched for the mostly dead.

The glut at the nocturne pulsed. I found Clive, wrapped myself around him, and thought, *I love you.*

Thank goodness. Where are you? You said you were just going for a run.

I did. To The Wicche Glass. I need the grimoire to fight Abigail.

I'm on my way.

No need. I'm fine.

Not if Galadriel finds you.

She did. The safe I opened had a message for her from Martha. She took it and left.

Still…

Up to you. I can run home when I'm done, or I can see you sooner. Win-win for me.

On my way.

If my eyes are closed, I'm trying to do something. Just leave me be.

After checking all the blips in the nocturne, in case she was hiding right under our noses, I went farther afield, looking for anything. I found a few of Clive's vamps out in the city, but not Leticia.

If she tried for another werewolf, the nearest pack was my family's old one in the Santa Cruz Mountains. Nope. I didn't see any vamps in the mountains, but there was a nocturne down in the city of Santa Cruz. I checked each of those vamps, and none were Leticia. How was she hiding from me?

Frustrated, I pulled the grimoire into my lap and began to leaf through the pages. I wanted to stop and study every spell, but that would have to wait. Finally, handwritten on the last page were notes to me on necromancy. The first one froze my limbs.

Sam, the wicche glass I gave you will protect you from pain. But it comes at a cost. It will shield you, but it will also blunt your powers. I never needed a big punch all at once, so I was able to leave the magical imbalance in the wicche glass. I'm very sorry to say, for you it will be different. Before you try to take on Abigail, you'll need all the strength, all the magic, inside you. You need to right the imbalance. I think—understand, I don't know for certain—that you'll need to draw in that fireball of pain around your neck and let it balance the scales to make your magic as bright and sharp and true as it's meant to be. I am horrified to realize that in pulling the pain from the wicche glass, you'll be taking on decades of my pain, stored in the ball as well. If you survive, you'll be stronger, but…you can instead take this book, protect it, and run. I'm still searching for another way.

THIRTY

Why Does Pain Have to Hurt so Much?

But she *had* needed a punch of power. When Abigail attacked, she didn't have the magical object she needed to fight at her strongest. She'd been handicapped because she'd already given it to me.

I needed to find Leticia and I needed to fight Abigail. There was no choice. I wasn't going to run, not anymore. I'd done that for too long. I was hanging on to Clive and this life, no matter what. 'What,' unfortunately, was apparently a world of pain.

Nope. I wasn't giving myself time to get scared. It had to be done, and sooner rather than later. I'd suffered through the horrible headaches and blindness before I had the wicche glass, and I could do it again. I put the grimoire aside and stepped off the table. I had no idea what would happen, but lying down on the flagstones and moss seemed preferable to falling from four feet up. Why add to the trauma?

Okay, fuck it. Let's go. Slowing my breathing, I envisioned my magic like a thread, coiled in my chest. Wrapping the thread around the wicche glass, I began to pull the magical payment from the small glass orb. Fire spread slowly down my limbs. Teeth gritted, I forced myself not to scream.

Martha had said I could direct the payment. It didn't have to be blindness. Opening my eyes, I stared at the purpling sky above and directed the payment elsewhere. I didn't want to be trapped in the dark again, not like before… When I heard the high keening sound I was making, I knew this wouldn't work. I had to open wide the floodgates. I couldn't do this a little at a time. The pain would be too much and I'd stop, whether I meant to or not. Like a Band-Aid then, all at once.

And just like that, the scars covering my body were painted in fire, my head crushed in a vice. All thought gone, only horrific, unending pain. Back bowing off the ground, I screamed and screamed and screamed as my blood boiled and my skin crackled. A slow, ceaseless, hellish torture.

Sam!

And then I was huddled in a dark place, alone and cold. I needed to go away, to sleep.

"Sam! Where is it? Where are you hurt?"

Poor Clive. He sounded frantic. The black cocooning me muffled his voice, which was good. I didn't want him to hurt, but I couldn't go back there.

"What have you done to her?"

"I did nothing, vampire."

That was nice. Maybe Clive and Galadriel could become friends. He needed a friend. I was fading into the cool depths of nothingness.

"Look at this."

"Her heart is slowing. I don't care about the damn book. Sam, can you hear me?"

"*Read.*"

I was going to miss him. So much. My mate. My love. Oh, that was good. The screaming had finally stopped.

"I swear by all that's holy, if you die, I will bring you back!"

No. I didn't want to be one of those damn pissy vamps. I didn't even like black.

"I mean it, Sam! You come back right now. I have reason to know just how long an eternity is. I refuse to live it without you."

I wanted to touch him, to feel him, but that would mean letting in the pain, too. I didn't think I could do that. There should be only so much one person is forced to endure.

Go on, dear. It's time to go back. I'm sorry you had to live my pain, too. Martha's words came on a cool breeze, smelling of wisteria and moss. *Go on. Feel his hand on your face, his forehead against yours. Don't break both your hearts. Follow him back. He's waiting.*

It hurts.

I know, child. That's how you know you're alive. You still have work to do and a hand to hold. Don't give up now.

I waded back through the pain, every nerve ending alight with torment, but I felt Clive's hand on my face, a phantom ache.

"She's coming back."

"How do you know?"

"The screaming is getting louder."

"I don't hear—"

Eyes popping open, I gasped, and then curled up and shook. Clive was trying to take away my pain, but it was barely lapping at the shores.

Two cool hands rested on me at shoulder and hip. "Don't expect me to do this again. I hate Faerie."

The flames were snuffed out as pain drained from my body.

That's my Gad. Tell her I love her. Always have. Always will.

With a shudder, the last of it dissipated. I opened streaming eyes to see a pale, shaking Galadriel. She got unsteadily to her feet, headed for the bar door and the mirror beyond. Clive helped me sit up, his hands gentle as he pulled me into his arms.

"Galadriel?"

She paused at the door, not looking back.

"Thank you."

I heard a gust of breath and she stepped into the darkened Wicche Glass.

"Also, Martha says she loves you. Always has. Always will."

The only response was the sound of a sob before I felt her pass from this realm into the heart of Faerie.

Clive held me close and rocked. I put my nose against his throat and breathed, his scent settling me. After a while, I realized I was picking up on stray thoughts, not ones he was sharing with me, ones he was struggling with.

Leaning back, I stared him in the eye and said, "I mean it. I saw firsthand what the mixing of vampire and werewolf blood does. I don't want to be a vampire."

His fingertips traced the lines of my face. "I know," he finally said. "I don't think I'd be able to stop myself, though."

Standing, I held out a hand and helped him to his feet. "You're plenty strong enough. You have more self-control than twenty vamps. You know I don't want it, so you won't do it."

"I'm afraid you have more faith in me than I do in myself." Clive looked confused when I picked up the grimoire and climbed back up on the table.

"Galadriel cleared the pain. I want to try to find Leticia again."

"You're sure?"

"This is where my power's strongest." I closed my eyes and breathed slowly. When I felt Clive sit and rest his head on my knee, I smiled, running my fingers through his hair.

Wow. Okay. That worked. The ghosts were clearer, not a nebulous hazy fog, but individual smoky forms. The green blips felt like beacons now. I hadn't been able to sense her before, so I ignored all the glowing blips and instead searched for a faint vamp signature.

"Found her."

He squeezed my calf. "Of course you did."

"She's…" I laughed. "She's next door to Stheno and her sisters."

"And they haven't noticed a vampire in their neighborhood?"

"In their defense, they drink and fight a lot. Shh, I'm going to try to read her."

Wrapping myself around her vampy mind, I found a weak spot and wriggled in. When the pain hit, I gasped and then Clive soothed it. I was getting better at this, but it still felt like walking through a minefield.

After visiting memories of her feeding on that poor werewolf, I was braced for horror and instead found Clive. He was much younger, maybe an early teen. Leticia's heart was racing. She was sitting on a horse and terrified. Her mother had berated her for being afraid, sending her to the village on an errand, forcing her to ride her father's ill-tempered bay. The horse had tried to bite her on multiple occasions. She'd hated it.

She'd lost control, yelling as the horse had barreled down the path, headlong toward a craggy outcropping of rocks. She knew he was going to throw her, knew it in her bones. And then a handsome young man stepped out of the trees, dropped his scythe, and ran to intercept them.

He stepped directly in front of the charging horse, put out a hand, and shouted, "Ho!" The horse faltered at his command, slowing, dancing one way and then the other. A young Clive strode forward and took the reins, murmuring softly to the agitated horse.

Once the horse finally settled and blew out a breath, Clive leaned in and rested his cheek against the horse's. He nodded to an awed Leticia, staring wide-eyed at him.

"All right then, miss?"

"I hate this horse," she squeaked.

"Aye, and I venture he knows it." He patted the horse's neck. "He's a mite big for you. Do your parents know you've taken this beast?"

"I was sent to the village." Still terrified of the horse she was riding, Leticia only had eyes for Clive.

"Well, that's lucky then. I was headed there myself. I'll walk with you both."

Leticia glanced back at the edge of the woods where his abandoned scythe glinted in the sun and gratefully pretended she believed him.

The memory went dark and I moved forward, slipping into another.

Clive was older now, a young man. He was driving a plow pulled by oxen. His tunic hung from his waist, sweat glistening on straining muscles. Not that I wasn't enjoying the view, but why was I here? Glancing around, I found Leticia huddled behind a stand of trees at the edge of the field Clive was plowing.

She, too, was older, perhaps middle teens. Her face showed marks of a recent beating, a reddened cheek, blackened eyes.

A girl, younger than Clive, walked to him carrying some kind of pouch. She treaded carefully over the furrows in the soil. When he saw her, he called to the oxen and stopped, pulling up his tunic and wiping the sweat from his brow.

"Please let me help you. With Papa gone, it's too much for one." She held out the pouch to him and he turned it, drinking greedily before pouring some over his head.

Handing it back, he said, "Nay, Elswyth. If we have a good season, perhaps we can take on a hand."

"At least take a break from this sun. Dinner is ready."

Clive looked up, marking the sun in the sky. "At the end of this row, I'll eat and let them rest. I need to finish the field before dark if we've any hope of getting the crops on time."

"Aye." Elswyth looked sad as she turned to go.

"Hey, did you collect berries for me? I've been dreaming of them with honey."

Spinning, she smiled. "You'll just have to wait and see, won't you. The pottage is high fragrant. It'll fill your stomach right enough. As to the berries…" She turned back toward the small, squat cabin, a spring in her step.

Grinning, Clive called up the oxen and began the heavy work again. Leticia sighed, watching him.

And the memory went black. Trying to follow synaptic pulses, I jumped into another memory along the same neural pathway.

"Dead!" Leticia's mother Aldith screeched. "They're dead!"

Leticia cowered in the corner, happy the brutal men, who so casually beat her, were gone.

"It was that liar who accused your father and brothers of meddling with his whore of a sister. I know it was him. The farm's been abandoned. He's probably the one that done it. Blaming your poor father for his own wicked ways."

"He's…" Kind. She wanted to say kind, but quelled at the look in her mother's eyes.

"He's what?" Eyes narrowed, her mother waited.

"Gone. Almost a year now." Leticia's fingers worried the edges of her apron.

"And how would you know that?" Aldith looked at her daughter differently, as though just realizing she might actually know something.

"I used to see him in town from time to time. After his sister died and his mother took ill."

"How would you know anything about him? Their farm is miles away." Calculation had slowed her words.

"Gossip. Royse had her eye on him." Leticia shrugged, hoping her mother would go back to ignoring her.

"Whore," she spat before pacing the room. "I know t'were him. He'll wish he kept his lying mouth shut when I'm done with him."

THIRTY-ONE

A Thousand Year Vendetta Begins

L eticia's memory went black and then I was thrust into the next. Body alight in agonizing pain, lungs like stone, unable to breathe, the room awash in red.

Not me. I separated myself from the source of the pain, Leticia writhing on the floor of a bedchamber. Her mother, flickers of red in her cold, dead eyes, stood in the doorway, an old, red-faced man who seemed to be in shock locked in her steely grip. "Finally," she said before hurling the man across the room.

Leticia sprung, tearing into him as she fed.

"Now we're both widows," Aldith said as she walked away.

The memory went black and then flickered like an old movie reel. My head pounded horribly when I dropped into a new memory. This one was recent. Clive and Russell appeared as they did now, the clothing the same. Clive walked in the door and was met by Russell. The entry was empty but for the two of them. Leticia had to be nearby, though, for me to be here.

"And how is our resident werewolf these days, Sire?" The corner of Russell's mouth quirked up.

"Funny," Clive said as he walked to the study.

"What was the topic of discussion tonight?" Russell followed Clive down the hall.

Clive stopped and leaned against the doorjamb, hands in his pockets. His expression softened as he shook his head. "She was quite angry about a children's book."

"A children's book?"

"Yes. Something about a tree being cut down so a selfish boy could have everything he wanted. And then—this part seemed to incense her the most—the tree had to spend the rest of her truncated life with him sitting on her."

"The tree was gendered?"

Clive shrugged, grinning at his friend. "I have no idea. I know for a fact, though, that the boy was an asshole. She was quite clear on that point."

Russell chuckled. "I'm sure she's right."

"I'm sure she is."

"If I might suggest, Sire, perhaps next time you should join the conversation."

Clive's eyes lit with humor. "Now why would I do that?" Lost in thought a moment, his expression turned grim. "Silent and threatening is more my speed. Come, tell me what I missed."

The door of the study closed firmly behind Russell. I looked up and down the hall, trying to find Leticia. A moment later, I saw an eye peeking out from the salon across the hall. The door couldn't have been opened more than an inch or two, but the heartbreak was clear.

I supposed that answered our 'why now' question. After centuries of hoping and pining for her one true love, he defied logic and became smitten with a book nerd werewolf.

I pulled myself out of Leticia's memories, exhausted. Clive was waiting, still seated in front of me, hand still around my calf. It was disorienting seeing him now, all polish and sophistication, and remembering him then, sweating in the fields. One thing was true in either time, though. He was a good man.

I kissed him and then stepped off the table. "Let's go. I'll explain in the car." I wanted a soft bed as soon as possible.

Holding the grimoire in my lap, I tipped the seat back and let the cool night air wash over me. I pushed away the memory of the pain and focused on the chill I was feeling, the way stray hairs whipped around my face, Clive stripped and working in a field.

"It's unfair," I said sleepily.

"What is?"

"You. You never had an awkward age. Twelve? Adorable, earnest. Twenty? Holy crap. I'll be fantasizing about that for years to come. Undead? Gorgeous. Ergo, *ipso facto*, unfair." Thankfully—in this case—I had no pictures from my childhood. No middle school class photos meant I couldn't show him what awkward adolescence was supposed to look like.

"How—Leticia knew me in life?"

"Yup. She had a massive crush. Massive. Like I-refuse-to-kill-him-Mother-no-matter-how-much-you-torment-and-berate-me-even-if-you-turn-me-into-a-vampire-I-won't-do-it massive." I couldn't blame her. I was hopelessly in love with him myself.

"And then she said yes." He exited the freeway, twisting through dark surface streets on the way back to Pacific Heights.

"In her defense, she said no for almost a millennium."

"There's that."

I relayed everything I'd seen and then we sat in silence, each lost in our own thoughts.

"I don't remember her," he finally said.

"Why should you? It was hundreds of lifetimes ago. Knowing you and seeing you through her eyes, I also know kindness to a stranger wasn't unusual for you. You didn't mark her or her rescue because erring on the side of compassion is ingrained in you."

He glanced over, brow furrowed. "I'm not the hero, Sam. Tell me you understand that. I've lost count of the number of people I've killed. I lost count centuries ago. Stheno told you in New Orleans. I've lived as long as I have because I always put myself first. Always. Threats are eliminated immediately, so as not to become greater threats later. Cold-hearted bastard, I believe she called me. She wasn't wrong."

Downshifting, he drove through the gate being swung open by

one of his vamps. "Do you think I've become a master vampire by being sweet and cuddly?"

I laughed. I couldn't help it. "I know who you are. You may be ruthless and calculating and deadly and all the rest, but you temper it with intelligence and decency. You're not St. Germain or Lafitte, not even Cadmael or Liang."

He pulled into the garage and turned off the engine. "Meaning what?"

"You haven't lost your humanity." Unbuckling, I stepped out of the roadster, grimoire held to my chest.

He walked around the front of the car, took my free hand, and kissed it. "I feel hard-pressed to remind you I lost that a millennium ago."

"Nope. Dead-ish doesn't mean mindless or heartless. In your case, it's stripped away the daily concerns of planting and harvesting, of asshole bosses and paying rent. When all of that noise and drama is shed, what's left is what's true. And what's true is that you are a good man. Feared, yes, but also beloved. Russell and Godfrey willingly step between you and danger, not out of duty, but out of love and respect. Look at all the other masters calling you, volunteering to watch your nocturne while we went to New Orleans. That doesn't happen because you're so scary. It happens because they admire you and know you would offer your help if they were in trouble."

Shaking his head, he leaned in and kissed me soundly. "As you would say, boy, do I have you snowed. Come, let's get you cleaned up and in bed."

When we walked through the door into the hall, Russell was waiting. "She's right, Sire."

"No one asked you." Clive patted Russell's shoulder as he walked by. "Anything to report?"

"Nothing, my liege." Russell followed us down the long hall.

The *Sire* and *liege* could only mean one thing: People were listening.

"I'll be down shortly and then we'll begin our strategy. Sam has found where Leticia's been hiding."

"Thank you, Miss Quinn. We are indebted."

It was a bit of theater for the nocturne. Clearly, Clive and Russell were trying to get the vamps to appreciate me. I could have told them it'd never work, but it was sweet that they tried.

After a long, tepid shower—I couldn't handle heat right now—I looked in the mirror and saw a bright white streak in my hair. Starting at my right temple, it was an inch wide and went right down to the tips. Martha had told me I could redirect the payment. It didn't have to be blindness.

Tonight, when I absorbed the pain in the wicche glass and then spied on Leticia, I chose a different payment. I don't remember consciously choosing to lose the pigment in my hair. I have always thought the bride of Frankenstein's streaks were cool, though, so who knows? I blew dry the new hair, put on my pajamas, padded into our room, and found Clive sitting on the side of the bed.

"What are you doing here?" Not that I wasn't happy to see him.

"I live here." He rose and pulled me into his arms. "I gave Russell and Godfrey the brief overview. I was distracted, focusing on your heartbeat," he murmured, kissing my neck. "You scared me earlier." He toppled us to the bed. "I won't have it. The sound of your next heartbeat can't be the most important thing in my life."

"Sucker," I crooned. "You've got it bad." I dropped little kisses all over his face.

His nose grazed my throat, my jaw, before he rubbed his cheek against my own. Twisting a finger in the white hair, he studied it. "I like it."

I shrugged, self-conscious. "I redirected payment so I wouldn't go blind tonight."

"Smart. I thought this," he said, running the hair over his lips, "was because of the wicche glass." He sighed and then kissed me. "Whatever shall I do with you?"

"Better put a ring on it."

Bracing himself on his forearms, he studied me. "I'd do it right now, but the vicar might be put off by our shagging."

"I don't believe we're currently shagging. I'm pretty sure I'd know."

"Darling, I'm just getting started." In no time, he'd divested us of our clothing. "See?" he said, nuzzling my breast. "This might be embarrassing for the poor man." Trailing kisses down my body, he added, "And this."

When he settled between my legs, his tongue and fangs yanking a scream out of me, he said, "Honestly, I'm not even certain that's legal."

Panting and giggling, I pulled him up and rolled us over, shutting him up with my own mouth. I rose, taking him in on a moan. He dragged his hands from my hips to my breasts, rolling and plucking at my nipples as I rode him.

"Think of how red in the face he'd be right now, trying to remember his dearly beloveds."

"Clive."

"Sorry, darling." He rolled us back over, his arms snaking under my legs to keep them spread open for him. Letting the joke go, he showed me exactly what supernatural strength, speed, and skill could do to a person.

Spent, vibrating, muscles like jelly, I clung to him. "I do."

Sliding his fangs from the crook in my neck, he kissed my throat. "As do I."

I WOKE TO CLIVE'S THUMB BRUSHING BACK AND FORTH AGAINST MY stomach.

Smiling, I curled into him. "I love winter."

His hand skimmed up my body before settling on a breast. Lips at the back of my neck, he said, "Whatever shall we do with all these longer nights?"

"Nothing," I said, scrambling out of bed, "until I brush my teeth." Clive followed for the most erotic teeth brushing of my life.

Much later we were cleaned, dressed, and headed downstairs.

Wait. It couldn't be. I knew that voice!

With a whoop, I raced down the hall and leaped over the balustrade, dropping down through the narrow gap between staircases and gallery walks. In the two seconds it took to drop, I left my stomach on the third floor and cursed my own idiocy, but I had to get to him as quickly as possible. I would have been fine, but Dave snatched me out of the air and held me a foot above the tile.

"What the fuck?" he growled.

I took one look into those shark-black eyes and burst into tears. I wrapped my arms around him and sobbed into his shoulder, unable to form words.

"Damn it, Sam. We've talked about crying." He let go, no doubt hoping I'd drop to the floor, but there was no way I could stop hugging him.

Clive's hand slid up and down my back, soothing. "It's good to see you again."

"Can you do something about this?" His pissed-off grumble brought joy to my soul.

"In a minute. Sam has been quite concerned—more than I realized—that she'd killed you or sent you to a parallel universe from which you'd never return."

"She did." He patted my back. "Good job on that. Now let go."

Shaking my head against his shoulder, I continued to cling like a demented spider monkey.

"Perhaps we should move this discussion to my study."

Dave sighed and then strode down the hall, doing his best to ignore the werewolf attached to him.

Once in the study, Clive pried me off Dave and then held me close, sitting us together on my bench. Taking deep breaths, I wiped off my face and let it sink in. He wasn't dead.

"I'm sorry." I pointed to the scars across his face.

"Eh." He shrugged. "Sorry I tried to kill you."

I waved my hand, erasing his apology. "No big deal."

Shaking his head, Clive patted my leg. "Come," he called.

The study door opened. Russell and Godfrey entered, followed by a vamp whose name I didn't know carrying a tray holding a beer, a cranberry juice, and a goblet of blood.

When the as-yet-still-unnamed vamp left, Russell took the chair beside Dave and Godfrey moved one over from the table on the other side of the office. Before we got started, I downed the juice and grabbed Clive's now empty goblet, taking them to the wet bar counter. I tapped through Clive's tablet to start the music playing.

"Can you tell us what happened?" Clive didn't need a position-of-power seat. Relaxed on the bench, my hand in his, he commanded the room.

"Shit, the headaches started as soon as George took Owen away. She's good. I'll give her that. I didn't realize what she was doing until it was too late." He smoothed a hand over his bald head. "It was constant. This throb behind my eyes. Really negative shit kept cycling through my thoughts. Maggie and I got into it and she kicked me out the night I attacked you. That just added fuel to the fire."

"I'm so sorry! I can talk to her for you. Explain what my aunt is like. I—"

"I talked to her before I came here. If you need a banshee to help take down your aunt, you got one." Dave tipped up his glass and finished his beer.

"Is it wrong that the idea of a banshee screaming in my aunt's ear makes me warm and giddy?"

Dave smirked. "Anyway, the negative shit racing around in here"—he tapped his forehead—"it was all about you and what a huge fucking asshole you are."

"Understandable," Godfrey said, expression serious, though I felt the humor under the words.

I tried to flick him between the eyes with my mind. When he flinched, Clive held up a hand and I high-fived him.

"After Maggie booted me, I knew you were at the root of all my problems. I wanted to kill you. Enough of me remembered that wasn't right, so I went to the bar to avoid you." He scrutinized me. "I thought I burned you."

"You did." Clive's voice dripped ice.

Oh shit.

THIRTY-TWO

A Small Hug?

I shook my head and waved my hand, trying to erase the accusation in Clive's voice. We weren't blaming Abigail's victims for what she forced them to do. "I got lots of help. See?" I lifted my head so he could see my unmarked neck. "I'm fine."

"Now," Clive added. "It was not without a great deal of pain on Sam's part."

I smacked Clive's hand. "Stop it. None of this is Dave's fault. None of it. You want to be pissed at someone, be pissed at Abigail."

"Oh, I am."

"Good. Dave fought her. Right to the end, I could see it. She was pushing him to kill me, and he was doing everything he could to hold back the flames." I stared him in the eye. "I know how hard you fought to protect me. And I'm not blameless here. Those scars across your face are because of me. I was so afraid I'd killed you or sent you to someplace you'd never find your way back from." I placed a hand on my churning, guilt-laden stomach. "I'm sorry."

He stood, shook his head, and began to prowl the room.

Russell studied Dave a moment and then turned to Clive. "How sure are we that Abigail is no longer in him, watching us?"

"Very," Dave said, stopping to lean against the conference table. "Sam sent me to Hell. Good on you for that one. And when someone is trying to kill you, you fight back any way you can. Do you think I give a shit about this?" He motioned to his face. "You've done me a favor. Fewer randos stopping me on the street asking questions."

Clive gave me an appraising gaze before turning to Dave. "Sam sent you to Hell?"

"Yeah. No big deal. They know me there." He winked at me, which was completely out of character for Dave. The big lug was trying to assuage my guilt. Then again…

I got up and crossed to him. When I was standing directly in front of him, I pulled at his arms, which had been crossed over his chest, and put his hands on my neck.

"Whatcha doin'?" Eyebrows raised, he waited.

"You winked."

"I did."

I stared him down. "Super unlike you."

"Ah. Maybe I'm not choking you because she's smart enough to know that if I tightened my grip a centimeter, three vampires would try to kill me."

"She wouldn't care what happened to you as long as she hurt me."

"Good point." He patted my shoulders, turned me around, and then shoved me back toward Clive. Rude.

"You need to practice that spell. It was a good one. Anyway, since I was there and I still had her in my head, I was able to trace the demon she's been working with."

My hand flew to my mouth. "You found him?"

"I did," he said. "She only stayed with me for a second or two after I made my descent, but it was enough." He shrugged his broad shoulders. "Lower-level demon. I unmade him. It'll take an eon to reform."

"That's wonderful, but couldn't she find another?" Russell asked.

Something occurred to me as I noticed the now vacated seat beside Russell. It was uncomfortable for a predator to have another predator at his back. I guessed that was why Dave was now standing on the other side of the room.

"She could, but she doesn't know she's lost her symbiont. I called in a favor. Junior-level demon. He'll keep tabs and fulfill the role in all ways except one. He won't allow her to act against you. When the time comes, he'll cut her off so she'll be flying solo with no warning." The grin that spread across Dave's face sent a chill down my spine.

I raised my hand.

Lifting one eyebrow, he waited for me to speak.

"I know you said no hugs, but I *really* want to hug you right now. Are you in more of an I'll-put-up-with-it-but-I-won't-like-it place or is it a hard I-will-yank-out-your-arms-and-beat-you-with-them head space?"

"Why don't you hug me instead? I believe Dave has been through enough." Clive opened his arms and I dove in, hugging the life, sort of, out of him.

"You know what this means?" I asked, getting myself under control. "The tide is turning. I may actually have a shot at this. She's lost her demon and we just added a banshee!"

"Don't forget. You're now a friend of the dragons," Clive added, his eyes glowing as he took me in.

"What is it?" I whispered. He seemed even happier than I was.

He squeezed my knee. "The more people on your side, the longer I get to keep you."

"That's it," Dave grumbled. "When vampires start getting mushy, it's my cue to go." He put up both hands, warding me off, when I started to get up. "Don't even think about it," he warned and then walked out.

"I'm hugging you in my mind!" I shouted as the door slammed shut.

"So," Godfrey said after a moment, "now that we have a handle on the Abigail situation, what are we doing about Leticia?"

"I could call Stheno and ask her and her sisters to watch the house. Keep an eye on her for us while we plan?" I patted my pocket and then remembered. "But before that, I need to replace my phone."

Clive pointed to his desk and grinned. "Russell already got you one. The box is in my top drawer."

"I picked up a few extras while I was at it," Russell assured me in all seriousness.

"Oh, sure. Everybody yuck it up."

"And," Clive interrupted, "I spoke with Stheno last night. She said they would watch their neighbor." He paused, brow furrowed and then stood abruptly, Russell and Godfrey in his wake as he rushed for the door. "Apparently, they're visiting us now," Clive called back.

I caught up to the boys at the front door. Stheno and her sisters were standing on the other side of the closed gates while the vamps on guard duty looked anywhere but at them.

"Listen, you little shits, if you don't welcome us with over-flowing cups and dancing boys, we will tear these gates off their hinges and create a fanged sculpture garden." Stheno was pissed and her sisters weren't far behind.

"Stheno," Clive called as he crossed the courtyard, "Euryale, Medusa, we are honored to have you visit."

The vamps were already opening the gates, so Clive didn't need to pause before leaning over Stheno's hand to kiss it. He did the same for her sisters, the very image of a handsome prince bestowing courtly attentions.

"Please, come with us." Clive offered his arm to Stheno, who took it with a wink at me. Russell and Godfrey offered theirs to her sisters, escorting them in.

As the library was right out, Clive chose a salon decorated in blues. I'd seen the room but hadn't spent any time in it. It was really quite lovely, all soft watercolors. The ladies were left to choose their seats while the vamps went to the sideboard to pour glasses of wine.

The women sat in the chairs, leaving the sofa for the vamps, which was such a funny power move. Grinning, I sat in the middle of the sofa and extended my arms along the top of the cushions. When the men turned around, there was the briefest of hesitations before they passed out the wine.

Clive sat beside me while Russell and Godfrey remained standing by the wet bar like wine stewards. Unerringly, Clive reached over his shoulder, grabbed my arm and pulled it forward so it was draped around him.

Stheno lifted her chin at me. "What's with the hair?"

"Oh." I touched the streak self-consciously. "It's nothing." At Stheno's continued scrutiny, I added, "I don't lose my sight anymore."

She nodded. "Good trade-off."

"Come."

A vamp walked in with a tray of fancy hors d'oeuvres he offered our guests—not me— and then left the tray on the coffee table.

"Thank you for the visit," Clive began. "I don't believe I've seen you all together like this since the late eighteen hundreds. Chicago, wasn't it?"

Euryale and Stheno stared at their sister while Medusa threw her head back, laughing. "Damn, that was fun. We should go back there next time. Everybody who'd remember us is dead."

"No." Euryale's tone put a stop to Medusa's musings. "When you burn down a city, you do the people the favor of not returning."

"Listen to Miss Manners over here." Medusa rolled her eyes and grabbed another snack off the tray. "And we've met in Athens loads of time." She glanced at us. "The ruins speak for themselves."

Leaning forward, I grabbed what looked like smoked salmon, cucumber, and some white stuff. Mmm, delicious.

"What do you think, Sam?" Stheno asked as I reached for another one.

"Really good," I said, popping it into my mouth. When I looked up, I realized she was glaring at Clive.

"I can't help but notice your surprise at the appearance of food or that the bloodsucker didn't offer you any." Her expression was thunderous. "We had this conversation in New Orleans. You said you'd do better."

"No, no, I'm fine. See? Jeans fit perfectly. And his assistant offered to get me whatever I want. It's going to be a fully stocked kitchen soon."

"Soon," Stheno echoed, not taking her eyes off Clive.

"So," I said, desperately trying to change the subject. "Have you guys seen Leticia in the neighborhood?"

Medusa held up her glass for more wine and Godfrey filled all three glasses.

"The vampire?" Euryale had been watching the exchange between her sister and Clive closely. "We haven't seen her. The house appears closed up and empty. Medusa's sure she heard a racing heartbeat last night, though."

"It was two or three in the morning." Medusa picked up the story. "I was having a drink on the deck, avoiding these two and listening to the ocean. I thought I saw movement in the water. The moon was bright, but there are trees between the properties. It sounded like something slapped on the dock.

"The ocean was roaring," she continued, "but I'm sure I heard footsteps. I was interested, so I was focusing on the house. I'm sure I heard a door close. A heart raced and then stopped. It could have been anything, a rabbit caught by a hawk. I don't know, but it *felt* like it was coming from inside the house."

We were silent a moment, considering.

"Do you think she has a minion, bringing her meals?" But why would someone just offer themselves up like that? If it came from the ocean, was she feeding on the fae now?

"You tell us. But eat more first." She slid the tray toward me.

"Oh." I glanced at her sisters. Were we telling everyone I could read vamps? Gorgons probably didn't give a shit, but it still left me feeling exposed.

"Now who's endangering her?" Clive said, all welcome and humor lost from his voice.

Stheno blew out a short breath and swore. "People need to tell me when things are secrets." She turned to her sisters. "What I told you about that one," she said, aiming a thumb at me, "forget it. The whole New Orleans story. Forget it."

The sisters looked me up and down before Euryale finally nodded and drank her wine. Medusa took longer, finally shrugging like an angsty teen, finishing her wine and holding up the empty glass to Godfrey.

I couldn't help but notice a shrug wasn't an agreement, but it was probably the best we were going to get. Toeing off my running shoes, I curled my legs up under me, leaned into Clive, and closed my eyes.

Throwing a mental net over San Francisco, I searched for Leticia. The immortals across from me registered as black with an almost ultraviolet halo, not that I'd ever tell them. That was the kind of info that would get me killed right quick.

I sorted through the vamps in the nocturne, the ones out in the city, and looked where I'd last seen her. She wasn't there anymore. How was she making her signature so dim? The only people who knew I could read vampires were the ones in this room, as well as Dave, Owen, George, and Meg.

Stheno's sisters had only known for a day or two. None of the others would betray me. How would she know she needed to hide from me?

THIRTY-THREE

The Panama-Pacific International Exposition of 1915

Opening my eyes, I turned to Clive. "What reason would a vamp have for feeding on other supernaturals, rather than humans?"

"You couldn't find her?" Brows furrowed, he thought a moment. "She may have left the area again."

"Hm? She's not at the house right now. I'll keep looking. I was thinking, though. She has no way to know I can do this, so drinking werewolf blood wasn't done to confuse me. Why does she do it?" There had to be a reason she was going to so much trouble.

"Kink? Taste preference?" Godfrey volunteered. "Of course, I don't believe she drank anything but bagged blood or the occasional human when she lived here."

"Strength," Russell added. "I didn't absorb any wolf-like characteristics, but your blood made me stronger than human blood, Miss Quinn." Russell's deep, measured voice always focused the conversation.

The hand holding mine flinched. Barely, but I felt it. Clive didn't like being reminded that Russell had once fed from me.

"Scent," Euryale volunteered. When she noticed the vamps and

I were staring at her, she pointed to Clive and said, "Your scent is different from theirs."

"I don't understand. All vamps smell different, just like you three smell different."

"Yeah?" Stheno leaned forward, suddenly interested. "What does that one smell like?" She pointed to Medusa.

I breathed in deeply. "Right now, she smells like new leather." I glanced down and found unmarked boots. "Sorry, but a sour tang of alcohol seeping through unwashed skin."

"Hey." Medusa looked equal parts outraged and embarrassed.

"We told you to get cleaned up." Stheno nodded to me. "What else?"

"Orange blossom shampoo, aloe lotion, the salmon she just ate, but now that I'm paying attention, you're right. The three of you do have a common underlying scent."

"Snake?" Stheno guessed.

"Yes." I turned to the vamps in the room. "But with these guys, I don't get anything—oh."

Nodding, Euryale said, "It's subtle, that coppery blood scent. The older and more feral the vampire, the stronger the stench. Polished, urban vampires like you three? It's barely there." She leaned forward and took another hors d'oeuvre.

Breathing deeply, I filled my lungs with the myriad of scents in the room. She was right. Blood was in there, but it was overpowered by the individual scents that made them who they were.

"Clive's always smelled like lemons and fresh linens drying on the line to me." I pulled his hand to my lips for a kiss. Strength, safety, and home. "Mine."

"That's very sweet, but he smells like you too," Euryale said. "He drinks from you. They don't. His coppery scent has a hint of fur."

"Really?" I kept Clive's hand trapped in mine. "That's fascinating. These guys have said that other vamps can tell we're together because of our scents, but I thought they meant because of sex—"

"We do," Godfrey interrupted. "You reek of it."

The gorgons nodded and my face flamed.

"Payback's a bitch," Medusa grumbled.

"Perhaps," Clive said, "we could get back to Euryale's theory on why Leticia is drinking the blood of supernaturals."

Euryale finished her glass and raised it again. At this rate, Godfrey was going to have a full-time job. He opened another bottle and refilled glasses.

"If this vampire doesn't know what Sam can do, then she's hiding from you," she said to Clive. "Has she ever seen you track by scent?"

"No, I—" He stopped to consider. "I don't believe so."

"1915?" Russell suggested.

Clive shook his head. "How would she know about that? It was local and had nothing to do with us."

Godfrey topped off the glasses and then placed three open bottles on the coffee table. "Ladies, my shift is over. I'll leave these here for your next server." With a grin, he dropped down on the couch next to me. "Everyone heard about that stunt you pulled."

Rolling his eyes, Godfrey elbowed me. "Your fiancé over there helped the human police track down a murdering pedophile who was kidnapping children from the Panama-Pacific Exposition."

"The San Francisco World's Fair? You were—right. Of course, you were here. I will *never* get used to how long you guys live. Ever."

"We, sweetheart, not you guys. Anyway, children were going missing but there was so much chaos. People were visiting from all over the country," Godfrey continued.

"And how would you know? You weren't living with us during that period," Clive said.

"My point. I was in Wales." He elbowed me again. "Now there's a good story. Ask me about it some time. Anyway, I'm in bleeding Wales and I heard about it, so you know everybody else did, too."

"*Somebody* tell the story. What happened in 1915?" I was

surrounded by six people with more lifetimes of stories than I could fathom, and I wanted to hear them all.

Russell picked it up. "I *was* here, so I can tell it." He pulled over a chair and sat while the sisters filled their own glasses. "The Pan-Pacific Exposition lasted almost a year. Close to twenty million people visited the city during that time. I'd never seen anything like it."

"I've only seen pictures," I interrupted. "To have been here and experienced it." I shook my head. "The Palace of Fine Arts is on all my running routes. It's magical. To have seen all the palaces, the entire exposition...mind rightfully boggled."

"I felt the same way, Miss Quinn. I spent many nights wandering through closed exhibits. It was"—he stopped to think —"before and after, an extraordinarily singular experience." He gave his head a wondering shake. "I wish you could have seen it. I have a feeling you would have been beside me, walking the halls, as enthralled as I was.

"As Godfrey said," he continued, "people visited from all over. Transportation and communication being what they were then, travelers were away from home for weeks, sometimes months, at a time. By the time anyone realized people were missing, it was far too late to investigate."

"Wait. That's like H. H. Holmes and the Chicago World's Fair."

Nodding, he said, "Exactly. It was fertile ground for serial killers. And pickpockets and rapists and con men."

"And vampires," Godfrey cut in.

"Indeed," Clive agreed.

Russell continued, "Unlike when adults go missing, when children disappear, it's noticed right away."

I pulled my knees up to my chest. "How many children disappeared?"

"We arrived in the evenings to feed," Clive said. "The sun went down and families gathered in meeting spots to walk back to their lodgings. We saw parents shouting children's names, but more often than not, a child would arrive, out of breath from racing through a flood of other visitors. We were still there, though, when desperate families were looking long into the night."

"No. Most of us fed and left. I stayed to walk the exhibits. You stayed to make sure the children were found." Russell tapped the arm of the sofa beside Clive. "It didn't take long to realize we had a human predator. The first child was found with his clothes torn and bruises around his neck. Clive found his body dumped behind the Horticulture Palace. It wasn't as though Clive could carry the child back to the family or the proper authorities. He couldn't insert himself into the investigation. Then, as now, we did everything we could to remain unnoticed."

"What happened to the child?" My voice was small and scared. Even I heard it. I knew something about what that child had gone through and I hated thinking of one so young…

Russell didn't answer my question. He didn't have to. Instead, he said, "Clive waited with the body, staying out of sight while mentally influencing the human authorities to look in the correct place."

"Not all of them. I'd fed from an officer the night before. Normally, the link doesn't remain once we walk away, but I tried. Eventually, he came around the corner of the building, saw the child, and began blowing his whistle. The poor man was shaking so hard, he had trouble getting the whistle in his mouth."

Clive rested his hand on my knee. "It was maddening. The children were being taken during the day. I found the bodies, but I couldn't catch the killer before he hurt them. I couldn't stop it from happening." When he squeezed my knee, I leaned into him.

"But he noticed something about their scents," Godfrey said. "Which brings us back to the point of the story. The children were covered in a million scents, all the places they'd been that day and the days before, as people didn't bathe daily then"—he glanced at Medusa—"or now," he added with a smirk, making sure to keep his eyes averted. "They also all carried the scent of candy apples."

"A few of them would have been reasonable," Clive took over the storytelling. "There were food carts scattered all over the exposition and it made sense that they'd smell of fair food, but all of them? No.

"I searched. I couldn't find the killer, but I had to wait for nightfall. One evening, I finally found the right cart, although it was manned by the wrong person. I could smell him, the man who'd left his scent on every dead child, but I couldn't find him."

Russell picked up the story again, "Frustrated, he wrote a letter to the chief of police—slipped under his front door—saying he knew who was killing the children. He gave them a description of the cart, told them the man only worked during the afternoons." Russell turned to Clive. "I believe you included the types of pomade and aftershave he used as well. It took two days—"

"And one more dead child," Clive cut in.

"But they caught him. Strangely, though, he didn't make it to trial. He was found dead in his cell, drained of all blood. It was quite the mystery for some time."

I kissed Clive's cheek, and he wrapped his arm around me. Those poor children. It was a hundred years ago but my heart ached for them, for their last moments of fear and pain.

"And you believe," Clive said to Godfrey, "that Leticia not only heard that story but is now trying to muddle her scent to confuse me?"

"Makes sense," Godfrey responded. "She probably thinks that's how you found her in that cave up the coast. I'd imagine she's feeling proper paranoid about your tracking abilities right about now."

"We're willing to help you look for her," Euryale said.

The vampires looked surprised by the offer, but I caught Stheno's eye and smirked.

"Fine," she admitted. "We're bored and can't stand another minute in each other's company. Give us something fun to do, please." Stheno finished off her wine and slammed the glass down —thankfully, not shattering it—ready to go.

Euryale's expression was pinched and Medusa looked bored, but they were all sitting here, willing to help.

"I haven't found her yet." Jeez, no pressure, though, right?

"Well, hurry up. In the meantime…" She held up an empty wine bottle and shook it in Godfrey's direction.

"Oh, that's what's going on here. You guys ran out of your own wine so you're 'visiting,'" I air quoted, "trying to drink all of theirs."

"How dare y—" Euryale began but Stheno smacked her arm.

"True, *but* we're willing to work for our wine, so tell us where to look."

"Come," Clive called.

A vamp entered carrying a case of wine bottles.

"Okay," Stheno said, "we're good." She waved her hand at me to hurry up. "Go find her."

I padded to the other side of the salon, dragged a high-backed chair into the corner, and sat, blocking out the voices in the room. Pulling my socked feet up, I rested my head against my knees, let out a long, slow breath, and revisited the mental net I'd thrown over the city. When my head started to throb, cool pain relief washed over me. Even while chatting with the gorgons, who were laughing uproariously, he was looking out for me.

I started with the Sea Cliff house but didn't sense her there. Slowly, painstakingly, I searched every corner of the city. Nothing. When I reached for the North Bay, my mind snagged on something odd and unnatural that twisted my stomach.

THIRTY-FOUR

Well, Shit. This Isn't Good

Wrapping my mind around an oddly colored blip, I checked to make sure I had Leticia and not some new creature I was unaware of. It was her, but she felt all wrong. Her mind was strangely chaotic. I heard her steady voice in my head, willing someone to relax, that all was well, while something else screeched. It was like nails on a chalkboard, if those nails were sentient and desperate.

I dove deeper, past the voices, and saw through her eyes. She was draining the life out of a mermaid, her arms clamped like iron bars around her victim. The mermaid was losing strength, the screeching now mere whimpers. When she was little more than a desiccated husk fading into nothing, Leticia dropped her and swam toward shore.

I tried what I had done in New Orleans, when those vamps had attacked Stheno and me in an alley. I envisioned my magic like a golden thread and wrapped it around Leticia's mind. Once done, I yanked, but the threads slid off. Confused, I tried again, doing exactly as I had done before. A few of the threads snagged as though they had caught hold, but then they slid through again.

I was a necromancer. I had no control over the fae. The only thing that made sense was now that she had glutted herself with fae blood, she'd altered her own chemistry to such a degree, I couldn't touch her. It wouldn't last. Vampires needed to feed regularly because their bodies—actually, I wasn't entirely sure how that worked, but I knew they needed blood on a daily basis. My only hope was to get her between feedings, when she'd be without the fae protection.

Opening my eyes, I turned back to the room, defeated. "Found her."

"Where?" Clive was already standing.

"The ocean." It sounded ridiculous. Given the way everyone was staring at me with varying degrees of confusion, they agreed.

"She's on a boat?" Medusa asked.

Shaking my head, I looked at Clive. "You guys don't need to breathe, right?"

All three vampires looked decidedly uncomfortable.

"She's—what? She's swimming around? Sitting on the bottom, watching fish go by?" Godfrey threw up his hands and walked across the room.

"She's feeding on the water fae. She just drained a mermaid dry. Do the fae disappear when they die?" If I couldn't kill her, maybe the vamps could catch her in the water.

Clive dropped back down on the couch, his head in his hands. "She's killing the fae," he said quietly to himself.

"Shit," Stheno breathed. "Even we don't fuck with the fae."

"Is there a way to contact an emissary, explain that this isn't us?" There had to be something we could do to distance ourselves from Leticia.

"Which us?" Godfrey asked as he dropped into a chair near me. "Vampires? San Francisco? All non-fae?" He dragged a hand down his face. "Can you imagine if Faerie decided to set her warriors against us?"

"You'd be annihilated," Euryale answered.

"Aye."

"Is that the goal?" I asked.

Clive lifted his head and turned to me.

"I mean, you all seem to know what a bad idea it is to piss off Faerie, so is Leticia doing it to burn it all down, you included? Her mom's back in England. Maybe the plan is to stir up apocalyptic shit here and then hop across the pond to wait out our destruction."

"What about your great-aunt's wife?" Russell asked. "Would she be willing to act as an envoy, to explain we're hunting Leticia, that she isn't one of us?"

Clive shook his head.

"I'm not her favorite person and she's currently in Faerie, recovering from the last time she healed me."

"Liam?" Godfrey suggested.

"He's not really happy with me, given what my aunt did to him." This was hopeless.

"You said there was a door into Faerie at the Wicche Glass. Could you step through and talk to someone?" Russell ventured.

"No!" Clive and Stheno responded as one.

"You do not step foot in Faerie without an invitation and guarantees of safety. Too many would love nothing more than to eat you," Euryale explained.

"How do we get an invitation?" I asked.

Godfrey leaned forward, bracing his forearms on his thighs. "You said earlier that Sam is now considered a friend of the dragons. Would they fly her in, vouch for her?"

Clive stood, his face drawn. "Sam is not going into Faerie, and certainly not alone."

"Couldn't you just hurry up and kill the bloodsucker? Then you could give Faerie the body and say, 'See? We took care of it.'" Medusa suggested.

"She'd be a pile of dust," I said.

"Okay, even better. Get her close to death and hand her over. Then Faerie gets to do the honors." Medusa filled her cup again.

"Maybe we should go talk with Coco and George's grandmother again. See what she thinks?"

Clive nodded slowly, taking his phone out of his pocket. "I need to call first."

I'd felt the pull through that mirror in The Wicche Glass. Faerie wanted me. I was terrified I wouldn't get back out if I went in. My life was here: Clive, my friends, the bookstore and bar. It was all here. I didn't want to visit Faerie for what seemed like an afternoon, only to return home and find everyone hundreds of years dead. I needed to go to keep everyone safe, but in doing so, I might lose them all.

Clive walked back, nodding. "She'll see us."

Knowing what a stickler for etiquette the matriarch of the dragon clan was, I ran upstairs and changed into a long, soft, slim-fitting sweater dress in a rich wine color. I was sitting on the side of the bed, sliding into black leather boots when Clive strode in.

"You always look posh," I said. "You don't need to change."

He distractedly looked down at himself. "No. I don't want to set this plan in motion. I don't want to make Faerie aware of you. She's capricious and vicious. She could decide she likes you and engage you in a conversation you believe to be an hour long, only to return to this realm sometime in the next century. Or she could take a dislike to you and give you to one of her monsters—like that thing that attacked you in The Wicche Glass—to eat."

He paced across the room. "I have no power, no influence in Faerie. None. If anything, she hates vampires, as we're considered unnatural."

"The Unseelie Court—or the dark sidhe, or whatever the proper term is—aren't exactly flower fairies," I said.

"No, but they're part of the natural order. Light, dark, day, night; in our literature we separate them into seelie and unseelie, good and evil, but it's never that simple. The fae wield extraordinary power and adhere to a code of ethics that's foreign to us."

He ran his hand through his hair, a rare sign of agitation for him. "It would be like attributing evil to a snake. It acts as it was designed to act. Good and evil don't factor in its behavior. The fae are self-serving. Beneficence is not prized. Trickery is. If they can mislead you, get you to agree to something you believe is right, but then twist it to cause harm, they'd celebrate the deception and glory in your destruction. They tricked you and won."

"I thought the fae couldn't lie."

"Who knows?" He sat beside me on the bed. "It may be lauded as superior strategy and manipulation to deceive while speaking truth. It's just as possible that their inability to lie is a tale they've spread far and wide to make us think we stand a chance against them. Only the fae know what they're capable of."

"Okay, let's stop and think this through. The goal is not to survive a visit to Faerie, but to keep her from attacking us because of Leticia. Let's find out how to send a message to Faerie explaining the problem, and then let's stop Leticia before she causes war between the realms. None of us needs to actually enter Faerie."

Clive blew out a breath. "Good. Come." He took my hand and pulled me to my feet. "We'll ask Benvair for advice."

The street and house were much the same as before: clean, wealthy, exclusive. A few windows in Benvair's home glowed in the night. Clive parked on the street in front of the mansion. He met me on the sidewalk and took my hand.

Squeezing it, he held my gaze and said, "Faerie can't have you."

"Who says she wants me? Lord knows you didn't. Remember? You kept finding ways to ditch me." I forced a laugh, trying to lighten the mood, even though my stomach was sinking. I did not want to enter Faerie. With any luck, we'd figure out how to avoid it.

He lifted our hands, turning them so my engagement ring shone in the dim light. "Bad example."

Before we reached the porch, the front door swung open. Fyffe in his black suit stood in the light and then stepped out of the way. "This way, please." Shutting the door behind us, he led the way back into the sitting room we'd met in last time.

Benvair was already seated, a cup of tea in her hand. Looking every inch the queen she was, she wore a gold silk blouse with black trousers and heels. Canary diamonds glittered at her ears and on her finger.

When Clive and I sat, she motioned to the tea service. Fyffe poured and handed us each a delicate cup. The scent was amazing. I breathed deeply, savoring, before I took a sip.

Clive drank and said, "Good. My package arrived." He never missed a trick, already sending her that super expensive tea he'd mentioned last time.

"It did." She held her cup like she was protecting her newest treasure.

Clive put his down. "Thank you for meeting us on short notice." At her nod, he continued. "We seek your knowledge and advice."

Raising her eyebrows, she waited.

I struggled not to grin. The woman was such a badass, I wanted to shake her hand for making the great Clive measure his words so exactingly. As I was on Clive's side, though, that seemed rude.

"There is a vampire—not one from my nocturne—who is attacking the fae."

Benvair's hand paused as she brought the cup to her lips. It was brief, but for a woman so in control, it screamed shock. "I now see the reason for the late-night visit."

"The vampire's name is Leticia, and her goal is to kill me. She's feeding on supernaturals, a werewolf and now the fae, in an effort to alter her scent, to make herself more difficult to hunt."

Benvair tipped her head to the side. "I've never heard of that."

"Nor had I." *May I tell her?*

I wasn't sure what he planned to tell her, but we needed her help, and I was kind of in awe of her, so I said, *Yes.*

"It was Sam who put it together. You know she's a necromancer and can speak with the dead. It seems vampires are dead enough to qualify."

Benvair returned her cup to its saucer on the coffee table, her gaze pinning me to the couch. "Explain."

Clive opened his mouth and she flicked her hand to silence him. She pointed at me. "You explain."

When a woman whose other form is the size of this room, probably a few rooms, latches her predator's focus solely on you…it was a lot. "Ma'am, I'm able to sense vampires. If I concentrate hard enough, I can sometimes hear their thoughts, like I can with the dead."

"It's not without pain," Clive said.

Benvair barely spared him a glance. "Did you find the vampire?"

"I did, but it was far more difficult than usual. The first time I located her, she was up in Bodega Bay—"

"You could sense her that far away?" Benvair leaned forward in her chair.

"Yes, ma'am. Her signature was off though. She didn't feel like a vampire, not completely. When I tried to read her, I realized why. She had a werewolf held captive and was feeding solely on him, trying to turn him, actually."

"And did it work? Was she able to create a werewolf-vampire hybrid?"

Careful.

"No. What she created was a horrible, mindless monster, neither wolf nor vampire. It tried to attack anything it saw. She had it chained down."

"You killed it?"

"Of course."

Nodding, she leaned back. "Good. Continue."

THIRTY-FIVE

Of Dragons and Teas and Terrifying Things

"She was holding him in an extremely remote place and we lost her. I found her again tonight, but she wasn't reading up here," I tapped my forehead, "like a vampire. I'm sorry. It's hard to explain."

I set my cup down as well. "I'd searched the city and found all the rest of the vampires, but not her. I began to search in the North Bay again and felt something odd in the ocean. The signature was off. It wasn't a vampire and yet I could see it. I realized it was Leticia and she was in the process of draining all the blood from a mermaid. When she shoved the body away, it began to dissolve into nothingness."

"Dead fae return to Faerie. So, you not only hear vampires' thoughts, you can see through their eyes." She sat back, appraising me.

"I'd really appreciate it, ma'am, if you kept that between the three of us."

Benvair stood abruptly and crossed to the fireplace, absently picking up a figurine. "Can you locate dragons as you do vampires?" The reluctant hope in her voice had me exchanging glances with Clive.

"I'm sorry. I can't. Only the dead. Or mostly dead," I added. "The living are beyond my abilities."

"I see." The cold indifference in her voice now couldn't quite hide the disappointment. Who was she looking for?

She went back to her chair and picked up her cup of tea. "If you found her, why is she still alive?"

"Glutting herself on fae blood changed her. She was still a vampire, obviously, but I didn't have the same control over her."

Benvair's finger lightly tapped the rim of the teacup, lost in thought. Fyffe returned a moment later to refill it for her.

"Your concern," she said to Clive, "is that Faerie not hold you or all of San Francisco responsible for what this vampire is doing, is that correct?"

"Yes."

She took a sip, staring out the window. "You could send a note, but she could very easily interpret that was disrespectful and dismissive. Her people are being killed by one of yours." When Clive opened his mouth, she continued. "She won't care whether or not this vampire is a member of your nocturne. She's a vampire. You will all be blamed for not controlling your own. If she's in a bad mood, she may cast her net more widely and blame all of us."

She blew out a breath and shook her head. "You can't go," she said to Clive. "The existence of vampires offends her." She pointed at me. "You go and plead the case."

"No," Clive said, jumping to his feet. "That's unacceptable."

"You draw in this Leticia and kill her while Sam speaks with the queen." She turned her attention to me. "You show her respect by informing her of the threat to her people and what you're both doing to end the threat."

Clive strode to the window overlooking the moonlit ocean, his back to us. His emotions were in upheaval, but he appeared unperturbed.

"We've been trying to catch her for a while. How does Clive draw her in?" I took another sip of the now tepid tea, hoping my calm would help settle Clive.

Benvair's gaze caught on my ring. "Throw an engagement party. A big, lavish party. Invite everyone. Make it a masquerade, so she thinks she's hidden. You said she wants to kill Clive. She'll come, hoping to hide in plain sight and attack. Instead, you take her."

"Yes," Clive said, nodding slowly at his reflection in the dark glass. "That could work."

"And while the vampires are neutralizing that threat, Sam visits Faerie."

"Sam needs to be at the party with me."

"No. The party will take time to set up, decorations, food, invitations. In fact, *I'll* throw it for you here. You'll pay for it, of course."

"Of course," Clive said.

"That way, it will appear even less like a trap. Don't fill it with vampires. It will be a who's who of the local supernatural community. You should have someone roughly Sam's size and build at your side. We'll draw her in, and you end it."

She resumed tapping the rim of her cup. "While we plan and set up, Sam crosses into Faerie and begins the long trek to Una's court."

"Una? That's Faerie's name?" Everyone kept referring to the queen by the name of the realm. It was confusing.

"The Fairy Queen, Mab, Titania, Gloriana, Una, Queen of Elphame, Morgan, Maeve, Tanaquill; she goes by many names, though most refer to her as Faerie itself. All fae swear their allegiance to her."

"No king?" I desperately needed any and all information I could get.

Benvair shrugged, her lips pursed. "I suppose. He was going by Finvarra last I heard. He's always scheming to steal her power, but make no mistake, the power is hers."

"Okay." Nodding, I turned to Clive's back. "This could work." When he remained stiff and unyielding, I said, "What's the alternative? Race up and down the coast, trying to catch her? Let her kill more innocents as she desperately tries to keep your attention? Ms. Drake has graciously offered us her home to set a trap. You take care of the imminent threat. I'll chat up the queen and try not to incite an incident."

Clive turned, eyes vamp black, expression forbidding. I rose and went to him, wrapping my arms around his waist. "You don't think I'm going to be just as worried about you? You're making yourself bait for a woman who will do anything to get close to you. Her childhood crush is now her obsession. I have to leave you here and hope for the best."

Squeezing him, I said, "Will I be scared? Of course, but Ms. Drake will tell me what I need to know, and I'll be my most polite as I explain our predicament. I'm a lowly, humble book nerd and bartender. I'm just the messenger. I'll slip in, explain what we're doing to protect her people, and slide right back out again."

Black eyes blazing, he said, "No."

I laid my head on his chest and breathed in his scent. "It's not your choice, love. It has to be done and it can't be you. Partners, remember?

"Oh, hey," I said, extracting myself from his grip. "I can call Grim and ask for advice. Tankards of mead for life if he gives me the inside scoop on surviving Faerie. This'll work," I assured him, patting his shoulder and returning to my seat. I needed Benvair to tell me everything she knew.

THE FOLLOWING AFTERNOON, I AWOKE TO CLIVE'S ARMS WRAPPED tightly around me. I couldn't wiggle out. Finally, after assuring him over and over I wouldn't leave until he awoke, his muscles relaxed enough to release me.

Showered and ponytailed, I stood in the closet and considered. I was meeting a powerful queen, but comfort and ease of movement seemed the more important consideration. If I needed to run,

I didn't want a dress or heels to trip me up. I was a messenger, after all, not a visiting dignitary.

Jeans, running shoes, and a hoodie it was. I grabbed my old threadbare backpack, stuffed in spare clothes and toiletries, and then went to the kitchen to raid its recently filled cabinets. Protein bars and jerky went in, along with two bottles of water. My image of Faerie was one of lush greens and babbling brooks, so more water shouldn't be a problem. Then again, Benvair made it quite clear I was not to eat or drink in Faerie, no matter what. I could eat the food I brought in, but not hers.

Adding more water, I searched the shelves for high-calorie, high-protein foods I could live on for a while. I had no idea how long this journey would take. Stepping through the mirror and into the heart of the realm was easy enough. It was getting back out that had me in a cold sweat.

Once full, I dropped the backpack to the side of the stairs, intending to be there when Clive awoke, but he was already coming down, expression hard. I turned and led the way back to the kitchen, grabbing blood from the refrigerator and pulling down a goblet for him. No one else was awake yet and we needed to talk before they were.

Handing him the goblet, I took his free hand and walked him to his study, nabbing my backpack on the way. If the other vamps woke before I got back for it, food might go missing. They didn't actively want me dead. Too much. But if I got trapped in Faerie, well, was that really a tragedy?

I took the now empty goblet from his hand, leaving it on his desk, before making him sit on my bench. Straddling his knees, I sat and stared him straight in the eye. "I'm going to be careful and I'm going to come home to you."

"You can't know that. Anything could happen and I wouldn't be able to stop it. I'm being asked to sit safely in my fortress while you risk your life because of vampires. Damn it, Sam. I won't *know* if anything happens to you."

"Lots of fae come into the bar. They like me fine. I'll be okay." I leaned in and kissed him, wanting to reassure him. He was right, though. Neither would know if the other was safe. We'd each need to wait and hope.

"The fae you've met have chosen to live in this realm, rather than Faerie. They've acculturated. The fae you will be dealing with in Faerie have no interest in nor any experience with passing as human." He pulled me in, crushing me against him. "You will come back to me, safe and healthy. That's an order."

I grinned against his neck, breathing in his scent, trying to store it for the journey ahead. "So strict."

"We haven't had nearly long enough together." He leaned back and framed my face with his hands. "I mean it." His thumbs brushed my cheeks. "It won't do if you're not here beside me." He pulled me forward, his lips claiming mine. Longing and fear mixed with love and passion.

When we finally broke apart, I stood and held out a hand. "We should go now." Clive was going to drive me to The Wicche Glass and watch me step through.

"Wait. I have a gift for you to give the queen." He went to his desk and pulled a velvet bag from his top drawer. "Here. Hopefully, she'll see it as a worthy gift."

There was some weight to it. "Can I see?"

"Of course."

I opened the bag and tipped it over. A round, green stone dropped into my hand.

"It's imperial jade, carved centuries ago. One of a kind."

Turning it over, I saw one side was a smooth, intense green while the other was intricately carved, amazingly so. The leaves of a tree appeared to be hanging over the recessed scene of a fairy drinking from a pond. The detail was extraordinary. Staring, I felt like I was being drawn into the cool shadow of the sheltering branches.

It was delicate and perfect and now I was terrified I was going to break it before I had a chance to give it to her. "Do I want to know how much this thing is worth?"

"No. Hopefully, it will be enough to ensure your safe passage home."

Russell and Godfrey met us at the garage door. In a rare show of emotion, Russell handed me the sword I'd been practicing with and then hugged me. Godfrey, on the other hand, hung back, looking concerned.

Sword and sheath in hand, I asked, "Do I need this? I have my claws and I don't want to appear hostile."

"We don't know if they'll work, do we?" Godfrey said.

"If what'll work?"

"Your claws, Miss Quinn. We have no idea if you'll be able to shift in Faerie." Russell nodded toward Clive. "The Master can adjust that for you." He bowed a moment later, Godfrey a half second behind. "We are indebted. You are once again risking your life for our kind."

He was good, playing it up for anyone who was listening. Poor Russell and Clive. They really seemed to think they could get the nocturne to stop hating me. Good luck with that.

The drive to Colma was far quicker than it should have been. When Clive parked, it took all the courage I could muster to open the door and step out. I needed to be confident and controlled. Clive was worried enough for the both of us.

When we went through the gate, I heard low voices. Had The Wicche Glass opened again? Dang. Stepping through the mirror was going to be tricky now.

When we turned the corner into the courtyard, I stopped short. "What are you doing here?"

THIRTY-SIX

The Fellowship of the Sam

"Och, it's about time. No lollygagging. Let's go." Maggie, Dave's beautiful banshee girlfriend, was standing, arms crossed, expression annoyed. I hadn't seen her since she'd accused me of sleeping with Dave a few months ago. Pale Irish skin, long black hair, and big blue eyes, she'd been spitting mad and I'd been horribly confused. And terrified she'd let loose her banshee wail and crack the glass wall of The Slaughtered Lamb that held back tons of seawater. It had been a big misunderstanding, but I knew she'd felt guilty for the accusation afterward. It was probably why she was here today.

Chairs scraped against the slate tiles as Grim, the grumpy dwarf who'd been sitting on my last stool since my bookstore and bar had opened, and Liam, my kind selkie friend who was still recovering from his possession, stood.

"I don't understand. What are you all doing here?"

"As you said this evening"—Clive wrapped his arm around me —"you have fae friends. These three volunteered to go with you."

My eyes flooded. I wasn't alone.

"None of that!" Maggie shouted. "He's paying us, so keep the tears in check." She pointed to the huge, gnarled tree roots. "There's a pixie that wants to talk to you. Then we go."

I moved toward Martha's grave and saw Pippin standing on the topmost root. "Hello."

"I'mgoingwithyou."

As before, it took a moment for my mind to translate his fast, high-pitched words. "With me?"

"Oh, no you're bloody well not, pixie man. I won't have your chirpy little voice in my ears the whole way." Maggie glared at Pippin.

"Gofuckyourself,banshee."

"Well, this ought to be fun." As Grim and Liam looked rather miserable at the prospect of our journey, I added, "Regardless of what you promised Clive, you don't have to go if you don't want to."

Clive's arm tightened around my waist. "Yes they do."

"Wedon'tneedanyofthem.I'lltakeyou." Pippin hopped off the root and swaggered over to me.

Clive went down on one knee and looped the sword sheath around my waist and thigh, his hands lingering on my hips, not wanting this final task to be done. Reluctantly, he stood.

"Okay, so we're all clear. We're just going to tell the queen we're hunting down Leticia. We're trying to keep the fae safe and then we're out of there, right?"

At their nods, we all moved to the tavern entrance.

"The mirror's on the back wall," I said.

"We can feel it," Grim grumbled as he stomped through the doorway.

Clive held me back, pulling me into his arms. "I know you," he whispered in my ear. "When you're thinking about doing some horribly selfless thing, remember you have become necessary for my survival." Kissing my neck, he took my hand and led me toward the others who were gathered around the mirror.

"It's strong, isn't it? That pull?"

My four fae traveling companions all turned to me. "You feel it?" Liam asked.

"Of course."

He turned to Clive. "Do you feel it?"

Shaking his head, he said, "Nothing."

Liam's head tilted to the side as he studied me. "Odd."

Grim leaned over and picked up Pippin, letting him ride on his shoulder. They were the first to step into the mirror. The surface rippled, like a large stone had been dropped into a still lake. Maggie didn't give us a backward glance before she followed them in.

Liam paused. Eyes averted, he said, "We'll look after her." Then he, too, was through the portal.

"Looks like it's my turn through the looking glass."

"Just make sure you hurry home, Alice." Clive checked my backpack and sword again, reticent to say goodbye.

"I'll be back in no time." Please, let that be the truth. "We have a wedding to plan, after all. I'm sorry I'll miss the engagement party."

"Don't remind me," he groused. "You better go. Time is different in Faerie. They might already have been waiting a few days for you."

"Jeez, I hope not. Maggie already hates me."

"She doesn't hate you. She's afraid of leaving Dave, of not getting back. The same as we all are."

"Right." I kissed him with all I could muster and then stepped into the frame. "I love you!"

The words were echoing in my head as I looked around. Meadow. I was in a meadow blanketed with wildflowers: purples and blues and pinks and whites. Remembering, I spun around, looking for a way out and finding the massive trunk of an enormous tree. It was like the one on our side, the one they hollowed out for The Wicche Glass. Was this the backside of that same tree? Did it straddle the realms?

I pushed on the trunk, trying to find the portal, but only found bark.

"Isearchedthetree.Can'tfindawayback." Pippin sat on a high branch, watching me.

"It can be done, though. When that monster was beating the crap out of me, a warrior stepped through the mirror from this side and dragged the body back."

"Hmm." He popped up and raced around the tree again. "Don'tcallthemmonsters.Theyhatethat." Hopping over huge gnarled roots a minute later, he said, "Maybe.There'sasoftspoton-theback.Can'tfigureouthowtopushthrough.Mightneedagiftfrom-HerMagestytodoit."

"Where are the others?" The meadow, with a sparkling pond on the edge, was surrounded by deep, dark woods. Tiny, colorful creatures flitted over the water. "Are those fairies?"

Pippin followed my gaze. "Aye."

"The others?" This was idyllic, but we had a job to do.

"Searching.Noneofushaveusedthisentrance.They'retry-ingtofindwhichwaytothepalace." He tapped my ankle and pointed up. "CanI?"

"Oh, sure." I reached down to pick him up and he scrambled up my arm to sit on my shoulder. "Okay?"

"Aye."

"Couldn't we just ask the fairies which way to go?" I took one step into the meadow and Pippin yanked my earlobe. "Hey!"

"Watchwhereyou'restepping.Flowerfairiesareeverywhere.Y-ousquishone,andtherestwillhuntyoudown."

"Oh." I stepped back onto the moss at the base of the tree. "Will the others be back soon?"

"Theysetoutrightbeforeyousteppedthrough.Beaminute."

While we waited, I tried to find Clive in my mind, assure him I was all right. There was nothing. I was completely cut off from the dead. Mostly. There was something there, something I couldn't quite reach.

"Got it," Grim's deep, gravelly voice broke the silence. He pointed past the pond. "That way. Not too far."

A few minutes later, Liam and Maggie returned. Grim pointed and we headed out. I thought I was being careful where I stepped, but still Pippin pulled my ear every time I was about to step on a mushroom or a tree root. The others seemed to instinctively know where they could place their feet, so I followed in their footsteps and stopped getting my ear pulled.

The forest was thick in all directions. Lush and green. Trunks were festooned with flowering vines. They hung like garlands between trees. The forest floor was covered in moss, dotted with tiny white flowers.

The path turned and we were walking through a much darker, denser portion of the woods. An icy breeze was at my back, making me shiver. Breathing. I was hearing breathing and felt someone's eyes on me. When I turned my head, searching for the source, Pippin tugged my ear and quietly whispered, "Don'tlook."

A vine dropped from a branch above. I lifted my hand to brush it out of the way but received another tug. Understanding in that second that the vine would have snatched me away had I touched it, I ducked underneath and kept going. Pippin patted my shoulder.

My four companions and I were silent. We all felt the menace studying us, deciding, so we tried to do nothing to incite its ire. Thankfully, ten very tense minutes later, the path turned again and the dark presence weighing on us lifted.

Just to be safe, I waited a few more minutes before saying, "Thank you guys for coming. Without you, I'd still be in the meadow, getting pummeled by fairies for stepping on flowers."

Maggie forced a laugh, glancing uneasily around. "Those little hussies are right vicious."

Grim grunted at that.

When I got too distracted by the beauty around me, Pippin would flick my ear, reminding me to pay attention. We'd only walked a half mile or so when the light changed. The trees were farther apart. Dappled sunlight led the way out.

I'd started hearing the buzz of voices a while ago, but as we stepped out from the trees, I was hit with a dizzying array of creatures: all shapes, sizes, and colors. Although many had a humanoid form, certainly not all did. Some resembled nothing so much as a rhino or a gorilla. Fairies in an array of glittering colors flitted this way and that. Someone who looked very much like a horse trotted by, nodding to the vendors who called out to him.

Colorful pennants flapped in the breeze, leading the way to the white palace. Vendors had stalls along the sides of the dirt road: food, drinks, fabrics, jewelry, oils, herbs…I could have spent the afternoon exploring their goods, but there was no time. When I appeared a bit too interested in a jewelry stand, I was given an ear flick. Right. Focus.

Scanning the crowded, chaotic road ahead, I looked for my companions and realized I'd lost them. I was hurrying to catch up when a man stepped into my path. He was tall and quite thin, with a long face and razor-sharp cheekbones. Large black eyes and a bluish cast to his skin, he wore a black tunic and trousers with a complicated belt that held two daggers.

He looked me up and down hungrily, and I tasted bile at the back of my throat. "And who do we have here?"

Heart lodged in my throat, I searched for my companions again but couldn't find any of them. Stupid. I let Faerie cast its spell and distract me. "I come seeking an audience with the queen. I have a message from…the human realm."

He moved closer, inhaling my scent. "Why don't you give me the message then?"

I stepped back and tried to move around him, but no matter which way I went, he was right in front of me.

"Whydon'tyoufuckoff?" Pippin said, brandishing his tiny sword.

It was too fast. Even I could barely register the movement. I felt a breeze at my neck and then his dagger was back in his belt and Pippin was no longer on my shoulder. No! Frantic, I spun, looking for my pixie friend. *Please, don't let him be dead.*

Finally, I saw him on the top of a vendor's cart. He was holding his head, but he was alive. "Pippin, are you okay?" I tried to move forward, to get him back, when long, thin, steely arms slid around my waist.

A voice breathed at my ear, "You turn your back on me? That's going to cost you."

I froze, trembling, terrified.

His nose caressed my cheek. "I'll just have to think of a way for you to make it up to me."

The people around us showed no interest; indeed they were all looking away from us. When one of his long, bony hands slid between my legs, I couldn't think past *never again*. My claws shot out, thankfully proving I could shift in Faerie. I stabbed them over my head, where I knew his head to be, and then yanked him over my shoulder, slamming him to the ground. Silvery blood was already running down his face. He was reaching for both knives when I sliced my claws though his neck, sending his head spinning away.

Silence. Every fae creature had stopped what they were doing and was silently staring at the dead fae at my feet. Then their gazes fixed on me, wobbly, hyperventilating me. *Fuuuuuuucccckkkk*. One job. I had one job.

Marching feet were moving in my direction. I couldn't run. I had no idea where to go. Besides, I still needed to talk with the queen. And where were Grim, Liam, and Maggie? Had we been separated on purpose?

I plucked Pippin off the cart and moved toward the palace. The fae stared but got out of my way. "Maggie!" I ran through the tents and around vending carts, looking for my friends. "Grim! Liam!"

When I made it back to the main road, I didn't get more than a few steps before a wall of warriors was blocking me. The wall consisted of three warriors, but they were quite broad. The ones on each side had their swords drawn. The one in the middle had his arms crossed over his impressive chest, studying me.

"You have taken a life. Yours is now forfeit," he declared, voice hard and cold.

Clive was going to kill me. "I've come to deliver a message to the queen. That man laid hands on me first. I defended myself."

"That may be true. It may not. Regardless, you'll come with us now."

"But—"

Something sharp poked my back. I spun and found two more warriors with their swords drawn. Understanding I had no choice, I turned back, nodded, and followed the men, though I still scanned the crowd, looking for the others.

The men were stripped to the waist, with a leather bandoleer holding daggers looped across their muscular chests. At their waists were sheaths for swords, one on each side. The bottom halves of their bodies were clothed in breeches tucked into boots.

They marched me past a dizzying array of fae, all of whom had given up even the pretense of doing anything other than watching them escort me to the steps of the white marble palace. It had domes and turrets and was everything a fairy-tale castle should be.

The soldiers shoved me to my knees and then stepped back, ranging around me, ready to attack if I tried to escape. The one in charge unsheathed his sword and motioned to my hands. "How did you do that?"

Assuming he meant my claws, I said, "I'm a werewolf."

"Yes, I know. You shouldn't be able to shift in Faerie, though. How did you?" He didn't sound angry, more curious.

It hit me then. I knew that face. I'd been battered and bloody, looking up at him from the tavern floor. He was the one who'd stepped through the mirror in the Wicche Glass to drag the Orc who'd attacked me back into Faerie. How had he come through in the opposite direction?

"I'm the last descendent of the origin."

"Is that how you were able to survive against my soldier?"

Damn, if that monster was a soldier, I could only hope he didn't have a platoon at the ready. Out of the corner of my eye, I saw movement. Maggie, Grim, and Liam were being herded to the palace steps as well.

"Why did you send a soldier to kill me?"

"Not to kill you. Test you." He glanced at my friends before focusing on me once more. "What message do you have for my mistress Gloriana?"

I hesitated a moment, not knowing if I should tell anyone other than the queen herself or if that would add to my crimes against Faerie. When Pippin flicked me, I said, "There is a vampire in our realm who is killing the fae."

The change in the warrior was immediate. He'd been ridiculously scary before. In that instant, his expression turned fierce and unforgiving. Muscles taut and ready to spring, he leaned in, forcing me to cringe back as I stared up into his enraged face.

"Who is killing my people?" The question dripped from his lips, one poisoned word at a time.

THIRTY-SEVEN

In Sheep's Clothing

"Her name is Leticia. We're hunting her, trying to stop her, but ingesting fae blood has changed her scent, her psychic signature. We'll get her, but we wanted the queen to know that we weren't ignoring the deaths of her people. Clive, the Master of San Francisco, is even now setting a trap for her."

Tilting his head, he studied me, still furious but confused now too. "Psychic signature?"

I shot a quick glance at my friends but found varying degrees of awe and fear directed at the warrior. *Fuck me. One job!* Since death was apparently imminent, I did my best to calmly redirect and relay the message properly.

"Clive is a vampire—"

The warrior hissed, disgust mingling with fury.

"—who has presided over the supernatural community of San Francisco—fae included—for hundreds of years. He is an honorable leader. Leticia, also a vampire, is trying to kill him, and is using fae blood to mask her scent, to hide from Clive, who is a skilled tracker. He's—"

"You love this vampire." He sheathed his sword and then crossed his arms over his chest again, baffled. "They're dead. Reanimated corpses."

"Yes and no, mostly no. I'm a werewolf, as you know, but I'm also a wicche. A necromancer, to be precise. I can communicate with the dead and all that, but as vampires are kind of dead, I can do the same with them."

Eyes intent, he towered over me menacingly. "Explain."

"The psychic signature I mentioned earlier. I can feel the vampires in my head, know where they are." When he eased back, I went on, sweat rolling down my spine. "Leticia has been hard to find because she's feeding on other supernaturals. At first, it was a werewolf, but I put him out of his misery and took that avenue away from her. Now she's attacking the fae. The supernatural blood changes her chemistry, making her hard to find, at least until her body absorbs the blood. We will find and kill her, though. I came to explain to the queen why it hadn't happened yet."

At the soft mutters behind me, I turned to see a crowd had formed. The warriors were still circled around me, but behind them was a multitude of fae, watching and listening. *Damn it.* There was no way I was getting out of here alive.

The warrior shoved my shoulder to get my attention and said, "And why shouldn't we march into your realm and kill every last one of you for what she's done to our people?" Fury once more danced in his eyes. The grunts and chest pounding behind me said they were all ready to go to war.

Swallowing, feeling lightheaded, I said, "We came at great personal risk because we wanted to show our respect for Faerie, to let her know that we would police our own in order to protect hers. We know your forces are great, but we're trying to avoid the destruction of innocents."

I paused, glancing at my travel companions. They looked terrified. Well, not Grim. He always looked grim, but Maggie and Liam appeared rightfully thunderstruck by the warrior.

"Perhaps I shouldn't have come. In our culture, communicating a problem right away, even if it casts us in a bad light, is a sign of respect and an acknowledgment that the problem is ours to resolve."

"And how do you plan to repay us for the lives lost?" His sword was once more in his meaty grip. I hadn't even seen him unsheathe it. Some in the crowd took up the question, demanding the payment of our lives for the ones lost.

I was going to get my friends killed. Stomach roiling, I tried to take long, slow breaths while my thumb worried the back of my engagement ring. Glancing around again, I saw a familiar face in the crowd. Galadriel stood to the side, watching, listening.

"A life can never be repaid. It's a gift, a fragile and ephemeral one. People are taken from us, most far too soon no matter the length of their lives."

I thought of my mother, the father I barely remembered, the great-aunt I'd only just met, and—no, I wouldn't grieve the loss of Clive until that sword the warrior kept fingering ran me through. "We're given a finite amount of time to live. In your realm, the life is much longer than in mine, but the loss is, I imagine, the same."

I thought a moment. "Do you have dandelions here?" At his blank face, I rushed on. "It's a kind of flowering weed. It looks like a puff ball on a long stalk, but if you look closely, you see hundreds of tiny, fuzzy stars, perfect and amazing. When a breeze blows, those stars are carried on the wind, far and wide.

"It's the same for a life. We grow in adversity, fighting to survive, often keeping that part of us that is unique and dazzling hidden behind the mundane. And like the dandelion, our lives reach far beyond what we guess. So," I said, shrugging, "can we repay your lost people? No. No one can repay a life. It's too great, too far-reaching a miracle to be reduced to payments."

I made the mistake of glancing again at Galadriel and found glassy eyes staring back. I wouldn't cry, couldn't show weakness. I had to make sure my friends and I made it out.

"A life for a life," he said, to the cheers of the crowd.

"I've heard that saying, too. It's a lie, though. Taking a life doesn't bring another back. It deprives the world of two lives. Killing me in payment for the mermaid helps no one."

"I disagree. It would help *me* a great deal," the warrior sneered, his guards chuckling.

Swallowing, I fisted my hands at my side, trying to hide the trembling. "It might make you feel better in the moment, but my death won't return that mermaid to the ocean. Deaths, like lives, affect many. I am beloved by an ancient and powerful being. Revenge begets more revenge."

"Perhaps."

"May I see your queen and deliver my message?" If I couldn't talk with the queen, this would have all been for nothing.

"And what would you say to her that you haven't already said here?" He backed up a few paces, as though getting out of the splash zone when one of his men ran me through.

Good question. "I suppose I'd ask Her Majesty if she could give us the time to right another's wrong. We know Faerie holds her own quite dear, so—"

"And what do you hold dear, Samantha?" The warrior had begun to pace in front of me. A plan was no doubt forming.

How did he know my name? "My friends here." I inclined my head toward where Maggie, Grim, and Liam were being held at swordpoint, before gesturing to Pippin on my shoulder. "They are, each of them, a credit to Faerie and shouldn't be punished for my own missteps or for what was done to that poor mermaid."

"The queen deals with her own people as she sees fit," the warrior grumbled.

"Of course."

"Nothing else?" he asked.

"I hold a great many things dear. Foremost is Clive. I love him with all my heart. We plan to marry soon."

He stopped pacing at that. "You'd bind yourself to a corpse?"

"He's only mostly dead." A grin threatened at our familiar joke. "I hold dear my bookstore and bar, my friends Dave and Owen, Meg and Stheno, Russell and Godfrey, George and Coco…" I was suddenly struck by how much my life had changed, how full it had become when I wasn't looking.

"If you had asked me even a year ago what I held dear, I'd have said my life and The Slaughtered Lamb." I glanced at the wall of guards, swords drawn, and shrugged. "I might be safer sticking to home, shutting everyone out, but even if you kill me on the spot, I will have experienced more, loved more, in these last few months than I ever thought possible. I'm standing in Faerie, jeered at by the fae, threatened by her warriors, and completely alive."

Back to pacing, he asked, "And what will your mate do if I decide to take your life in payment?"

I grinned now, not being able to help myself. "He'll cuss me out for getting myself killed." Tears formed, thinking of him on his own again. "He'll fly into a rage, gather an army of vampires, and declare war on Faerie. Regardless of whether or not they'd win, you'd have a legion of supernatural killers tearing through your people. Eventually, glutted with fae blood, he'll grieve, and that will be even more terrifying."

"You seem quite sure of yourself," he said.

I glanced back up at him, confused. "Not me. Him. I'm quite sure of him."

When he resumed pacing, I felt off balance. The warrior looked different. It was subtle, but he was shorter, thinner. When he turned back to me, I couldn't focus on anything but his eyes. They'd been dark brown only moments ago, but now they were a mesmerizing kaleidoscope of colors.

"And what would you give to avoid war?" His voice was higher, more melodious.

"Anything."

When he stopped in front of me and she finally dropped her glamour, I knew I was speaking with the queen herself. The crowd, who no doubt knew it was her all along, bowed when she showed her true face. I was like a deer in headlights, staring into her eyes.

"How about that pendant around your neck?" She leaned in, studying it.

I touched the carved dragon and shook my head. "I'm sorry. It's not mine to give. Benvair, matriarch of the dragon clan, loaned me this heirloom to keep me safe. I can't offer another's treasure as though it were my own."

Annoyance flitted across her face. "And that ring you haven't been able to stop touching since you arrived in my realm?"

I pulled it off my finger and offered it to her.

"So easily?" She took it from me and studied it, appreciation glowing in her expression, before slipping it on her own finger.

"Not easily, no, but it's a symbol, not the love itself. That ring means the world to me because Clive means the world to me. I gladly give it to you, though, in hopes of seeing him again."

She broke eye contact with me, flicked her fingers, and the swords pointed at my friends were sheathed. It was hard to look at Gloriana herself. She radiated power clothed in ethereal beauty. When she glided back to me, her hypnotic eyes filled my vision once more.

"You, Samantha of Clan Quinn, are one of mine," she whispered.

I hated to disagree with a queen. "Ma'am, I'm not fae. I'm werewolf and wicche."

I felt her anger boil my blood for an instant. "One drop of fae blood makes you one of mine. And you, little one"—she tapped my forehead—"have more than a drop."

All I could get out was, "How?"

"Did you know that the wicche who created werewolves was a Corey?" At my blank stare, she continued, "And did you further know the only reason she was able to do it was because she had fae blood running through her veins? All those in the original line of wolves carry her blood, which is my blood. It's why I sent my soldier to test you. I was curious. So many generations later, the first female, was my magic still strong in your blood?"

My stomach dropped. Every time I finally got my feet firmly planted, someone came along to sweep them out from under me again. "And is it?"

THIRTY-EIGHT

What Kind of a Psycho Wears a Hat?

S he beamed, her glittering radiance making my heart sing. "Oh, yes." She pulled a tiny gold band from her finger. "Take this in exchange for the ring you have offered me. With it, you will be able to find your way back into Faerie so that we may speak again."

It was a thin gold band, etched with symbols that sparkled in the sunlight. Her hands were far more delicate than my own, so I slid the ring onto my pinky.

"And I expect an invitation to the wedding."

Sound returned. I hadn't noticed its absence, but when the queen moved away from me, it was like a cone of silence had been lifted. Had the crowd seen us talking, the ring? I thought not, as Maggie, Grim, and Liam's guards were just now dropping their hands from the hilts of their swords. She'd given us a moment out of time to talk.

"You may go now," she said as she walked up the steps into her palace. "I give you safe passage. You will take care of this threat before I decide to do it myself."

I stood and bowed with her people. "Thank you. We will."

The journey back to the tree was delightfully uneventful. The queen had promised safe passage and none of the fae chanced her displeasure. Even that evil sentinel we'd encountered on the way in was absent on our walk back.

"Whyarewegoingbacktothetree?" Pippin chirped.

"Because Sam said she knew a way through. Now shut up about it. The question's been asked and answered twice." Maggie's patience was running thin.

We were all a little shaky. Clearly, I wasn't the only one who'd thought they weren't getting out of Faerie alive.

When we returned to the tree, we circled the massive trunk to the back, where Pippin thought there was a veil between the realms. "I have no idea if this will work, but just to be on the safe side, everyone hold hands." At their confused looks, I added, "In a chain. Pippin, hold my ear." I held out my left hand to Maggie. The queen's ring was on my right and I wanted to lead with that hand.

Once Liam and Grim had joined the chain, I touched the trunk where Pippin had indicated. The bark shimmered a moment and then the mirror appeared. Stepping back through the looking glass, I held tight to Maggie. Everyone had to make it back with me.

A moment later, the five of us were standing in The Wicche Glass Tavern. Pippin whooped and jumped off my shoulder, racing out of the dark tavern.

"Thank you so much for coming with me."

"Eh, I told you. We got paid." Maggie picked up her phone. She'd left it sitting on the bar. Tapping the screen, she said, "Two days." She glanced at Liam and Grim. "Far better than we were expecting."

"I'd thought a month, at least," Grim grumbled.

"Aye." Maggie grinned. "At the very least. So," she said, tapping on the screen again, "it's almost dead but there should be enough to call for a pickup."

While Maggie called Dave, I went behind the bar to see if there was anything left after Abigail and her demon had trashed the place. The bottles had been smashed, but the tap lines seemed to still be working. I found a mug in a cabinet and poured Grim a mead, sliding it down to the end of the bar that had no stools. He reached up, snatched the mug, and downed it in one. He drank the refill a little more slowly.

I went through the bar refrigerator and found a bottle of champagne. Our continued existence seemed reason for celebrating. I popped the cork and filled a chipped coffee cup, a dented tumbler, and a shot glass for Liam, Maggie, and myself. The three of us clinked containers—Grim couldn't be bothered—and we downed ours, as well.

On our second cup, Grim's third, heavy footsteps crossed the courtyard outside. Dave's muscular frame filled the doorway. When he stalked across the bar, eyes intent on Maggie, I had to look away. A moment later, she was in his arms as he continued to walk her back into the hall, out of sight. I poured Liam and me another cup, assuming we had some time.

Later, when Dave dropped me off in front of the nocturne, it was well past midnight. This was prime vamp time, but the place felt empty. There was only one guard at the gate, who reluctantly opened it after glaring at me for five full seconds. Asshole.

Walking through the front door, I reached out for Clive but didn't find him. I did, however, find Godfrey. He was sitting in Clive's study, his feet on the desk, playing on his phone.

"And Amélie really thought you wanted your own city." I shook my head as I walked in, remembering the ploy used in New Orleans to get Godfrey to betray Clive.

Godfrey grinned and popped up. "Thank God. It's been a yawn around here since you've been gone, and his highness has been in a right foul mood." He surprised me by pulling me into a hug. "How are you back so soon? Clive thought you likely gone for weeks."

"The queen took pity on me and gave us access to a shortcut." I dropped my pack and then remembered the delicate carving I was supposed to give Gloriana. Dropping to my knees, I unzipped the backpack, burrowing into soft tees, looking for the jade gift. I pulled out the cloth I'd wrapped it in, but it was empty. Something fluttered to the carpet. It was a folded note on white linen parchment. It read, *It's lovely. Thank you.*

Shaking my head, I pocketed the note. It's not every day Faerie herself gives you a thank you card. "So where are Clive and Russell?"

"Your engagement party."

"That's tonight?" I grabbed my bag and ran toward the door.

"Oh, sunshine," Godfrey called.

Skidding to a stop in the hall, I ducked my head back in.

"You're already there, remember?" Eyebrows raised, he leaned back on the desk and waited for me to find a solution.

"It's a masquerade party, right?" At his nod, I continued, "So I get all gussied up, wear a mask, slip in, and take over. We can pretend I'm a dick and needed to do a costume change."

"Pretend?" He tilted his head, considering.

"Ha ha. So who's playing me?" I hadn't thought to ask before.

"As you're the only werewolf-wicche around, we had to improvise. Medusa thought it would be a kick, so..." He shrugged. "She's wearing your clothes and is sticking close to Clive to muddle scents. Let's face it: Most have no idea what a gorgon smells like, so we thought it might work. Of course, there's a better than good chance the entire supernatural community thinks you're an unmitigated lush by this point."

Great. "But she's shorter and more built than me." We weren't the same body type at all.

"Eh. High heels, the right kind of dress, hat, mask."

"Hat?"

"Her hair's black."

"I'm walking around the party in a hat drinking straight from the bottle, aren't I? Jeez," I muttered. "Clive's marrying a real asshole." I started to leave again and then stopped. "You can drive me, right?"

He shook his head. "Sorry, love. I'm guarding the nocturne tonight."

"So I'm jogging in heels and an evening gown?" The euphoria of a minute ago was well and truly gone.

"I can have someone drive you."

"Hard pass. Your guys will wrap the car around a tree in the hopes of killing me. No thanks." I guessed I could hold the heels and jog over in running shoes. I'd still look stupid, but what choice did I have? I'd promised Dave I wouldn't drive alone. I couldn't wait to get my license and go anywhere I wanted.

"Audrey would never let anything happen to you."

Audrey? I hadn't thought of her. "Yes, please."

"Good." He nodded, tapping the screen of his phone. "You go get ready and Audrey will be waiting out front for you."

"Thank you!" I shouted, running down the hall. I raced up the steps, dumped my stuff in my bedroom, and then dove into the shower.

Wrapped in a towel, I went to the closet. Medusa had made a mess of the place. Discarded gowns were lying on the floor. What the hell? Who does that? I hung them back up and then looked for anything that wasn't horribly wrinkled.

There was one in the corner, still in a garment bag. I unzipped it and almost gasped. It was a deep indigo that turned to eggplant as it moved in the light. Long, slinky, it slid along my fingers like liquid. I was hesitant to touch it, let alone put it on. I pulled it out of the bag and hung it up beside the mirror. Stunning.

I found a box with heels the same hue. Knowing I'd need to do a lot of work to do this dress justice, I got to it. Buffing, polishing, moisturizing, blowing dry, brushing out, I used the good hair stuff Owen had recommended. Consequently, my brown hair now showed highlights of gold and red. It was glossy, with a bit of a wave. I wore it long, having no idea how to do a complicated updo.

Wait! I knew someone who could. I called Godfrey and asked if he could send Audrey up. While I waited, I did my best with makeup. My expertise tapped out at mascara and lipstick, though.

When there was a knock at the door, I was in the dress. Closing my eyes, I checked first. No need to let in a bad guy. It was Audrey.

She *did* gasp. "Oh, miss. You're pretty as a picture."

Grinning, I spun. The form-fitting column flared at the bottom. "Isn't it beautiful?"

"Aye. That fabric." She reached out to touch and then stopped herself, no doubt remembering I was the Master's fiancé. "Sorry, miss."

I held out my arm for her to feel the soft, shimmering fabric. "I have no idea what it is, but I'm having a hard time not staring at it, myself." Moving out of the doorway, I waved her in. "I hoped you'd be willing to do me a favor."

"Anything, miss." Audrey almost stopped herself from bobbing in a quick curtsy. Almost.

"Could you make my hair look as good as this dress?"

Smiling shyly, she said, "I've been itching to get my hands in your hair for quite some time. Now," she said, ushering me to my own vanity, "we need a style that matches this gown. Sit." She ran her hands through my hair, thinking. "The streak is natural?"

"Yeah. Long story." Grimacing, I added, "Sorry. I only have rubber hair ties." I opened the drawer to show her a pile of colorful bands.

She waved that idea away, closing the drawer and pulling a thin case from her pocket. "I always have my hair things with me, miss."

Not wanting to bug her, I sat straight and kept my mouth shut.

After a few minutes of Audrey playing with my hair, she said, "I've an idea."

"Great. You do whatever you want back there." How odd it must have been to have had a ladies' maid, hovering and fussing all the time. Of course, it was darn handy right now.

Sooner than I would have thought possible, she had loosely braided my hair like a headband and then pulled up the weighty mass into a curly, messy bun. I assumed she was going to do one of those sleek chignon styles that Benvair preferred, but she went the other way.

"Your hair should complement the dress, miss, but all of it needs to complement you. You're not a cold, sophisticated person. The loose, sexy bun is you. This isn't a costume. This is fun, sexy Sam, all dressed up." She patted my shoulder. "Trust me, miss."

"I do. Completely." She was right. About all of it. I looked like me, just gussied up.

"What jewelry are you going to wear?"

I pointed to the box on the shelf to my left. She pulled it down and opened the top. It was embarrassing. Every time I turned around, there were new pieces. In fact, that wasn't even the same box. This one was bigger.

Audrey closed the box as quickly as she'd opened it and continued to look on the shelves.

"So, no?" I was confused.

"That was everyday jewelry. We're looking for the good pieces."

I thought those were all really good pieces.

She opened a drawer and nodded. "Here we are." Opening and closing thin cases, she finally said, "These, miss." She handed me square opal earrings, surrounded by triangular diamonds. They matched the dress and the ring I'd given the Faerie Queen.

The dragon pendant was thin and rested against my chest under the neckline. The wicche glass hung between my breasts, so neither was visible. "Do I need a necklace, or are the earrings good?"

Audrey started to roll her eyes and then caught herself. "The questions you ask, miss." She drew out a diamond choker. My stomach dropped at the thought of wearing something so expensive. Exquisite, the necklace looked like an Art Deco masterpiece. Audrey slipped it around my neck, and it sat right over the neckline of the dress. Perfect.

"The clasp is strong, right? It's not going to fall off and get lost?"

"No, miss." She touched up my makeup. A few strokes and my face was as dressed up as the rest of me. Glancing around the dressing room portion of the closet, she said, "You need an evening bag." Opening another drawer, she found an array. She chose two and offered them to me. One was a beautiful, brushed silver and the other a fan of blues, greens, and purples like a peacock feather. I went with the peacock.

"I'll wait for you downstairs, miss." Audrey left and I studied myself in the mirror. It was a far cry from my baggy jeans, zombie tees, and braids, but I guessed this was me too. When I began to feel adrift, I remembered that Clive liked me best in running shoes and my racing heart settled. No one was trying to change me. Marriage to Clive didn't mean losing myself. I was still me, just more formally attired this evening.

Of course, if I'd realized then how the night would turn out, I'd have ditched the jewels for running shoes.

THIRTY-NINE

The Thing About the Ring

When I got in the car, I sent a text to Owen and George, telling them I was on my way and to maneuver Medusa toward the front door. I also told them not to alert Clive. I wanted to surprise him.

"Thank you, Audrey, for everything." As she pulled to the curb, I studied the mansion. "I don't want to embarrass Clive." I touched my hair. "You made sure I won't."

Opening the door, I stepped out and then heard, "Miss?"

I leaned in the door. "Yes?"

"Well." Her hands fidgeted on the steering wheel. "It's just, I know what the others say, what they think about you and the Master." She looked up then. "I don't hold with any of that, miss. The Master's lucky to have found you, and that's that." Giving a decisive nod, she added, "You have a lovely evening."

"Thank you, Audrey." I closed the door, my throat tight as she drove away.

Texting Owen and George again, I let them know I was on the front porch. A few minutes later, the door swung open, Owen and George hustling Medusa out between them. She was wearing a long black gown with an enormous wrap in a watery green color and a half mask that matched. All of that would have been fine if she hadn't topped it off with a black knit beanie.

Medusa looked me up and down, huge wine glass filled to the brim in her hand. "Thank the gods. This party is boring as fuck. I thought there'd be strippers. What kind of party doesn't have strippers?" Shaking her head, she walked down the stairs.

"Wait. I need the mask."

When she flung it over her shoulder, George leaped down the stairs to catch it.

I stared after the retreating gorgon as she headed down the sidewalk toward the house she and her sisters were renting. "What. The. Hell? How did anyone believe that was me?"

"They didn't," George said as he handed me a mask that smelled strongly of red wine. "Everyone in there is convinced Clive killed you, either accidentally or by design. No one wants to call him on it, though. They're taking bets as to when he announces you ran away or got into a car accident."

"Wow. Nice to know people give a shit I was turned into a vampire juice box." I wasn't sure I wanted to go in anymore. Where were the pitchforks? The angry mobs looking for vengeance? Jeez. Serve people drinks for seven years and they step over your corpse for fancy hors d'oeuvres.

Owen approached me nervously. What was that about? "I'm really sorry for the way I acted before, the things I said to you."

It took me a minute. "Holy crap, Owen, that wasn't your fault. *I'm* the one who's sorry for having an asshole aunt who tried to possess you." I pulled him into a hug. "None of this was your fault. None of it."

George ran his hand up and down my back, no doubt thanking me for letting his fella off the hook.

"Look at it this way," I said, finally letting him go. "Dave actually tried to kill me, burned my neck and everything. You just said some harsh stuff." I shrugged. "And nothing I didn't deserve." I handed him the mask. "Can you get this on me so it doesn't mess up the fancy hair Audrey gave me?"

He did and then all three of us waltzed into my engagement party. As we walked through the entry, George leaned over and whispered, "And those of us that would have killed Clive for hurting you were in on the plan."

Good point. I was feeling better when I spotted Clive across the crowded living room. I'd barely stepped over the threshold, when he spun, eyes vamp black and stalked toward me. Everyone got out of his way.

And then he was kissing me and kissing me and kissing me. We held tight, both of us knowing how easily it could have gone the other way, how easily I might not have made it out of Faerie. When we finally broke apart, all the guests had moved to a different part of the house.

"How are you back so soon?" Clive's eyes had returned to their usual stormy gray. He leaned back, gaze traveling over me. "You are…a vision."

Grinning, I took a better look at him as well. Clive in a tux. *Damn.* He took my hand and led me through the room and out onto the deck. I heard the murmur of voices and went to the railing to look over. The rest of the guests had moved to the lower level. It sounded as though a string quartet played inside.

Owen and George, along with other couples, danced under the moonlight. Russell stood at the edge of the gathering, looking up at us. When I waved, he nodded. His expression remained stoic as hell, but I could feel his relief at seeing me.

Clive pulled me into his arms and then we, too, were dancing. The moonlight's pull was strong. Full moon tomorrow. I couldn't wait to ditch this form and run, feel the earth under my paws as I raced through the forest.

He kissed me again, more softly, reverently. "I was worried."

"Me too."

Glancing over his shoulder at the moon, he turned back to me and whispered, "Soon. Your eyes have lightened since we've been out here."

"Soon," I agreed. And then we were dancing again, my head on his chest.

When I felt his lips on my forehead, I realized I'd started to drift. I was so sleepy. Snapping straight up, I looked around. Was my aunt screwing with me again?

"Problem?" Clive spun me around and danced me toward the opposite end of the deck.

"I started to fall asleep. I wasn't tired before."

He stiffened, his arms like metal bars around me. "Abigail?"

"I'm not sure, but it feels like her. Dave said her demon isn't allowed to hurt me." I patted my chest. "And I'm wearing Benvair's pendant." I thought about it a moment. "Sleep isn't violent. It might not be considered hurting me."

"Sleeping Beauty?"

I shrugged, leaning into him. "Maybe."

"Any sign of Leticia?"

Embarrassed, I internally face palmed. I'd forgotten why we were here. I was so happy to be home and with Clive, I'd neglected my role in the ruse. Tipping my head to his shoulder again, I reached out, searching for her. The vamps at the party popped into my mind immediately. The green glut at the nocturne was as it should be. A few vamps were on the town. I continued to hunt, though, for that odd, fae-colored overlay of the cold, green vamp blip. I shook my head, frustrated.

"Are you hungry?"

"Famished."

He'd started to walk me back into the house when I caught it. I pulled him back, wrapped my arms around his neck, and drew him into a passionate kiss. *There!* I felt the snap of anger and jealousy at the water's edge.

She's in the water, at the edge of the lower dock. I wormed my way into her thoughts and saw us from her perspective. Hey, we looked good together. I tried to yank her mind out, as I'd done with other vamps, but she'd recently fed on a kelpie. Damn kelpies, nothing but trouble.

Clive must have communicated with Russell because soon the people below ambled back in with talk of champagne and cake. They were trying to lure her in. It was too easy for her to disappear in the ocean. They wanted her on land so there was a fighting chance of catching her.

Clive nuzzled my cheek and then kissed my neck.

"I can't help but notice," he murmured, "your left ring finger is lighter than it should be."

"Oh. That." I tilted my head back, giving him better access. While his lips slid along my jaw, I considered how to break the news. "Here's the thing," I began. When his fangs grazed the side of my throat, I shivered and all thought drained from my head. What the man could do with his mouth…

"The thing?" He ran his nose along my temple, breathing me in as I often did him.

"Thing?" What thing?

"The ring thing," he prompted.

"Oh. Gah. Stop that. I can't think when you do that." Instead of stopping, he sunk into a long, deep kiss that had my body going up in flames and my brain shorting out.

Has she moved in?

What?

Leticia. Has she moved from the water?

Right. Shit. I had a job I was supposed to be doing. Reaching out, I found her right away. *Tree behind you.*

And like that, he winked out of sight. From the side of the deck, a vamp flew at me. He was one of Clive's, so I didn't want to kill him until I was sure he wasn't trying to rush me out of harm's way. When he tackled me, throwing us both over the rail, I was less understanding.

In the two seconds it took to hit the slate patio below, I had two thoughts: If he ruins this dress, I will kill him; and if I lose this necklace, I will kill him. Basically, his death was a done deal, but then I heard Leticia's voice in his head. Damn it! How was she controlling Clive's vamps?

I shouted at Russell in my mind, *Help Clive now! Tree. North side of the deck.*

It shouldn't have worked. I didn't have a connection with Russell as I did with Clive. It was possible Clive called him as well. Whatever the reason, I only saw a blur as Russell leaped off the deck into the huge cypress that separated the Drake estate from its neighbor.

I had the vamp who'd attacked under my control. He lay, gazing blankly up at the stars while I listened to branches creaking overhead. As I contemplated how Clive could reclaim his vamp, two more hopped the fences on either side of the yard and rushed me. Damn it! How many did she have?

I took control of both before they could touch me. Three lay at my feet when I felt two more vamps racing toward me from inside the house. When I dropped to my heels, taking control as they flew over my head, I heard a frustrated scream from above. Poor Leticia. She'd probably spent years putting these vamps under her power, and all for nothing.

It was then I noticed two sets of red eyes glowing in the dark. Two hulking black forms emerged from the water, lurching toward me. What the hell were they? The plip plop of water hitting the patio tiles reminded me of something. It niggled in the back of my mind. One of the hunks blew an annoyed breath through its nose and it all came back.

The Slaughtered Lamb had still been under construction when a kelpie used the ocean entrance to hunt up a late-night snack. He'd found me in the cavernous worksite, looking through book catalogs. I'd thought him a dream, believed I must have fallen asleep. How strange it had been to have a horse standing in my soon-to-be bar. It was the plip plop of seawater that had broken the spell then, too.

With each step, their hulking mass shifted until what was standing five feet from me was a pair of huge black horses with glowing red eyes and razor-sharp teeth glinting in the moonlight. Claws sliding from my fingertips, arms bulking up, jaw distending, I'd learned a few tricks in the intervening years. I wouldn't be running this time.

One put his nose down and snorted, like a bull getting ready to charge. Fine by me. When he pounced, I leaped, flipping onto his back. I raked my claws through his neck as he transformed, but he wasn't fast enough.

As the first faded into nothingness—Gloriana better not hold this against me. They started it—the second snapped, tearing flesh from my arm. It burned like a mofo but my arm still worked, which was all I cared about at the moment.

He backed away, trying to circle around me, no doubt looking for a weakness. I had a moment, less than, to realize how badly I'd fucked up. I'd been so distracted by the kelpies that I'd dropped my control of the five vamps at my feet. They flew at me from behind as the kelpie charged from the front.

There wasn't enough time. I was fast, but so were they. I spun, taking the first vamp's head, but couldn't complete the sweep before the other two had their fangs in my neck. Before one could rip my head off, I dove into their minds and yanked hard, channeling the pain into the wicche glass. I couldn't deal with pain and a kelpie at the same time.

The vamps dropped dead—for real this time—at my feet, and the kelpie lunged for my stomach, tearing away a chunk of flesh. Stifling a scream, I slammed the claws of both hands through the top of his head and struggled, muscles straining, as I ripped, inch by inch, through his skull, tearing his head in half.

When he winked out of existence, I dropped to the slate tiles. *Shit, that hurt!* There was movement above me, a blur really. Three silhouettes flew from branch to branch in the tree above. They grappled, branches creaked, and then Russell was thrown across the balcony. Leaping up, he raced back into the fray. None were giving an inch. It had to end tonight.

As the blood flowed from the kelpie's bites, I became colder and more numb. I wouldn't call Clive for help, couldn't distract him. He needed his total focus on Leticia.

"Sam!" Owen's shout broke the relative silence of the night. Leticia glanced down and then threw back her head, laughing. Clive ripped her head from her shoulders, the laugh turning into a strangled gurgle before her dust blew away in the wind.

Owen's gaze darted skyward, no doubt looking for dive-bombing vampires. George carried me inside, not even seeming to mind that I was bleeding all over him. Clive dropped to the patio a moment later, pursuing us into the house.

Reaching up with my good arm, I touched the diamond choker. *Whew*. Still there.

FORTY

Effing Kelpies!

I must have passed out for a minute because I awoke to raised voices.

"Why is Sam lying on a cold stone floor?" Clive ground out.

"I told my grandson to put her down. One surface is much the same as another when the patient is unconscious, and these floors are far easier to clean than bed linens and mattresses."

Heels clicked across the marble tile. When I opened my eyes, I saw Benvair elegantly dressed in a champagne-colored gown, studying me with a look of mild annoyance. No doubt my blood loss was wrecking her party.

"Sorry." I wasn't sure how she did it, but one disapproving look from her and all I wanted to do was quickly back out of the room, bowing and apologizing.

Clive dropped to his knees beside me. "Perhaps it wouldn't be too much to ask for a towel." He was seething and if he didn't calm down, he was about to alienate the dragon clan. "I can assure you a replacement will be delivered later today."

Benvair's eyes flashed and then she walked to the other side of the room.

"Stop," I whispered. "I'm fine."

"You're not, no. I'm kneeling in a pool of your blood. Again, I might add. And your hand is like ice."

That wasn't good.

"Russell has called Dr. Underfoot." Clive picked me up, cradling me in his arms.

"Fyffe is bringing something to staunch the bleeding," Benvair said.

"You made your choice, and now I've made mine." He spared her one look that had her backing up, and then he raced out the patio doors. Carrying me as gently as he could, he rounded the side of the house and stopped at the curb where Russell was waiting with the car. Carefully, he slid us into the back seat. "Go."

"You shouldn't piss off dragons." My voice was weaker than I'd thought, but he heard me.

"No, darling. *She* shouldn't piss off *me*." The cold fury in his voice made me shiver. "Russell, turn up the heat."

We were driving through the gates a moment later, so I may have passed out for a couple of minutes. Once the vehicle stopped, the doors flew open and Godfrey was helping Clive move me.

"Where?" Godfrey asked.

"Her bench in the study. Get bandages and blankets. A pillow."

It was weirdly disorienting being rushed through the nocturne. My head was flopping on Clive's arm, so I only saw snatches of things: a light fixture, a painting, flowers, two black-eyed vampires, an open doorway, a bookcase, Clive's desk, the study ceiling.

"I think my blood is exciting your people," I whispered.

"Go downstairs and feed," he called toward the open door.

Godfrey appeared with a pillow and a blanket. That was nice. When Russell stepped forward, he blocked the overhead light, so I could stop squinting. Cold and numb. When the kelpie first bit me, it was all fire and pain. Now I felt like I was drifting down a river in winter, floating this way and that as the currents swirled around me. I'd been hurt lots of times. Why was everyone so upset?

"What's th—" *matter?* My voice had given out, but I knew Clive would understand.

"You're not healing on your own. We don't know why." Clive turned to Russell and asked something about the doctor.

It was easy to ignore their voices. The rush and gurgle of the river filled my head.

"What's happened to you?"

I turned at the melodious and all too familiar voice. "Your Majesty."

"I heard your heartbeat slow. I thought these vampires were taking care of you." She spared an annoyed glance at the men who spoke nearby.

None of them turned to see that Faerie herself was with us. Maybe only I could see and hear her. Maybe this was a dream. "Damn kelpies attacked me."

"My soldiers did this to you, after I assured you safe passage?" She became incandescent with rage.

"It was on this side. They stepped out of the ocean." I didn't want her to think people in her own realm were ignoring her commands.

"They are ALL my subjects!" Her scream shook the windows.

The vamps stopped talking, gazes trained on the glass.

Dr. Underfoot rushed in behind Gloriana. He took one look at the back of his infuriated queen and dropped to his knees. The vamps as one turned to him, wearing matching expressions of confusion.

Gloriana barely glanced over her shoulder at the dwarf bowing at the door. "Yes, yes. I hear your heart giving out." She paced in front of the bench. "There is something wrong, something poisonous in this realm and it is infecting my people. You"—she pointed, my engagement ring on her finger—"will find the source of the problem and fix it."

"I'll do my best."

"You will make sure to do better than that." She flipped up the blanket covering me, laid one hand on my stomach and the other on my arm, the places where the kelpie had taken out chunks. Power and light shot through me. A flood of golden bubbles sparkled inside me. The cold river was gone and I was lying in a sun-drenched meadow.

She leaned over, her face, her incomparable beauty all I could see. "Don't expect me to come running again. You have a quest. I suggest you get up and start working on it."

An impact tremor shook the air and then sound returned.

Wonder bright in his eyes, Clive took my hand and sat on the edge of the bench. "Your heart. It slowed to a stop for a moment and then started again, healthy and strong."

Dr. Underfoot slowly got to his feet. He approached us warily, clearly not sure what to make of Faerie paying me a visit.

I caught Underfoot's eye. "I'm okay now."

"Of course you're not. Let him bandage your wounds." Clive laid his hand on the side of my face. Joy, relief, love, all of it was loud and clear in his touch.

"I doubt she left wounds," I said, sitting up. Clive tried to stop me from moving, but I patted his arm, scooted up, and then dropped my feet to the floor. "I didn't stain the bench, did I?"

Studying the torn and bloodied dress, I sighed. "Damn. I loved this one." Remembering, my hand shot to my neck. Diamond choker still in place. Fingers flying to my ears, I checked the opals too, and breathed a huge sigh of relief when they were both in place. I was not cut out to wear expensive things.

Sliding the blood-encrusted fabric aside, I looked at my arm and stomach. Both wounds were perfectly healed, skin like new, my scars a memory. I looked up and found Clive staring at my stomach as well. "Is it better or worse to have patches of unscarred skin?" I imagined it looked odd.

Clive rested his hand on my stomach. "How?"

"You'd have to ask Faerie." Ha. I felt it. Clive flinched. I doubt anyone saw it, but with his hand on me, I felt it.

"The windows rattling, our good doctor here on his knees, that was Faerie?" He was doing his best to sound calm and reasonable, but I could tell he was shook.

Nodding, I said, "Gloriana herself stood in your study." I nodded at the dwarf who still hadn't spoken. "Dr. Underfoot saw her."

He cleared his throat. "I did. Yes."

"Thank you so much for coming, but as you can see, I'm perfectly fine." I tapped Clive's arm. "Maybe we can get someone to drive you home, sir."

Underfoot blinked a few times in quick succession, checked his pockets, picked up his bag, and turned to the door. "Not at all," he mumbled as he walked out.

"Miss Quinn, it might be helpful if you explained to those of us who apparently cannot see the queen what happened." Russell closed the study door after the doctor and waited.

"Sure thing." I kicked off my heels—they miraculously still looked like new—and sat crossed-legged on the bench, both knees poking through holes in my dress. "Before we begin, though"—I turned to Clive—"is there any chance you can get a replacement on this dress? I really loved it."

"Anything you want." He shook his head in wonder and leaned back. "You were saying?"

I relayed everything that had happened in Faerie, her two guises, what she'd said to me, the exchange of rings, and then I explained what had just happened.

"Wait," Godfrey began. "Gloriana expects an invitation to the wedding?" Laughing, he plopped down in one of the chairs.

"You're part fae as well?" Russell asked, confusion clear on his face.

Shaking my head, I said, "No. I don't—maybe? It sounded like the Corey wicche who created the first werewolf used fae magic in order to complete the spell. Only members of the original line— Quinns—possess the magic or the blood." I shrugged. "She didn't explain it all. There's some tie between Quinns and the fae." I thought about it a moment. "And Coreys and the fae. Huh." Uneasy, I pushed that aside.

Glancing between Clive and Russell, both of whom looked off balance, I waited for someone to fill *me* in. When neither did, I finally said, "I saw you take Leticia's head. She's well and truly dead, right?"

"Unfortunately." Clive squeezed my hand and then rose to pace behind his desk. "I wanted her captured alive—wanted to question her—but I couldn't touch her with my mind."

"Because of feeding on the fae?"

"Unclear. Sometimes we inherit gifts from our makers. Sometimes the dark kiss enhances what is already ours. My maker possessed strong mental gifts. They were different from mine— more like Leticia's ability to keep Audrey enthralled for over two centuries—but I believe they augmented my own natural..." He paused, considering.

"Empathy?" Russell suggested.

Clive moved a shoulder and continued pacing. "If you like. I hadn't considered, though, that if we shared a maker, our unique powers would be in conflict."

"I'd assumed Aldith had turned Leticia. You think it was the same vamp who turned you?" I needed an undead family tree so I could keep all the connections straight. Ooh, maybe I'd make a big tapestry on a loom outlining all the relationships. It could—nah, too much work. I'd end up like one of those psycho guys with thousands of pictures plastered to a wall, different colored threads tracing paths between them.

"It stands to reason. We often stay with our sires for years, sometimes centuries. We need to learn, of course, but past that, we've been banished from our old lives, become the stuff of night-mares. Having a companion—even one you despise—can be preferable to being alone. The sire can set the..." He searched for a word.

"Tone," Godfrey said.

Nodding, Clive said, "All right. A sire—or dame in my case—

can set the tone for one's undeath. Garyn, my creator, wanted a kind of new family. She wanted us to remain forevermore in each other's company."

"Sad." That sounded like a horribly lonely existence, turning people in hopes of finding a companion.

"She was, yes. I only stayed with her for a few months. I needed to understand this new life, and I needed control. Once I had it, I set out to find the Atwoods and kill the men who had taken my sister. She was desperate to keep me with her, but I'd accepted the kiss to exact retribution, not to find a new friend."

"And once you had, Aldith just happened upon the same vampire? That seems far-fetched." I mean, what were the chances?

Clive opened his mouth to respond and then closed it.

"That," Godfrey said, "makes more sense. She followed you when you left her. You'd probably told her about the Atwoods." He waited for Clive to confirm. At his nod, Godfrey continued, "So she follows, sees what you did, and then offers her services to the woman and child left on their own. She may have even wanted someone to commiserate with, someone who understood what a right bastard you were. They'd spend their undeaths bitching about you. Instead, she got another one hell bent on revenge."

"It makes a strange sort of sense, Sire. If this Garyn turned all three of you, it could explain why your mental powers didn't work," Russell said.

"I've known fledglings from the same creator battle it out. I bet it was the fae blood she was drinking," Godfrey said.

"What about how she was able to turn our people against you? If it was more than just sowing seeds of doubt, if she was actually messing with their heads—"

"Don't forget," Godfrey interrupted. "St. Germain was messing with our people too."

"Right," Russell agreed, getting up to pace on the opposite side of the room. "It was part of the deal. He'd turn Clive's people against him and Amélie would make sure he was given Sam."

"She's still doing it," I reminded them. "Five of your vamps tried to kill me tonight." At Clive's stony silence, I ventured on. "I've been thinking. She was pretty darned adept at using blood to hide, to control, whatever. I don't know all the vamp rules, but is it possible she was feeding your people her own blood to create ties with them, to strengthen her mental suggestions?" I let the question hang, as all three vamps wore similar expressions of concern.

"I've never heard of that," Russell said.

"Nor I," Godfrey said.

"I have." He stared at me and then shook his head. "I'd forgotten. After I'd been turned, Garyn told story after story, helping me to learn control"—he distractedly ran a hand through his hair—"to keep me from wiping out an entire village when the thirst hit. One of the stories was about a nocturne on the continent somewhere. Italy, France…"

He shook his head. "I could barely think then. I remember her talking of a nocturne that had been stolen from the Master by one of his fledglings, one who had fed the other vampires his own blood in order to break old ties and forge new ones."

"If Garyn told you this story," I said, "it stands to reason she told the same one to Aldith and Leticia."

FORTY-ONE

A New Plan

"With Leticia and St. Germain working against us, it's amazing we have any people left," Godfrey groused.

"Again, no idea on the rules, but couldn't you just do a new blood thing with your people to get them all back under your control?"

Godfrey grinned. "Yes, Sire, do a blood thing, would you?"

"The whole nocturne at once?" Clive sat at his desk. "I could, yes, but I'd essentially be in a coma afterwards." At my look of horror, he added, "Until the following evening or perhaps the one after that."

"Well, that's doable. I mean, we'll miss you, but it would be nice not to be attacked by our own people."

Clive checked his watch. "The sun will be up soon. When we wake, assemble the nocturne in the training room. I'll need all the novitiates present. I can't do this properly with bagged blood."

"There are currently only four novitiates. That won't be enough for a nocturne this size." Russell's gaze darted to me before returning to Clive. "Godfrey and I will go at sunset to secure more donors."

Nodding, Clive drummed his fingers on the desk. "Six. I'll need six more. Young, healthy."

Russell moved toward the door, Godfrey in his wake. "We'll leave you now, Sire, and tell the nocturne we'll be assembling this evening."

"We should find a frat party," Godfrey suggested as he left. "When they come to, they'll assume they got drunk and passed out."

Clive rose and took my hand. "Come. Let's get you cleaned up."

"You're kidnapping people to drain?" I snatched up my shoes before he pulled me toward the door. "No, no, no! Bad vampire!"

"Kidnapping, yes. Draining, no. I don't need to drink as much as I would if I were turning the living, but I do need to reestablish the blood bonds." We started up the stairs. "The people they secure for me will be paid well and their memories will be altered so they have no recollections of their evening."

"Super uncomfortable," I said as we crossed a landing.

"Your idea," he reminded me.

Once in the room, we went straight for the shower. I was a bloody mess. I had Clive return the jewelry to its boxes first and then I sadly pulled off what was left of my shredded dress.

Clive started the shower and was undressing as I stepped into the spray. Ah, it felt so good. Oh, damn. I'd forgotten the hairpins.

Clive brushed my hands away when I reached up to find them. "I've got it." It took him only a few seconds to find them all and then my hair was tumbling down.

We took turns washing and shampooing each other. It had been a scary night. The tending was necessary for both of us to settle. We were okay. Better than okay. When Clive held me, just held me, I understood how close he'd thought he was to losing me.

Lifting up on my tiptoes, I rained kisses on his wet face. "I'm all better."

"Only through the intervention of the fae queen." He crushed me in his arms. "Who was only aware of the problem because you crossed into Faerie and she decided to swap rings." He pulled back, framed my face with his hands. "What are the chances all of

296

those pieces line up exactly as they did and lead to you standing here breathing?" He shook his head. "It's astronomical. In every other scenario, you die."

"But I didn't," I reminded him.

"But you could have," he said, expression stricken.

I grabbed his wrists and squeezed. "I can't guarantee I'll never die." When he opened his mouth, I plowed on. "But I can guarantee to do everything within my power to survive. There's no point in worrying over what might have been."

I pulled his hands down and clasped them. "My parents might have lived. I might have grown up in a loving, stable home. I might have gone to college. I might be in another city, starting a career. We might have never met."

I shrugged. "There are endless might have beens. What matters is this. We're here. We're alive. Ish. We're in love. And we're clean. So," I said, leaning into him, "what should we do to celebrate?"

Let it be known that Clive celebrated me into unconsciousness. My body was delightfully sore and still trembling with aftershocks as we both fell into a deep sleep.

When I woke the next day, I felt off. I'd slept well and yet my nerves were buzzing. *Shit.* Full moon. Part of me couldn't wait to shift to my other skin and hunt down a rabbit. The other part, though, worried about missing the blood thingy tonight.

It had to happen. Clive needed his people loyal. It meant, however, that I'd be without backup while we still had a predator circling our territory. Abigail knew my usual running spots, the Presidio and the North Bay woods.

I considered running on the beach, maybe taking a break and trotting up to the house Stheno and her sisters were sharing. Medusa would no doubt pour me a bowl of wine and I could hang with them before I got back to it. Grinning at the silly thought, I dressed and went downstairs.

As I was heating up a plate of enchiladas, I considered my options. Too many people could be found in Golden Gate Park at night. That wouldn't work. I could run laps inside the nocturne walls, but that sounded both sad and boring. I could—long, rolling fields of gravestones popped into my head. I could run in Colma. People didn't hang out in foggy graveyards at night.

I could undress and shift at The Wicche Glass. That way I wouldn't need to worry about racoons stealing a roll of clothes hidden in a bush. The damn little thieves had done it before. The more I thought about it, the more I liked it.

Me: Hello 1/3 of the Lush Sisters! How goes it? Have you killed each other yet? It's full moon, which means lots of furry running for me. If I'm still feeling energetic afterward, can I run by your place for a visit?

Stheno: Hell yes. Follow the smell of red wine and the sound of drunken singing. What time?

Me: No idea. Abigail (AKA psycho aunt) knows my usual spots. I think I'm going to run near The Wicche Glass. Being close to the dead makes me stronger. I'm wondering what that means for my other half.

Stheno: Don't trip on a headstone

Stheno: Wait. Aren't you supposed to have a guard with you?

Me: Normally, no. With all the craziness of the last couple of months, probably. But the vamps are busy tonight. I don't want to ask Owen or Dave. Abigail already screwed with both of them. No one but you knows where I'm going. If you promise not to rat me out, I should be fine.

Stheno: I can go with you.

Me: Thanks, but as neither of us drives, you'd have to jog with me ten miles each way.

Stheno: That's a hell no.

Me: That's what I thought

Stheno: Ask that harpy

Me: Fury. And a good idea. Hopefully, I'll see you later.

Stheno: Bring more wine.

When I was done eating, I walked through the library. Reconstruction had begun. Nerves jangling, fur pricking under my skin, I sat in the window seat, equal parts pissed off and sad.

Abigail had taken The Slaughtered Lamb away from me again, this time by attacking my friends. Leticia and her bomb-wielding minion had taken away the library. Villains had no respect for books!

I pulled out my phone and dialed Meg.

"What?"

"Really? That's how you answer a phone?" What was it with ancient cranky people?

Click.

Jeez. Ask one question. I dialed her back.

The line opened but she said nothing.

Okey-dokie. "Meg, it's full moon. Can you hang out with me tonight?"

"Why would I need to do that?"

"Well, my aunt is still gunning for me, so…" I paused, remembering someone bigger and stronger had told her to step aside the last time I was being attacked. This was probably a bad idea. "I'd like someone nearby in case I'm ambushed. Only if you'd actually intervene, though. On my side, that is."

She made a click of annoyance in the back of her throat. "Where and when?"

"Do you know The Wicche Glass?"

"That fae bar in South San Francisco?"

"Colma, and yes. Can you meet me there tonight?" The fact that Meg could fly over the top of where I ran made her the perfect candidate for guard duty, if she'd do it.

"I'd heard it had closed. The owner died."

"Yes, that was my great-aunt Martha. It was horrible. Abigail and her demon killed her." Maybe this was a bad idea. Perhaps Coco would be willing to fly over the forest. Her other form would be a lot harder to hide than Meg's, though. "Never mind, Meg. I don't want to bug you. Have a good ni—"

"I didn't say I wouldn't do it. If your aunt knows about this place, why are you going there?"

"Open green spaces with little to no humans are hard to find.

Abigail already knows about my usual spots. I've never run in Colma before, and the cemeteries back up on a state park."

"Fine." *Click.* Ever the charmer, that one.

Shaking it off, I walked out, jogged up the steps and back to our bedroom. Clive had said he felt a moment of panic every time he woke up and I wasn't there. With my scent in his head, he'd reach for me and find my side of the bed empty. If I was around at sundown, I liked to be there when he woke.

Kicking off my shoes, I snuggled up next to him on top of the comforter. Too restless to relax, I traced a finger down the planes of his gorgeous face, outlined his mouth.

"What are you doing?" He hadn't opened his eyes yet, but I felt his consciousness bloom to life in my mind.

"You're so pretty," I crooned.

Grinning, he rolled me over, his stormy gray eyes taking in every detail. "Handsome. I'm devastatingly handsome. I'm not pretty."

"Says you."

"You are a little spark plug of energy right now. You're practically vibrating. What—ah, full moon tonight."

I ran my fingers through his hair. "Yup. Much running on the agenda."

"Hmm, I think I can help take the edge off." He dragged his lips over my jaw and down my throat, letting his fangs glide over my skin. Trembling and needy, I flipped him, pinning him to the mattress and demonstrating the benefits of a werewolf mate. All that energy had to go somewhere.

Later, feeling great but definitely late, I put on running tights and shoes, with a long-sleeved tee.

"Where are you going? Your usual spots have been compromised." Clive slid into one of his millions of snow-white dress shirts, tucking it into charcoal gray slacks.

"Wicche Glass. I'll stash my stuff there and then run through the cemeteries and into the San Bruno State Park beyond it. I'll be fine and Meg said she'd keep an eye out."

Nodding, he stepped into his shoes. "Good. If Meg is guarding you, I won't worry."

"I'm the one who's worried. How dangerous is this vampy blood thing tonight?"

Shaking his head, he said, "That word."

"Blood? I thought you liked that one. Anyway, could you have Russell or Godfrey text me when it's done and you're okay?" I hugged him hard. "I know you said you'd be out of it by then, but I want to know as soon as I shift back that you're okay."

"As you like," he said, kissing the top of my head, "but you must do the same. I know you need to run, but I can't help thinking this is a bad time for you to be out running on your own."

FORTY-TWO

Comeuppance

When I stepped out of the nocturne door, I found Dave leaning against the hood of his shiny black muscle car, texting. "What are you doing here?"

He glanced up and then went right on texting. "Your boyfriend asked me to guard the nocturne while they're doing their secret shit."

"He's my betrothed, and that was nice of you to agree. It's just..." How did I put this?

"What?" His annoyance knew no bounds.

"It's just—If someone wanted to sneak in, couldn't they just hop the back wall while you're standing here texting by the main gate?"

"Sure, they could. But then they'd die." He held up his phone to me. "I've got the security loaded on this. I get an alert if anyone on the sidewalk gets too close to the property."

"Ooh cool. Can I see?" When I stepped closer, he held up a hand, stopping me.

"No. Go use all that energy to run and stop bugging me."

I wondered who he was texting. "Is Maggie okay?"

A grin pulled at his lips. "She's perfect." He looked up then. "Thanks for getting her back so quickly. She said you and Faerie had a little chat, that you made sure everyone got out safely." He nodded his thanks.

Pointing at his car, I said, "If you're feeling grateful, you can give me another driving lesson."

"What did I say about bugging me? Go away," he grumbled.

"Fair enough." I took off at a sprint and kept going, skirting the edge of what was believably human speed. I could be an Olympian in training. They didn't know.

I was only a few blocks from the nocturne when a car screeched around the corner and gunned it down the street toward me. I barely had time to dive for the grass of Lafayette Park when the car jumped the curb and rammed into a streetlamp. Heart pounding, I cautiously made my way back. The driver was slumped over the steering wheel.

Abigail. It had to be.

"Oh, my God. Are you okay?" A woman walking her dog rushed up. "Is he drunk? He went straight for you." Her little dog growled at me, keeping safely behind his owner's legs.

"I have no idea," I said, pretending to be far more shaken than I was. "I was just going for a run when I heard squealing tires behind me." I put my hand over my mouth. "I'm going to be sick." I raced around a wall of bushes bordering the park.

The woman already had her phone out and was calling 911. As she spoke to a dispatcher, I moved farther away. If the driver woke up and continued to come after me, it would be very hard to explain.

The joy I'd felt at the beginning of the evening had evaporated. Abigail would never stop. She would continue to hurt innocents until she finally came for me herself. This had to stop. I had to stop her.

When I ran through the gate at The Wicche Glass, I found Meg waiting in the courtyard at a table.

"You're late."

"I never gave you a time." I paused to brush a leaf off Martha's grave marker and then raced into the tavern. "Be right back." I undressed quickly, rolling up my stuff and placing it behind the bar.

I was about to shift when I remembered the queen's ring on my finger. *Shit.* It was too valuable of an object to leave here, but too awkward to remain on my paw while I ran. I tried unclasping the dragon chain so I could string the ring on it, but the clasp wouldn't open. It had probably been magicked shut so I wouldn't lose it. Benvair was not a trusting soul.

The wicche glass was on a chain just long enough to go over my head. Spinning it through my fingers, I realized it had no clasp. Not having another option, I took it off and threaded the chain through the delicate ring. It dropped. Being a bit smaller than the ball, it encircled the top like a halo. Good enough. I slipped the chain back over my head.

Once on my hands and knees, I finally let the moon call my other side. Fur burst through my skin as my jaw elongated. Muscles straining, my body shifted and reformed. I braced for a blinding moment of pain but didn't feel it. Panting on the barroom floor, I grinned a wolfy grin. My necromancer side was stronger here. It allowed me to shift with far less pain.

Standing, shaking off the aftereffect, I took stock. The wicche glass and the dragon carving were still around my neck. The dragon chain was tight, but when I shook again, it settled next to my skin, leaving me breathing room.

Trotting out to the courtyard, I found Meg gone. Leaves rustled. I peered up into the perpetual twilight of this border land and found Meg standing on a branch of the massive fae tree. I gave a quick woof and headed toward the gate.

The evening was chilly, the wet of the fog soon beading on my fur. Pausing behind a parked car, I listened intently. An owl, a dog bark, cars on the distant highway, little scurrying animals, but no humans. I bolted across the road and into the cemetery, weaving between headstones, heading for the state park beyond.

I'd expected to have to scale fencing of some kind, but either there was none or I happened upon a fenceless section of the border. Once past the roads and buildings, I raced over the park land, down ravines and up steep hills, dodging the brush too tall to leap over. Through it all, the moon shone down, lighting the way.

When I skirted close to a large stand of trees, I smelled the sweet scent of prey. Spinning, I crashed through the wooded area, sending birds and small woodland creatures racing away. It was a dick move, but I loved it. Zeroing in on the rabbit I'd smelled a moment before, I dove into the small shrub I knew he was hiding beneath and came out the other side with him between my jaws. One quick snap and I was pausing for a snack.

"Hurry up. That sounds disgusting." The shadow of Meg's wings circled above. Tearing into the small rabbit, I made quick work of the meal and then was up and running again. A few miles later, I found a stream and drank greedily.

I gloried in the night, in being one with nature. Of course, being an apex predator had a lot to do with my enjoyment. If I were a rabbit shifter, the evening would have sucked.

Meg's shadow crossed the moon often enough for me to know she was keeping close. After a few hours, as the moon began to set, I headed back toward the cemeteries, stopping once again at the stream to drink my fill and wash off the blood of the second rabbit I'd found.

Sated, happy, and tired, I trotted back through the gravestones. Pausing at the edge, I stilled, listening to the sounds the world made when it slept. Ghosts hovered nearby. I could feel their desire to be close to me warring with their confusion over my current form.

Bolting across the street, I ran through the gate and into the safety of The Wicche Glass. The dark, foggy night once more became soft and fragrant in the perpetual dusk of this almost-fae hinterland.

No pixies had been playing with my stuff, so I shifted and dressed. Normally, I'd shower first, but the stream had taken care of most of the dirt and debris. I was just reaching for my phone when a fire roared to life in the hearth.

I turned, wondering if I had an angry Galadriel to deal with and instead found the dark silhouette of a far more petite woman standing before the flames. Flickering light from the fire left most of the tavern in shadow. A chill ran down my spine. I might not have been able to see her, but I knew exactly who she was.

"That was grotesque. You may look human now, but you're nothing but a vile animal, an abomination to the name Corey."

"Quinn." I hated to admit it, even to myself, but the fear I felt was bone deep. I'd been taught for as long as I could remember to hide from this woman. My mother's fear of her sister was that great.

"Don't remind me of that beast," she spat. With a flick of her wrist, lanterns hanging from the ceiling lit, throwing the room into relief. The disgust I'd heard dripping from her every word was mirrored in her expression.

"Why do you care? I mean, really, why have you made it your life's work to kill my mother and me? Such a miserable life you've chosen for yourself." She'd set up my rape and torture—had orchestrated a second attempt before I'd killed the wolf she'd set on me. Her twisted obsession knew no bounds.

She twitched her fingers and I felt a hard shove but instead of flying across the room, I staggered, keeping my feet under me. Balance regained, I felt stronger. Weird.

"Not as big and bad as you used to be, huh?"

She wore a momentary look of shock but covered it quickly with a sneer. "A mutt, that's all you are, like your father before you." She shook her head. "My sister, so special, the chosen one." She spat on the floor. "The Crone decreed it at her birth. The Mother sanctified the choice. My perfect sister was the next in line, the Maiden joining the Mother and the Crone." She paced, anger getting the better of her, hair floating and sparking about her head. "Rulers of the Corey Clan. My sister," she ground out, "married a

306

dog and then gave birth to another one. Turned her back on her destiny."

The fear lingered, but I was seeing her differently, like seeing something from childhood and realizing it was much smaller and dingier than remembered. "I get it now. You were hoping if you got rid of your sister, you'd become a power player. Of course, that doesn't explain your fixation on me—" It was in the eyes. I saw her expression change and knew exactly what it meant. "Aww, they still didn't want you, did they? They wanted me." Shaking my head, I leaned against the bar. "How much do they have to hate your guts to choose me, sight unseen? Ouch."

Screaming, she shot her hands out and my chest seized. Lung, heart, everything stopped. And then it didn't. I took a deep breath and Abigail's eyes went round. The magic I kept coiled in my chest felt different, stronger. My fingertips tingled with a ready spell.

Ignoring for now the way her spells were being claimed by my own magic, I said, "So, being the petulant little sociopath that you are, you decided torturing innocents was the price the world would pay for not giving you what you wanted."

Flicking her fingers again, I was knocked sideways into the solid wood of the bar. My ribs hurt, but nothing was broken. Again, a spell danced along my skin, down my arm, and along my fingertips. And then it hit me. I remembered a passage I'd read in the family grimoire and *finally* understood the Corey Curse.

Be warned. If hand is raised and Corey slew
Powers, born and learned, shall be stripped from you
Treachery, like a poison, has weakened our clan
We, the three, have enacted a plan
Once great, we are too few
Slaughter and you will be unmade. We spake true.

"You didn't recognize her, did you? The woman you tortured in that back room?" When she flicked her fingers again, I put up my hand and caught the spell like a softball lobbed to me. I held it tight in my fist and then let go, feeling it gambol up my arm, settling in my chest.

"She was your aunt." There. I saw it. A flicker of fear in her eyes before she flicked her wrist again. I felt nothing and she knew it. "Not as powerful as you used to be. Remember when you shattered my mind? It rained glass in my head. Damn, *that* was impressive. Now," I said, shrugging, "I believe this is referred to as comeuppance."

Chanting under her breath, she stalked toward me, her hands readying a complicated curse. With a grunt, she sent it flying. Freezing cold gripped my limbs. Sneering, she said, "You will die worse than all the others. I'm going to watch as your skin is peeled one strip at a time from your bones."

The cold drained from my limbs, becoming one with the magic coiled tight in my chest. "Killing your aunt, your spells sliding right off me, this must be that Corey Curse I've heard so much about."

Abigail's face turned red. "No!" She hit me before I could dodge the spell. It was the one that had put me down a couple of months ago, the one that felt like glass raining in my skull. Instead of dropping to the ground, I held tight to the bar, remaining upright. As shards of glass tore at my brain, a door opened...

I was walking through someone's mind. The dark, the occasional sparks of synapses firing nearby, memories lighting and then dimming, was there a vampire with us? Whose mind was I in?

When a light flared to life beside me, I stepped in. It was the last apartment my mother and I had shared. She was shoving me into a tiny closet. I was tripping over jumbled shoes.

"Shhh. No matter what you hear, love, you stay here and be quiet." She patted the pendant she'd made me that hung around my neck. "She won't sense you. Remember, never take this off."

Shorter than me, she rose on her tiptoes and kissed my forehead. "I love you forever, my girl."

The front door flew open and my mother stood a little straighter. She flicked her wrist in my direction and then closed the closet door. When I tried to open it, to find out what was going on,

I couldn't move. She'd spelled me. The latch was old, though. If you didn't pull up on the handle when you closed the door, it fell open. It was only an inch or two, but I was able to see out.

A woman who looked very much like my mother stalked into the room. Their voices were muffled, like they were talking underwater. I couldn't make out the words, not clearly. My mother's spell was trying to protect me from all of it.

Abigail's hand flew out and my mom was hit with a spell that sent her reeling. When my mom hit back, Abigail staggered and then lifted both hands up in the air and threw her head back, shouting. Behind her, a shadowy form rose from the floor. Her face a mask of insane fury, Abigail pointed at my mother.

Mom backed away from the demon, holding up the protective amulet she wore around her own neck. The demon moved out of sight and came back with a struggling man who appeared to be living hard, clothes stained and ill-fitting, face dirty, hair matted. He held the man by his neck and then walked into him, becoming one with the homeless man. The man's expression, two parts confusion and one part inebriation, turned horribly focused and gleefully sadistic.

Abigail handed him a knife. He tested the weight and then almost faster than my eye could register, he'd thrown it, pinning my mother to the wall through the neck. Blood spattered the room as he tore her apart. Frozen, I couldn't close my eyes.

Blood dripping from her smug face, Abigail said something in Latin and the demon sunk back down. Wiping her face with her sleeve, she stared down at what was left of my mother. "Always the fucking perfect one, weren't you? Not anymore. The power is mine now."

It wasn't until I watched her sail out of the apartment that I realized I'd heard her words, that I could move. The spell had ended when my mother's life had.

Eyes blinking, memory fading, I stared into that same smug face as the wicche glass heated up around my neck. Eyes alight in malevolent intent, she said an incomprehensible word and then began to chant again. Behind her, a black form rose from the floor-boards. The inky black form took the shape of a man, a tall, muscular man. She shouted something while pointing at me.

No. She'd done enough damage in this life. It was time to end her. I called the dead to me, asked that they leave the in-between place where they resided and come to me. Abigail's eyes shone with a zealot's gleam as the dead gathered around me in numbers too high to count.

In my mind, I asked them to visit on her the pain they'd experi-enced in their deaths. The flames behind her roared to life as a whirlwind of spirits raced past me and enveloped Abigail. Eyes bulging in terror, she spun, trying to see her invisible attackers.

Convulsing in pain, she howled, "What are you doing?"

I didn't care if the Corey curse came back to slap me down for killing a relative. Too many had lost their lives because of this one woman's insane jealousy.

Gurgling words to the demon, she struggled, in a panic now that she was the one in pain. Dave had promised the substitute demon wouldn't hurt me. I guess we'd see if that was true.

Claws out, I lunged forward and was immediately snatched back. Hanging from the demon's meaty grip, I watched Galadriel step through the mirror, pull her sword from its sheath, and raise it over her head. She took only a moment to look into the eyes of the woman who had tortured and killed her wife and then the sword was arcing through the air, firelight glinting on the elven metal as she sent Abigail's head spinning.

Galadriel lifted the bloody sword and licked the flat of it, drinking the blood of her enemy. With a short bow to me and the demon, she stepped back through the mirror and returned to Faerie.

The demon dropped me, picked up the head and body, winked in a Dave-like way, and returned to Hell with Abigail as his spoils.

Left alone with countless ghosts, I thanked them all for their help and gave them a gentle push away. I couldn't think with so many surrounding me.

Abigail was dead. The woman who had haunted me my entire life was dead. It didn't seem real. And my mother...she'd done everything in her power to protect me—*had* protected me—and was slaughtered by her own sister out of bitterness and envy. How did any of that make sense?

"Was that really a demon?"

I jolted at the voice, causing my ribs to throb. Scanning the room, I found Charlotte, my ghost assistant, staring at the floorboards Abigail had disappeared through.

Holding my side, I went behind the bar to grab my shoes and phone. "Yep."

"And he really..."

"Dragged Abigail, body and soul, to Hell? You bet." I checked my phone first, looking for a message. It was short and sweet. *He's fine.* Clearly Godfrey had sent the text.

"That thing around your neck is glowing."

I glanced down and realized it wasn't the wicche glass that had been heating up earlier. It was the ring encircling it. Gloriana must have tipped off Galadriel that Abigail was here. I pulled the necklace off and tapped the ring, worried it might still be hot.

It was warm, not hot, so I unthreaded it and returned it to my pinky finger. It pulsed in time with my heart, once, twice, and then settled down.

"You don't need to—" stay. Where'd she go? Huh. I guess Charlotte was more freaked out than I'd thought. Using one of the wicchey spells Lydia had taught me, I doused the fire and then closed the door.

"Are you done now?" Meg was back up in the branches.

With my run? With my aunt? "Yes. And thanks so much for your help in there," I added sarcastically.

She swooped down, encircled me in an arm, and then beat her huge wings, lifting us up into the air. "Did you actually need it?"

Stomach swooping at the height, I closed my eyes and thought about that a moment. I was surprised to say, "No, I didn't."

We rose quickly into the fog and then shot forward. I was freezing, terrified by how far away the ground was, but the ride got me home faster so I could check on Clive myself. I appreciated the text, but it had been short on details.

"Thanks for staying with me tonight. I'm sure you had better things to do." My teeth were chattering so hard, I wasn't sure if she got all that.

"I did. I think you should pick up my bar tab for the next year."

Blinking rapidly against the icy wind, I studied her wings. They were a thing of beauty, the feathers every shade of black, white, and gray. "One month," I countered.

"Six months." Her long gray hair streamed out behind her in the wind.

I considered not just tonight but the fact that she'd gone to New Orleans to help us battle vamps. Honestly, Owen, George, Stheno, and Dave should probably be getting free drinks as well. No. Not Stheno. She'd put me out of business in no time. "Okay, six months."

She flew over the walls of the nocturne and released me five feet from the ground, jolting my ribs and knees. Damn, Fury.

"Make that five months!" I yelled after her.

FORTY-THREE

Ding, Dong, the Wicche Is Dead!

The vamp at the gate who witnessed my awkward landing turned back to his guard duty with nary a sneer. Huh. You know what? I'll take it. No sneering was a huge improvement. When I reached the front door, it was opened before I could touch the knob. The butler waited, face blank, for me to pass and then shut the door and disappeared down the hall. Okay, now they were freaking me out.

I ran up the stairs, wanting to check on Clive before I found someone to give me a better update than 'he's fine.' When I got to the third-floor landing, I saw Russell standing guard at the bedroom door.

"Everything okay?" If the vamps were back under Clive's influence, why the need for a guard?

"Good evening, Miss Quinn. Yes, the Master is well, just resting. He was inquiring after your whereabouts. Please, go in. I'm sure he'd like to speak with you." His tone was even more formal than usual.

When I opened my mouth to ask a question, he gave an almost imperceptible shake of his head and opened the door for me. Trying to follow his lead, I said, "Thank you for your help, Russell. We do have a lot to discuss."

He patted my shoulder as I walked by. As Russell wasn't given to gestures of affection, I worried I was about to find Clive in far more dire straits than I'd been prepared for.

Instead, he was sitting on the couch, feet on the coffee table crossed at the ankles, an open book in his lap, eyes closed. "Hey, handsome. How was your night?" I said in a normal voice as I hurried across the room to kiss him, laugh at something he said, and then close the drapes behind him.

I was ten steps behind but understood we were pretending that Clive was up and everything was normal. Sitting beside him, I took the book in his lap, moved it to the table, and then took his hand in mine. His skin was colder than normal, but I felt the buzz of his lifeforce, so I didn't panic. Much.

Closing my eyes, I searched for vamps. The nocturne was full... except for Godfrey. Where—oh, he was returning frat boys to a party. I wrapped myself around Clive's blip. *Hello, love. Can you hear me?* I didn't want to delve into his mind. It was too invasive for someone I loved. *Are you okay?*

He squeezed my hand—barely—but again, I'd take it. I rested my head on his shoulder. News of the night could wait. He needed to recover.

When I felt him sink more deeply into sleep, I got up and took a shower. Clean and dressed in my softest pjs, I went back to the couch, picked up Clive, and carried him to the bed. Werewolf strength came in quite handy.

Undressing him first, I slid him into our bed and then hopped over him to snuggle at his side. With any luck, he'd wake tomorrow and we'd share our news. I wasn't sure what excuse we could make if he needed another day to recover. One crisis at a time, though.

Exhausted, I wrapped my arms around him and dropped off almost at once. My dreams were filled with memories from my childhood, memories I'd thought lost forever. My mother and me singing in the car, our sparse belongings in the trunk and backseat as we moved yet again.

She did everything she could to make our lives as normal as possible, but we moved constantly. When we were lucky, we were able to stay one place for four months, maybe even six. Sometimes, though, we were back in the car only a few days after we'd moved in.

My mother used a scrying mirror to keep tabs on her sister. When she was getting too close, off we went. She could use any reflective surface to do it, but when I was eight or nine, I found the perfect mirror. We'd been shopping in a thrift store for a new pair of jeans for me—I'd had another growth spurt—when I saw an antique dresser set. The silver was tarnished, but the etchings on the mirror, brush, and comb felt special. I didn't understand what it was about the set, but I asked my mother to buy it.

The lady in the shop said she'd recently picked it up from an estate sale. It was pretty pricey for us, as we lived on the cheap, but the lady threw in a silver polishing kit. Later, as Mom drove, I polished.

Mom began using that mirror exclusively when scrying. She said it was more powerful, that it had retained some magic from its previous owner, who she believed was some type of fae. Perhaps even then, something about the fae drew me. I had no idea what had happened to the set. Probably burned like the rest of our belongings in that…

Wait. There'd been no fire. After Abigail and her demon had left that day, I'd called the police, told them I'd come home to find my mother dead and that poor homeless man covered in her blood. He hadn't survived the demon's possession. I'd heard one of the EMTs say heart attack.

I didn't want to remember losing her, living it all over again.

Pushing my mind in a different direction, I remembered ice cream cones. No matter where we were or how broke we were, Mom always scraped together the money for ice cream. She'd stop the car at an interesting-looking shop. We'd hop out, pick our flavors—they changed every time— and then we'd take our cones and walk around the neighborhood, discussing whether we should look for a vacancy or move on.

I awoke to Clive rolling me over and gazing down at me, his eyes alight with humor. "Ice cream? You dream about ice cream? How did I not know that?"

I put one hand over my mouth and the other on the side of his face. "You're okay?"

"I am." He kissed the back of my hand. "What are you doing?"

"I need to brush my teeth," I mumbled behind my hand.

"Ah." He rolled off me and flipped the comforter back. "Get to it then."

I bolted into the bathroom and took care of a number of things. A few minutes later, I was crawling back into bed and on top of Clive. Resting my chin on my hands, I settled in for story time. "Tell me what I missed."

"It went as planned." A corner of his mouth tilted up. "Russell and I agreed it was best you weren't there."

"Hey." I mean, he was right. The vamps neither needed nor wanted a random wolf in their midst, but he could have prettied it up a little.

Leaning forward, he dropped a kiss on my forehead. "It was a night filled with fangs and blood. You probably would have been too nauseated to stay."

"Yeah, there's that. The frat boys were okay, though, right?"

"No worse than they were at the beginning of the evening. Godfrey left them with money in their pockets and bottles of orange juice in their hands." His fingers kneaded the muscles in my shoulders. He knew where I held tension.

"Does the nocturne feel different? Did it work?" Hopefully, it wasn't a huge waste of time and blood.

He rolled me over and kissed me deeply, scattering thoughts and questions. When he finally drew back, he said, "My beautiful mate is also brilliant. Yes, renewing the blood bond eradicated the poisonous voices some of my people have been dealing with."

"No more Leticia screwing with your people and no more

Abigail screwing with mine. Huzzah! We should celebrate." I wrapped my legs around him.

"No Abigail?" Brow furrowed, his gaze was intent on me. "What did *I* miss?"

I relayed the events of the previous evening, my heart filling with joy at the thought of reopening my Slaughtered Lamb.

Clive slid to the side, his hand on my abdomen. "Your ribs?"

"Still sore, but they healed while we slept." I had to admit, it was ouchie having him on top of me, but I preferred the pain to his absence.

"You know what this means, don't you?" He grinned, the weight of the world lifting from his shoulders.

Heart fluttering, I said, "Slaughtered Lamb," at the same time he said, "A wedding." I pivoted, cringing. "I mean, a wedding!"

Rolling his eyes, he propped his head on his hand and looked down at me. "You do still want a wedding, right?"

"Marriage? Yes. A fancy wedding in a big dress with lots of people staring and judging? Not so much."

"All right. I can work with that. How about an intimate gathering of friends?"

That might be nice. Just Owen and George, Dave and Maggie, Russell, Godfrey, maybe Audrey and Meg. Stheno was still in town...

"Tonight."

It took me a minute. "Tonight? This night, tonight? As in now?"

"Are you busy?"

My mind went blank. Completely blank. "Now?"

"Look at the terror in your eyes. I doubt you were this scared dealing with your aunt last night. Come on." He dragged me from the bed, my limbs not working. He got me to my feet, but when I started to drop back down to the bed, he picked me up and walked me across the bedroom.

Married. Tonight. I struggled to breathe properly. Now. I was getting married now.

He placed me back on the floor but kept his arms around me.

"What do you think?" There was a dress hanging under a light, positively glowing in the closet.

"Oh." When I moved toward it, he let go and followed me. It was stunning. The top was a delicate white flowery lace. It reminded me of the meadow blanketed in wildflowers in Faerie. The handwork was so fine, I hesitated to touch it. Tiny pearls were sewn into the flowers. It had a crew neck and long, tapered sleeves.

At the waist, the lace dropped to the floor in an airy overskirt that was open at the front revealing a slim, form-fitting, white silk underskirt beneath. White silk slingback heels stood on the floor beneath the dress.

His arms slid around me again as he kissed my neck. "Well?"

"I'm afraid to touch it." I'd never seen a more exquisite garment in my life. I put my trembling hands over his. "You're sure?"

Holding me tight, he kissed the shell of my ear. "I've never been more sure of anything in my very long and storied life."

And just like that, my stomach settled. The ceremony made me nervous. Spending the rest of my life with Clive at my side? It was all I wanted. "I was thinking."

"Hmm?"

"We should probably get married tonight." When he picked me up and spun me around, I giggled uncontrollably. Gasping, I asked, "Is there time to put it all together?"

"Leave it to me," he said, sailing out of the closet. "We'll aim for two o'clock."

"You'll need pants," I called.

The bedroom door he'd just opened was closed abruptly. "I will, won't I?"

FORTY-FOUR

Dear Reader, I Married Him

I took a long, hot shower and instead of the panic I expected, uncontrolled giddiness kept bubbling up. I buffed and washed and moisturized, all the while being surprised anew each time I remembered that Abigail was gone. She'd been a specter haunting me my entire life. Gone. That death threat had been taken off the table and in its place was a marriage to a man I loved more than was rationally advisable.

As I tied on a robe, I heard a knock at the door. Old habits were hard to break, so I checked in my mind to see who was on the other side of the door. Audrey. Perfect.

"Good evening, miss," she said as I swung the door open. "The Master asked me to help you get ready, if that's all right."

I waved her in. "If you don't mind doing it, I'd welcome the help. Thank you." I led her to the vanity and sat on the bench, grateful someone who knew what she was doing was going to be in charge of me. I didn't think a ponytail was the best look for a wedding.

"Not at all, miss. I'm happy to do it. In fact"—she paused, looking embarrassed—"if it's not too much trouble—afterwards— could I see the pictures of the wedding? If you wouldn't mind, that is." She rested a hand over her heart. "I do so love weddings and I haven't been to one in more years than I care to count."

"You'll come to mine." I picked up my phone to text Russell, to let him know Audrey was to attend.

Audrey looked stricken. "Oh no, miss. The Master didn't invite us. I could never."

"I'm inviting you." I caught her eye in the mirror. "Truly. I'd love for you to be there—wherever there is." I laughed and turned on the bench so I wouldn't need to talk through a reflection. "I have no idea how any of this works. Clive said he'd arrange it all and that I just needed to show up. There's going to be some sort of blood ceremony, though. Knowing I had a friendly face in my corner would really help. Would you come, please?"

"Oh, miss. Are you sure no one would mind my being there?" She positively glowed.

"Not at all, and I insist."

While Audrey worked on my hair, I texted Owen to tell him about the wedding. Apparently, he and George had already been contacted. Clive really was taking care of everything. He even had a vamp bring me food. It was true love.

I contacted Coco, asking her to please take back the dragon necklace. She arrived shortly and was escorted up by Godfrey. She appeared quite uncomfortable, but I wasn't sure if it was because she was in a house filled with vampires or because her grandmother had spelled the necklace so it wouldn't come off.

Coco whispered, "Could we do this alone?"

Godfrey held out his arm for Audrey and they departed.

"Sorry," Coco said. "It's just that Grandmother used a spell that requires dragon blood to unlock. I didn't want to prick my finger with two vampires in the room."

"Understandable."

In no time at all, the necklace was slipping from my neck and Coco was off to return it to Benvair.

Hours later, hair, makeup, and nails perfect, I stepped into the dress—which involved ridiculous gymnastics, as the enclosures were cleverly hidden so as to not interrupt the line of the lace. I had a moment of worry it was too small and then Audrey adjusted the dress and it fit like a glove. The man never missed a trick.

Audrey pulled out a blue velvet jewelry box. "The Master says these are the jewels you should wear." When she opened the box, we both sucked in air. "Oh, miss. I've never seen anything so beautiful."

The platinum pendant was an Art Deco design. It was a domed circle of filigreed, diamond-encrusted swirls that ever-so-subtly reminded me of flowers. At the center was a large stone of intense violet blue. The earrings were tear-shaped drops that mirrored the design of the pendant. They were stunning.

When she pulled out a second box, I almost stopped her. It was all too much, but then she was sliding a matching cuff bracelet over my hand. I stared at my wrist, unable to take it all in. "Are these sapphires and diamonds?" Good Lord, this set had to cost a fortune.

"Blue and white diamonds, miss."

I stared at the stones in wonder. "I didn't even know there *were* blue diamonds." Shaking my head, I turned to Audrey, straightening the perfect dress, touching the pendant. "Okay?"

Eyes downcast, she did a quick curtsy. "Perfect, mistress."

My phone buzzed with a text from Godfrey: Your carriage awaits.

Audrey flitted around me on the stairs, adjusting the skirt, fluffing the lace to float over the silk beneath it. The first floor was empty, so I didn't need to walk through any disapproving vamps on my way out. As I was crossing the entry, I remembered a promise. Holding the fae ring to my lips, I whispered, "I'm getting married."

Godfrey waited by the open back door of the Mercedes. After more fussing than I would have thought possible, Audrey had pulled the lace overskirt up, so I wasn't sitting on it. Granted, I'd soon be leaning back on it, but she seemed to believe that was preferable to sitting. As I had no opinion on the matter, I deferred to her.

"Where are we going? I thought the ceremony would be in the nocturne."

Godfrey drove down the hills of Pacific Heights toward the Marina. "Patience."

When he drove around the Palace of Fine Arts and then turned into the parking lot, that giddiness I'd been feeling earlier bubbled up again. He'd remembered.

Getting out of the car proved every bit as precarious as getting in. This time, though, I had Godfrey to pull. Audrey took a moment to adjust the dress and check my hair, and then we were walking up the colonnade toward the center rotunda.

Heart racing, I was blinking back tears and trying to take it all in. The rotunda jutted out into the pond, its dome rising over a hundred feet into the air. Tiny white lights encircled the thick columns holding up the dome. White orchids and soft, romantic peonies in every shade of pink stood on pedestals along the edges of the curve. What had me blinking back tears wasn't the impromptu beauty of this spot. It was all the people who had shown up in the middle of the night with little to no warning, dressed to the nines.

Owen and George, Coco and Benvair, Grim, Liam, even Ule for goodness' sake. Stheno and her sisters keeping their distance from Meg. Lydia and Lilah...everywhere I looked I saw friends from The Slaughtered Lamb.

Standing silently to the side were Rémy and Cadmael, joined by vamps I'd never met. Dave broke away from Maggie and walked to us.

"I've got her," he said to Godfrey, who took that as his cue to leave.

A violin began playing. I located the source and found Grim with the instrument tucked under his chin.

"What did I say?" Dave's gruff voice was in my ear. "No crying and no hugs."

Right. Blinking back the tears, I took a deep breath and straightened my shoulders. Audrey handed me a bouquet of orchids and peonies and then slipped back into the crowd.

"Ready?"

I pulled at his arm, whispering, "My head is filling with white noise and little black spots. Don't let me pass out."

"No crying, no hugs, no fainting." He studied me a moment and then patted my hand. "Do you love him?"

"More than I ever thought possible." I was feeling light-headed and may have been hyperventilating.

"It's a gift, you know. Not everyone finds their one perfect love. Are you really going to let fear stand in the way?" His shark-black eyes took in the crowd, some of whom had seen us and were starting to move out of the center.

"No," I said, taking a deep breath. "I'm going to get married." Gripping the flowers, I prayed I didn't trip.

"Good choice." As we moved into the rotunda, the fountains in the pond beyond sprang to life, illuminating the dark water.

The rest of the crowd separated, giving me a clear view of Owen and Russell standing side by side, framed by columns, water sparkling behind them while Clive waited for me. Gloriana was standing to his side, though I don't believe he knew. The vamps all seemed oblivious to her presence. The fae guests, however, kept shooting her sidelong glances. I bowed my head as I passed her, and she smiled beneficently.

I gripped Dave's hand hard when we stopped. Shocking no one more than me, he leaned down and kissed my forehead before moving back to Maggie's side.

Clive took my hand and we turned to face Russell and Owen. I felt, rather than heard, movement behind us. When I turned, I saw the whole nocturne had arrived. Clive's vamps filled in spaces, showing their respect for their Master.

Clive nodded to his people and turned back. I felt his heart lighten beside me and it made me want to hug every one of those damn vamps who'd shown up for my guy.

"Dearly beloved, we are gathered here to join Clive Fitzwilliam and Samantha Quinn in matrimony," Owen began.

"And to tie them to one another for all eternity," Russell added.

That probably should have scared the shit out of me, but something rattling around inside me fell into place instead.

"Now, some of us may have questioned the advisability of our Sam marrying the big, scary vampire—no offense intended." Owen swallowed and then continued. "But it was clear to anyone with a brain that he was devoted to her. And just as clear, though she tried to hide it, that she felt the same." Owen paused and looked at Russell.

"I knew it before they did," he said.

Owen grinned. "In the presence of friends, who are the family we chose, Clive and Sam will recite their vows."

Clive had sent me what I needed to say for the blood ceremony. Nervous as I was, I'd memorized the words as Audrey did my hair. The vows I'd planned for the wedding, however, flew right out of my head.

"Sam," Clive turned and spoke to me, "I promise to stand beside you through life, to be your sword when you need one and your shield when you don't. I promise to listen to what you say and even more closely to what you don't. I promise to be a hand to hold in the dark. And I promise," he said, squeezing said hand, "to love you every day of our very long lives."

He took a ring from his pocket and placed it on my finger. It matched the jewelry, a filigree dome set with a large blue diamond in the center. *Shit!* I totally forgot I was supposed to have a ring ready for him. And just like that, one appeared between my hand and the bouquet I held. I glanced at Gloriana, who raised her eyebrows at me.

Clive let go of my hand, removed the cuff link on his right wrist, turned up his sleeve and held his wrist out to Russell. "I vow on my blood to cleave only unto you until my dust is scattered in the wind."

In answer, I held the ring tightly in my hand and passed my bouquet to Stheno, who was standing nearby. I pulled up my left sleeve a few inches and offered my wrist to Russell. "I vow on my blood to cleave only unto you until I've breathed my last, and probably after that too."

Clive's lips twitched as Russell cut both our wrists and then placed Clive's over mine, tying them together with a red braided cord. "With the giving and receiving of blood and the vows you have made, you are joined forevermore in this life."

I slipped the ring onto Clive's finger and echoed his words. "And I promise to love *you* every day of my life. I promise to be your claws when you need them and your bartender when you don't. I'll be the one you confide in, the one who always takes your side, and the one who snuggles with you in the library window seat. I promise to make your enemies my own and to do everything in my power to always pull you out of danger. Understanding, though, that I'm often the one pushing you into it."

"And I wouldn't have it any other way," he interrupted.

"I promise to remind you to thank people," I continued. Russell smiled at that one. "To be the last person you see before daybreak and the first one you see at nightfall. Whenever possible, because that can be difficult if I'm working."

At Clive's bland look and the scattered chuckles around us, I decided I probably needed to wrap this up. "Wolves mate for life. However long this insanely beautiful life ends up being, you'll have my heart every day of it."

"And by the power vested in me by the Universal Church of the Interwebs, I now pronounce you husband and wife." At the sound of applause, Owen added, "You may now kiss the bride."

When Clive kissed me, the last piece, loose and rattling around in my chest, dropped into place. My mate and I were pledged to one another forever more. It was electric and perfect and over far too soon.

Music began again and Clive spun me in his arms as tiny lights twinkled above. Couples joined us in dance, and all was right—for the moment—in the world.

"How does a honeymoon in England sound?" he asked, his lips skating over my cheek.

"Perfect." *We're going after Leticia's mother, aren't we?*

"My beautiful, brilliant wife."

Epilogue

THE RE-RE-OPENING OF THE SLAUGHTERED LAMB BOOKSTORE & BAR

Even in the middle of the night, people tended to notice large groups of well-dressed people partying at The Palace of Fine Arts. The fact that no cops had come to roust us probably meant Clive had made some donations. As we had a ready supply of food and drink at The Slaughtered Lamb, though, we changed the venue.

Tables were moved to create a dance floor on one side of the bar. Clive and I swayed to Grim's violin, while Owen and Audrey held down the bar. Apparently, in life, Audrey had an uncle who ran a pub. She'd helped out when she was quite young, before she'd gone into the lady's maid biz. Owen was teaching her how to mix cocktails, but none of us could build a pint of Guinness with her expertise. I felt a twinge of guilt as Clive spun me around, a guest working, but she seemed to be having a ball.

"Leticia kept her isolated and smothered. Her life is finally her own again and she's exploring. Let it go, Sam." Clive kissed my temple and spun me back in the other direction.

Dave and Maggie pushed through the kitchen door, each holding a large platter weighed down with delicious smelling hors d'oeuvres. When Dave passed, I snagged two.

Godfrey came down the steps carrying a three-tiered wedding cake that was a work of art.

"Tell me you didn't just steal that." I didn't want some poor couple to be cakeless at their wedding tomorrow.

He grinned and winked, saying nothing. I was just about to make him return it when Clive intervened.

"We have bakers in our community. I ordered this hours ago." Chuckling, he pointed to the toppers. "Although I didn't order those." Instead of a traditional bride and groom, there was a scary, red-eyed vampire leaning over a wolf, howling at the moon.

Godfrey. It had to be.

"Again with no strippers?" The look of disgust on Medusa's face as she hit the bottom step and surveyed the room was priceless. Shaking her head, she turned around and walked back up the steps, her oldest sister in her wake.

Only Stheno continued down into The Slaughtered Lamb. She gave me a wave and then sidled up next to Godfrey.

"Is that going to be a problem?" I had no idea about the love lives of the rest of the vamps. They were remarkably discreet.

"Hmm?" Clive followed my line of sight. "Not for me. Speaking of which, where is…ah. Excuse me, darling." He gave me a quick kiss. "I need to speak with Russell."

I moved to the side, leaned against the wall, and took it all in. This was the reopening we should have had. Friends crowding the bookstore and bar, the sounds of laughter and clinking glasses filled the air. I almost ducked behind the bar to help Owen and Audrey, but they seemed to be having so much fun, I didn't want to mess it up. Clive was right. Audrey was finally living her life on her own terms, and tonight she wanted to learn how to mix cocktails.

Joy was new to me, and I wasn't sure how to deal with it. All night I'd been bracing myself, waiting for the next shoe to drop, the next spell to be cast, and next attack to be launched, only to realize the danger had passed. For now. Of course, without the peril, Clive and I wouldn't have started working together. If that memory I'd plucked from Leticia was correct, though, maybe we'd have ended up here anyway. Maybe.

Feeling suddenly off-kilter, I looked for Clive. My husband—I doubted I'd ever get used to that—was a master at getting me out of my head. I wished Martha could have been here, could have seen my place, met Clive. She understood that true love found a way. Whether it be between a wicche and an elf, or a vampire and a werewolf, it found a way.

Clive and Russell were locked in an intense conversation. Stoic Russell appeared angry. As I made my way across the crowded bar toward where they were speaking in the bookstore, Clive smiled and patted Russell on the shoulder. Russell inclined his head and walked away, almost bumping into me as I came through the doorway.

"Is everything all right?" I placed my hand on his forearm, stopping him.

"Of course, Miss—Mrs. Fitzwilliam." His expression softened. "Best wishes to you both." Leaning down, he kissed my cheek before heading up the stairs and out of The Slaughtered Lamb.

"Mrs. Fitzwilliam," Clive echoed, "can I have this dance?"

"There's no music." Grim was taking a well-earned break and drinking a tankard of ale.

"In my head, there's always music." He led me back to the dance floor and pulled me into his arms. Humming, he swayed with me in the corner.

"Oh, husband mine, you're keeping secrets." Something was going on between him and Russell, and I didn't like the look of it.

"Am I? How very like me. I have many secrets, you know. My own and others. For instance," he whispered, his mouth dropping to my neck, "I know how you shiver when I do this." His fangs glided down the column of my neck and I shivered uncontrollably. Stupid know-it-all vamp.

"Quit trying to distract me. What's going on with Russell? He looked upset."

"Did he? How very *un*like him. He normally has an excellent poker face." He kissed me again. "It's nothing bad, my love. I didn't wait a thousand years to marry just so everything could go back to the way it was. Lots of changes are coming. Russell needs to make peace with that."

"Bad changes?" I thought about his expression as he'd spoken with Clive.

Clive laughed. "Only Russell would think so." He spun me around when Grim began playing again. Lips at my ear, he added, "He'll also have to make his peace with the nocturne calling him Sire."

Shocked, I leaned back so I could see him clearly. "Now?"

Shaking his head and spinning me again, he said, "Soon. I need to clean up my own mess first. Now," he said, tone changing, "how do you feel about beginning our trip in Paris?"

Dear Reader

Thank you for reading **The Wicche Glass Tavern**. If you enjoyed Sam and Clive's third adventure together, please consider leaving a review or chatting about it with your book-loving friends. Good word of mouth means everything when you're a new writer!

Love,
Seana

Acknowledgments

Thank you to books, the healing restorative power of books! The pandemic threw me off my reading game. Thankfully, I was still able to write. Whichever side of the page we're on, story gives us a place to escape, a place to explore the human condition, a place to visit with old friends, and a place to meet new ones. To all the storytellers in the world, thank you!

Thank you to my incredibly kind and loving husband Gregory and our amazing daughters Harper and Grace. Too many early mornings, weekends, and vacations have been taken up with me behind a laptop. Thank you for always cheering me on!

Thank you to friend and critique partner extraordinaire C. R. Grissom. You are one of the gifts that writing has given me. Your unwavering support means the world to me.

Thank you to Roseann Rasul and Norma Jean Bell. My beta readers have fifty years and half a country between them, but they each understand character and story deeply. If either tells me something doesn't feel right, I know I've taken a misstep.

Thank you to Peter Senftleben, my insightful and gifted editor. If you like it, I know I'm on the right track. And thank you to Susan Helene Gottfried, my wonderfully knowledgeable proofreader. I love your track comments of *Webster's says____ but Oxford says____. I think it's clearer, though, if you___.*

Thank you to the amazing team at NYLA! Natanya Wheeler is a wonder and makes the whole publishing process easier. Cheryl Pientka went out and sold Sam, ensuring the books were also available in audio. My fabulous agent Sarah Younger understood how much this character and her story meant to me and never stopped trying to bring it to the world.

Sneak Peek at THE HOB & HOUND PUB

SAM QUINN, BOOK 4

The City of Lights...and Shadows

Paris is my new favorite city! Granted, I haven't been many places but still. I'd thought we were headed straight for England to hunt down Aldith. Instead, we flew into the City of Lights. Russell and Godfrey continued on without us to do some reconnaissance and get us a place to stay. Cadmael, an ancient Mayan warrior and Clive's vampy friend, was watching the San Francisco nocturne. Audrey, Leticia's former lady's maid who had been turned into a vampire to keep her in service in perpetuity, was covering for me at The Slaughtered Lamb. Owen said she was having a ball and the customers were starting to relax around her.

With Abigail, my homicidal aunt, and Leticia both gone, San Francisco was the safest it had been in quite a while. Aldith, Leticia's mother and the woman who had declared war against Clive almost a thousand years ago, was in England. We needed to skewer the heart of the hydra or more vamps would be coming for us. And we *would* soon, but not now.

Now we were strolling hand in hand around a glowing glass pyramid between fountains at the entrance to the Louvre. I stopped at one of the smaller glass pyramids to look down into the museum. I had to keep pinching myself. I was in Paris!

It was after hours, but Clive knew a way in, one Rémy, his French vampire friend, said still worked. The massive high baroque palace surrounded us on three sides as Clive walked us away from the lights toward a shadowy corner between the Richelieu and Sully wings. Once the expansive courtyard had cleared out, Clive swung me around so I was clinging to his back and then scaled the wall to the roof.

We jogged along the narrow metal beam between the stone façade of the building and the newer glass domed roof. I followed, not looking down, as heights were not my friend. Clive ducked behind a statue and circled to the back of the gorgeously ornate attic of the pavilion centered in the wing.

"The last time I was here," he whispered, "these were government offices. The finance department, I believe."

He took my hand and led me to an ornamental hexagonal medallion. It appeared fixed in place and yet when he pushed, it swung in. "The museum used to be one long wing." He pointed to the wing opposite us, across the courtyard. "Remy said this wing was gutted and remodeled to expand the museum."

A grin flashed in the darkness. "Let's take a look."

He sat on the lip of the opening, his legs dangling into the darkened hall below. "No heartbeat. The guard is in another wing." He pulled me onto his lap, my legs swinging beside his own, his arm tight around me. A moment later, we were dropping forty feet. Clive took the impact before he loosened his grip and my boots hit the polished floor.

I looked up at the open panel, a tiny piece of starlit sky visible. "You left the hatch open," I whispered.

"All the doors are alarmed. That's how we're getting out. Now, where to first?" He took my hand and we strolled down the huge airy halls, pausing to study paintings and sculptures.

I knew there were guards walking the museum with us, but Clive's sensitivity to heartbeats meant he heard them coming long before they appeared, giving us time to hide behind a tapestry or wall.

We wandered for hours, only seeing a small portion of the vast collection. It felt almost religious, this realization over and over of the greatness, the near divinity of some. We all leave a mark on the world, through our relationships, our actions, our words, our creations, but some have created art so remarkable that tens of thousands flock to experience it daily. It was staggering.

I enjoyed the surprises too. The *Mona Lisa* was small and roped off to keep visitors far away. Clive and I didn't want to trip any silent alarms, so we stayed behind the lines. It was beautiful, if a little underwhelming.

The *Winged Victory* sculpture, however, was magnificent. She stood atop a staircase in a large open hall, an artery for other galleries and floors—easily seen by guards entering from every direction. I couldn't tear my eyes from her. Power, glory, confidence, she awed and inspired me. I wanted to hold her essence deep within myself, to call upon it in moments of darkness and fear.

I was studying the marble statue one minute, the folds and movement of her skirt, the detail and lift of each feather in her wings, when I was picked up and raced down multiple halls, turning this way and that. When Clive finally put me down, we were standing in front of Botticelli's *Venus and the Three Graces Presenting Gifts to a Young Woman.*

"What the heck?" I whispered.

"Guards from different sectors were all about to converge on that hall. We have a little time before the guard for this sector returns." He pointed to the painting. "And I thought you'd enjoy this one."

Moving in closer, I tried to take in the fresco, the soft colors, the delicate beauty of the women in their billowing robes. The age and cracking of the plaster did nothing to diminish the beauty. If anything, it lent to it.

Turning to Clive, I said, "And you were around when this was first painted." It hit me at the oddest moments. My new husband was ancient. One thousand being the new thirty, if you were a vampire.

He quirked an eyebrow at me. "Problem?"

I shook my head and shrugged, turning back to the fresco. "Decrepitude looks good on you." I'd just leaned in to study the bride's features when I was snatched up, thrown over his shoulder, and carried down darkened passages again.

When my feet hit the floor, we were tucked away in a shadowy corner, away from the art. Clive's mouth was at my neck, his hands dragging down my body.

"Decrepit?" His lips skimmed my jaw.

"Elderly." I gasped when he nibbled my earlobe. "Infirm." One of his hands snaked up my sweater and palmed a breast. Breath uneven, I added, "Frail." The last word ended on a moan as he unzipped my jeans and slid his other hand into my panties.

Clive took my mouth to muffle the sounds I was making, his hands and lips working me over like a virtuoso.

I crushed him to me as I flew apart. Panting, I rested my head against the wall, trying to recover. My knees almost buckled when he did some kind of secret, vampy finger twirl as he slid out.

He leaned in, his lips hovering an inch from mine. "Decrepit?"

"Doddering." I rezipped my jeans with shaky hands.

"That's it." And just like that, I was thrown over his shoulder and we were racing down darkened halls again.

Giggling silently, I smacked his butt. "I want to see the Egyptians before we go."

A few minutes later, I was put down again, my hand in Clive's as we walked through the gallery holding Egyptian antiquities. Glass cases held sculptures, jars, jewelry. Some pieces towered over us; some were kept safely behind glass. I studied hieroglyphs longer than I should have, as I had no idea how to read them, but the idea that a story was being told drew me in.

Rows of sarcophagi were lined up in a case, some gorgeously painted, inside and out, others without decoration save the faces carved at the top, the etchings on the chest. They were—each of them—extraordinary examples of skilled workmanship.

Sometimes it made my head hurt to think I was looking at pieces fashioned by hand four thousand years ago. "Hey, do you know any Egyptians?"

Clive was studying a small cat sculpture with ruby eyes. "Of course."

"I mean one who was alive in ancient Egypt."

Straightening up, he turned to me. "Yes. Well, one, really."

I rolled my eyes and kept walking. "And let me guess. You dated."

Catching my hand in his, he walked with me. "Actually, no. He's quite striking, but not really my type." He twisted our hands so the blue diamond in my wedding ring glinted in the low light. "For some unknown reason, my type seems to be bookish bartenders who give me far too much lip."

I spun him around and kissed him soundly. "You mean like that?"

His eyes had gone vamp black, so I knew I was a heartbeat from being thrown over his shoulder and taken back to the hotel—which, granted, would have been lovely—but I wasn't done. I extricated myself from his arms and went in search of a mummy. I was sure they had to have one here.

Perhaps my necromantic abilities were on overdrive in this gallery, but it was almost like I felt him calling to me, waiting behind a row of sphinxes. He was extraordinary, nothing like the mummies described in books or depicted on film. Linen strips had been woven in a geometric pattern over his face. He also had pieces—a neckband and an apron—laid over him that had been painted with such precision, it was a wonder.

"Nenu," I breathed.

"Hmm?"

"His name was Nenu…and he was loved." Someone had taken painstaking hours to weave his wrappings as they had, someone who grieved his loss.

I was stepping away when I saw movement out of the corner of my eye. Nenu's faceless head had turned toward me, the fingers of one hand twitching.

Shhhhiiiiiiiittttt.

"Um, just to be clear, I didn't read from the book." Yes, much of my mummy knowledge came from a movie. What's your point?

Clive had his head tilted toward the arched entrance of the hall, listening. "You didn't what?" he asked absently.

"Clive?"

When he turned, he found my shaking finger pointing at a mummy, one who now showed movement in both hands.

His eyes widened. "Oh, good Lord."

We both watched in horror as an arm moved, causing the neckband to slide off and into the side of the glass box.

"Fix it, darling. Now. We are not setting a mummy loose in Paris. We'll never be allowed to return." His elbow nudged me, hurrying me along.

"I don't know how to—" The head lifted an inch and then dropped.

"Figure it out. And hurry. The guard is coming back."

I closed my eyes and sought out the dead, not all of them, just the one right in front of me. *Rest, Nenu. Your time on this earth is done. Return to Osiris. Go.* I pushed on the last word and felt his spirit leave this realm.

"A bit of a time crunch, my love."

"Done."

Clive snatched me up and raced us through the halls, eventually stopping where we had started. I looked up into the hole in the ceiling. It looked impossibly far away. Clive adjusted his hold on me so I was clinging to his back, my arms around his neck.

"Hold on," he said, patting my wrist.

When he flexed his knees to jump, I said, "No way."

He leaped straight up, catching the lip of the opening. "Climb up and out, ye of little faith."

I scrambled up his body and out the hexagonal opening in the dome. Once I was back on the roof, Clive pulled himself through. He pushed the decorative panel back in place and then grinned at me in the dark.

"What shall we do now?"

To preorder
THE HOB & HOUND PUB
Sam Quinn, book 4
click here.

Want more books from Seana?

If you'd like to be the first to learn what's new with Sam and Clive (and Owen and Dave and Stheno...), please sign up for my newsletter *Tales from the Book Nerd*. It's filled with writing news, deleted scenes, giveaways, book recommendations, and my favorite cocktail and book pairings.

The Slaughtered Lamb Bookstore & Bar
Sam Quinn, book 1

Welcome to The Slaughtered Lamb Bookstore and Bar. I'm Sam Quinn, the werewolf book nerd in charge. I run my business by one simple rule: Everyone needs a good book and a stiff drink, be they vampire, wicche, demon, or fae. No wolves, though. Ever. I have my reasons.

I serve the supernatural community of San Francisco. We've been having some problems lately. Okay, I'm the one with the problems. The broken body of a female werewolf washed up on my doorstep. What makes sweat pool at the base of my spine, though, is realizing the scars she bears are identical to the ones I conceal. After hiding for years, I've been found.

A protection I've been relying on is gone. While my wolf traits are strengthening steadily, the loss also left my mind vulnerable to attack. Someone is ensnaring me in horrifying visions intended to kill. Clive, the sexy vampire Master of the City, has figured out how to pull me out, designating himself my personal bodyguard. He's grumpy about it, but that kiss is telling a different story. A change is taking place. It has to. The bookish bartender must become the fledgling badass.

I'm a survivor. I'll fight fang and claw to protect myself and the ones I love. And let's face it, they have it coming.

The Dead Don't Drink at Lafitte's
   Sam Quinn, book 2

I'm Sam Quinn, the werewolf book nerd owner of the Slaughtered Lamb Bookstore and Bar. Things have been busy lately. While the near-constant attempts on my life have ceased, I now have a vampire gentleman caller. I've been living with Clive and the rest of his vampires for a few weeks while the Slaughtered Lamb is being rebuilt. It's going about as well as you'd expect.

My mother was a wicche and long dormant abilities are starting to make themselves known. If I'd had a choice, necromancy wouldn't have been my top pick, but it's coming in handy. A ghost warns me someone is coming to kill Clive. When I rush back to the nocturne, I find vamps from New Orleans readying an attack. One of the benefits of vampires looking down on werewolves is no one expects much of me. They don't expect it right up until I take their heads.

Now, Clive and I are setting out for New Orleans to take the fight back to the source. Vampires are masters of the long game. Revenge plots are often decades, if not centuries, in the making. We came expecting one enemy, but quickly learn we have darker forces scheming against us. Good thing I'm the secret weapon they never see coming.

The Hob & Hound Pub
Sam Quinn, book 4

I'm Sam Quinn, the newly married werewolf book nerd owner of the Slaughtered Lamb Bookstore and Bar. Clive and I are on our honeymoon. Paris is lovely, though the mummy in the Louvre inching toward me is a bit off-putting. Although Clive doesn't sense anything, I can't shake the feeling I'm being watched.

Even after we cross the English Channel to begin our search for Aldith—the woman who's been plotting against Clive since the beginning—the prickling unease persists. Clive and I are separated, rather forcefully, and I'm left to find my way alone in a foreign country, evading not only Aldith's large web of hench-vamps, but vicious fae creatures disloyal to their queen. Gloriana says there's a poison in the human realm that's seeping into Faerie, and I may have found the source.

I knew this was going to be a working vacation, but battling vampires on one front and the fae on another is a lot, especially in a country steeped in magic. As a side note, I need to get word to Benvair. I think I've found the dragon she's looking for.

Gloriana is threatening to set her warriors against the human realm, but I may have a way to placate her. Aldith is a different story. There's no reasoning with rabid vengeance. She'll need to be put out of our misery permanently if Clive and I have any hope of a long, happy life together. Heck, I'd settle for a few quiet weeks.

And for something completely different...
Welcome Home, Katie Gallagher

Want more books from Seana?

This romantic comedy was my first book published. Remember, don't judge a book by its (truly hideous) cover.

Nobody said a fresh start would be easy

A clean slate is exactly what Katie Gallagher needs, and Bar Harbor, Maine, is the best place to get it. Except the cottage her grandmother left her is overrun with woodland creatures, and the police chief, Aiden Cavanaugh, seems determined to arrest her! Katie had no idea she'd broken his heart fifteen years ago...

About the Author

About Seana Kelly

Seana Kelly lives in the San Francisco Bay Area with her husband, two daughters, two dogs, and one fish. When not dodging her family, hiding in the garage to write, she's working as a high school teacher-librarian. She's an avid reader and re-reader who misses her favorite characters when it's been too long between visits.

She's a two-time Golden Heart® Award finalist and is represented by the delightful and effervescent Sarah E. Younger of the Nancy Yost Literary Agency

You can follow Seana on Twitter for tweets about books and dogs or on Instagram for beautiful pictures of books and dogs (kidding). She also loves collecting photos of characters and settings for the books she writes. As she's a huge reader, young adult and adult, expect lots of recommendations, as well.

twitter.com/SeanaKellyRW
instagram.com/seanakellyrw

Printed in the USA
CPSIA information can be obtained
at www.ICGtesting.com
LVHW021639170924
791331LV00011B/563